POISON PRINCESS

KRESLEY COLE

POISON PRINCESS
The Arcana Chronicles

SIMON AND SCHUSTER

First published in Great Britain by Simon & Schuster UK Ltd, 2012

A CBS COMPANY

Originally published in the USA in 2012 by Simon & Schuster Books for Young Readers, an imprint of Simon & Schuster Children's Division, New York.

1 3 5 7 9 10 8 6 4 2

Simon & Schuster UK Ltd
1st Floor, 222 Gray's Inn Road
London WC1X 8HB

www.simonandschuster.co.uk

Simon & Schuster Australia, Sydney
Simon & Schuster India, New Delhi

A CIP catalogue record for this book is available from the British Library

Hardback ISBN 978-0-85707-918-3
Paperback ISBN 978-0-85707-919-0
Ebook ISBN 978-0-85707-920-6

Printed and bound by CPI Group (UK) Ltd, Croydon, CR0 4YY

TO ZAREEN JAFFERY,

my incredible young adult editor, for your
help with *Poison Princess*. You made all the
difference in the world!

ACKNOWLEDGMENTS

Thank you to my friends and family in Louisiana who helped with the flavor of this book (and especially to Jonah T. for your assistance with all things Cajun). Couldn't have done it without you!

Many thanks to Lauren McKenna for your fantastic insights with this story.

To the brilliant doctor sisters, Bridget and Beth, much gratitude for all your technical expertise.

Thanks to my wonderful agent, Robin Rue, for your enthusiasm for this project and for finding the perfect home for it.

And thank you, readers, for taking the plunge with me into the world of the Arcana Chronicles!

TAROT: *n.* a specialized deck of illustrated cards, now used mainly for fortune-telling, often associated with the occult. The twenty-two trump cards of the deck, the Major Arcana, are distinctly symbolic, depicting scenes and characters from ancient times.

POISON PRINCESS

PROLOGUE

She's so lovely, so fragile. Those haunted eyes. Those rosebud lips . . . they'll scream so prettily.

I gaze out my door's peephole, willing the girl to come closer. A *female* so near! *Come to me.*

In the ash-filled twilight, she paces the sidewalk fronting my charred Victorian home, wrestling with the decision of whether to approach.

Chill winds toss her heavy mane of blond hair. She wears frayed jeans, battered hiking boots, and has her hands buried in the pockets of a threadbare hoodie.

Her clothes are no match for the temperature outside, which has only recently dropped from the punishing heat we've had all winter. The weather *worsens* as summer nears. . . .

She glances up. Has she caught the food scents carrying from my home? I have canned beef stew simmering atop a wood-burning stove. Does she note the smoke curling from the chimney?

She looks hungry; after the Flash, they're always hungry.

Everything about my lair is meant to lure her to me. If the brightly glowing kerosene lantern isn't enough of a beacon for travelers, I have a poster-board sign—written in marker and covered with plastic wrap— pinned by the door:

VOICES OF THE FLASH

HOT MEALS, SAFE SHELTER, JUST TELL ME YOUR STORY OF THE APOCALYPSE.

My house is ideally situated at a crossroads in this ghost town. Most of my guests tell me their lives are at a crossroads too. This girl's obviously is as well.

Earlier, she followed me from a distance, watching as I pruned away wasted plant life to uncover the town's singed welcome sign. *Requiem, Tennessee, population 1212.*

The Flash whittled that number down to single digits. Now it's just me and mine.

As I worked on the sign, I whistled a jaunty tune for effect. She'll think I'm a decent person, trying for normalcy.

Now she stills, looks straight at the door. Her mind is made up. I can see it in the set of her slim shoulders.

As she nears the front entrance, I make out her features more distinctly. She's maybe a couple of inches over five feet tall. Her willowy figure and delicate face tell me she can't be more than sixteen. But the hint of womanly curves I detect beneath that hoodie indicates that she's older.

Her eyes are a cornflower blue—the color bold against her pale cheeks—but they're heartbroken. This waif has known loss.

Who hasn't since the apocalypse?

She's about to know more. *Come closer.*

She hesitates to set foot on the front porch. *No, come to me!* After taking a deep breath, she makes her way to my door; I shudder in anticipation, a spider poised on its web.

Already I feel a connection to this girl. I've said this in the past—others like me have spoken of a bond with their subjects—but this time I do feel an unprecedented tension.

I want to possess her so badly I barely stifle a groan.

If I can get her inside, she will be trapped. The interior half of the doorknob is missing; the only way to open it is with my pliers. The windows are made from clear sheeting, unbreakable. All the other doors to the outside are nailed shut.

She raises her hand and knocks lightly, then retreats a skittish step. I wait for several seconds—*an eternity*—then stomp my feet as if I'm approaching.

When I open the door with a broad smile, she relaxes a touch. I'm not what she was expecting. I don't look much older than my early twenties.

Actually, I'm younger. Closer to her age, I'd imagine. But my skin has been weathered from the Flash. My experiments have taken their toll as well.

Yet the girls below, my little rats, assure me I'm the most handsome boy they've ever seen. I've no reason to think otherwise.

Ah, but my mind feels ancient. *A wise man in the guise of a boy.*

"Please come in out of the cold," I tell her, opening my arm wide. "Look at you—you must be freezing!"

She warily peers inside, gaze darting from wall to wall. The interior is cheery, candlelit. A homemade quilt stretches over a couch arm. A rocking chair sits directly in front of the crackling fire.

My lair looks safe, warm, grandmotherly. It should; an old woman lived here before I slaughtered her and made it my home.

The girl eyes that rocking chair and fire with longing, yet her muscles are still tensed to bolt.

Feigning sadness, I say, "I'm afraid it's just me. After the Flash . . ." I trail off, letting her assume that my loved ones were lost in the apocalypse.

Pity me. Until you first set eyes on your new collar.

At last, she crosses the threshold! To keep from roaring with pleasure, I bite the inside of my cheek until the tang of blood hits my tongue. Somehow I manage an even tone when I tell her, "I'm Arthur. Please take a seat by the fire."

Her fragile form is trembling, her eyes stark as she gazes up at me. "Th-thank you." She heads for the rocking chair. "I'm Evangeline. Evie."

Behind her, I furtively pocket my pliers and close the door. As it clicks shut, I smile.

She's mine. She will never leave this place.

Whether she remains alive or dead within depends on her. "Are you hungry, Evie? I've got stew simmering. And maybe a cup of hot chocolate?" I can all but hear her salivating.

"Yes, p-please, if it's not too much trouble." She sits, raising her hands to the flames. "I'm starving."

"I'll be right back." In the kitchen, I ladle stew into a bowl, arranging the dinner carefully on a TV tray. It's her first meal with me. It must be perfect. In things like this, I am fastidious. My clothing is spotless, my hair neatly combed. My organized sleeve of scalpels sits tucked in my blazer pocket.

The dungeon, however, is a different story.

Beside the bowl, I add a steaming cup of cocoa, made from my dwindling water stores. From the sugar dispenser, I pour one teaspoonful of white powder—*not* sweetener. With each sip of her drink, she will relax more and more until her muscles fail her, yet her consciousness will remain.

Unmoving yet aware. It's important that she experience our communion fully. My homemade concoctions never fail.

In fact, it's time for my own elixir. I collect a stoppered vial from my cabinet, downing the clear, sour contents. My thoughts grow even more centered, my focus laser-sharp.

"Here we are," I say when I return. Her eyes go wide at the bounty. When she licks her plump bottom lip, the tray rattles in my quaking hands. "If you'll just grab that stand . . ."

She all but lunges to help me set it up, and in no time, she's digging in. I sit on the couch—not too close, careful not to crowd her.

"So, Evie, I'm sure you saw the sign out front." She nods, too busy chewing to utter an answer. "I want you to know that I'm delighted to help you. All I ask is that you share some information with me." *And cry as I touch you, flinch whenever I near you.* "I'm archiving folks' stories, trying to collect them for the future. We need a history of how people's lives were rocked by this catastrophe."

This is essentially true. I tape my girls' stories—background on my subjects—and later their screams. "Would you be interested in sharing?"

She eyes me cagily as she finishes her stew. "What would you want to know?"

"I'd like you to tell me what happened in the days leading up to the Flash. And then how you coped with the aftermath. I'd record you with this." I point at the battery-operated cassette recorder on the end table and grin sheepishly. "Old-school, I know."

She reaches for her mug, raises it, blows across the top.

Drink, little girl.

When she takes a sip, I release a pent-up breath. She's drinking a toast to her own doom, to our beginning.

"So you'll just record me talking?"

"That's right." When I rise to remove the tray, she snatches her mug, holding it close to her chest. "Evie, I've got more in the kitchen. I'll bring back a whole pot of it."

By the time I return with a pot and my own mug, she's finished her drink. Her hoodie is now wrapped around her waist, and as she stokes the fire, her short-sleeved T-shirt molds to her breasts.

I clench my mug handle so tightly I fear it will break. Then I frown. I'm not usually so *lustful* of my subjects. Mixing business with pleasure is . . . messy. But her allure is intoxicating.

Earlier in town, when I first saw her, I'd desired her, imagining her in my bed, opening her arms to me.

Could she be the one?

She returns to her seat, breaking my stare. "Why do you want to know about *me*?" Her voice has a drawling southern lilt to it.

After clearing my throat, I answer, "Anyone who makes it here has a story of survival to tell. You included." I take my spot on the couch. "I want to know about your life. Before and after the Flash."

"Why before?"

To get a baseline history on my new test subject. Instead I say, "The apocalypse turned lives inside out, altering people. In order to survive, they've had to do a lot of things they never thought they could. I want as many details as possible.... You don't have to give your last name, if that makes you feel more comfortable."

Over the rim of her mug, she murmurs, "My life was turned inside out long before the Flash."

"How do you mean?" I reach over and press the record button. She doesn't seem to mind.

"In the weeks leading up to it, I'd just gotten home after a summer away. And things were strained."

"Where was your home?" I ask, nearly sighing as I gaze at the girl. Her lids have grown a touch heavier, and the blond waves of her hair shine in the firelight. She smooths the silken length over her shoulder, and I catch the faintest hint of her scent—sublime, flowery.

Even eight months post-Flash, and with all the lakes and rivers evaporated, she manages to smell as if she's fresh from a bath. Amazing. Unlike the fetid little rats in the dungeon.

"My home was in Louisiana, on a beautiful sugarcane farm called Haven." She leans back in the chair, gazing dreamily up at the ceiling, remembering. "All around us, there was a sea of green cane stretching forever."

Suddenly I find it imperative to know *everything* about this girl. Why is she alone? How could she have made it this far north with no male protecting her? If the Bagmen didn't get her, then the slavers or militiamen surely would have.

I realize she must've only recently lost her protector—which is why a girl this fine would be alone.

My gain.

"How were things strained at home?" Which will it be—a tale of strife with her parents, or punishment for staying out past curfew, or a messy breakup with the local high-school stud? "You can tell me." I give her an earnest nod.

She takes a deep breath and nibbles her lip. In that moment, I know she's made the decision to tell me everything.

"Arthur, I . . . I'd just been released from a mental institution." She looks up at me from under her lashes, gauging my reaction while seeming to dread it.

I just stop my jaw from dropping. "Mental institution?"

"I'd been sick the last quarter of my sophomore year, so my mom made me go to a clinic in Atlanta."

This girl's been heaven-sent for me! I, too, had been *sick*. Until I'd tested my concoctions on myself, eventually discovering a cure.

Her idea of sickness and mine would likely differ to a murderous degree . . . but I could *teach* her to give in and embrace our darkness.

"I can't believe I'm confiding this." She frowns, then whispers, "I couldn't tell him my secrets."

Him—her previous protector? I must know these secrets!

She gives me a soft smile. "Why do I feel so at ease with you?"

Because a drug is at work even now, relaxing you. "Please, go on."

"I'd only been home for two weeks and strange things were starting to happen again. I was losing time, having nightmares and hallucinations so realistic I couldn't tell if I was awake or asleep."

This troubled girl is as frail in mind as she is in body. *She's mine. Heaven-sent.* I know I can take the merest spark of madness and make insanity flare to life. I begin sweating with harnessed aggression.

She doesn't notice, because again she's studying the ceiling, thinking back. "A week before the Flash would have been the day the school year began, seven days before my sixteenth birthday."

"Your birthday was day one A.F.?" I ask, my voice high with excitement. She nods. "What was happening then?"

Drawing a foot up on the chair, she uses her other to gently rock herself. "I remember getting dressed for school Monday morning—my mom was worried that I wasn't ready to go back." She exhales. "Mom was right."

"Why?"

7

Evie meets my gaze. "I'll tell you. All of my story. And I'll try to remember as much as possible. But, Arthur . . ."

"Yes?"

Her eyes are glinting, her expression ashamed. So exquisitely wretched. "What I believe happened might not be what actually took place."

"How are you feeling?" Mom asked with an appraising eye. "You sure you're up for this?"

I finished my hair, pasted on a smile, and lied through my teeth, "Definitely." Though we'd been over this, I patiently said, "The docs told me that settling back into a normal routine might be good for someone like me." Well, at least three out of my five shrinks had.

The other two insisted that I was still unstable. A loaded gun. Trouble with the possibility of rubble.

"I just need to get back to school, around all my friends."

Whenever I quoted shrinks to her, Mom relaxed somewhat, as if it was proof that I'd actually listened to them.

I could remember a lot of what the docs said—because they'd made me forget so much of my life before the clinic.

With her hands clasped behind her back, Mom began strolling around my room, her gaze flickering over my belongings—a pretty, blond Sherlock Holmes sniffing for any secrets she didn't yet know.

She'd find nothing; I'd already hidden my contraband in my book bag.

"Did you have a nightmare last night?"

Had she heard me shoot upright with a cry? "Nope."

"When you were catching up with your friends, did you confide to anyone where you really were?"

Mom and I had told everyone that I'd gone to a special school for "deportment." After all, you can't prep a daughter too early for those competitive sororities in the South.

In reality, I'd been locked up at the Children's Learning Center, a behavioral clinic for kids. Also known as Child's Last Chance.

"I haven't told *anyone* about CLC," I said, horrified by the idea of my friends, or my boyfriend, finding out.

Especially not him. Brandon Radcliffe. With his hazel eyes, movie-star grin, and curling light-brown hair.

"Good. It's our business only." She paused before my room's big wall mural, tilting her head uneasily. Instead of a nice watercolor or a retro-funk design, I'd painted an eerie landscape of tangled vines, looming oaks, and darkening skies descending over hills of cane. I knew she'd considered painting over the mural but feared I'd reach my limit and mutiny.

"Have you taken your medicine this morning?"

"Like I always do, Mom." Though I couldn't say my bitter little pills had done much for my nightmares, they did stave off the delusions that had plagued me last spring.

Those terrifying hallucinations had been so lifelike, leaving me temporarily blinded to the world around me. I'd barely completed my sophomore year, brazening out the visions, training myself to act like nothing was wrong.

In one of those delusions, I'd seen flames blazing across a night sky. Beneath the waves of fire, fleeing rats and serpents had roiled over Haven's front lawn, until the ground looked like it was rippling.

In another, the sun had shone—at night—searing people's eyes till they ran with pus, mutating their bodies and rotting their brains. They became zombielike blood drinkers, with skin that looked like crinkled paper bags and oozed a rancid slime. I called them *bogeymen.* . . .

My short-term goal was simple: Don't get exiled back to CLC. My long-term goal was a bit more challenging: Survive the rest of high school so I could escape to college.

"And you and Brandon are still an item?" Mom almost sounded disbelieving, as if she didn't understand why he would still be going out with me after my three-month absence.

"He'll be here soon," I said in an insistent tone. Now she'd gotten me nervous.

No, no. All summer, he'd faithfully texted me, though I'd only been allowed to respond twice a month. And ever since my return last week, he'd been wonderful—my cheerful, smiling boyfriend bringing me flowers and taking me to movies.

"I like Brandon. He's such a good boy." At last, Mom concluded this morning's interrogation. "I'm glad you're back, honey. It's been so quiet around Haven without you."

Quiet? I yearned to say, "Really, Karen? You know what's worse than quiet? Fluorescent bulbs crackling twenty-four hours a day in the center. Or maybe the sound of my cutter roommate weeping as she attacked her thigh with a spork? How about disconnected laughter with no punch line?"

But then, that last one had been me.

In the end, I said nothing about the center. *Just two years and out.*

"Mom, I've got a big day." I shouldered my backpack. "And I want to be outside when Brand shows." I'd already made him wait for me all summer.

"Oh, of course." She shadowed me down the grand staircase, our steps echoing in unison. At the door, she tucked my hair behind my ears and gave me a kiss on my forehead, as if I were a little girl. "Your shampoo smells nice—might have to borrow some."

"Sure." I forced another smile, then walked outside. The foggy air was so still—as if the earth had exhaled but forgotten to inhale once more.

I descended the front steps, then turned to gaze at the imposing home I'd missed so much.

Haven House was a grand twenty-two-room mansion, fronted by twelve stately columns. Its colors—wood siding of the lightest cream, hurricane shutters of the darkest forest green—had remained unchanged since it'd originally been built for my great-great-great-great-grandmother.

Twelve massive oak trees encircled the structure, their sprawling limbs grown together in places, like hundred-ton hydras trapping prey.

The locals thought Haven House looked haunted. Seeing the place bathed in fog, I had to admit that was fair.

As I waited, I meandered across the front lawn to a nearby cane row, leaning in to smell a purple stalk. Crisp but sweet. One of the feathery green leaves was curled so that it looked like it was embracing my hand. That made me smile.

"You'll get rain soon," I murmured, hoping Sterling's drought would finally end.

My smile deepened when I saw a sleek Porsche convertible speeding down our oystershell drive, a blur of red.

Brandon. He was the most enviable catch in our parish. Senior. Quarterback. Rich. The trifecta of boyfriends.

When he pulled up, I opened the passenger door with a grin. "Hey, big guy."

But he frowned. "You look . . . tired."

"I didn't get to bed till late," I replied, darting a glance over my shoulder as I tossed my bag into the minuscule backseat. When the kitchen curtain fluttered to the side, I just stopped myself from rolling my eyes. *Two years and out . . .*

"You feeling okay?" His gaze was filled with concern. "We can pick up some coffee on the way."

I shut the door behind me. "Sure. Whatever." He hadn't complimented me on my hair or outfit—my Chloé baby-blue sleeveless dress with the hem no more than four regulation inches above the knee, the silky black ribbon that held my hair back in a curling ponytail, my matching black Miu Miu ankle-wrap heels.

My diamond earrings and Patek Philippe wristwatch served as my only jewelry.

I'd spent weeks planning this outfit, two days in Atlanta acquiring it, and the last hour convincing myself I'd never looked better.

He hiked his wide shoulders, the matter forgotten, then peeled down Haven's drive, tires spitting up an arc of shell fragments as we zoomed past acre after acre of cane.

Once we'd reached the highway, a seamed and worn-out stretch of old Louisiana road, he said, "You're so quiet this morning."

"I had weird dreams last night." Nightmares. Nothing new there.

Without fail, my good dreams were filled with plants. I'd see ivy and roses growing before my eyes or crops sprouting all around me.

But lately in my nightmares, a crazed redheaded woman with gleaming green eyes used those same plants to . . . hurt people, in grisly ways. When her victims begged for mercy, she would cackle with delight.

She was cloaked and partially hooded, so I couldn't make out all of her face, but she had pale skin and green ivylike tattoos running down both her cheeks. Her wild red hair was strewn with leaves.

I called her the red witch. "Sorry," I said with a shiver. "They kind of put me in a funk."

"Oh." His demeanor told me he felt way out of his depth. I'd once asked him if he had nightmares, and he'd looked at me blankly, unable to remember one.

That was the thing about Brandon—he was the most happy-go-lucky boy I'd ever met. Though he was built like a bear—or a pro football player—his temperament was more adoring canine than grizzly.

Secretly, I put a lot of store in him, hoping his normal could drag me back from my wasteland-visions brink. Which was why I'd fretted about him finding another girl and breaking up with me while I was locked up at CLC.

Now it seemed like at least one thing was going to work out. Brandon had stayed true to me. With every mile we drove away from Haven, the sun shone brighter and brighter, the fog lifting.

"Well, I know how to put my girl in a good mood." He gave me his mischievous grin.

I was helpless not to be charmed. "Oh, yeah, big guy? How's that?"

He pulled off the road under the shade of a pecan tree, tires popping the fallen pecans. After waiting for the dust to pass us, he pressed a button and put down the convertible top. "How fast you wanna go, Eves?"

Few things exhilarated me more than flying down the highway with the top down. For about a nanosecond I considered how to repair the utter loss of my hairstyling—*braid a loose fishtail over your shoulder*—then told him, "Kick her in the guts."

He peeled out, the engine purring with power. Hands raised, I threw my head back and yelled, "Faster!"

At each gear, he redlined before shifting, until the car stretched her legs. As houses whizzed past, I laughed with delight.

The months before were a dim memory compared to this—the sun, the wind, Brandon sliding me excited grins. He was right; this was just what I needed.

Leave it to my teddy bear of a football player to make me feel carefree and sane again.

And didn't that deserve a kiss?

Unbuckling my seat belt, I clambered up on my knees, tugging my dress up a couple of inches so I could lean over to him. I pressed my lips against the smooth-shaven skin of his cheek. "Just what the doctor ordered, Brand."

"You know it!"

I kissed his broad jaw, then—as my experienced best friend Melissa had instructed—I nuzzled his ear, letting him feel my breath.

"Ah, Evie," he rasped. "You drive me crazy, you know that?"

I was getting an idea. I knew I played with fire, teasing him like this. He'd already been reminding me of a promise I'd made right before I left for *deportment school*: If we were still going out when I turned sixteen (I was a *young* junior), I would play my V card. My birthday was next Monday—

"What the hell does that guy want?" he suddenly exclaimed.

I drew my head back from Brandon, saw he was glancing past me. I darted a look back, and my stomach plummeted.

A guy on a motorcycle had pulled up right next to us, keeping pace with the car, checking me out. His helmet had a tinted visor so I couldn't see his face, but I knew he was staring at my ass.

First instinct? Drop my butt in the seat, willing my body to disappear into the upholstery. Second instinct? Stay where I was and glare at the pervert. This was *my* morning, my laughter, my fast drive in my boyfriend's luxury sports car.

After a summer spent in a fluorescent hell, I *deserved* this morning.

When I twisted around to glare over my shoulder, I saw the guy's helmet had dipped, attention definitely on my ass. Then he slowly raised his head, as if he was raking his gaze over every inch of me.

It felt like hours passed before he reached my eyes. I tugged my hair off my face, and we stared at each other for so long that I wondered when he was going to run off the road.

Then he gave me a curt nod and sped past us, expertly dodging a pothole. Two more motorcycles followed, each carrying two people. They honked and cheered, while Brandon's face turned as red as his car.

I consoled myself with the knowledge that I'd probably never have to see them again.

To preserve his paint job, Brand parked in the back of the Sterling High parking lot. Even among the many Mercedeses and Beamers, his car attracted attention.

I climbed out and collected my book bag, groaning under the weight, hoping Brand would take a hint. He didn't. So, on an already stifling morning, I would be schlepping my own stuff.

I told myself I liked that he didn't help me with my books. Brand was a modern man, treating me as an equal. I told myself that a lot on our long trek toward the front entrance.

Probably just as well. I had my secret sketchbook in my bag, and I'd learned the hard way never to let it out of my possession.

When we reached the freshly irrigated quad, someone produced a football, and Brand's eyes locked on it like a retriever's. Somehow he broke his trained gaze to look at me with a questioning expression.

I sighed, smoothing my hair—frantically braided once we'd reached Sterling city limits. "Go. I'll see you inside."

"You're the best, Eves." He grinned—with dimples—his hazel eyes bright. "I figure even *you* can make it from here by yourself!"

I was, in fact, directionally challenged. For someone who didn't have a mean bone in his body, he tended to land some zingers.

I reminded myself that Brandon had a good heart, he just genuinely didn't know better. I'd begun to realize that he was a *good boy*, but not yet a *great guy*.

Maybe I could drag him over the finish line with that.

He planted a sweet kiss on my lips, then jogged off with one hand raised for the ball.

Heading toward the front doors, I passed a rosebush with double blooms of poppy red—my favorite color. A breeze blew, making it seem like the flowers swayed to face me.

Ever since I could remember, I'd loved all plant life. I drew roses, oaks, vine crops, and berry briars compulsively, fascinated with their shapes, their blooms, their *defenses*.

My eyelids would go to half-mast from the scent of freshly tilled pastureland.

Which was part of my problem. I wasn't *normal*.

Teenage girls should be obsessed with clothes and boys, not the smell of dirt or the admirable deviousness of briars.

Come, touch . . . but you'll pay a price.

A metallic-blue Beamer screeched into a parking space just feet from me, the driver laying on the horn.

Melissa Warren, my best friend and sister from another mister.

Mel was a hyperactive wild child who was a stranger to shame and had never acquainted herself with embarrassment. And she always leapt before she looked. I was actually surprised she'd managed to survive her summer overseas without me.

We'd been best friends for a decade—but without a doubt, I was the brains of that operation.

I couldn't have missed her more.

Considering her five-foot-eleven height, Mel hopped out of her car with surprising speed, raising her straightened arms over her head and snapping her fingers. "That's how you park a car, bitches." Mel was going through a phase lately where she called everyone bitches.

Her mother was the guidance counselor at our school, because Mel's dad had paid for Sterling High's new library—and because Mrs.

Warren needed a hobby. Most parents figured that if Melissa Warren was a product of her parenting skills, then they shouldn't put much stock in Mrs. Warren's guidancing skills.

Today Mel wore a crisp navy skirt and a red baby-doll T-shirt that had probably cost half a grand and would never be worn again. Her bright Dior lipstick was a classic red to match, her auburn hair tied with a navy bow. Prepster chic.

In short order, she popped her trunk, dragged out her designer book bag, then locked her keys in the car.

With a shrug, she joined me. "Hey, look over my shoulder. Is that Spencer in the quad with Brand?" Spencer Stephens III, Brand's best friend.

When I nodded, she said, "He's looking at me right now, isn't he? All pining-like?"

He was in no way looking at Mel.

"This year I'm taking our flirtationship to a new level," Mel informed me. "He just needs a nudge in the right direction."

Unfortunately, Mel didn't know how to nudge. She play-punched *hard*, titty-twisted with impunity, and wasn't above the occasional headlock. And that was if she liked you.

In a pissy tone, she added, "Maybe if your boyfriend would—finally—set us up."

Brandon had laughed the last time I'd asked him, saying, "As soon as you housebreak her." *Note to self: Put in another request today.*

Two of our other friends spotted us then. Grace Anne had on a yellow sateen dress that complemented her flawless café-au-lait skin. Catherine Ashley's jewelry sparkled from a mile away.

The four of us were popular bowhead cheerleaders. And I was proud of it.

They smiled and waved excitedly as if I hadn't seen them every day last week as we'd spilled deets about our vacations. Mel had modeled in Paris, Grace had gone to Hawaii, and Catherine had toured New Zealand.

After I'd repeatedly declared my summer the most boring ever, they'd stopped asking about it. I was pictureless, had zero images on my phone for three months, not a single uploadable.

It was as if I hadn't even existed.

But I'd dutifully oohed and aahed over their pics—blurred, cropped shots of the Eiffel Tower and all.

Brand's pics—of him smiling at the beach, or at his parents' ritzy get-togethers, or on a yacht cruising the Gulf Coast—had been like a knife to the heart because I should have been in all of them.

Last spring, I had been. He had an entire folder on his phone stuffed with pics and vids of us goofing off together.

"Great dress, Evie," Catherine Ashley said.

Grace Anne's gaze was assessing. "Great *everything*. Boho braid, no-frills dress, and flirty, flirty heels. Nicely done."

With a sigh, I teased, "If only my friends knew how to dress, too."

As we walked toward the front doors, students stopped and turned, girls checking out what we were wearing, guys checking for a summer's worth of developing curves.

Funny thing about our school—there were no distinct cliques like you saw on TV shows, just gradations of popularity.

I waved at different folks again and again, much to the bowheads' amusement. I was pretty much friends with *everybody*.

No one ever sat alone during my lunch period. No girl walked the hall with a wardrobe malfunction under my watch. I had even shut down the sale of freshman elevator passes on our one-story campus.

When we reached the entrance of the white-stuccoed building, I realized school was just what I needed. Routine, friends, *normalcy*. Here, I could forget all the crazy, all the nightmares. This was my world, my little queendom—

The sudden rumble of motorcycles made everyone go silent, like a needle scratch across an old record.

No way they'd be the same creepers from before. That group had looked too old for high school. And wouldn't we have passed them?

But then, it wasn't like the genteel town of Sterling had many motor-cyclists. I gazed behind me, saw the same five kids from earlier.

Now I was ready to meld into auto upholstery.

Each of them was dressed in dark clothes; among our student body's ever-present khaki and bright couture, they stood out like bruises.

The biggest boy—the one who'd leered at me—ramped over the curb to the quad, pulling right up on the side to park. The others followed. I noticed their bikes all had mismatched parts. Likely stolen.

"Who are *they*?" I asked. "Have they come to start trouble?"

Grace answered, "Haven't you heard? They're a bunch of juvies from Basin High School."

Basin High? That was in a totally different parish, on the other side of the levee. *Basin* equaled *Cajun*. "But why are they *here*?"

"They're attending Sterling!" Catherine said. "Because of that new bridge they built across the levee, the kids at the outer edge of the basin are now closer to us than to their old school."

Before the bridge, those Cajuns would have had to drive all the way around the swamp to get here—fifty miles at least.

Until the last decade or so, the bayou folk there had been isolated. They still spoke Cajun French and ate frogs' legs.

Though I'd never been to Basin Town, all of Haven's farm help came from there and my crazy ole grandmother still had friends there. I knew a lot about the area, a place rumored to be filled with hot-blooded women, hard-fighting men, and unbelievable poverty.

Mel said, "My mom had to go to an emergency faculty meeting last night about how best to *acclimate* them or something like that."

I could almost feel sorry for this group of kids. To go from their Cajun, poor—and adamantly Catholic—parish to our rich town of Louisiana Protestants . . . ?

Culture clash, round one.

This was actually happening. Not only would I have to see the guy who'd shamelessly ogled me, I'd be in the same school with him.

I narrowed my eyes, impatient for him to take off his helmet. He had the advantage on me, and I didn't like it.

He stood, unfolding his tall frame. He had to be more than six feet in height, even taller than Brand. He had on scuffed boots, worn jeans, and a black T-shirt that stretched tight over his chest.

Beside him was a couple on a bike—a kid in camo pants and a girl in a pleather miniskirt. The big boy helped her off the bike, easily swinging her up—

"Wheh-hell," Catherine said, "good to know her panties are hot pink. Shocked she's wearing them, actually. Classy with a capital *K*."

Mel nodded thoughtfully. "I finally understand who buys vajazzling kits."

Grace Anne, proud wearer of a purity ring, screwed her face up into an expression of distaste. "Surely she's going to get sent home with a skirt that short."

Not to mention her midriff-baring shirt, which read: I GOT BOURBON-FACED ON SHIT STREET!

Once he'd set the girl on her feet, she took off her helmet, revealing long chestnut-brown hair and a face made up to an embarrassing degree with glaring fuchsia lipstick.

The skinny boy who'd been driving her removed his own helmet. He had dark-blond hair and a long face, which wasn't *un*handsome but still reminded me of a fox.

He revved his motorcycle, startling two passersby, and his friends laughed.

Or rather a weasel. *Strike feeling sorry for them.*

Finally, the big one reached for his helmet. I waited. He yanked it off, shook out his hair, and raised his head. My lips parted.

Mel voiced my thoughts: "I kind of wasn't expecting that."

A tangle of jet-black hair fell over his forehead, with jutting tousles above his ears. His face was deeply tanned, with a lantern jaw and strong chin.

He looked to be older than eighteen. Overall his features were pleasing, handsome even. Though he couldn't hold a candle to Brandon's Abercrombie looks, the boy was attractive in his own rough way.

"He's *gorgeous*," Catherine said, her eyes lighting up with interest. We called her Cat-o-gram because she could never hide her reactions, displaying them for all to see.

People passed us in the doorway, speculating about the newcomers:

"My maid comes from Basin. She said all five of them are juvies with records."

"I heard the tall boy knifed two guys in the French Quarter. He was just released from a year's stint in a cage-the-rage correctional center!"

"The blond boy is a sophomore for the third *try. . . ."*

Weasel and the big one started for the entrance, leaving the other two and the girl to smoke, right out in the open.

The big one dug a flask from his back pocket. On school grounds? I noticed his fingers were circled with white medical tape for some reason.

While Weasel sneered at everyone he passed, his friend just narrowed his eyes with an unnerving resentment, as if he was disgusted by the kids at this school.

As the boys neared, I could make out some of their words. They spoke Cajun French.

My grandmother had taught it to me—before she'd been sent away—and for years I'd listened to the farm help speak it. As they'd stomped through Haven's fields in their work boots, I'd followed in my miniature boots, eagerly listening to their wild tales of life deep in the bayou.

I understood the dialect well. Not that this was something to brag about, since I could barely understand proper French.

I saw Weasel glowering at a nearby group of four JV cheerleaders. As he stalked closer, the girls grew visibly nervous; he yelled, "BOO!" and they cried out in fright.

Weasel snickered at the girls' reaction, but the other boy just scowled in their direction, muttering, *"Couillonnes."* He pronounced it *coo-yôns*. Idiots.

Any tiny lingering inclination to be friendly to the new students—as was my usual way—died. They were messing with *my* khaki tribe.

Then Weasel zeroed in on me with a smirk. "Ain't you dat *jolie* girl in dat Porsha?" His Cajun accent was as thick as any I'd ever heard. "Turn around, you, and hike up dat dress, so I can tell for true."

My friends' shocked expressions had me squaring my shoulders, refusing to be cowed by either of these boys. They'd come into our domain, acting like they owned the place.

With a sunny smile, I said, "Welcome to *our* school." My tone was part bubbly, part cutting—a mash-up of sugar and snide so perfected I should TM it. "I'm Evie. If you need assistance finding your way around *our* campus, just let someone—else—know."

If possible, Weasel's leer deepened. "Well, ain't you sweet, Evie. I'm Lionel." He pronounced it *Lie-nell*. "And this here's my *podna* Jackson Deveaux, also known as Jack Daniels."

Because of the flask? How delightful.

Jackson's eyes were a vivid gray against his tanned skin, and they were roaming over my face and figure like he hadn't seen a girl in years—or hadn't seen *me* minutes ago.

Lionel continued, "We doan need no ass-is-tance finding our way, no, but there're other tings you can ass-ist us with—"

Jackson jammed his shoulder into Lionel's back, forcing him along. As they walked down the hall, the big Cajun snapped under his breath, *"Coo-yôn, tu vas pas draguer les putes inutiles?"*

My eyes widened as understanding hit me.

Catherine said, "Did you see the way that boy was looking at Evie?"

"I didn't understand a word of that gibberish they were talking," Mel said. "And I just got back from Paris." She turned to me. "So what'd the big one say?"

Grace asked, "*You* speak Cajun?"

"A little." *A lot.* Though I didn't particularly want everyone in Sterling to know I spoke the "Basin tongue," I translated: "Idiot, you're not going to chat up one of those useless bitches?"

Catherine gasped. "You lie."

As I watched Jackson striding down the hall, I noticed with amazement that the flask was not the only thing he kept in a back pocket of his jeans.

I could clearly make out a knife, a folded blade outlined in faded denim.

Then I frowned. Was he heading into *my* homeroom?

Grace said, "Wait a second. What did that boy mean about you hiking up your dress in a Porsche?"

For lunch period, Mel and I were lying out on a blanket in a sunny spot in Eden Courtyard, sleeves and skirts rolled up.

All around us, roses and gardenias bloomed. A marble fountain gurgled. Brand and Spencer were playing a pickup game in the adjoining quad with other boys, laughing in the sun.

And Jackson Deveaux?

He was loitering just outside our courtyard with the other Cajuns, sipping from his flask while the rest smoked. And he was staring at me.

Ignore him. I was determined to enjoy the rest of lunch relaxing with my best friend; never would I take for granted this precious freedom.

I exhaled. Okay, so maybe I wasn't precisely *relaxing*. I'd been on edge since I'd woken this morning from another nightmare of the red witch.

In each one, I seemed to be present with her, watching from a short distance away, forced to witness her evil deeds. Last night, she'd been in a beautiful golden field, surrounded by a group of cloaked people, all on their knees. She was tall, towering over their bowed heads.

With a laugh, she'd cast bloody grain in front of them, demanding that the people lap it up, or else she'd *slice their flesh to ribbons and choke them in vine.*

As she'd bared her claws, sinister purple ones that looked like rose thorns, her victims had wept for mercy. She'd given them none.

In the end, their flayed skin really did look like ribbons. . . .

Eager for distraction, I turned to Mel, but she had her earbuds in, absently singing an angry female rock song. She loved to sing; her voice sounded like two cats in heat sparring in a traffic cone.

With the right makeup and lighting, her face looked stunning, all haughty cheekbones and flawless skin. Right now, she was cute, with her mouth a touch too big, her eyes a bit wide, her expressions comical instead of come-hither.

We'd been best friends ever since kindergarten, when a little punk kid had kicked my shins. Mel had swooped in to save the day. Lisping through her missing front teeth, she'd demanded, "Wath he mething with you?"

I'd nodded up at her, sensing a sympathetic hug on the way and eager for it. But she'd marched off and handed that boy his ass.

Now she leaned up on her elbows, removing her earbuds with a frown. "Okay, nobody's ever accused me of being perceptive or anything, but even *I* can feel that Cajun staring at you."

He had been at it for a day and a half. "Imagine having three classes with him." English, history, and earth sciences. Not to mention that Jackson and I were practically locker mates.

"*And* homeroom." Mel was still pissed that she and I weren't together, that I'd been exiled from all my friends.

But hey, I'd scored both Jackson and Clotile Declouet, the Cajun girl.

I sat up, twisting my hair into a knot, sneaking a glance to my side. Yet again, I found myself in his sight line. He was sitting atop a metal table, scuffed biker boots on the attached bench, with his friends gathered around him.

Jackson had his elbows on his knees and his gaze fixed in my direction, even as he spoke French with the others. Occasionally Clotile leaned over to murmur to him.

"You think she's his girlfriend?" I asked, immediately regretting it when Mel shaded her eyes to blatantly study them.

"Normally, I'd say they were *perfect* for each other."

Klassy, meet Good-Natured.

"But if they're together, then why does he keep staring at you? Like he hasn't deposited enough mental images into his spank bank by now?"

"That in no way makes me feel better about this situation, Mel."

"What are they talking about?" She'd been delighted that I was uncovering all kinds of dirt on our enchanting new students.

Though I'd never considered myself a big eavesdropper, it wasn't like I could turn off my French, and the Cajuns kept talking in front of me, completely unguarded. "They're debating whether to pawn their school-issue laptops."

Mel snorted, then grew serious. "How much do you think they'd go for . . . ?"

In homeroom yesterday, when a TA had passed out the computers, Clotile and Jack had stared in astonishment; then Clotile had smoothed her fingers over hers, wistfully murmuring, *"Quel une chose jolie"*—such a pretty thing. As if it was the most precious possession she'd ever owned.

With an involuntary pang, I'd realized it probably was. Their town was basically a big swamp filled with leaky-roofed shacks, many without power.

As mind-boggling as it seemed to me, these kids wouldn't have computers—much less their *own* computers. When I'd comprehended how hard it must be for her to adjust to this new school, I'd caught her eye and mouthed, *Hi*, with a smile.

She'd frowned over her shoulder, then at Jack—who'd canted his head with puzzlement. . . .

"Well, what's the verdict?" Mel asked. "Pawn or not?"

"Lionel and Gaston plan to cash in *tout de suite*. Clotile and Tee-Bo are going to hold. Jackson has *parole* concerns."

"I knew the rumors about him were true!"

When they'd eventually finished drinking/smoking and meandered off, Mel's attention focused on Spencer. "He *really* likes me. I can tell."

"Uh-huh, sure thing." I'd asked Brand yet again to set them up, even if just on a friends double.

"I *am* a sure thing," Mel said. "Why *wouldn't* Spence like me?"

Sometimes when she said stuff like that, I couldn't tell if she was kidding or not.

"So what are you going to do about Brandon's hymen safari?"

"I have no idea." I'm sure everyone in school was wondering—I had a sixteenth birthday coming up and an older, much more experienced boyfriend.

As Mel had summed up my predicament, "Once a racehorse learns how to run, you can't expect to keep him hobbled for long."

I watched Brand laughing with some other guys, his face flushed against his white button-down. He looked utterly gorgeous.

And yet I just didn't feel this grand passion to experience sex with Brand, no overwhelming curiosity about the deed either. Though I felt *meh* about the whole subject, I didn't want to lose him.

It has to happen sometime. "I just don't like being pressured." Even if I'd made that promise to begin with. But I'd been desperate to keep him faithful all summer! "I . . . I'll think about it later," I trailed off in a defeated tone, feeling even more exhausted.

"What's up with you? You usually have tons of energy."

I shrugged, unable to tell her that my pills left me drained.

"If you're going to be lame, I'm going to go creep on Spencer."

"Have fun," I muttered. "No biting. Wake me before the bell."

She skulked off, and soon enough I heard her laughing theatrically at one of Spencer's jokes.

But I couldn't drift off, still feeling like I was being watched. I scanned the area again. Everyone was going about their lunch as usual.

I made myself close my eyes. *Stop being paranoid, Evie. Enjoy this place, the blooms. . . .*

Their scent reminded me of my Gran's beloved rose garden at

Haven. She'd planted it beneath one of the windmill water pumps, tended it religiously before her breakdown.

I didn't remember a lot about my grandmother, but since I'd returned home, I'd been thinking about her more and more. I was eight the last time I'd seen her. On a sweltering Louisiana summer day, she'd told me we were going to get ice cream. I remembered thinking it must be the best ice cream in the state, because we drove and drove. . . .

I frowned. The scent of roses was growing stronger, overwhelming. Was someone holding one in front of my face? Was it Brand?

I peeked open my eyes, blinked in confusion. Two rose stalks had stretched toward me, delicate blooms on either side of my head. As I watched, dumbstruck, they inched closer to my face, to *touch* my cheeks.

Dewy, soft petals were caressing me as my mind flipped over and I worked up a scream—

"Ahhh!" I scrambled to my feet.

They retracted just as quickly. As if in fright—of me.

I glanced up. Saw students staring at me. Mel shot me a quizzical look.

"Th-there was . . . a bee!" *Oh, God, oh, God!* I snatched up my purse and rushed inside, heading for the bathroom.

In the hall, sounds seemed muffled. I passed people without speaking to them, ignoring anyone who approached me.

When I reached the sink, I splashed my face with water over and over. *Get hold of yourself. Reject the delusion.*

Was I getting sick again? I'd thought I was cured!

Leaning forward, I studied my face in the mirror. I barely recognized myself. But I didn't look crazy; I looked . . . scared. *Am I going to lose everything?*

I gripped the edges of the sink. Maybe I'd fallen asleep and had been experiencing another weird dream?

Yes! That was it, I'd simply dozed off. My medicine prevented delusions. I hadn't had one in Atlanta. Not a single episode.

This made sense. After all, I hadn't experienced my usual hallucination symptoms. Last spring, whenever I'd been vision-bound, I'd felt a bubbly sensation in my head and nose, as if I'd drunk a carbonated soda too fast—

"What the hell, Greene?" Mel charged in. "You're scared of bees now?"

I shrugged, hating to lie to her. Would she notice my shaking?

"You have been acting so weird since you got back from Hotlanta. Even slooowwwer on the uptake than you were last spring. Nervouser, too." Mel's eyes widened. "Oh, I get it. Did your friends at deportment school learn you good about high-dollar drugs?"

I rolled my eyes.

"I'm serious. So help me God, if you are doing drugs"—Mel pointed to the ceiling—"without me, there will be consequences, Evie Greene!"

"I swear to you that I'm not doing illicit drugs."

"Oh." She backed down, appeased. "Are you okay?"

"I'm fine now. I fell asleep, and when I woke up there was a bee right on my face." The lie tasted like chalk in my mouth.

"Oh, shit! Why didn't you say so? I was about to schedule a carefrontation with you."

"I don't . . . just a bee . . ." I trailed off because ivy was climbing through the raised window behind Mel. Growing before my eyes, it began to slither down the wall.

Like a long green snake—

The bell rang. The ivy retreated, taking with it a big chunk of my sanity.

"I'll go get our things," Mel said. "Meet you at your locker." But at the door, she turned back. "Hey, buck up. You look like somebody died." As I tried to move my lips in a response, she breezed out the door.

Evie Greene, version 1.0, RIP.

DAY 4 B.F.

As I sat waiting for Mr. Broussard's history class to start, I sketched in my contraband drawing journal and tried to ignore Jackson, sitting a couple of rows behind me.

Easier said than done. Everything about him seemed to demand my attention. Especially since he and that boy Gaston had started talking about girls—namely Jackson's *many* lady friends, his *gaiennes*.

So in the Basin, Jackson was a player? *You're in a different league now, Cajun.*

I resumed drawing my latest nightmare. Three out of the last three nights, I'd dreamed of the red witch's gruesome killings.

Drawing was not something I did for fun, but more a compulsion—as if I feared a bad memory had to mark a page or it would stain my brain.

As my thoughts drifted, my pencil began to move. I flicked my wrist for slashing lines, slowly shading elsewhere, and the witch's latest victim took shape—a man hanging upside down from an oak limb, trapped in thorny vines.

Unlike the delicate, shy ivy I'd encountered in the bathroom yesterday, the ones that bound him were thicker, barbed lashes that coiled around him like an anaconda. And the witch controlled them, making them squeeze tighter each time the man released a breath.

Those thorns bit into his flesh, a thousand greedy fangs. I

painstakingly carved edges as I darkened those barbs, sharpening them.

The witch forced the vines to constrict, tighter, tighter, until his bones cracked—and blood poured.

She wrung it from that man like water from a rag. . . .

Cracking, squeezing. He had no breath to scream. One of his eyeballs burst from its socket, tethered to his skull by veins. As I sketched that, I wondered if he could still see out of it.

With drawings like this, it was easy to see why my journal had been my downfall before.

When I'd first complained of tingling sensations in my head and blurred vision, Mom had taken me to a slew of doctors for CT scans and tests, all negative. Throughout it all, I'd been able to disguise from everyone how bad the hallucinations had been. Then Mom had discovered my journal.

I'd trusted her, coming clean about my apocalyptic delusions. Big mistake.

After gaping in horror at page after page—of ash and devastation, of slimy bogeymen teeming among blackened ruins—she'd begun connecting the dots. "Don't you understand, Evie? Your hallucinations are things that your grandmother *taught* you when you were little. Those doomsday kooks you see on the street? She's not much different from them! Looking back, I can see that she . . . she *indoctrinated* you with these beliefs. I know, because she tried to do it to me!"

I'd been sunk. You can deny being insane all you want, but when a parent has hard copies of your crazy on file—and you've got a family history of mental illness—you're screwed.

Mom had yanked me out of my sophomore year a couple of weeks early, then driven me to CLC. The docs there had stuck me in the same track they used for kids rescued from cults.

My deprogramming had started with a single question: *"Evie, do you understand why you must reject your grandmother's teachings . . . ?"*

I'd given that doc an answer, slurring from the mind-altering meds they'd pumped into me. But I couldn't quite recall my reply—

Gaston distracted me again, asking Jackson about his latest *doe tag*. Cajun for scoring?

I sneaked a glance at Jackson over my shoulder. On his desk, he had only the history text, a few sheets of loose-leaf paper, and a single pencil clutched in his big, taped fist. His expression was smug as he replied, *"Embrasser et raconter? Jamais."* Kiss and tell? Never.

I gazed heavenward with irritation, then turned back to my journal, finishing another detail on my sketch—the man's other eyeball succumbing to the pressure, dangling beside the first.

But Gaston's next question drew my attention once more. *"T'aimes l'une de ces filles?"*

Did Jackson like any of the girls here?

His deep-voiced answer: *"Une fille, peut-etre."* One, maybe.

Again I felt his eyes on *me*. Earlier Mel had asked, "Does he really think he's got a shot at you?"

I kind of believed he really *did*.

Yesterday, I'd decided to give him a wide berth. Not so easily done. Unlike most boys, Jackson returned to his locker after every class. To be fair, his stops could've been for flask refills.

But sometimes he would take a drink, then turn to me with his lips parted, like he was about to ask me something.

I always gave him a cool smile, then strode off. And the Cajunland player seemed *surprised* that I was immune to his charms. Granted, he was attractive—some girls *sighed* as he passed them. . . .

Acting like I was fascinated with the classroom's many wall maps, I glanced over my shoulder to gauge his looks once more.

His gaze was already on me. As we took each other's measure, sunlight beamed through the window, striking his handsome face, highlighting his gray eyes and chiseled features.

With those cheekbones, squared jaw, and raven-black hair, he probably had Choctaw or Houma ancestry.

No wonder he has so many gaiennes.

Where had that thought come from? I faced forward with a blush.

33

Even if I didn't have a boyfriend, I'd never go out with a parolee biker. Who, if rumors were to be believed, was the ringleader behind a new rash of thefts in Sterling.

Back to the drawing. I blanched at my ghastly depiction. *Slice you to ribbons, choke you in vine.* So totally disturbing—but I had no one to confide in, no one to tell me things would get better.

If my crazy was anything like what Gran had gone through, I wished we could talk about it. Yet Mom had forbidden me to contact her, didn't want me even to think about her. . . .

"Everybody settle down," Broussard said. "Today we're going to learn a little about the French Acadians or Cadians—more commonly known as Cajuns."

He could do all the Cajun PR he wanted to; everybody had already made up their minds about the transfers.

Whenever Clotile sashayed down the hall in her microminis and cutoff T-shirts, boys stopped and stared, jamming traffic. The guys in this town had just never encountered a girl so blatantly available for sex, and it was making them a little wild.

Most students steered clear of Jackson, whose steely gaze and buck knife had done nothing to dispel the cage-the-rage rumor.

The three other Cajuns were just as troublesome, punching students' books out of their hands or tripping them.

"They were originally French settlers in Acadia," Broussard began, "what's now known as Nova Scotia." He raised a wooden pointer to indicate Canada on a map. "When the Protestant English who controlled that area gave them ultimatums—one of which was to change their religion or leave—the fiercely Catholic Acadians migrated to Louisiana, to settle bayou lands that everyone else had deemed worthless. Acadian—Cadian—Cajun. Get it?"

I couldn't have been less interested in this subject. I only tuned back in once Broussard had finished his lecture and began outlining our junior paper on local history.

Making up 40 percent of our grade, it would be a partnership effort.

I listened without concern as he announced the sixteen partnerships; I could work with fairly much anyone in this class.

"Jackson Deveaux and Evie Greene."

The. Hell.

Paired with the boy who'd been staring at me for days? I bit my lip, glancing back at him. He gave me a chin jerk in acknowledgment.

Broussard said, "For the last half of this class, you'll sit with your partner, working out meeting and research schedules for the semester."

Meeting with Jackson *for an entire semester*? Obviously I'd have to write the whole paper. But something told me the drunken biker who'd ogled my ass in the Porsche might insist on us "researching" together.

When everyone else began moving desks, he patted the vacated seat next to him with a cocky smirk.

Did he expect me to trip over myself to get near him? To become a doe tag?

I didn't need this! Already my classes were going to be grueling, without having to deal with a lecherous parolee on a regular basis.

A drop in grades was one of the signs my mom was supposed to look for that might indicate a relapse.

When I imagined returning to CLC, my hand shot up. Broussard ignored me.

I cleared my throat. "Mr. Broussard, can I . . ." My voice trailed off when he turned on me, his thick brows knitted with irritation.

"Evie, start working on this. *Now.*"

I decided to endure the next thirty minutes, then talk to Broussard after class—

Jackson slammed into the desk next to mine, his gray eyes furious. I hastily shut my journal, but he must've gotten a peek because he frowned for a second before saying, "You doan even *know* me, and you're angling for another . . . podna?"

I knew *podna* was hard for him to say, because it also was Cajun for *friend*. "Wouldn't you rather work with Gaston?"

"I asked you a question. Why you want to switch?"

"Fine. Because when you drove by us Monday, you were leering at me like a registered SO."

"A blonde pulls up her skirt and bends over for me? I'm goan to pay attention."

My eyes darted. Had anyone heard that? Under my breath, I snapped, "I was not bending over for you!"

"You been *leering* at me just as much, girl."

"Me?" Inhaling for composure, I said, "Come on, Jack, be realistic. You know that someone like you and someone like me would never be able to work together."

His voice scathing, he said, "You doan call me Jack, no. Only my friends do."

Anger issues, much? I was starting to believe the knifing rumor. "There are a thousand other things I'd prefer to call you."

My nose began to itch, which set me even more on edge. The room darkened. Maybe we were *finally* going to get some rain. There hadn't been a drop of precipitation all summer.

With a glare for good measure at Jackson, I glanced outside—

The sun was . . . gone.

Night was falling. And across the sky, ethereal lights flickered, crimson and violet, like Mardi Gras streamers. I gaped as flames arced over the school, those eerie lights like a twinkling crown above the fire.

Across the grounds, a river of snakes slithered over each other, their scales reflecting the lights above. Panicked rats scurried alongside the creatures that usually *ate* them.

Those flames descended, searing them to ash, everything to ash.

The apocalypse. Just like my visions from last spring. I'd thought . . . I'd thought I was *cured*, at least of these. But that shivery feeling in my head told me otherwise.

Reject the delusion. Center yourself; you're in control, focused.

I told myself that, but all I could think was: *You're freaking out, about to hyperventilate, where the hell is center?* Damn it, I'd taken my medicine!

I jerked my gaze away, inwardly chanting, *Not real, not real.* Everyone else in class was talking, Broussard reading with his heels kicked up.

Jackson was staring down at his fists, taking deep breaths. Caging the rage? He opened his mouth to speak. . . .

Another peek at the window. A *boy* was strolling through the flames outside, stopping fifteen feet or so away from the line of windows. Though fire raged all around him, he was untouched.

He had even features, a mop of dark brown hair, and deep brown eyes. He was tall, with a swimmer's physique, leanly muscular. An attractive boy.

I'd never seen people in my delusions before! Unless you counted the blood-drinking bogeymen—

"Evie!" The imaginary boy was speaking to me!? *"Where are your allies? So much to learn. Know no plays! Allegiances forming!"* he said, his demeanor harried. *"Beware the old bloodlines, the other families that chronicle. They know what you are! Beware the lure: a wounded creature, a light in darkness, a feast when your stomach cleaves. Allies, Evie! Beware!"*

He was . . . *talking* . . . to *me.* Maybe the real test of crazy was if I talked back?

I dimly heard Jackson saying something to me as well. What? What? I felt off-kilter, like the ground was teetering. *Act normal, Evie. You remember how to do this. Respond to the Cajun like nothing's wrong.* "I, uh, I s-suggest we talk to Broussard after class and get ourselves reassigned."

He scowled. "You doan know anything about me."

"I know enough . . ."—*finish your sentence*—"enough not to trust forty percent of my grade to you." That had come out way harsher than I'd meant it.

His expression turned menacing. "Are you even listening to what I've been saying, you?"

"You don't prepare," that imaginary boy murmured sadly. *"I go over the edge, the dog at my heels, but the moon is waxing, Empress. You must be ready. Field of battle. Arsenal. Obstacles. Foes. It begins directly at the End. And the Beginning is nigh."*

Empress? The word dredged up forbidden memories of Gran ask-ing, *"Does Empress Evie want some ice cream?"*

Outside, the landscape was changing. The school's gardens had been incinerated. Everything was dead. I might as well have been look-ing at the surface of the moon. Nausea churned.

"Behold the field of battle," the boy said, motioning toward the waste-land of cinder. *"Arsenal?"* he queried in a hopeful tone. *"Obstacles? Foes? No? Ah, you listen poorly!"* Then his face brightened. *"Next time I'll talk* louder. *And louder. And louder."*

He—and the entire scene—vanished.

Louder? I couldn't handle this, much less *louder*! I clasped my shaking hands in my lap as I struggled to hide my panic. Had Jackson just said something else?

Again, I told him, "We'll get new partners."

He was silent for long moments before grating, "You doan think I can do the work, doan think I'm smart enough?"

My third day of school. The apocalyptic visions had returned. I was insane.

Two years and out? I wouldn't make two weeks. I gave a bitter laugh.

"You're *laughing* at me?" He clenched those big, taped fists like he was just dying to hit something. Most likely my face.

"What else would I be laughing at?" I questioned sharply, defen-sively. It took me a second to realize that I'd just insulted the hell out of the Cajun.

I felt like sobbing. The medicine wasn't working, I wouldn't make two years till college, and I'd just been hideous to Jackson, even if I hadn't completely meant to be.

Maybe I could apologize later, tell him I hadn't been feeling well—

"Tu p'tee pute," he sneered to my face. You little bitch.

I stiffened. Scratch that apology.

Unable to help myself, I glanced at the window again. That boy was gone, and the sun had returned to shine over green grass and achingly brilliant blooms.

Maybe I'd dreamed that wasteland. Maybe all of this day was a dream! A side effect of my medicine was a sense of being outside one's body.

I felt a million miles away.

Or maybe that scene was like a residual hiccup from last spring—a sign, a *test*—to see how committed I was to being normal.

If this was a trial by fire, I'd pass. I'd *excel*.

Jackson scowled at me, clenching that pencil in his fist until I thought it would snap. The tension between us groaned as I battled the urge to take out my journal, to draw that cryptic boy's face.

The clock on the wall ticked like a bomb.

How would I manage to hide this latest development from my eagle-eyed mother during one of her interrogations? For most of my life, Karen Greene had been the ideal mom—funny, kind, hardworking. But lately, it'd seemed like a stranger had taken her over, one determined to bust me for something.

If she discovered I was hallucinating again, I had no doubt my mother would lock me up in a place like CLC indefinitely.

Because she'd done it to her own mother eight years ago.

At last the bell rang. Once the rest of the students had filed out of class, Broussard pronounced to Jackson and me, "The assignments stay the same. You two have to work it out."

Jackson's pencil snapped in his fist.

Brandon was waiting on me at my locker, casually eating an apple, so blissfully immune to drama or doubts. Between bites, he said, "What's the matter? You look like you're about to freak out."

Ding, ding, ding. Then I reminded myself that what I'd just suffered was a mere residual vision. So what was there to freak out about? "I'm fine. I just got partnered in history with Jackson Deveaux. Broussard won't reassign me."

"Deveaux shoved his shoulder into mine yesterday," Brand said. "Don't know what his problem is. You need me to talk to him?"

Brand was a lover, not a fighter. "I don't want you to do anything that will get you kicked off the team." Plus, I suspected Jackson would mop the floor with him. "Those Basin kids are driving me up the wall."

He nodded. "I hate those four punks." Startling words from Brand. Normally, he was like me, getting along with everybody. "The girl seems all right, though."

Does she, then? Yesterday after biology, I'd smiled to find Brand waiting for me, but he'd turned, agog, as a braless Clotile sauntered past—before I cleared my throat with an arch look.

Even more embarrassing? Jackson had seen the whole thing, smirking over the rim of his flask.

Now Brand seemed to be awaiting something from me. *What?* My brain was soup.

Jackson stormed up to his locker then, Lionel following him. As Jackson tossed his history text inside, he shot me a killing look. I slitted my eyes before I turned back to Brand.

"I've got an idea I want to run by you," he murmured, his lids growing heavy.

Oh. Back to that. Ever since I'd returned, I'd been avoiding the subject of My Promise, hoping Brandon would take a hint.

In texts, he'd actually begun counting down the days left until my birthday—like he had a cherry countdown widget.

When I caught him sneaking a glance at my chest, his expression one of longing, I remembered a movie where one of the heroines had likened boobs to smart bombs. I'd laughed. Now I marveled at how right she'd been.

I scraped up a placid smile. "Let's talk after practice."

He leaned in. "Spence's parents are going out of town, not this weekend but the next. So it'd be after your birthday . . ."

Jackson was too close, could overhear this private conversation!

". . . you can tell your mom you're spending the night with Melissa, then stay with me."

"Brandon, we'll meet *later*. I'll let you know then."

"Okay. Yeah, sure." When his friends called for him, he dipped down to give me a peck on the lips, then jogged off.

As I collected my books, I heard Lionel say in French, "Surprised you didn't make a run at that one." He indicated me with a jerk of his chin. "She's not your type, but she's pretty."

Jackson's *type*? He probably preferred drunken Bayou Bessies who put out *before* the crawfish boil.

"She's ice-cold and she's a conceited bitch," Jackson replied in French, his voice rumbling with anger. "Just a useless little doll—pretty to look at and not a damn thing more."

While Lionel snickered, I gritted my teeth, determined not to let them know I understood.

Oh, I'm more than a useless little doll, Cajun. I'm a damaged one. And if you knew what went on inside my mind, you'd make the sign of the cross and run the other way.

Yet Jackson was sharp. His gaze took in my stiffened shoulders and clenched jaw.

With narrowed eyes, he faced me while continuing to address Lionel in French, "*You* should make a run at her, and be sure to take her down a peg while you're at it. Never met a girl who needed it more."

I tried to school my reaction, didn't know if I succeeded.

When the bell rang and Lionel shuffled off, Jackson grated to me, *"Tu parles le Français Cadien?"*

I hesitated a moment, looked up, then glanced over my shoulder. In a confused tone, I said, "Are you talking to *me*?" Advantage Evie.

Jackson looked thunderstruck. *"Tu parles Français!"*

"Huh? What are you saying?"

He stalked closer, looking dangerous, making me crane my head up to hold his gaze. "Like you doan know, you."

Matching his fuming tone, I enunciated, "I do not speak *Basin*." It came out even snobbier than I'd intended, but I was okay with that.

After unending moments, Jackson turned toward his class, but he looked back, pointing at me with a taped finger. *"Je te guette."* I'm watching you.

DAY 3 B.F.

I lay in bed with my books spread out all around me, my buzzing cell phone in my open palm, my TV on, volume muted.

On Thursday nights, Mel and I always watched *America's Next Top Model* together, texting commentary. She opened with: I'd totally do the ginger model.

But I had no energy to respond.

R U there?

I finally texted, U'd do the dress dummy.

HAHAHAHAHAHA bitch

I grinned sleepily, then turned back to my homework. I'd been reading the same sentence again and again with no comprehension. Ultimately, I gave up, collapsing onto my back. Sprawled like a casualty, I gazed around me.

After my stint in the bleak, no-frills CLC, I was still unused to the luxuries of home. My room here was spacious, with a walk-in closet you could get lost in and a Sotheby's auction worth of antique furniture. The astronomical thread-count of these yummy sheets made me want to purr.

I'd even missed my wall mural. Before I'd gone round the bend last spring, when things had been so hopeless, I'd drawn the blackest, most ominous storm clouds, then rendered them aglow with lightning bolts. I found myself staring even now. . . .

A text chime distracted me. Spence hasn't called. WTF Greene?

Working on it, I texted with a wide yawn. Though so much was riding on my grades, I still couldn't motivate myself to study. Convincing myself that I'd never have a pop quiz tomorrow—I mean, what were the odds?—I decided to go to sleep.

With one lethargic leg, I shuffled books off my bed. My journal was already tucked safely under my mattress.

I texted: C-P. bout 2 pass out, tlk 2moro? My responses to Brandon's messages had been equally lame.

But U never miss ANTM

Though I could *hear* the hurt in her text, I still wrote, Nite. Phone and TV off.

In the dark of the night, our old house settled with ghostly groans, shrouded in fog. The moisture swelled the boards, making the frame shift like it was trying to get comfortable.

On nights like this, a ship at sea was quieter.

Haven was the only home I'd ever known. I could feel its history, could feel the farm suffering now. Since I'd been back, the weather had been like a near-sneeze, rain clouds building and building, only to dissipate with no payoff. The drought wore on. . . .

But when I shut my eyes, I found my thoughts drifting to another source of worry. Jackson Deveaux. Courtesy of the Cajun, my week had deteriorated even more. As promised, he'd been keeping his eye on me, scowling the entire time.

Like he was being forced to investigate something he particularly hated.

In English yesterday, he'd glowered at the kid behind me, taking the swiftly vacated desk. While I'd sat stiffly, he'd leaned forward until awareness of him had permeated my senses. I'd been able to hear his breaths, to smell the medical tape on his hands and a woodsier male scent that made my skin flush. The room had been dark and close as another teasing storm front had rolled into the parish.

Then he'd started murmuring *le Français Cadien* to me, telling me

43

that he knew I could understand him, and that he'd prove it. Wanting to thwart him in any way possible, I'd shown no reaction, even when he'd said in a husky tone that I smelled *comme une fleur*, like a blossom.

Why wouldn't he leave me alone?

Just as he'd studied me, I'd tried to analyze him. One thing I'd noticed? When he didn't think anyone was looking, his gaze turned restless, as if he longed to be anywhere but where he was at that moment. And he would absently run his fingers over the tape on his knuckles. Why did he wear it?

I threw my arm over my face. Why was I musing about Jackson? Instead of my own boyfriend?

I wasn't thinking clearly! God, I just needed one good night's sleep. Though my bitter little pills hadn't prevented yesterday's hallucination— or, rather, my *residual blip*—they still succeeded in making me sleepy.

I glanced over at my pill bottle. *Desperate times . . .*

Later that night, I woke to find myself standing in my driveway in my underwear, with no memory of how I came to be there.

I blinked several times. Surely this was a dream, or even a hallucination.

Last I remembered, I'd been tanked on pills, drifting off in my bed. So, any minute now, I'd *really* wake up.

Any minute . . .

Nope. Still standing there, barefooted on my oyster-shell drive-way, wearing nothing but boy-short panties and an old cheerleading camp T-shirt.

Shit.

I squinted through the mist to get my bearings, but I could barely see a few feet in front of me.

The fog was as thick and wet as breath on a mirror, dimming the heat lightning above. Yellow bolts the color of a cat's eye forked out above me.

Assuring myself that there was a perfectly logical reason why this hallucination was more lifelike than the others, I started back toward the house, wincing as the razor-sharp shells sliced my tender feet. Naturally, our driveway was raised, flanked by two drainage ditches all the way to our lawn. Which meant I was stuck halfway down the mile-long drive.

A stable person might ask herself why she had no cuts from the trip out here; it wasn't like I'd been plopped here from the sky.

Maybe because this is just a dream? I told myself that, even as I cussed and sputtered my way across the shells.

And to make the situation worse, I again felt like I was being watched. I ran my hand over my nape. *Ignore it—*

A horse shrieked. I jerked my head around, peering through the fog, but couldn't determine the direction.

Another frenzied shriek—that couldn't possibly have come from my gentle nag dozing in the barn. I quickened my pace.

My eyes went wide when I made out the sound of hooves crushing the shells; a horse was speeding toward me. From behind me? Farther down the drive? I couldn't tell!

This isn't real. You're in control, focused!

Hard to focus when my feet were getting sliced! "Shit, shit."

Hooves pounded closer . . . *closer* as I hopped and yelped my way down the drive like a cartoon character.

Then I heard metal clanking against metal, almost like the sound of *armor?*

My instincts got the better of me. Ignoring the pain, I began to seriously run.

Finally the end of the drive was in sight. To my right, Haven House loomed. To my left was the edge of our front cane field.

The house was safer.

The field was closer.

How much of a lead did I have on the rider? The heaving breaths of that horse sounded directly behind me. How close was he?

A memory of Gran's voice drifted through my mind: *"The fog lies, Evie."*

As soon as the driveway dumped into the front lawn, I veered off, sprinting toward the field. This close to harvest, the cane was mature, twice as tall as I was. I could lose anyone in those rows. I craned my head back but saw only a blur of a rider.

Running . . . running . . .

I heard a whistle, as if something was slicing through the air. A sword? Even in my panic, some memory was tickling my brain.

The cane was twenty feet away.

Ten feet.

When I heard that whistling directly behind me and felt a sudden breeze on my nape, I dove for the edge of the cane rows, arms out-stretched in front of me.

Amid the stalks, I scrambled to my knees, but the rider didn't follow. His horse reared with another shriek, front legs stabbing the air with sharpened hooves.

I gaped up at my pursuer. He wore black armor with a fearsome helmet. The weapon he'd wielded was a scythe; it now sat glinting in a saddle holster. His pale stallion had red eyes.

As he spurred that mount to stalk back and forth at the edge of the field, I fought realization.

Scythe. Black armor. A pale horse.

This was . . . Death. The classic image of the Grim Reaper.

His horse's mane was blowing in a wind that I could not feel. The feathery leaves of the cane above me were still.

As I stared at him, the regular soundtrack of the farm—my own horse whinnying in sleep, katydids chirping—gave way to the sounds of gravel crunching underfoot, that breeze picking up, and the occa-sional . . . hiss?

Behind Death, Haven House began to disappear, transformed into a space of gleaming black, cluttered with crushed pillars and piles of rubble. Like ancient city ruins?

I sensed that this was his barren, soulless lair, and his plane seemed to be pressing against my own.

Would he find my half of the world—all green and misty with sultry night air—as incomprehensible as I found his?

If he left, would my house come back? Would my *mother* inside come back? This delusion had gone from mind-blowingly wrong to horrifying. *Can't process this!*

He dismounted and strode to the edge of the field, but he wouldn't enter the cane. *Why?*

His jet-black armor was clearly from olden times, yet sported no chinks. Because no one had landed a blow against him? He had two wicked-looking swords, one sheathed at each hip.

Finally, I found my voice. "Who are y-you?"

"*Who am I*, she asks." My question amused him? "Life in your blood, in your very touch"—his voice was as raspy as the dry leaves, his accent foreign, though I couldn't pinpoint it—"and yet no one told you to expect *me*?" There was a light shining behind the grille of his helmet, as if his eyes *glowed*.

"What are you talking about?" I demanded with as much bravado as I could. "What do you want?"

Another hiss came from his lair, from among those ruins behind him.

Death removed his spiked metal gloves, revealing a man's hands, pale and perfect. "You know me. You always know, well before my blade strikes you down."

"You're insane," I whispered, though he felt so familiar to me.

He dropped to one knee at the edge of the cane and reached for me. "Come to me, Empress."

Empress Evie, Empress Evie . . .

His hand was mere inches from my arm, but I was paralyzed, transfixed by the light coming from behind his helmet—until something drew my attention.

Behind Death, I spied a hideous horned boy—more like a hunchbacked beast—skulking among the ruins. Ropy lines of spittle dangled from his bottom lip.

Death followed the direction of my gaze. "Don't mind Ogen," he said. "El Diablo is an old ally of mine."

"I'll make a feast of your bones," Ogen hissed at me as he sharpened one of his horns against stone. The grating sound was unbearable, shaking the rubble like an earthquake, making me want to scream. *"Suck the marrow dry as you watch."*

"Ignore him. Think of me alone." Death reached closer. "I've waited so long to face you again. Aren't you ready to have done with this?"

The cane bent unnaturally around me, as if to cage me in. Hadn't Gran always called the stalks "soldiers at attention"?

Was the cane trying to protect me?

"It begins directly at the End, Empress." Another seeking reach.

I scrambled back from him, wincing as pain ripped down my legs. Bloody stripes dripped down the sides of my thighs.

How had I cut myself? I raised my hands, and gasped with horror.

My nails were razor-sharp, a purplish-red color. I'd seen that sinister shade a thousand times before—that triangular *shape* before.

They looked like rose thorns.

"Oh God, oh God . . ." My heart thundered, my breaths shallowing until I was panting. Thorn claws like the red witch's? Blackness wavered in my vision, blurring Death, his lair, his hideous ally.

I started to laugh, hysterical sounds bubbling up from my chest, drowning out Death's promises to return for me, to finish our battle once and for all. I was still laughing when I collapsed backward, head smacking the ground—

At once, I shot upright in my own bed, covered in perspiration. My eyes darted around my room, flitting over the hand-painted walls. Death was gone, Ogen too.

"J-just a dream?"

Right when I was about to yank off the sheet to examine my legs and feet, I heard footsteps clipping down the hall.

I dropped back, closing my eyes an instant before my mother

entered. Without even a courtesy knock. "Evie, are you up?" Light flooded in from the hallway.

"Mom?" I said, trying to sound sleepy as I took a frantic mental inventory of my body. Were my feet bleeding, my legs? Was I covered in dirt? Had my fingernails returned to normal?

But all I felt was numbness, as if my entire body were immersed in Novocain.

"I thought I heard you cry out." Her tone had that alarmed edge to it. *Sherlock senses crazy. . . .*

"Huh? I must have been dreaming."

Still dressed for the day, she sat at the end of my bed, her diamond studs flashing. "Your face is so pale. Are you coming down with something?"

"Nope. Not me." Oh, God, if there was blood on my legs, would it soak through my sheet? If my mom saw those parallel slices, she would probably think I was a closet cutter, like my former roommate at the center.

"I'm worried about you," she said. "We need to talk about how you're doing now that you're back at home."

"Mom, I told you, everything's fine." My legs *were* bleeding.

Another furtive adjustment of the sheet. Three stripes of crimson were soaking through. *She'll see, she'll see. . . .*

Adjust the sheet, overlap it. There. Better.

"You've been back for nearly two weeks, but I haven't heard you laugh a single time. You always used to joke around, just like your dad." Her brows drew together. "Evie, what's . . ." She laid the back of her hand against my damp forehead. "Are you trembling?" She wrapped her arms around me, rocking me. "Baby, I'm here. What's wrong?"

What's right? I'd doubled up on my meds tonight—and I was now *worse* off. "I-I think I just had a bad dream."

She drew back. "A hallucination?"

"No! I was sound asleep."

"Honey, just *tell* me, and I will make this better."

You didn't last time. The cure didn't take! Yet I was so freaked out, I was tempted to reveal all once more.

Instead, I dug deep, resolved to make a stand. I met her gaze, steadying my tone. "I will tell you when I need your help."

She was taken aback by my demeanor. "Oh." Because, for a brief moment, I'd sounded just as steely as she usually did. "Um, okay."

"I've got a big day tomorrow. And I've really got to get some sleep." *I'm already going to be up for hours, convincing myself that I dreamed those claws.*

Mom rose, her gaze wary, almost startled. "Of course. Uh, sweet dreams, honey."

Once the door closed behind her, I yanked the sheet away, grimacing in advance at what I'd see.

The skin on my thighs was crusting with blood, but my feet were clean and free from gashes.

Maybe I'd just cut myself with my fingernails in sleep. I wanted to latch on to this reasoning, to ignore how realistic Death's visit had been.

When I recalled his armor, my fingers itched to render his likeness. I reached under my mattress, dragging out my drawing journal.

Pencil flying over the paper, I whispered repeatedly, *"Two years and out, two years and out."* A tear dropped onto the page, then another and another—three blurred spots over Death's otherworldly image.

By the time I'd finished the drawing, the storm pressure was ebbing. No rain for our crops tonight.

And because I was insane, I ached *with* them.

I gazed down at one of my legs, convinced that I'd merely cut myself during my nightmare. With a curse, I flicked the crusted blood away.

The skin beneath it was . . . unmarked.

I spent my free period on Friday in Eden Courtyard, sitting at the tiled cement table, licking my wounds in private.

On the verge of tears, I tried to ignore the fact that a bed of daisies had turned their faces toward me—instead of the direction of the sun.

At least the roses and ivy were still.

Last night, before I'd gone to sleep—the first time—I'd wondered, *What are the odds that I'll have a pop quiz?*

I hadn't had one today.

I'd had *two*. And just to add insult to injury? When we'd handed our English quizzes up the row, Jackson's paper had all the answers, scribbled in bold handwriting.

Though I'd never before gotten below a B+ on *anything*, I'd accumulated two Fs this week. At the thought, my eyes welled with tears. I laid my flushed face against the cool stone, struggling not to cry.

Today when I'd asked my teachers for makeups . . .

Bitches said *no*.

My stomach churned. *A drop in grades.* I couldn't go back to CLC, would never go back.

I had to wonder where the bottom was for this. What was that SAT word for the absolute rock bottom? The *nadir*. Where was my nadir?

How much more could I fail/lose/hallucinate/unravel? After last night's date with Death, I might've thought that I'd get a time-out from creepy. Not so!

Once we'd finished that quiz in English, I'd fallen asleep, dreaming again of the red witch. I began sketching her now. Naturally, she'd been fresh from a kill. Her vines had been smearing the blood of her victims over her skin; she enjoyed wearing it.

I'd been able to see more of her than ever before. Her pale face was round, her skin marred only by those two shimmering tattoos running the length of her cheeks. No, not *tattoos*, but *glyphs*—like glowing green brands. Though she had girlish freckles across her nose, she looked older, maybe midtwenties? Her eyes were gleaming green, pure evil.

I'd watched as she'd advanced on a magnificent rosebush, stabbing her thorn claws into one of its stalks. Somehow she'd leeched energy from it, siphoning its life into herself as she'd thrown back her head and shrieked with pleasure.

The plant writhed, as if in death throes, but she was merciless, sucking it dry, leaving it a withered husk. She was like a parasite, enslaving the very things I loved.

When I'd jerked awake, everyone had been packing up their books—except for Jackson.

Then I'd realized he hadn't been looking at my face, but at my hands, at my knuckles gone white as I clenched the edges of my desk. I'd released my hold at once.

"Nightmare?" he'd asked with a nod.

Had he seemed sympathetic? Unable to help myself, I asked, "Do you . . . do you have them?"

"Yeah." He'd sounded like he was about to say more, only to remember we weren't friends. He'd just repeated, "Yeah."

"What do you do?"

"I sleep with one eye open." He'd taken a pull from his flask and strode away.

I'd be happy just to sleep at all.

My phone chimed with a text from Brandon. If this was more pressure, I was going to primal-scream.

Kick-back on Sat. 4 couples. Ur friends & mine. Spence & Mel

He'd come through with Spencer? Finally something positive! I seized on this, excitedly texting: Where?

Sugar mill

I frowned. On the back, back, *back* forty of Haven there was a crumbling mill on the banks of the bayou. It was so old, only the brick walls and a smokestack remained. There was no glass in the porthole windows, so it kind of looked like an old Roman coliseum.

If folks thought Haven might be haunted, they were convinced the mill was. Rumors of gory deaths inside the cane crushers abounded.

But thinking of Mel, I knew I would agree to go—

"And you Sterling girls make fun of Clotile for wearing short skirts?" Jackson said, striding across the courtyard, raking his gaze over me in my cheer uniform.

I hastily closed my journal, putting it with my other books.

"Um, um, *UM*, Evie. Just seeing you in that getup makes me feel more . . . cheerful."

When I'd walked into homeroom this morning, he'd taken one look at me and smirked over the rim of his flask. He'd accused me of being like a doll. As I'd gotten ready for school, putting on my bright-red skirt and V-neck vest, with an oversize hair ribbon to match, I'd kind of felt like one.

Over my shoulder, he said in a goading voice, *"Je t'aime en rose."* I like you in pink. Then he sat uninvited beside me.

Huh? I wasn't wearing anything pink. Nothing but my bra—

He'd been looking over my shoulder, straight down my top! Did he have *no* boundaries?

And I couldn't say anything about it, or else I'd lose our battle of wills. I didn't need this! But I refused to leave my table, to give in to this bully.

"Tell me how you learned our tongue," he said, sounding . . . not irate.

"Once again, I don't understand that ridiculous gibberish you keep murmuring. And more, I'm done talking about it." I began to text my answer to Brand.

"You typing to that beau of yours?" Again Jackson got that frustrated look on his face. His moods were so changeable.

"*Texting*. Yes."

"He doan want to fight me after I called you a bitch?"

Sounds goo— My thumbs paused on my keyboard.

"Of course, I said that in French," Jackson continued. "But now I've had to go back and think of anything else you might've understood."

I tried to keep my expression neutral. "Whatever. All I know is that Brandon won't fight you."

"Because he knows I'll hand him his ass." Jackson gave me a mean smile.

"No, because he actually has something to lose by fighting."

Jackson didn't like that comment *at all*. His gray eyes blazed.

I realized where I'd seen that color before. On my bedroom wall.

Those ominous clouds in my mural, the ones aglow with lightning . . . that gray was the color of Jackson's eyes when he was angry.

"You think you and Radcliffe and all your stuck-up friends are so much better than everybody else." His fists clenched, his hands swelling. Tape ripped on one, revealing a deep gash across his fingers. All around it, grisly scar tissue had formed.

Our fight forgotten, I cried, "What happened to your hand?"

With a cruel look in his eyes, he pinched my chin and eased his other fist toward my face like he was throwing a punch in slow motion. "The teeth," he sneered, baring his own. "They cut like a saw blade."

He'd been in so many fights, he had scars growing over scars. I jerked back from him with a gasp, and he dropped his hands, his expression suddenly unreadable.

But I'd received the message loud and clear. This boy was dangerous. I turned away, finishing my text.

Jackson snagged my sketchbook, shooting to his feet, putting distance between me and his new prize.

As I scrambled from my seat, he opened the journal, frowning as he tilted a page to a different angle.

"Give it back, Jackson!"

"Ah-ah, *bébé*." He held it above my head, walking backward, taunting me with it. "Just let ole Jack see."

"I want it back—NOW!"

Suddenly he staggered, barely righting himself before he fell. The journal flew out of his grasp, landing on the ground.

I darted forward and scooped it up. "The bigger they are!" I snapped at him.

Lucky for me he'd tripped. Maybe he'd backed over the monkey grass.

My lips parted. Strands of it were still coiled tight around his ankles, dropping to the ground one by one.

Behind him that line of green was rippling, though there was no breeze. Jackson didn't seem to know why he'd tripped, but I did.

Those strands had shot out and *bound* his ankles. The plants were *interacting* with another person?

Plant movement had been *my* crazy—confined to my reactions, my confusion. I'd found it utterly terrifying to see.

But were they helping me? Like last night, when the cane had caged me in protectively?

Now the monkey grass had nearly felled my foe, saving my sketchbook. I started to laugh. *Helped a girl out, did you?*

Jackson again thought I was laughing at him. A flush spread over those chiseled cheekbones of his. He straightened to his full height, gave me a threatening scowl, then stalked off.

Once he was gone, I knelt in front of the grass, wanting to fan my fingers over it, but still too scared to. I stared at the daisies, then the roses.

Because I was round the bend again, I could ask myself some truly bizarre questions.

What did the monkey grass *want* in return for helping me? Did the ivy have an agenda? Roses: friend or foe?

One way or another, I needed to figure out what was happening to me.

I decided that once I got home, where no one could see me, I was going to test out the cane.

When Brand dropped me off at my house after school, he parked out of view of the kitchen window. "Is everything all right, Eves?" He drummed his fingers on the stick shift. "You've been acting weird ever since you got back."

"Everything's fine," I said, impatient to get to our field.

"Good deal," he said simply, taking me at my word, though my demeanor screamed, *Everything's futhermucked!*

He rested his hand on my thigh, high enough to make me frown up at him. He had a smile on his face, but it was strained. He traced circles above my knee.

"So have you thought about us going to Spencer's next weekend?"

"Probably not as much as you have."

"My brain's on shuffle," he said, tapping his temple. "Evie, football, Evie, football."

"At least I come first."

"Always," he said easily, flashing me his movie-star grin.

"I'll tell you my answer sometime this weekend, I promise." *Giving myself less than forty-eight hours to decide?*

Once he'd driven off to get ready for the game tonight, I headed toward the cane before I lost my nerve. I was determined to get to the bottom of this. Two equally catastrophic results awaited me. Either I was delusional. Or . . .

I didn't even want to go there.

Squaring my shoulders, I swallowed, and reached for the cane.

And damn if it didn't reach back.

I staggered away a few steps. Deep breath in. Deep breath out. *You're focused. Centered.*

I forced myself to reach for it again. Once more, it stretched toward my hand. This time it gently closed around my palm.

That curling leaf hadn't already been curved. It was *moving*. Like an infant grasping a parent's finger.

Oh, shit.

I hadn't experienced that tingly feeling in my head during any of the plant interactions because I hadn't been hallucinating. This was no vision—no delusion; this was real.

Right?

Straightening my shoulders, I stepped into the field, among all the cane. At once, the crop seemed to *sigh*, the leaves whispering around me.

I followed a row, deeper and deeper, those leaves ghosting over my face. My lids went heavy, as if a friend were brushing my hair.

The cane arched and danced toward me, and I went dizzy from pleasure, from the staggering sense of unity.

If they truly were my soldiers at attention, then I had the largest army in the world—six million stalks strong.

I could picture them moving in certain ways, and immediately they would respond. Bend, shimmy, sway. Left, right, up, back. Because we were utterly connected.

Among this number, I was safe, a chessboard queen surrounded by her pawns. And with this easing of tension, memories started trickling over the mental levee that CLC had helped me construct. I recalled more snippets of stuff my grandmother had told me.

On that last day I'd spent with her, as she'd driven us out on the big highway toward Texas, she'd said, "I'm a *Tarasova*, Evie, a chronicler of the Tarot. I know things that nobody else on earth knows. And you're the Empress. Just like the card in my deck. One day, you'll control all things that root or bloom."

I'd been barely listening, dreaming about the ice cream she'd promised me.

Empress? Was that why I loved plants so much? Was that why they sighed to be near me? Both Death and the cryptic boy had called me Empress as well.

How insane all of this sounded! What was more likely? Plants moving on command? Or a teenage girl—with a history of mental illness—experiencing a delusion?

I slowed my steps, doubts arising. Hadn't I had nightmares about the red witch controlling plants, hurting them? Was all this connected in my overwrought brain?

Maybe none of this was real. Maybe I was getting worse because Gran *had* spread her crazy to me—and I wasn't fighting hard enough for the life I desperately wanted back.

Evie, do you understand why you must reject your grandmother's teachings . . . ?

I gazed at the stalks swaying. I could be hallucinating—right at this moment.

I turned toward the house in a daze. On the front porch, I readied to face my mother. Easier said than done.

Mom really could be fierce. A regular Frau Badass. Which was great in some instances, such as when she'd taken over the farm from Gran and grown it into the parish's largest in less than a decade.

Not so great in others—such as when she'd resolved to get me well.

At the front door, I took thirty seconds to compose myself. *I need to learn how to whistle.* My roommate at the center had taught me that trick. Parents never suspected their children were unhappy/delusional/high when the kid was whistling. Their minds just couldn't reconcile it.

As I slipped inside, I puckered my lips, blowing soundless air. Whistling sucked.

I heard my mom on the phone in the kitchen. Was she upset? I froze. She had to be talking to Gran. Every now and then, my grandmother managed to elude the orderlies and ring home.

"I will fight this tooth and nail. Don't you dare try to contact her!" Mom said, then paused for long moments. "You won't convince me of this!" Silence. "Just listen to yourself! You hurt my little girl—there is *no* forgiveness! Cry all you like, this number will be changed tomorrow!"

When she hung up, I joined her in the kitchen. "Gran?"

Mom smoothed her hair. "It was."

I opened my mouth to ask how she was doing, but Mom said, "Anything you'd like to tell me, Evangeline Greene?"

I *hated* it when she asked me that. I liked that question as much as I liked self-incrimination.

Where to begin?

Grades, schmades, bitches, think I'll just flunk this year. For the first time in months, I've been having delusions. Or else I can make plants do tricks. Can't decide which scenario I'm hoping for. I'm tempted to play my V card defensively, just to get this gorgeous, usually wonderful senior to back—the hell—off.

Instead, I told her, "Um, no?"

"You haven't spoken to your grandmother?"

"Not at all." Not since I was a little girl, and Mom had dispatched her to a home on the Outer Banks of North Carolina. Or at least, the court had, in a plea deal.

I remembered Mom had once tried to reassure me, calling it "*the* place to send relatives with dementia." I'd gaped in horror.

Even if Gran had managed to call my cell phone, I would never have answered. My own release from CLC was conditional on two things: medication compliance and zero communication with her.

I'd agreed to both. Readily. By the end of my stay at CLC, my deprogramming had worked; I'd been convinced that Gran was merely disturbed.

Instead of prophetic.

Now I was questioning everything. "I haven't spoken to her in eight years."

Mom relaxed a shade. "She's a very sick woman, Evie."

Then she needs to be home with us, I almost said. *No, two years and out.* "I understand."

"I don't think you do. She's very convincing. She's got an answer for everything. Hell, she could get anyone spooked about this drought, connecting it to her crazy doomsday scenarios."

"What did she say?" I asked quickly.

Mom narrowed her gaze, blue eyes flashing. "Wrong question. We are *not* concerned with what she says." She pointed a finger at me. "She forfeited any consideration from us the day she tried to . . . kidnap you."

I glanced away, part of me wanting to dredge up memories of that day, part of me fearing to. "I know, Mom."

"She got you to the Texas state line before the cops pulled her over. God knows where she was taking you. Do you remember any of that?"

"I remember the arrest." To her credit, Gran had gone with the officers peacefully, her expression satisfied. In a serene voice, she'd murmured, "I've told you *all you need to know*, Evie. You'll do just fine. Everything will be just fine."

But *I* had been hysterical. When they'd cuffed her, I'd kicked the men, screaming.

I glanced up at Mom. "I don't remember much of the drive, though." I didn't remember *all I needed to know*. If I believed in Gran, then that meant I *wouldn't* do just fine.

Nothing would be just fine. Unless I remembered. *But no pressure, Evie.*

"I'm sure she was filling your head with nonsense."

Yes, of course. Nonsense. The docs had told me that I'd internalized some of the things she'd said. That sounded about right. Maybe?

"Her mother was sick before her, my great-grandmother too."

I hated being reminded of that. I snapped, "I filled out the CLC family history, Mom." I already knew I was the latest generation in a bloodline that had been boiling with madness for ages.

"Evie, listen, we're on the right track. We *can* make this work. You've just got to trust me."

A breeze blew, ruffling my cane. "And what about the farm? What happens if we don't get rain?"

"What happens is that your mother will figure something out. You don't worry about anything except school."

School. Studying. The idea of cracking a book left me nauseated. "But, Mom—"

"I *will* figure something out." Her shoulders went back, chin up, eyes bright with determination—a force of nature. Frau Badass.

I could almost feel sorry for the drought.

A family friend had once told me that when my dad disappeared during a fishing trip in the Basin, Mom had taken up the search herself. She'd journeyed deep into the million-acre swamp, determined to scour every inch for her husband, a kindhearted, jovial man she'd adored.

To no avail. He'd vanished without a trace. I'd been only two years old.

Though Karen Greene had a genteel facade, with her flawless hair and manners, I could easily imagine her in waders steering a johnboat, staring down alligators.

And to think I'd once shown signs of being just like her. I'd wanted so badly to make her proud. Until my platform-dive fall from grace.

Now I was just the latest crazy girl to live in Haven House.

DAY I B.F.

As Mel ushered me into a seat in front of my mirror, I demanded, "*This is how I'm supposed to compete with Clotile?*"

With borrowed clothes—a shimmery red Versace halter, black micromini, knee-high Italian boots—and flashy makeup?

Lipstick color: Harlot Letter.

Mel was over at my house, prepping me for date night because she felt the need to sluttify my outfit so I could stand a chance against Clotile's "free-balling lady lumps."

The girl had shown up at the game last night in a *tube top* and skin-tight boy shorts.

I told myself Brand would've missed those plays anyway. Hey, we'd still managed to eke out a win.

But even Grace Anne had trotted up to me on the sidelines and said, "You're going to have to sleep with Brandon to keep him."

As if that weren't enough to worry about, I'd had another vision. In the middle of a routine, I'd experienced that shivery feeling in my head. At the very top of the bleachers, I'd spotted a strange girl, sitting in profile, her face too blurry to discern features.

She held a longbow and quiver in her lap and she'd seemed to *glow* even under the stadium lights. Her hair had been like backlit silver— not gray, but shimmery.

When she'd nocked an arrow to her bow and set her sights on some target in the distance, my skin had crawled. I'd almost missed a step. Forcing a smile, I'd ignored her, bounding along the sideline, cheering, "Go Stars!" *Going crazy!*

Visions coming so quickly meant I was *escalating*. As two out of five Atlanta shrinks had predicted.

Might as well enjoy my few remaining days at Sterling. The way things were going, they were numbered.

Now I told Mel, "Shouldn't I wear whatever makes me feel most comfortable? Instead of this . . ." I motioned to my top—a bright swath of clinging material that tied at the neck and across the open back.

Mel scoffed. "Eves, on the scale from wholesome to whoresome, you're practically Amish."

I glared.

"You have two choices, grasshopper. Out-slut Clotile—or go Springer on her ass. I'm down for the assist in both scenarios."

The idea of competing with Clotile left a bad taste in my mouth. And yet I'd gone along with Mel as she chose my wardrobe and designated accessories: black chandelier earrings and a wide scarlet ribbon to work as a headband—because she'd decreed big hair for me.

As she began diffusing it, turning waves into wanton curls, I asked, "Mel, is this really necessary?" Though I'd never admit it, the lipstick was kind of fun.

"Stow it, Greene. You're lucky I'm not brandishing Aqua Net. 'Cause I could've gone there."

"When are *you* going to get ready?"

"Please. It takes me five minutes. You can't improve on perfection." Then she began chattering, outlining her plot to seduce Spencer.

Though we were curfew-free—I'd told Mom I was spending the night at Mel's after our double date, and Mel had told Mrs. Warren that she'd be home "whenever my happy ass walks through the door"—I was nervous about tonight.

As I tried to pin down the source of my unease, I only vaguely responded to Mel's plan. *Yeah, sounds good, maybe.*

"Seriously, Evie. What is *wrong* with you?" She laid down the diffuser. "You've been acting weird all week. Is there something up with me and you?"

"No! You're my best friend."

"Duh. But something's up. You're acting all *Girl, Interrupted*." She studied my expression in the mirror, having no idea how close that was to the truth. "You don't text with me. You missed *ANTM*, which is required viewing. You blow me off after practice."

She hoisted herself up on my delicate dresser. It groaned in protest. "And what happened this summer? You couldn't spare *one* call? All I got was lame letters from you. Who the hell writes letters? Why didn't you just send smoke signals, or pigeons with little furled messages?"

I burned to tell her everything. But even as I imagined how I'd explain it, I remembered that another word for *delusional* was . . . *psychotic*. "Look, my mom is freaked over the drought. Brand is pressuring me. School is going to be impossible this year. I've already gotten two Fs! I'm a shit show!"

Let's take a week's tally, shall we? Hallucinations: two confirmed, perhaps more. Nightmares: countless. Homework assignments completed: zero.

New superhuman/possibly imaginary powers: I'd sprouted thorn claws, controlled plants, and spontaneously regenerated my skin from injury.

Maybe.

Mel waved away my concerns. "Ignore your mom, put out for Brandon, tank your grades. If you fail, I'll flunk with you. *Su fail-a, mi fail-a.* Case dismissed."

I wished it were so easy. "What if I don't *want* to give it up to Brand yet? Huh? I don't respond well to pressure!" Exhibit A: my wild-eyed look in the mirror. I took a calming breath. "I just feel like everything's slipping away. I'm constantly scared of losing him, losing all my friends."

"Losing your popularity, you mean?" Mel asked with a shrewd look, and I grudgingly shrugged. "Is it *that* important to you—" She stopped herself. "If popularity is your My-Little-Pony gumdrop-forest of a dream, then so be it. Who am I to piss on your dreams? But know this: The school would freaking shut down without you, and that isn't going to change just because you're slow on the uptake and doing drugs without your bestie."

"I walked past people all week without saying hi! I blew through the hall like a zombie."

"Everyone will just figure this week was Evie's red-light at the Y. When I'm OTR, I scourge the halls like Godzilla. Your little la-la-land thing is *cute* compared to the breathing of actual fire."

Next week, maybe I *could* turn everything around. Hell, I'd almost gotten used to the plants. Take that fear out of the equation, and maybe . . .

"The most important thing to remember is that you're *my* best friend," Mel said, her voice the sweetest it'd ever sounded. "Do you know how rare and wondrous that makes you?"

I sighed, turning to hug her. "Aw, Mel . . ."

But she pulled me into a headlock, rubbing her knuckle into my hair. "You've always kept me on the straight and narrow, Greene. Don't go breaking up with me or anything, okay?"

"This is hella creepy," Mel said as we waded through dried-out brush near the mill.

We'd driven as close as we dared in her Beamer, then started walking into the withered woods. The fog was so thick I could barely see where I was stepping. Another of Gran's sayings surfaced: *Be wary of droughts—snakes slither about.* "This was not my idea, Mel."

"I should seriously hope not. Two cheerleaders going out into the woods, at night, to a supposedly haunted mill?"

"I can't decide if it sounds like the beginning of a joke or a horror flick."

"Hey, you've still got your endangered hymen. Which means you'll make it to closing credits—I'm s.o.l."

"Do you think the others are already here? Maybe they parked on the opposite side? I should try to call." Then I remembered I'd left my overnight stuff and phone locked in her car, along with my precious sketchbook. I turned, but couldn't see the Beamer through the fog.

"Call?" Mel hastily said. "Don't be silly. We're almost there, right?"

As we neared what was left of the mill, I murmured, "Did you hear something?" I rubbed my nape, again feeling like I was being watched—

Lights blinded me. Bodies lunged at me, faces rushing closer.

I shrieked at the top of my lungs.

Shouts of "Surprise!" faded, dozens of students startled into silence by my reaction. Grace Anne, Catherine. *Brandon.* All of them looked stunned.

Oh. My. God. This is a surprise birthday party. Someone had strung up lights all over the walls. Speakers perched atop rusted cane crushers. Kegs sat in aged iron kettles.

I'd just humiliated myself in front of all of these people.

Mel's jaw had dropped at my scream. Just when I was about to burst into tears, she recovered, saying loudly, "Evie! You totes knew about this, didn't you, bitches? Freak out the surprisers?" Then she imitated my shriek, punctuating it with a yodeled *"Lay-hee-hoo."*

When people started laughing, I forced a smile. "Yep. I totally knew. Been waiting all day to do that!" *Keep smiling, Evie!*

Now everyone relaxed, some giving me play punches on my shoulder like I'd just done something cool, a funny prank. *Good save, Mel.*

Out of the corner of her mouth, she muttered, "You had no idea, did you?"

"None-point-none."

"Carefrontation?"

"Probably unavoidable."

"Then have fun tonight, little soldier. 'Cause tomorrow, shit gets real."

Brand swooped me up then and swung me around until I was truly laughing. "I hope you don't mind."

I bit my bottom lip. Maybe if the party didn't get any bigger or the music too loud.

A horn honked then. And another. Mel, Brand, and I gazed out the front entrance. Down an old tractor trail, headlight after headlight shone through the fog. It looked like a mass evacuation was pointed directly at the mill.

The last thing I needed was for my mom to call the cops, not realizing it was her daughter throwing the rager. "Look, guys, maybe this isn't such a good idea."

Mel and Brandon blinked at me in confusion. Evie Greene didn't often utter those words.

"It's not like we're going to trash your house," Brand said. "It's outside."

"My mom—"

"Will never know. We've got, like, miles between us and your house. Plus the walls keep the sound down."

Mel said, "He's got a point. And think of the pics! You could get some serious uploadables from a party like this." Then she added, "*Popular* girls celebrate their birthdays by having a rager in a haunted sugar mill."

Hadn't I just been worrying about losing my popularity? Wouldn't it be *ab*normal for me to not have a sixteenth-birthday kegger? Hell, Mom might take it as a good sign. She'd been rebellious with Gran and usually wasn't too strict with me.

On the other hand, she might reconsider Brandon being "such a good boy" or hit her limit with Mel's hijinks.

Earlier tonight, Mel had called her "Woman Who Spawned Evie" to her face. Mom had been unamused.

I didn't know what I'd do if she outlawed either of them.

"I promise you, it'll be okay," Brand said. "Scout's honor." Instead of the three-finger Scout salute, he held up a peace sign.

I chose to think he was making a joke.

I was wavering when Brand dug into his pocket. "Oh, I almost forgot! Your birthday present. Was saving this for Monday, but I thought you might want to wear it tonight." He handed me a wrapped box with a crushed ribbon.

I ripped it open to find a huge solitaire on a white-gold chain. *Stunning.* It would match my diamond earrings perfectly.

Mel clasped her hands over her chest, saying in a cajoling tone, "And all he wants is to throw a rager in your sugar mill?" Then she frowned. "Wow. That sounded raunchy."

"Do you like it?" he asked, seeming nervous. Which was so adorable.

Game. Set. Match. "I love it. And I love my surprise party." I stood on my toes to give him a quick kiss. "Thank you."

He grinned, handing me a sweating Solo cup of beer. "Cheers, Eves!"

I raised my cup, hesitating. Would alcohol act wonky with my pills? But hey, how much worse could my head get? Perhaps I might even start . . . hallucinating? *Ha-ha.*

My time here was short anyway. "Cheers, guys!"

For the next hour everybody partook heartily of keg juice, until we were—in Brand's estimation—"fitshaced!"

More and more people showed up, turning my party into a wild and woolly kegger. I saw faces I didn't recognize, spied letterman jackets from other schools.

Over the course of the night, I'd watched several of Mel's ill-fated attempts to flirt with Spencer. Yet now, as she danced with me up on a ledge, he was actually checking her out.

She and I sang so loudly I was losing my voice, danced so madly to the thumping music that the world was spiraling. For once, I didn't fight it. We were laughing at something when I saw Jackson Deveaux leaning his shoulder against the crumbling brick wall in the back.

Then I noticed the other transfers beginning to mingle with the crowd. Clotile's outfit tonight *still* made mine look Amish.

But I couldn't muster any outrage that they were all here. With a shrug, I thought, *This ought to end well.*

As I danced, Brand's eyes were glued to me, *not* on Clotile. I cast a smug look in Jackson's direction; his darkened gaze was locked on me as well.

Flustered, I reached out two arms for Brand, prompting him to come help me down. But he swung me up instead, twirling me around in his arms. I laughed, throwing my head back. Spinning . . . spinning . . .

Tingling nose?

I suddenly saw the cryptic boy. He gave me a defiant kind of shrug—like he'd done something I might get mad at?

On my next rotation, he'd disappeared, but I saw that blurry-faced girl once more.

I gasped, then caught a glimpse of movement in the tree limbs above. There was another boy! He was dressed in old-timey clothing, with long black hair and jet-black *wings.*

A last kid joined the rotation, a boy with electricity sparking all around his body.

The girl and those two boys looked like they lay in wait for me, ready to pounce.

I twisted in Brandon's grip until he let me down. With a hearty laugh, he said, "Evie, you about to yuke, or what?"

Or what! Or what!

I put my hand to my forehead—because now as my gaze darted around, I saw nothing out of the ordinary. Those characters had disappeared like mist.

Someone was climbing the stairs to my hidden spot.

After I'd disentangled myself from Brandon, assuring him I'd be fine with a short breather—again he took my word for it—I'd climbed to a ledge near the old smokestack, needing to be alone, needing to *keep watch*.

I'd taken a seat, hanging my legs over the edge, careful not to crush the clover growing between the bricks. From here, I'd been able to look down on the party, like gazing at a living dollhouse.

Time passed, the crowd still swelling.

Disconnection. Why couldn't I be down there having fun like a normal teenage girl? Why did I always have to feel threatened? Under fire?

And why was my raucous birthday party still going strong—without me?

As if to illustrate, a football player mooned the crowd, with full-on junk shot. I sighed. I couldn't *unsee* that. Ever.

Then I'd sensed someone on the stairs. Who would even know how to get up here?

Jackson. With two plastic cups in hand.

I exhaled a disappointed breath. "How did you find me?"

"Not many black miniskirts escape my notice, *cher*." *The Cajunland player.* He sat beside me, offering me a cup. "Here."

I reluctantly accepted it, peering at the contents. "Is this roofied?"

"It can be." Was he slurring? He definitely seemed buzzed tonight, his accent more pronounced, his dark hair tousled.

"Lovely." Was *I* slurring?

Apparently. Because Jackson said, "Goody Two-shoes Evie Greene got herself pickled, for true. If I'd known you were such a juvenile delinquent, I might've asked for a new history podna."

"Juvenile delinquent? Hmm. Aren't your initials J.D.? If the shoe fits . . ."

He took a drink from his beer, but I could tell his lips were thinned with irritation. "So here we are, the Cajun JD and a Sterling High cheerleader who draws weird Goth shit. I figured out all these other fools easy enough, but you . . ." He shook his head. "Something ain't right with you, no. I doan like unsolved puzzles. *Evangeline*," he added significantly. "You got a Cajun name—you part Cajun? That's why you can speak my tongue?"

"How'd you find out my full name?"

He gave a shrug with one palm up, the most maddening of Cajun retorts, then took another drink.

"What are you doing here, Jackson?"

"Are Sterling parties off-limits to Cajuns?"

"I just didn't expect you and your friends at my birthday party."

"This is *yours*? We heard about a blowout in a different parish, followed the free drinks."

"A regular rager." I pulled my hair over my shoulder, fanning myself.

When he fell silent, I turned to him, found him staring at my neck with hooded eyes. "Damn, Evie, you smell good."

Why did everybody keep talking about my scent? Even Mel had asked to borrow my perfume earlier. One problem: I don't wear any.

Jackson was still staring at me. Flashing him a wary look, I scooted farther away.

He blinked, then coughed into his fist. "Why aren't you down at your own party?"

"I needed a quick tee-oh."

"Uh-huh." He drained his cup, chasing it with a shot from his flask.

I smelled the bite of whiskey on his breath, but didn't find it unpleasant. "You're at that thing constantly. And yet I never see you really drunk."

"You want to get me drunk, you? Take advantage of ole Jack?"

"I'll start referring to myself in third person before I take advantage of you, Jackson."

"Heh. So, *cher*, now that you've set up this rendezvous with me, what are your intentions?"

I sipped from my cup. "You are firmly on the pipe."

"I see the way you look at me, undressing me with your eyes."

"Riiight. I have a boyfriend."

"Then how come he's not with you right now? How come he doan carry your books at school?"

Why had Jackson noticed that? "Should Brand? Just because I'm a girl? I'm his equal, would just as soon carry his as he'd carry mine."

"Where I come from, a man carries a woman's things 'cause it's polite—and to let other beaux know she's taken. How's anyone to know you belong to him?"

"I don't *belong* to anyone. Did you crawl out of a swamp—or a time capsule?"

He leaned forward until our faces were mere inches apart, then purred, "Now, dat's not nice, Evangeline. Doan you want to be *doux à moi*?" Sweet to me. He dipped his finger down my halter top between my breasts—

"Jackson!" Then I realized he'd lifted up my new necklace.

"Pretty penny for this, no?" His gaze was shuttered.

"It's an early birthday present from Brandon."

"And I know just what you're goan to give him." He dropped the chain.

"You don't know anything about me. Do you understand me? *Nothing.*" One of the clovers curled over my knuckles, which was strangely soothing.

"I'm starting to get an idea. Does Radcliffe know you?"

"Of course," I said, though I had doubts. Why couldn't he sense how much pressure I was under? Why add to it?

"Une menterie." A lie.

"None of what you say matters. I know my boyfriend and I are solid."

He gave a scornful laugh. "As long as you doan mind sharing him with brunettes of the Cajun persuasion. He's been sniffing around Clotile, for true. And you know it, too. That's why you're dressing like this." He waved unsteadily at me.

"Like *what*?"

Another shuttered gaze. Another drink from his flask. "Different."

"Brandon's not doing any . . . sniffing. He *loves* me. He told me he thinks about me constantly." As much as football! "And aren't you concerned about your girlfriend?"

"Girlfriend? Hell, Clotile's probably my sister."

My lips parted. *Probably?* Jackson and I weren't just from different worlds, but from different universes.

"Look at Radcliffe down there. You think you're on his mind right now?"

Brand was surrounded by a bevy of slores as he drank from the keg like it was a water fountain. The life of the party, worshipped and adored.

Where was Mel? Normally, she'd be throwing elbows at those other girls. I hadn't seen her—or Spencer—for a while. I rose at once, stepping over Jackson to go look for her.

"Where you goan, Evie?"

Though I ignored him, he followed me down the stairs. Back on the ground, I saw a shadowy figure skulking among the parked cars. I squinted, but couldn't see through the fog. Another hallucination?

I cautiously eased closer to get a better look, but Jackson stepped in front of me. I shimmied to the left; he blocked me.

"I don't have time for this."

He began edging me toward the mill.

"Stop it, Jackson," I snapped when my back met a brick wall. The bass pumped so hard that I could feel the vibrations through the stone.

He leaned in, his brows drawing together. "You got on some kind of expensive perfume? Never smelled anything like you."

"I don't wear perfume."

He looked at me like I might be lying. "You smell almost like . . . honeysuckle."

"I'm *not* wearing anything."

"My fondest wish." The corners of his lips curled—the first time I'd seen his expression even come close to a genuine smile.

Despite myself, that half grin affected me, made my heart speed up.

Was Jackson *flirting* with me? Like a normal boy might? And not just to make me uncomfortable?

Too bad. Between Brandon, Death, and the cryptic boy, my dance card was full.

And this flirtatious side of Jackson made me wary. Even though the Cajun was attractive in a too-rugged kind of way, I probably trusted Death in armor more. "Just leave me alone."

"I will as soon as you do two things. Admit you speak French, and show me the rest of your drawings."

I was already gazing past him, done with this conversation. "Why are you acting so interested? Why are we even *talking*? You hate me, remember?"

"*Mais* yeah." For sure. Pressing his palm against the wall beside my head, he leaned in, murmuring, "But maybe I want you a little, too."

I'd just learned something I'd never known. A boy could desire to have sex with me and not like me at all. In fact, he could even hate me.

"Maybe I've decided to forgive you for making me *la misère*." Causing me trouble.

I exhaled, sick and tired of these games. I was sick and tired of *everything*. "Jackson, listen—"

"Call me Jack."

"No. Because we're not friends." Imitating his accent, I said, "And only your friends call you Jack, no."

He grinned down at me again, his teeth even and white. "We may not be friends, but I'm about to get real friendly with you." I could feel the heat coming off his body. He smelled delicious, like the woods, a little wild.

He had some unknowable look in his eyes. He seemed to be silently promising me something, but I didn't know what.

"Friendly with me?"

"I'm goan to kiss you, *cher*."

My thoughts scattered. Though the moment had begun to feel like a dream, I didn't want to be a cheater. "I need to get . . . back to Brandon." I laid my hands on Jackson's chest to push him away, but his muscles flexed under my palms, that heat drawing me like a magnet.

"I woan *let* you go back to that boy—not until you give me one *bec doux*." A sweet kiss. Then he reached forward, unlacing the ribbon from my hair.

"What are you doing?" I murmured.

"Souvenir." He put it in his pocket, and for some reason that struck me as the sexiest thing I'd ever seen.

Energy began filling me. *Sick and tired?* No longer. I felt excited and alive for the first time in months.

Where was the *meh* I'd been feeling about kissing and boys and sex?

At that moment, I was *dying* for this Cajun boy to kiss me. I didn't care about my reputation, the friends I'd disappoint, the popularity I'd lose, or the bragging rights he'd win.

I had to know what the look in his eyes promised.

He was staring at my lips, and before I could think better of it, I'd wetted them.

"That's it, *bébé*," he said in a coaxing rasp. *"Ma bonne fille."* My good girl.

He wrapped one of his arms behind my back, cupping my chin with his free hand. "Evangeline, I'm goan to kiss you until your toes curl, until we're breathing for each other."

That was the promise. . . .

As if from a great distance, I heard someone yell, "Jack!"

He ignored the voice, inching even closer to me.

"Jack!"

Our lips were about to meet—

"JACK DANIELS!" I realized Lionel was yanking on his arm.

As Jackson turned, he flashed Lionel the most frightening look I'd ever seen on a man. *"What you want?"* he thundered.

"Time to go, podna."

Jackson shook his head hard, his arm snaking tighter around my lower back.

"We're done here. Time—to—go," Lionel repeated.

Whatever that meant. Yet Jackson was listening to him.

Lionel said to me, "They're looking for you inside, Evie."

"Oh. Oh!" I shimmied out of Jackson's grasp, but I couldn't stop from glancing over my shoulder.

When I bit my bottom lip, I thought he might come after me, but again Lionel hauled back on his arm. Jackson growled at his friend, *"Want a taste of dat girl, me."* The look in his blazing eyes . . .

Lionel said something I didn't hear.

Something that made Jackson scowl. "Go on, Evie," he snapped. "Now! Go back to your friends."

His curt dismissal stung, bewildering me even more. I hurried back inside, pressing my fingertips to my lips. Oh, God, I'd almost kissed another boy. I'd nearly cheated on Brandon, who didn't deserve that.

I stopped in my tracks.

Clotile was slinking up to Brand, and he looked thrilled, holding out his hand for her. My jaw dropped as he helped her do a keg-stand, with all the wardrobe malfunctions that entailed. Football players cheered.

The humiliation! And in the midst of this embarrassing crisis, one mental plea stood out from all the rest: *Please don't let Jackson see this.*

I shoved through the crowd toward the keg. When Brandon caught sight of me, he flushed red, helping a giggling Clotile down.

I was mortified that everyone had just witnessed this scene—and pissed off. Feeling reckless, I gazed up at Brandon. "Hey, big guy. Why don't you give your *girlfriend* a kiss?"

"Here? In front of everybody?" he asked.

Hesitating? "Yes. *Here.*"

Finally, Brandon leaned down to slant his mouth over mine, once and again. With a stifled groan, he deepened the kiss, and I let him for a second, let him cover half of my ass with his palm. Then I smiled against his lips, nipping his bottom one with my teeth.

But instead of chuckling, he drew back, his lids heavy. "Ah, Evie, you don't know—"

"Walk me to the river?" I interrupted.

With a dazed look on his face, he murmured, "Girl, I'd follow you into hell itself."

Outside the mill, my satisfaction over my little victory dwindled—because now I had a drunken, hard-up boy to deal with.

As soon as the water was in sight, Brandon pulled me close. "You smell so good, Eves."

When he began to kiss my neck—urgently—I peered up through the fog. I'd found my *meh.*

No, Evie, be smart about this. I reminded myself how easy it was to read Brandon, how open he was, how carefree. He was the type of boy I *needed* in my life.

I couldn't lose him. Especially not to another girl. "Hey, hold up."

"Uh-huh." He didn't hold up.

I grabbed his face with two hands and made him meet my eyes. "I've made my decision."

His body shot tight with tension. "Yeah?"

"I've given the matter a lot of consideration, and I—"

Sirens blared.

A chorus of screams rang out: *"Cops!"*

My eyes went wide. The sheriff was here? "Oh, shit! Brandon!" As the music went dead, I swayed on my feet.

He caught my elbow. "Eves, I've got this! I'll tell the sheriff that it was just me and some other football players, and the party got out of hand."

"They'll arrest you!"

"Doubt it. My dad plays golf with the sheriff. Everything's gonna be fine! You were *never* here." He cast me a drunken grin.

In that instant, he looked utterly heroic to me.

"Just wait right here. I'll find Mel and tell her to meet you." He turned, jogging away.

"Brandon?" I called. When he glanced over his shoulder, I started to say *I love you*, but all that came out was: "You're the best."

He gave me a wobbly salute, then set off for battle.

Alone, I nibbled my lip. Could Brandon keep this under wraps? I half expected more sirens to wail, or maybe a convoy of big vans to show up for arrests.

My first impulse was to call Mel, but my phone—along with all my stuff—was locked in her car!

A cool breeze swept over me, clearing the fog and sending leaves cartwheeling across the surface of the river. I rubbed my arms, suddenly freezing in this outfit.

On the heels of that wind, angry clouds moved in. An approaching thunder boomer? In Louisiana we got microbursts all the time. I wasn't too concerned, would love to have the rain.

No, not too concerned—until chills skittered over the back of my neck.

Every rustle or animal call around me seemed amplified. I turned in a circle, but saw no one. Still I couldn't shake the feeling that I was being watched. Just paranoia? Just another symptom?

Then came that tingling sensation once more. Oh, no, no! *Ignore it. Resist it—*

A lightning bolt forked down not twenty yards from me.

I screamed, temporarily blinded, waiting for the deafening crack of thunder. None came.

When another silent bolt landed even closer, it zapped the ground with so much force that soil and sparks erupted into the sky.

I stared, dumbfounded. Smoking specks of dirt wafted on the breeze, the sight rousing me into action. I took off running, sprinting down to the river's edge.

A third bolt drove me closer to the water, into the moccasin-infested reeds. "Shit, shit!" My footfalls landed in the muck, the shallow mud sucking at my boots. I shifted my steps, running on my toes.

As more lightning struck, I realized it seemed to be *following* me.

This couldn't be real. Because instead of bolts, I now saw spears—like javelins. They were sparkling silver, engraved with symbols, but they exploded like lightning upon impact.

Not real, not real, I repeated hysterically, pumping my arms for speed. *Reject the delusion!*

One sizzled just inches from my last footfall. Someone was trying to kill me! I lurched around, heading back toward the mill. I'd rather be arrested!

"Oh God, oh God!" I blundered around trees, dodging branches that seemed to be going out of their freaking way to reach me, to hold me still. "Ugh!"

I risked a glance over my shoulder. Someone, or *something*, was definitely after me. I noticed that my thorn claws had returned, almost more upsetting than the—

I ran right into a man's solid chest.

9

I nearly bounced back onto my ass, but a taped hand caught my arm. I craned my head up.

Jackson. "What's wrong with you, girl?"

I gazed up at his face, catching my breath. "There's l-lightning!" I curled my fingers to conceal my claws, waiting as they slowly returned to normal.

"You got spooked by a little lightning?" He looked at me peculiarly, like he was disappointed in me. "I knew you were soft, but damn, Evie."

That look stung. I backed away from him, fearing that I was about to cry in front of this boy. "The bolts were so close."

"Shouldn't expect nothing else from a Sterling girl."

"No, this was different! It was . . ." *Like lightning, but not. Electric and sizzling, but cool.* Yet when I looked above me, the sky was clear, the night still.

"You out here alone?"

I gave a shaky nod. "I'm supposed to meet Melissa."

"Everybody's scattered."

"Then what are you doing back here?" I actually felt safer in his presence. I didn't sense a threat from him, and he *was* a hardened criminal with lots of experience fighting. I knew he'd landed at least some of his hits. "I thought you left."

Gazing down at me, he said, "Maybe I came back to claim my taste of you."

Between gritted teeth, I said, "Again, I have a boyfriend."

"Again, I couldn't tell. Seems Radcliffe ditched you in the woods. If you belonged to me, I'd never let you out of my sight—much less leave you alone out here."

What was his fixation on girls *belonging* to boys? "Brandon went back to smooth things with the sheriff!"

In a voice dripping with scorn, Jackson grated, "Of *course* he did."

"I'm going to find my friends."

"Now, wait a minute. You can't go back there, no. You'll get pinched." At my blank look, he added, "Arrested, on roll call, gaffled."

"Wow, you expect me to speak Cajun *and* Juvie."

He raked his taped fingers through his hair. "I doan s'pose I can leave you here." He started squiring me away from the mill. I thought. I was so turned around I couldn't get my bearings.

"Why are you being decent to me?"

"I'm not. I just want to get you on my bike, with you in that skirt. Where am I driving you to?"

I blinked at him. "I live here."

"You live on *this* farm? In that eerie mansion up the way? No wonder you're touched in the head."

I didn't deny the eerie description—or the touched-in-the-head comment. *Fair's fair.* "You've seen my house?"

He gazed past me as he said, "I saw it from the road once, after harvest. When I was little." He scrubbed his hand over his mouth, clearly wanting to be somewhere else. "I'll take you home." I realized we'd stopped near his bike, parked in the woods.

Where were *his* friends? Where was *Clotile*? "Wait, I can't go home! I've been drinking. I'm supposed to spend the night with Mel."

He raised his brows with an *I should care about this why?* look. "Two choices, *peekôn*."

I frowned. *Peekôn* meant "thorn."

"I can drive you home. Or I can leave your ass here. Alone."

What if there was more lightning? I didn't want to be out here by myself, at least not until I reached the cane fields. But I couldn't ride a roaring motorcycle home. "Neither of those choices will work for me."

He took a pull from his flask. "Nothing *else* will work for me."

"Then leave." Surely he wouldn't abandon me.

"Bonne chance, peekôn." He turned and strode toward his bike.

"Wait, Jackson! I can't ride with you! My mom hates motorcycles, and she'll hear me trying to sneak in." I studied my muddy Italian boots as I mumbled, "Will you walk with me? Just as far as the cane fields?"

He exhaled with undisguised irritation. "I'll stay with you that far." He disengaged the kickstand, pushing his bike.

Tendrils of fog drifted in as we walked in silence.

Though he was buzzed, Jackson somehow seemed alert. He was also so clearly begrudging that I was tempted to snap, "God, just leave!"

But the lightning still had me spooked. Even if it hadn't been real.

I hated that I was afraid. I hated that I wanted him close by.

As we continued, I peered up at him from under my lashes, struggling to understand the excitement I'd felt when he'd been about to kiss me—versus the *meh* I'd felt when Brandon had *actually* been kissing me.

I pictured Brandon's clean-cut good looks, his wavy brown locks, his letterman jacket and bright future.

Jack's prospects? The state penitentiary in Angola. Just a matter of when he got sent there.

If Brandon was a good boy but not yet a great guy, Jackson was a bad boy—and already a bad guy.

And yet with the Cajun, I'd gotten a taste of what it was like to desire a boy, *really* desire. . . .

He offered me his flask.

I declined, asking, "Why do you drink so much?"

"You're a fine one to talk, you." When he saw I was waiting for an answer, he said, "Give me one reason not to."

"It's bad for your health."

"You think I'm goan to live long enough to die of the effects of alcohol? Cheers to that."

I tilted my head at him, musing on all the rumors that swirled around him—the knifings, the correctional center, the thefts in Sterling. "Jackson, are you as bad as everyone says?"

At the rim of his flask, he said, "A thousand times worse, *fille*."

Thunder rumbled in the distance, as if to punctuate his statement.

Once we'd reached the dirt track that ran between two large cane fields, I said, "Thank you for seeing me this far. I'm good from here."

"I'm not goan to leave you in the middle of a field," he grumbled, yet with every step deeper into the cane, he seemed to grow more uneasy. "In the bayou, folks think this place is haunted." He again cast me that studying glance. "Is it?"

"Maybe a little." When the cane whispered in the windless night, I edged closer to the rows, running my splayed fingers over the stalks, taking comfort after my hallucination. Here I was safe.

A calm descended over me. I soaked up the sultry air, savoring the insect chatter, the sweet smell of dew, the animals at play all around us.

Everything was so alive, *teeming* with life. I sighed, my lids going half-masted.

"*Drôle fille*," Jackson muttered. In proper French, *drôle* meant *funny*. In Cajun? *Weird*.

"What did you say?"

"It's a foggy night and we're walking by these rustling canes. A *p'tee fille* like you strolling along without a care in the world? Shouldn't you be hanging on to my arm?"

"Hardly."

When something stirred nearby, Jackson said, "This cane doan . . . unsettle you?"

"I love it. You're probably just hearing raccoons." *Or snakes.*

I noticed that he hadn't hit that flask once since we'd been surrounded by cane. Maybe he sensed that something wasn't right with me, with this place. Maybe he believed the tales of hauntings and wanted to be on his guard.

When I could make out Haven's lights in the distance, I asked, "Are you superstitious, Jackson?"

"*Mais* yeah. Just 'cause I'm Catholic doan mean I can't be superstitious," he said, exhaling with relief once we'd emerged from the cane. Then he immediately whistled low at the sight of Haven House. "Even bigger than I remember."

I tried to see it from his eyes. The gaslights flickered over the twelve proud columns. Night-blooming jasmine ascended the many trellises, forever reaching for the grand old house as if with lust. Those majestic oaks had already caught it; they encircled the structure protectively.

Jackson's gaze darted over the place with such keenness that I figured we were due for a break-in directly.

"You know what I think?" he finally said. "I think you are just like this house, Evangeline. Rich and fine on the outside, but no one's got a clue what's going on inside."

He really could be surprisingly perceptive at times. "You think I'm fine, Cajun?"

He rolled his eyes, as if we were retreading established ground. "And both you and this place are a lot weirder than you have any business being."

You've got no idea, Cajun. No. Idea.

With a shrug, I turned toward the barn. He eventually followed, catching up. When I opened the door, the horses nickered a welcome. Well, all of them except for my sweet old nag Allegra—named *before* that allergy medicine had taken off; she snored.

Outside the door, Jackson parked his bike, leaning against it. "A big ole mansion like this, and just you and your folks live here?"

Though only Mom's silver Mercedes SUV was parked out front, I let him think I had a father on-site.

"You really are the richest family in the parish, then?"

"No. Everybody knows the Radcliffes are."

A muscle ticked in his cheek. "Are you goan to stay out here? Woan you get scared?"

Scared? *Six million strong.*

"If you asked me nice, I might stay and be your bodyguard."

When I gave a scoffing laugh at that, he scowled. "You love to laugh at me, doan you, *peekôn*? Enjoy it now, 'cause it woan always be that way."

"What does that mean?"

He just narrowed his eyes at me, looking dangerous in the gaslights.

"Feel free to leave at any time, Jackson. Because I don't need a bodyguard, and I won't be scared. I don't have a choice anyway, since you refused to take me to find Melissa or Brandon."

"Radcliffe again?" With a grated curse, Jackson pushed up from his bike, striding to the doorway. "Even though he helped Clotile with that keg-stand? After that, I thought for true you'd be reevaluating your definition of *solid*."

"You . . . you saw that?"

"*Everyone* saw that. And at your own birthday party, too. They also saw you trying to win his attention back. Looked desperate, if you ask me."

Bile rose in my throat. Jackson had said that I needed to be taken down a peg. Mission accomplished.

"I just doan know *what* he thinks Clotile has over you. You're pretty to look at in that skirt of yours, you're good at dancing, and you smell like a flower. What's not to like?"

When he smirked at me, I hit my limit. *Enough!* "You're enjoying this!"

"De bon cœur." Wholeheartedly.

"You *would*. Because you're a cruel, classless boy who gets off on other people's unhappiness." I held his gaze. "Brandon is twice the man you are. He always will be."

Jackson's expression turned more menacing than I'd ever seen it.

Done with him, I slammed the door in his face, then marched into the office at the back of the barn. Fuming, I paced. *Reevaluate your definition of solid?*

I wanted to strangle him!

No, no, I didn't need to be thinking about Jackson Deveaux; I needed to focus on who—or what—had attacked me.

Or at least to determine *if* I'd actually been attacked. When I reviewed every detail I could recall—and damn, I'd been *buzzed*—I concluded one thing. I was screwed.

I could accept the plants—hallucinations or not, they'd begun to comfort me. But the lightning javelins? Death on a pale horse? Seeing the cryptic boy in class?

Screwed. Two years and out would never work. Change of plans. Yes, I'd promised my mom that I wouldn't contact Gran—but I was CLC-bound anyway.

Death had said, *"No one told you to expect me?"* Maybe someone had? I would sneak a call to my grandmother tomorrow.

As I wondered how I'd begin our first conversation in eight years, my head and face started tingling. Then *hurting*. The barn soon faded away. "No, no!"

Too much! I can't take any more of this! I squeezed my eyes shut, as if that would do anything.

When I opened them again, I was standing in a windowless room, with beanbags on a tiled floor and *Star Wars* posters on the walls. A basement playroom?

Then I spied the cryptic boy, standing just before me!

"You must prepare, Evie," he said.

The bubbly sensation I usually experienced now felt more like a migraine, as if this vision were being shot into my skull with a nail gun. "J-just leave me alone!" Then to myself, I muttered, "How many visions can I have in one night?"

"Many," he answered. "It's the eve of the Beginning. Much work to do!"

Great. He was going to make as little sense as he had the first time I'd seen him. "Who are you?"

"Matthew Mat Zero Matto. Easier to think of me as the Fool Card."

A card. Ah, God, I *had* internalized my gran's Tarot teachings. A character from the deck she'd always played with was now talking to me. "And I suppose the reaper who visited—the one who wants to kill me—was the Death Card."

He nodded. "Major Arcana."

Hadn't Gran once explained the Major Arcana to me? They were special cards, maybe the trump cards of the Tarot?

Wasn't there a time when I'd shuffled through her deck, the cards feeling so big in my little hands . . . ? I couldn't remember!

"And the red witch?" I demanded. "What card is she? How can she"—*we*—"control plants?" That was the extent of our similarities.

I was good and she was evil. Period. I'd be a Glinda the Good Witch of plants—all peace, love, and unity with them—and she would be our hated scourge.

Death himself said that I was all about life—and the witch was clearly all about death.

I pinched the bridge of my nose. As if *any* of these characters were real!

"Red witch?" Matthew frowned. "Ah, she arises. We'll deal with her when the time comes."

"Deal with her? You mean *fight* her?"

"She's strong. You are *not*. Yet."

The pain in my head grew excruciating. My eyes watered. "Matthew, this *hurts*!" I tasted blood running down the back of my throat, increasing my nausea.

The pressure eased a little, but not all the way. "I don't want you to hurt," he said gravely.

"Why do you keep appearing?"

"Field of battle. Arsenal. Obstacles. Foes. I've taught you each; you listen poorly, take pills, drink."

When blood trickled from my nose, I pressed the back of my hand against it. "I'm about to go under, kid. I mean screaming, hair-pulling, whackadoodle cracked. I can't keep having these visions."

He gazed at me with solemn brown eyes. "I *won't* fail you. Evie, you are my only friend."

His heartfelt words took me aback. He did seem so familiar. Just when I was wondering why I felt a measure of trust in him—he'd done everything imaginable *not* to deserve it—I reminded myself that he didn't exist.

I shook my head hard, clearing just enough of the vision to escape. I made for the door, snagging a horse blanket, then out toward the cane. Rainclouds had gathered above the field; thunder rumbled.

"No, Evie," he called. "Not under the clouds! *Rain . . .*"

I glanced back. He looked frightened, unable to follow. Scared of precipitation?

He didn't need to know that Sterling's clouds were two-faced scammers, hadn't delivered on their promise all summer. I marched on.

"You aren't ready!" he called after me. "Your eyes will go bright if you look at the lights!"

"Just leave me alone, Matthew!"

"Turn away from the lights. Turn away! Want you safe!"

"So—do—I!"

Right before I reached the edge of the cane, he warned once more, *"The Beginning is nigh. . . ."*

When I hadn't heard from Mel or Brandon by noon, panic set in. Why wouldn't they pick up their phones?

Surely the two of them hadn't gotten . . . gaffled.

Especially when no one else seemed to have been. Without my cell, I'd been on my laptop, scouring students' posts online for info.

All morning, I'd looked at keg-party pics and Solo-cup shares. I'd read updates from kids bragging about being at the party of the year.

Not a word about the cops. And apparently, Mom hadn't heard anything either. . . .

I'd woken at dawn in the middle of the cane field, having slept soundly for hours. Surprisingly, I hadn't been hungover—a miracle considering how tanked I'd been, so drunk I'd hallucinated worse than ever before.

I'd been desperate to shower and brush my teeth, but I hadn't wanted Mom to see me in the clothes I'd gone out in. After a while, I hadn't cared.

She'd been so distracted by the drought, on the phone with another farmer, that she hadn't even noticed I was wearing a Versace halter and a moth-eaten pair of last year's jodhpurs.

Mom would've heard about the bust by then, yet she'd said nothing, just absently kissed my cheek before running off to another emergency farmers' meeting.

After I'd showered and dressed, I'd begun to feel confident that my boyfriend had truly hushed the situation.

Just as he'd said he would. My drunken knight in shining armor had won his battle.

Now I patted the enormous diamond solitaire around my neck, realizing that Brandon Radcliffe was not just the type of boy I *needed* in my life; he was the one I *wanted*—dependable, happy-go-lucky, easy to read.

Not brooding, mysterious, and impossible to decipher.

I decided to get something locked down with my boyfriend, so I'd stop thinking stupid thoughts about Angola-bound Cajuns.

With that in mind, I called Brandon's cell from my home line yet again, intending to leave a message this time.

"Hey, Brand, I hope everything's okay. Starting to worry." I nibbled my bottom lip, debating how to begin this. "Last night, about our conversation . . . we got interrupted—when you went off to save the day for me. And I just wanted to tell you my decision."

I paused, knowing there was no turning back from this. "My decision is . . . yes. I'll spend the night with you next weekend." *Done. Locked down.* "I . . . I'm . . ." Relieved? Nervous? "Um, call me. At home."

He still hadn't called by three in the afternoon, when Mel sauntered into my room.

"Where in the hell have you been?" My mood was *foul.* My plans to talk to Gran had been thwarted. I hadn't dared to call her from the house phone. "What happened to you last night?"

"Spencer and I went to his car, totally hooked up. I threw one over on him, released some steam, and he's puppy-dog whipped now." She made a whip-cracking sound. "Melly's got mojo—he wants an ER."

Exclusive relationship? Already? I felt excitement for her, before remembering I was pissed.

"Just when we were finishing up, the cops came," Mel said. "We drove out the back way."

"Why didn't you come here to find me?" I demanded.

She blinked. "I just did. So what happened to you, Eves?"

"Hmm. After Brandon left to go smooth things over with the sheriff and *find you*, I sat alone in the woods." *I was attacked and terrified.* "Eventually, I walked miles to get home—with that annoying Jackson Deveaux—and spent the night in the barn." Or rather, in the cane field. "You just left me out there, Mel. You chose bros over hoes," I said, drawing blood.

She gasped. "I thought you were with Brandon! I'll break up with Spencer as penance!"

The thing about Mel—she truly would. How could I stay mad at her when I'd been lying to her so much? In the end, I muttered, "You're forgiven."

"Thank you, Greene! I didn't want to bwake Spencey's wittle heart." She lay back on my bed, adding mischievously, "Not *yet*."

My laptop chimed. "An e-mail from Brandon?" Strange. We texted 99 percent of the time. He basically used his cell phone as his computer.

everything's cool w/ the cops. bout to get lecture from Dad tho. talk later.

"That's weird. Why didn't he just text? He doesn't know that I got stranded without my phone." And why hadn't he even mentioned my voice mail?

"He couldn't text you," Mel said, raising her hands in the air to study her nails. "Everybody's phones got stolen."

"What?" I shot to my feet.

"Why do you think I didn't call all morning?" She rose with a frown. "Somebody snatched wallets and cells right off of people. And they broke into all our cars. But don't worry, your bag didn't get taken."

I bolted out of my room, scrambling down the stairs to reach Mel's Beamer. *My journal!*

"What's wrong with you, Evie?" she demanded, trotting behind me, easily keeping up.

When I reached her car, I frantically slapped the door until she clicked it open. "Jesus, Evie, *chill.*"

My hand trembled as I reached for my bag. Surely a thief wouldn't leave it but then steal the journal. *Please let my drawings be inside—*

I reeled on my feet.

My sketchbook was . . . gone. The one filled with rats and serpents under an apocalyptic sky, bodies mangled in thorn barbed wire, and horrific sack-faced bogeymen. I'd drawn one lapping blood from a victim's throat. Like an animal at a trough.

My tear-blotted drawing of Death on a pale horse was dated from just a couple of nights ago.

It was the journal that Jackson had repeatedly angled to see. My eyes shot wide. The figure skulking among the cars last night—it was *Lionel.*

He'd stolen the phones *and* my sketchbook. My very own one-way ticket back to CLC.

And Jackson had kept me occupied, had acted interested in me . . . so that Lionel . . .

Oh my God.

Struggling not to throw up, I told Mel, "I know who's got our phones. And if you help me, I'm going to get them back."

"You've had better ideas," Mel muttered, squinting to see out of her bug-splattered windshield. At dusk the insects swarmed, and their squashed bodies had meshed till they were like tar on the glass.

"Maybe so, but I have to do this." I'd never been so incensed in all my life, and I'd be damned if I let Jackson get away with this. "Can't you go any faster?"

The sun would set soon, and we hadn't even made the parish levee yet. It'd taken us hours to find the Cajun's address on Mrs. Warren's computer, and then I'd wasted even more time persuading Mel to drive me into the Basin.

"You're lucky I'm in for this one at all, Greene. I'm not losing my license because of a fifth ticket this year. . . ."

She still hadn't stopped grumbling by the time the towering levee loomed. "Let's just call the cops."

And then they'd confiscate my journal. "Jackson only did this because he's a bully and because he *can*. No one ever calls him out. But it's time somebody did."

"How do you know he'll have the phones? You said he just served as a lookout."

I hadn't told Mel exactly how good Jackson had been at his job, only that he'd kept me talking to him while Lionel snatched our things. "I just know, okay?" Which wasn't precisely true. He might not have the phones, but he'd have that sketchbook, which was my main priority.

Not that the phones weren't a big deal. Though I code-locked mine—good luck accessing any of my info—Brandon *never* locked his phone. And he had all our private texts over the last seven months, not to mention a folder filled with countless pics and vids of me.

Were those Cajuns even now ogling images of me in my bathing suit, or snickering over the goofy faces I'd made for Brand's camera? The corny jokes I'd told.

Had they listened to my voice message from earlier? *"Yes, I'll spend the night with you."* My face burned, my fury ratcheting up to new heights.

When we came upon the new bridge, stretching over acres of swamp, my lips thinned. Without this line of dull gray cement, I'd never even have *known* Jackson Deveaux.

Once we reached the end of the bridge, we were officially in a new parish. Cajun country. Bayou inlets and smaller drawbridges abounded. A pair of wildlife agents in their black trucks sat chatting on a shoulder.

Mel exhaled. "Why are you forcing me into the voice-of-reason role? You know that never works out for us."

"I need to do this," I said simply. When I'd realized Jackson had played me, that the almost-kiss had been a ruse—it'd *hurt*. Even though I'd never wanted his kiss to begin with.

Why did he have to act as if he'd liked me? It was a mean-spirited, cold-hearted prank. How he and Lionel must have laughed at my gullibility!

"It's getting really dark," Mel said as we approached the Basin turn-off. She didn't just mean daylight-wise.

Ominous clouds were back-building over the swamp. "Yeah, but what are the odds that it'll actually rain?" Those clouds reminded me of the scene I'd painted on my wall, and of the blazing eyes I'd soon see.

Folks didn't usually drive to *lower* land when faced with a gale like that. I didn't know which storm would prove worse—the weather or Jackson's anger.

Didn't matter; I was bent on seeing this through *tonight*. I directed Mel to turn onto the dirt road that led to the Basin.

After a few miles, she said, "We're not in Kansas anymore."

We saw shrimp boats, bayou shacks, and shipyards filled with rusted heaps. Statuettes of the Virgin Mary graced every other yard. I'd known how Catholic the Basin folk were, but even I was surprised.

We neared the end of the road, closing in on Jackson's address. There were fewer structures down here, but more palmettos, banana trees, cypress. Trash had collected all around the ditch lilies.

By the time the marsh was visible, it was dark and the car lights had come on. Red eyes glowed back from the reeds. Gators. They were so thick, some of the smaller ones lay on top of the others.

Pairs of beady red dots, stacked like ladder rungs.

Mel nervously adjusted her hands on the wheel, but she drove onward. The car crept deeper under a canopy of intertwined limbs and vines, like a ride going into a haunted tunnel.

When the road surrendered to a rutted trail, Jackson's home came into view—a shotgun house, long and narrow, with entrances on both ends. The clapboard framing was a mess of peeling paint. A couple of gator skins had been tacked over the worst spots.

The roof was a rusted patchwork of mismatched tin sheets. In one section, a metal garbage can had been battered flat and hammered down.

This place was as far from proud Haven as possible. I thought I'd seen poor. I was mistaken.

"That's where he lives?" Mel shuddered. "It's horrid."

Suddenly I regretted her seeing this, as if I'd betrayed a secret of Jackson's, which didn't make any sense.

"Evie, my car'll get stuck if I drive any farther. And it's not like we have our phones on us."

"Not *yet*. Just stay here, and I'll walk it. Be back with our stuff."

"What if he's not even here?"

I pointed out his motorcycle, parked under an overhang beside the rickety front porch. "That's his."

When I opened the car door, she said, "*Think* about this."

I had. This entire situation was so unnecessary. None of this had needed to happen. All because Jackson had stolen from me! He'd violated my privacy, had possibly seen and heard my intimate exchanges with Brandon.

And he'd seen my drawings.

That freedom I'd vowed I would never take for granted? His actions were threatening it!

Remembering what was at stake made me slam the car door and venture forth. Yellow flies swarmed me, but I kept going, wending around tires, busted crab traps, cypress knees.

Closer to his house, there was no cut lawn, there wasn't even grass. In these parts, some folks who couldn't afford a lawnmower "swept" their yards, keeping them free of vegetation—and of snakes. His yard was a giant patch of hard-packed earth.

As I neared, I saw tools hanging from the porch roof. A machete and a saw clanked together in the growing breeze.

I crossed a dried-out depression in front of four wobbly-looking steps. The first stair bowed even under my weight. How did a boy as big as Jackson climb them?

There was no knocker on the unpainted plywood door, just a rusted lever to open it. The bottom was shredded in strips.

From when animals had scratched to get in?

With a shiver, I glanced back at the sky, saw the clouds were getting worse. I gazed at Mel in the distance, pensive in her car. *Maybe this is . . . stupid.*

No. I had to get that journal back. I found my knuckles rapping the wood. "Hello?"

The door groaned open wide.

"Mr. or Ms. Deveaux?" No answer. "I need to talk to Jackson," I called as I stepped into the house.

I saw no one inside but still got an eyeful. *Just as bad as the outside.*

The main living area was cramped, the ceiling hanging so low I wondered if Jackson had to duck to walk around. Dangling from it was a single lightbulb, buzzing like a bee.

The sole window had been boarded up. The door to a room in the back was closed, but I heard a TV blaring from inside.

On the left wall was a ridiculously small kitchen. Six fish lay cleaned beside a sizzling pan. Some kind of game was chopped in chunks, already breaded in cornmeal. Had Jack angled, trapped, or shot everything on that counter?

Why leave the stove on? "Jackson, where are you?" With a despairing eye, I took a closer look around the room.

Lining the wall to the right was a plaid couch, with cigarette burn holes pocking the arms. Frayed sheets had been spread over the sunken cushions.

His boots sat on the floor at the foot of the couch. *This is where he sleeps?*

My lips parted. He didn't even have his own room.

A *Spanish for Beginners* book lay on the floor, spine cracked and opened in the middle, with a worn copy of *Robinson Crusoe* beside it.

That novel wasn't on our reading list. So he read for enjoyment? And wanted to speak another language?

I felt something tugging inside of me. As much as I thought of him as grown, he was an just eighteen-year-old boy who would have a boy's plans and dreams.

Maybe he imagined running away to Mexico or sailing away from this hellhole.

It struck me how little I really knew about him.

As my anger faded, I reminded myself that what little I knew, I *hated*. Still, I found myself trudging forward to turn off the stove before the place caught fire.

I nibbled my lip. *Where is he?* What if my sketchbook was at Lionel's? I didn't see any of the phones here either.

After I turned off the burner, I heard yelling from the back. Not the TV?

Suddenly a harsh drumming pelted the tin roof. I gave a cry of surprise, but that noise drowned it out. "Just the rain," I murmured to myself. "Drops on tin." Finally!

Water started beading along bulging seams in the ceiling, dripping down to the floor, over the couch. Jackson would have nowhere dry to sleep tonight.

I jumped when stomping sounds shook the house, as if someone was bounding up a back set of stairs. When a door slammed in the back, the connecting door creaked open.

Morbid curiosity drew me closer. *One peek and I'll slip out. . . .*

On a stained mattress, a middle-aged woman lay sprawled unconscious, her long jet-black hair a tangled halo around her head. She was nearly indecent, her robe hiked high up her legs. A rosary with glinting onyx beads and a small gothic cross circled her neck.

Her arm hung over the side, an empty bottle of bourbon on the floor just beneath her fingertips. A plate of untouched scrambled eggs and toast sat atop a box crate by the bed.

Was that Ms. Deveaux?

A tall, sunburned man in wet overalls came into view. He started pacing alongside the bed, yelling at her unconscious form, gesturing with one fist and his own liquor bottle.

Was the man her husband? Her boyfriend?

I knew I needed to leave, but I was riveted to the spot, could no more look away than I could quit breathing.

Then I saw Jackson on the other side of the bed, pulling her robe closed. Shaking her shoulder, he urgently muttered, *"Maman, reveille!"*

She slurred something but didn't move. The way Jackson gazed at her face, so protectively . . . I knew he'd cooked her that breakfast this morning.

When the drunk lumbered toward her, Jackson smacked the man's arm away.

Both began yelling in Cajun French. Even with what I understood, I could barely follow. Jackson was trying to kick him out, telling him never to return?

The man reached for Ms. Deveaux again. Jackson blocked him once more. Then the two squared off at the foot of the bed. Their voices got louder and louder, bellows of rage as they circled each other.

Did the idiot not see that glint in Jackson's eyes? The one promising pain?

Instead of heeding that warning, the man clutched the neck of his bottle, busting the end on the windowsill. With surprising speed, he attacked with the jagged end. Jackson warded off the blow with his forearm.

I saw bone before blood welled. I thrust the back of my hand against my mouth. *Can't imagine that pain!*

But Jackson? He merely smiled. *An animal baring its teeth.*

At last, the drunk clambered back in fear. Too late. Jackson launched his big body forward, his fists flying.

A stream of blood spurted from the man's mouth, then another, and still Jackson ruthlessly beat him. The strength in his towering frame was brutal, the wildness in his eyes . . .

Why couldn't I run? Leave this sordid place behind?

Leave these horrific *sounds* behind—the angry rain on tin, the woman's slurring, the drunk's grunts as Jackson landed blow after blow.

Then . . . one last punch across the man's jaw. I thought I heard bone crack.

The force of the blow sent the man twirling on one foot, drooling blood and teeth as he went down.

With a heartless laugh, Jackson sneered, *"Bagasse."*

Cane pulp. Beaten to a literal pulp. I covered my ears with my forearms, fighting dizziness.

Now that the man had been defeated, Jackson's wrath seemed to ebb. Until he slowly turned his head in my direction. His brows drew together in confusion. "Evangeline, what are you . . . ?"

He swept a glance around his home, as if seeing it through my eyes. As if seeing this hellhole for the first time.

Even after Jackson's display of raw violence, I couldn't stop myself from pitying him.

He must have seen it in my expression, because his face reddened with embarrassment. His confusion evaporated, that rage returning. His gaze was almost *blank* with it. *"Why in the hell did you come here?"* The tendons in his neck strained as he stalked toward me. *"You tell me why you're in my goddamned house!"*

I could only gape as I retreated. *Don't turn your back on him, don't look away. . . .*

"A girl like you in the Basin? *C'est ça coo-yôn! Bonne à rien!* Good for nothing but getting yourself in trouble!" I'd never heard his accent so thick.

"I—I—"

"Wanted a look at how the other half lives? That it?"

I backed across the front threshold, almost to the porch steps. "I wanted the journal you stole!"

Lightning flashed, highlighting the lines of fury on his face. Thunder boomed instantly, shaking the house so hard the porch rattled. I cried out and swayed for balance.

"The journal with all your crazy drawings? You come to take me to task!" When Jackson reached for me with that injured arm, I recoiled, scrambling backward into the pounding rain.

That loose step seemed to buckle beneath my foot; pain flared in my ankle.

I felt myself falling . . . falling . . . landing on my ass in a puddle. I gasped, spitting mud and rain, too shocked to cry.

Strands of wet hair plastered my face, my shoulders. I tried to rise, but the mud sucked me down. I swiped hair out of my eyes, coating my face with filth.

Blinking against the rain, I shrieked, "You!" I wanted to rail at him, to blame him for my pain, my humiliation. And all I could say over and over was *"You!"* Finally I managed to yell, "You disgust me!"

He gave a bitter laugh. "Do I? I didn't last night when you were wet-tin' your lips, hoping I'd kiss them, no. You wanted more of me then!"

My face flushed with shame. Then I remembered. "You tricked me so your loser friend could steal our stuff. You acted as if you liked me!"

"You didn't seem to mind!" He raised his uninjured arm, shoving his fingers through his hair. "I heard your message to Radcliffe! You goan to kiss me? Then let that boy have you just days later?"

"Give me my journal!"

"Or what? What you goan do about it? The little doll got no teeth."

Frustration surged, because he was right. The Cajun had all the power; I had none.

Unless *I* could choke someone in vine or slice them to ribbons?

As my nails began to transform, I felt something akin to the blissful unity that I'd shared with the cane. I was awash in an awareness of all the plants around me—their locations, their strengths and weaknesses.

Above Jackson's house, a cypress tree shifted its branches over me. In the distance, I sensed kudzu vines hissing in response, slithering closer to defend me.

And for a brief moment, I experienced an urge to show him who really had the power, to punish him for causing me pain.

Punish him? No, no! At once, I struggled to rein back the fury I'd unleashed.

"You want your drawings?" Jackson stormed inside, returning with my journal. "Have them!" He flung the notebook like a Frisbee. Pages went sailing out, all over the muddy yard.

"Nooo!" I cried out, watching them scatter, about to hyperventilate.

By the time I'd managed to crawl to my hands and knees, I was breathing so hard I choked and coughed on raindrops. I reached for the pages nearest me, but every handful of paper made a vision sear my mind.

Death. The bogeymen. The sun shining at night.

With each page, I jerked again and again, yelling up at him, "*I hate you!* You disgusting brute!" His handsome face hid violence, seething ferocity.

Even though he'd been protecting his mother, he'd *liked* beating that man unconscious. Jackson had just proved how heartless a boy he truly was. *Bagasse . . .*

"HATE you! Never come near me again!"

He blinked at my face, his expression turning from murderous to disbelieving. He shook his head hard.

What was he seeing?

"Evie!" Mel cried. She'd come for me!

As she looped an arm around my shoulders to help me stand, she yelled at Jackson, "Stay away from her, you lowlife trash!"

With a last dumbstruck look at my face, he turned to stride away.

Just as he slammed inside that shack, my vines reached his porch. Mel was too busy checking me for injuries to see, but I watched them sway upright like cobras, waiting for me to command them.

I whispered, "*No.*" At once, they raced back into the brush like plucked rubber bands. Then I told Mel, "I-I need these drawings. All of them."

Without a word, she dropped to her knees beside me.

Both of us in the mud, collecting my crazy.

"You're being so quiet," I told Mel as she helped me up to my front porch. The rain was receding, the screen door open to the night breeze. We were both still coated with mud. "I hate when you go quiet."

On the way here, I'd told Mel about CLC, my visions, my mom, my gran—though not about the plants—finishing just as we'd pulled up.

Now, after my confession, I felt battered, like one of those dolls that always bounces back up when hit. But here's the thing—those silly dolls get hit all the more for it.

When will this day end? My bottom lip trembled as I fought off tears.

"I'm waiting for you to tell me what happened in the Cajun's shack," Mel said. "I mean, your expression was unforgettable—you were all like, *'Pa, I seen something behind the woodshed.'*"

"Maybe one day I'll tell you." Right now the memory was too raw.

"How come I'm, like, the last to know you have visions? The woman who spawned you knew before me. And that hurts."

"I didn't want you to look at me differently." When we reached the door, I said, "I understand if you don't want to be friends anymore." I motioned for my backpack, stuffed full of sodden pages.

With a roll of her eyes, Mel handed over my bag. "And miss my opportunity to sell your disturbed little drawings on deviantART.com? No way, my freaky, cray-cray minx." She curled her arm around my neck, dragging me down so she could rub her knuckles in my muddy hair. "I'm going to be rich! So get me some more drawings that aren't soaking wet with Cajun funk all over them."

"Stop!" But amazingly, I was about to laugh.

"You sure you don't want me to come in?" Mel asked when she finally released me.

"I've got it," I told her. "I'm probably about to ugly-cry."

"Look, grasshopper, we'll figure out all of this tomorrow," Mel assured me. "But check this—you are *not* going back to that CLC place. Ever. If we have to, we'll run away together, get married in a civil union, and live off your art."

And there went my bottom lip again. "You've always been there for me, putting up with my crap."

Mel glared at me. "You're being *wank*, Greene. Cut out all this sentimental b.s. and ask yourself: What choice do I have? *Hellooo.* You're my *best* friend. Now, get inside before I take off the filter."

With a grave nod, I limped into the house, turning to wave as Mel drove off with her iPod blaring and her signature three-honk salute.

When I hobbled into the kitchen, Mom was making popcorn. "Hi, hon," she called over one shoulder, her tone cheerful. "Can you believe it rained—" Her eyes went wide at my appearance. "Evie! What happened to you?"

"I tripped in the mud. It's a long story."

"Are you hurt?"

I shrugged, gripping the strap of my backpack. Define *hurt*. "My ankle's a little sprained."

"I'll get some ice and Advil." Had Mom's attention darted past me to the door? "And then you can tell me what happened."

While she wrapped ice in a dishrag, I plunked myself down in a chair, keeping my bag of drawings close. "It's not a big deal, Mom."

As I debated how to explain away this mishap, the winds picked up, blowing through the screened door.

Though we'd gotten rain, the breeze felt hot and dry. Like a scarf out of the dryer rubbed against my cheek.

When it blew again and harder, Mom frowned. "Um, just let me check out the Weather Channel really quick." She grabbed the remote for our kitchen TV and turned it on.

The screen was divided between three harried-looking field reporters, the trio talking over each other. One of them was the guy who'd been all blasé while at ground zero for Katrina.

So why was he sweating profusely now? "Sightings of bizarre weather phenomena in the eastern states . . . get a shot over my left shoulder . . . just look at those lights, folks . . . is that the *sun* rising?"

The second reporter looked like he hadn't blinked in a week. "Temperatures spiking . . . fires in the Northeast . . . there's no cause for panic," he said in a panicked voice. "Radiation spikes . . . reports of aurora borealis as far south as Brazil . . ."

The third guy's microphone shook in his trembling hand. "We've lost contact with our London, Moscow, and Hong Kong bureaus . . . all reported similar events"—he pressed his ear com—"what's that . . . New York? *DC?*" he said, his voice scaling an octave higher. "M-my family's in Wash—"

One by one, the feeds cut out. *Blip. Blip. Blip.*

"Mom?" I whispered. "What's going on?" *Why is your face paler than I've ever seen it?*

She glanced past me; suddenly her fingers went limp. The ice cubes clattered to the floor.

I lurched to my feet, my ankle screaming in protest. I was too scared to look behind me, too scared not to. Finally I followed Mom's gaze. Across the now-clear night sky, lights flickered.

Crimson and violet like Mardi Gras streamers.

I'd seen this very thing during Matthew's first visit. It was the aurora borealis. The northern lights in Louisiana.

They were utterly mesmerizing.

As Mom and I both crept toward the front door, that hot wind intensified, beginning to howl, rattling the wind chimes around the farm. The horses shrieked in the barn. I could hear their hooves battering their stalls, wood splintering.

They sounded terrified—

But just look at those dazzling lights! I could stare forever.

From the east, the cane rustled. A mass of fleeing animals burst from the fields. Raccoons, possums, nutria, even deer. So many snakes erupted from the ditches that the front lawn looked like it shone and rippled.

A wave of rats roiled in flight. Birds choked the sky, tearing at each other or dive-bombing the ground. Feathers drifted in the winds.

But the lights! So magnificent they made me feel like weeping with joy.

And yet, I didn't think I should be looking at them. Had Matthew said something, warned me? I couldn't think, could only stare.

The massive Haven oaks groaned then, distracting my attention. Mom didn't seem to notice, but they were *moving*, tightening their rain-soaked limbs around us. They spread a shield of green leaves over our home, as if readying to defend it.

My cane seemed stunned, standing rigid, even in that wind. *As if shell-shocked.*

They know what's coming. They know why I should . . .

Turn away from the lights! "Mom, don't look at the sky!" I shoved her back from the door.

She blinked, rubbing her eyes, as though coming out of a trance. "Evie, what is that noise?"

A roar was building in the night, the loudest, most harrowing sound I'd ever imagined.

Yet Mom's demeanor grew icy cold. "We are not going to panic. But we will be locked inside the cellar within thirty seconds. Understood?"

The apocalypse . . . it was now. And Mel was out there alone.

"I have to call Mel!" Then I remembered she didn't have a phone. "If I drive across the property, I can try to catch her!"

Mom clenched my arm and swung me around toward the cellar.

"I'm not going down there without Mel! I have to get to her!"

I lunged for the front door, but Mom hauled me back, her strength unreal. "Get in the cellar NOW!" she yelled over the roar. "We can't risk it!"

The sky grew lighter—*hotter*. "No, no!" I shrieked, fighting her. "She'll die, she'll die, you know she will! I've *seen* this!"

"You both will if you try to go after her!"

I flailed against Mom, but couldn't break her hold. Arms stretched toward the front door, I sobbed, thrashing in a frenzy as she dragged me back to the cellar stairs.

When I clung to the doorway, she yanked on me, peeling my fingers from the doorjamb. "No, Mom! *P-please* let me go after Mel—"

Then came a shock of light—a blast of fire that shook the ground— my eardrums ruptured—

A split second later, the force of the explosion hurled us down the stairs, the door slamming behind us.

DAY 246 A.F.

REQUIEM, TENNESSEE

"Arthur, what was that?" Evie asks.

I blink. And again. I'd been utterly caught up in her tale of the Flash. "What was *what*?"

She shakes her head hard—as if to throw off her drug-fueled fog.

Good luck with that. I am a master of concoctions, unparalleled in chemistry; the only reason she is still awake is because I *want* her to be.

Everything is moving along according to my schedule.

"I thought I heard a thud downstairs."

She likely had. I use the spacious cellar as my lab and containment facility. One of the little bitches down there was probably straining to reach the waste bucket. I'd left it just close enough to give them hope.

I never miss an opportunity to demonstrate the godlike power I wield over my subjects.

"Probably rats," I tell this one, inwardly laughing at my joke. "Just ignore it. Please go on." I'm eager to hear more of Evie's story.

Even though I believe little of it.

She tilts her head and gives me an appraising glance. "Arthur, what were *you* doing before the Flash?"

I'm taken aback. None of my visitors has ever asked me this before, and for a moment I grope for an answer before settling on a lie. "I was preparing to go to college in the spring. Majoring in chemistry at MIT."

Ever since I can remember, I've been interested in chemical concoctions, in the transmuting of one substance into another. A chemistry degree would've given me a good base for what I truly wanted to study.

Alchemy—the ancient occult art of potions and elixirs.

"I'd intended to be a chemist." An *alchemist*. But MIT wouldn't have me. Apparently, my entrance essay on the criticality of human testing had "raised red flags."

"Wow." Evie is genuinely impressed. Her expressions are so telling. "You must be really smart."

"I prepared all my life," I say with false modesty. My intelligence is off the scales, unquantifiable by even the most sophisticated measurements. "So now I study on my own, still working toward the dream." My own independent research—conducted in the cellar of my stolen lair.

God, I love to . . . learn.

But I don't want to speak about myself any longer. Evie will have plenty of time to discover exactly what I am—and what I do. "On the side, I compile these histories. Are you ready to recount more?" When she nods, I press record. "What happened to you and your mother after the Flash?"

"I was knocked unconscious from the explosion. When I woke up, we waited in the dark for hours. At dawn, we peeked out. You can imagine what we saw."

I could. Laserlike shafts of sunlight had blasted the earth for the course of one entire global night. Those fields of green cane she remembered dreamily would've been charred to ash. Anything organic—any living thing caught outside shelter—was incinerated.

And so many people, transfixed by the pretty lights, had wandered from their homes, drawn like moths to flame.

As if by design.

All the travelers who have visited me at these crossroads—those who've involuntarily surrendered to me their clothing, food, and even a rare daughter on occasion—brought tales from their regions. Before I slew them.

Certain details remain uniform.

Bodies of water flash-evaporated, but no rain has fallen in eight months. All plant life has been permanently destroyed; nothing will grow anew. And only a small percentage of humans and animals lived through the first night.

In the ensuing days, hundreds of millions more people perished, unable to survive the new toxic landscape.

For some reason, most females sickened and died.

An unknown number of humans mutated into "Bagmen"—contagious zombielike creatures, cursed with an unending thirst and an aversion to the sun.

Some call them hemophagics—blood-drinkers. I believe they are *anything* drinkers, but without water to be found, they've turned to people, walking bags of liquid.

They drink and drink but can never be slaked. Like my quest for knowledge. "Why do you think it happened, Evie?"

She shrugs, and curling golden locks tumble over her slim shoulders. Again, I am spellbound.

For a moment, I truly consider keeping her as my helpmeet, my companion. Though I am devoid of compassion, I do have *some* emotional needs.

Loneliness preys on me. Perhaps I have at last found a girl who can understand my genius, the importance of my work.

Maybe she will excuse my eccentricities, since she herself has tasted of sweet madness.

Or perhaps, I muse darkly, *she will try to distract me from my studies.* I ruthlessly eliminate distractions.

"All the theories I've heard of make sense in a way," she says. "I guess it was a solar flare."

Yes, but we'd had them before, often. What made this one so catastrophic? Why has the entire planet gone barren?

Some say the very tilt of the earth's axis wobbled, disturbing the balance of our world, lowering its defenses. Others claim that the depleted ozone layer—already a peeling scab—ripped open, leaving us vulnerable to heat and radiation.

Basically, we know as much about the Flash as medieval quacks knew about the black death. Will the answer turn out to be something as simple as disease-carrying fleas spread by rats?

"I really don't know what to think," Evie says. "I try not to dwell on things I can't control."

Smart girl.

"What's your theory, Arthur?"

"I'm in your camp. Best not to obsess over it," I say, though I obsess over it continually, fixated with how perfectly organic matter was destroyed, while at least some homes and buildings were spared. My theory would only frighten her; and I'm not ready to put her on edge. Yet. "Did any of your friends survive? Your boyfriend?"

Her eyes mist with tears. "None of them lived. Mel . . . she never made it home." Evie glances down, beginning to rock in the chair again. I've noticed that she rocks more whenever she feels particularly unsettled. "She died alone, without her family nearby, out on a lonesome highway."

"How do you know?"

"Her car was in a ditch. The door was open, and inside there was . . . ash."

"I see." Piles of ash had become the gravestones for much of the world's population—until the winds had come, dispersing the remains into the air, for all the rest of us to breathe. "I'm sorry for your loss," I say, though I'm not.

My lack of empathy is a boon for a scientist like myself. It allows me to experiment without hesitation. I experience only *joy* when my scalpel divides flesh—like two curtains, revealing secrets to my probing gaze.

Somehow Evie stems her tears. What a brave little girl. It will be all the more rewarding when I bring her to sobs.

"Did you lose all of your family to the Flash?" she asks, again surprising me with her interest.

"Yes, in the Flash." I muster a grieving look.

She offers me one of compassion. "This was your childhood home?"

I nod, though this is my sixth home since the apocalypse. I've moved like a hermit crab, from shell to shell. In the past, I would exhaust all the resources in a given place, then abandon it.

But I like this crossroads town, like that resources come directly to me.

I plan to stay for some time.

Another knock sounds in the basement. Evie tenses, cocks her head. My hands clench. *Those little bitches . . .*

I reach for the recorder, turning off the tape. Barely containing my rage, I rise, saying, "I'll go check my mousetraps really quick." I'm so incensed that I fear I'll do murder and get blood on my corduroys. "You stay put." As if she could possibly escape. "I'll be right back."

I pull out my key ring on the way to the cellar door, quietly unlocking it. As I descend the darkened stairwell, I hear the hushed voices of my test subjects. They know they're supposed to be silent unless I address them.

Disobeying me? Mindful of my spotless corduroys, I grapple for patience.

When I enter my dimly lit lab, the familiar scent calms me to a degree. All along the workbenches are bubbling vials and distilleries, flasks simmering on Bunsen burners. Myriad body parts are preserved in jars of formaldehyde.

The loose eyeballs in one jar always seem to follow my movements, which amuses me.

In one crystal vial, I've distilled a new potion that will spike my adrenaline, giving me a concentration of strength and speed. Another flask holds the key to accelerated healing.

I've weaponized other formulations. Bagmen—rumored to be allergic to salt—will stand no chance against my sodium chloride spray.

If any of the numerous militias roll through this town, they'll be in for a surprise when I launch my stoppered vials of acid at them. . . .

The other half of the cellar is screened by heavy plastic curtains. I call it the dungeon. This is where the dirty work gets done. There's an oversize butcher block, a stainless-steel operating table, drain fields, and anatomical tools.

I keep my stable of girls shackled in there as well. I currently own three of them, each between the ages of fourteen and twenty, each collared and chained to a wall.

Healthy young females like Evie have become rarities, *resources*. Like everyone else alive, I hoard resources.

It makes no difference that I'd begun doing this before the apocalypse. I *need* them, using them to test my concoctions.

Some might say I torture simply because I myself was tortured by my father, a tyrant who'd tried to "beat the evil" out of me. I'd been a mass of healing fractures and repeated contusions for all of my childhood—up until the day I chloroformed him, chained him in a storage tub, then leisurely dissolved him in hydrochloric acid.

He'd awakened in time to meet the evil up close.

And my mother, the woman who'd done nothing to stop him, even blaming me for triggering his ire?

She fared worse.

But my past experience is irrelevant. I use these girls only to further my research. This is my life's work. I don't set out to harm them, per se. The fact that I enjoy inflicting pain on them is incidental.

No, the research is all that matters.

When I head toward the dungeon, the trio falls silent behind the plastic curtain, their chains rattling as they scurry back toward the wall.

I push past the plastic, turning up the battery-powered lantern on the wall. As they shield their eyes from the light, I stare down at them one by one.

Clad in soiled garments, they cower on the packed earthen floor, their hands caked with dirt. They've been digging into the ground, making little nests in which to keep warm when they sleep.

A maggot-ridden corpse lies curled up in one nest, still attached to her chain. That one succumbed to my last experiment: a potion I'd designed to lessen the body's need for fluids.

For weeks, it'd worked faultlessly. Then it . . . didn't.

I view her remains dispassionately. The congealing blood, tissue, and organs used to be a *person*—a former Merit Scholar at an Ivy League college. That pile of meat used to embody a soul.

Now it's just a collection of elements.

Evie will take the scholar's place. Perhaps she'll live longer than a month. Perhaps my newest elixir—immortality in a bottle—will finally cheat death.

It must.

Why does everyone assume we've seen the worst of the apocalypse? I will be ready.

I clench the chain of the oldest girl, yanking her to her feet. "Why has there been noise?" I demand, spittle spraying.

The ring of blisters circling her neck runs with watery blood. All of them get neck wounds from the rusty iron collars. This one needs more of my salve. I won't give it to her now.

She considers answering, then thinks better of it. She'd been rebellious at first, *sassy*. Now she's hollow-eyed and quaking.

"If I hear another sound, I'll make you drink the gold elixir." It's a pain potion that rips through their intestines. I relish their stricken looks. "Understood?"

They mumble, "Yes, Arthur. . . ."

When I return upstairs to Evie, I find her relaxed in her chair, staring at the fire. Her heavy-lidded gaze follows the flames.

The last fire she'll ever see. *Enjoy it for now.*

"Sorry about that," I tell her. "A pack of rats seems to have moved in over the winter." I hope that my statement doesn't sound conceited. A rat infestation these days is a bounty. "If only they'd stop knocking over empty paint buckets. Now, where were we?" I turn the recorder back on, taking a seat. "Tell me what those first few weeks were like."

"My hometown used to have a few thousand people. Almost all of them watched the Flash—less than a handful lived. Directly after, they holed up in what was left of the still-smoldering church, but not Mom and me," Evie says. "When none of the cars worked, we took our one surviving horse, hooked up a cart, and went raiding."

She leans forward, growing a bit more animated. "Half of the grocery store had burned by the time we got there. So we hit the remaining aisles. Mom tossed back my graham crackers and potato chips, teaching me to go for calorie-dense food, like peanut butter. The pharmacy had burned down completely, so we ransacked the vet's supply of antibiotics. We looted guns and ammo from Flash victims' homes. We were like locusts."

Evie says this with pride. She should. If it wasn't for enterprising souls like her, I'd have no supplies to appropriate.

"Though Mom was convinced that the army would ride into Sterling and save the day—government and the rule of law returning, or whatever—we prepared like we were on our own. We worked ourselves to the bone, until our basement was stockpiled. Then we stood arm in arm, surveying the thousands of cans, the bags of beans, the canisters of weight-gain powder."

Shaking her head ruefully, she says, "I remember thinking our supply would last us *years*. As soon as Mom had prepared us as best as she could, she . . . broke down."

"What do you mean?"

"She was eaten up with guilt that she'd sent her mother away, that she'd sent *me* to that awful place in Atlanta. Can you imagine it? Her mother had been right all along, and her daughter's visions had proved pretty much spot-on. My 'bogeymen' were *Bagmen*, pale-eyed and slimy. Not to mention the details of the Flash. . . . Well, Mom's entire concept of the world got a violent reboot. Her confidence was obliterated."

"Did your grandmother impart anything to her that she could pass on to you?"

"Mom had blocked out Gran's doomsday preachings—like

aggressively blocked them out. So she didn't know a lot. And anytime I pressed her to try to remember more, she'd cry. She was no longer the steel magnolia I'd always known."

"There must have been something?"

"Mom knew only three things. My clairvoyance had to do with Tarot cards somehow. My call sign, of sorts, was the Empress. And I might be destined to"—Evie mumbles the next—"save humanity."

I inwardly laugh at this. This girl is weak in body and in mind, as defenseless as she is gullible; if the fate of mankind rests in her hands, we are all utterly doomed. "That's a lot to put on a sixteen-year-old girl's shoulders, isn't it?"

"I know! It was so frustrating. If Gran was right and I actually was some empress, then what was the freaking point? Could I have saved my friends? Was that what the visions had been for? I had guilt of my own to haunt me."

"Did the visions"—*hallucinations*—"continue after the Flash?"

She gives her head a clearing shake, blinking for focus. "The ones of different characters were rare, but I did see Matthew about once a week. Each visit, he seemed even more incoherent. Still, I was desperate to see someone my age, so I welcomed him, migraines, nosebleeds, and all. But I had a whole new symptom to deal with. I was hearing voices in my head. The Flash brought me a perfect storm of crazy—nightmares of gruesome deaths, visions, voices."

Voices? That would correspond with her pathology. "What did they say?"

"For months, I heard only whispers and gibberish. Nothing that made sense. They grew clearer each day, but that also meant they got louder. Everything bad kept building on itself." She rocked faster. "Stress, hunger, nightmares, voices. Always *building*."

Evie was alone on that farm with only her mother, as good as stranded on a deserted island. It's no wonder she conjured voices, to give her a sense of belonging. Like imaginary friends.

And naturally, she fabricated those superpowers for herself. In a world filled with peril, where girls like her are targeted at every turn, she *needs* to feel powerful.

I would diagnose her as a paranoid schizophrenic with delusional features. It's because of my own madness that I can so readily identify it in others. But mine is a divine madness, a spark that flared to godhood.

With my elixirs coursing through my blood, I *am* a god. Soon Evie will kneel, awestruck, as I reveal my true nature.

In comparison, her madness grows tedious. A garden-variety schizo won't hold my interest for long. "So what did you make of those voices?"

"Again, I didn't know!" She frets one of her delicate, shell-pink nails—hardly the *thorn claws* she described. "They started the day after the Flash. Eventually, they grew into warnings." She raises her head, meeting my eyes.

Seeing if I'm buying this? I cast her a sympathetic expression—or as close to one as I can manage.

"And with those warnings came the feeling that I was supposed to be out in the world doing *something*. Both Death and Matthew had said, 'It begins with the End.' Something had begun, but I couldn't say what."

"What about your other . . . abilities? Did you retain them?"

"There were no plants around for me to control. My skin regeneration was hit or miss. But sometimes when I had a scary vision, my nails would turn."

I raise my brows at her hands, a silent request for her to demonstrate this.

"Oh, I have to be really emotional. I can't just make them appear." She splays her pale fingers for me. "You don't believe me, do you?"

"Honestly? I'm not certain." I am 100 percent certain that she is either lying or delusional. The spontaneous plant movement she described is biomechanically impossible—not to mention the morphing of her fingernails into a plant's attribute.

Science can explain all the other events of the apocalypse—but not Evie's "powers."

Which have conveniently vanished. Since the earth has gone barren, and she isn't "emotional," there is no way to prove or disprove her tale.

I begin to wonder if I'm not being played, if perhaps the girl isn't spinning a tale on the fly, picking up cues from my home, from my personality. The boredom I'd felt dissipates as I consider the prospect.

Will she talk about fires—because of the flames she was just regarding—or stew, like the one she ate earlier?

"I feared you'd tell me that you believed me, even if you didn't," Evie says. "I appreciate your honesty, Arthur." She holds my gaze, as if to really make me understand how serious she is. "Lying is the worst, you know?"

So says the girl whose lips spill untruths. But I have to wonder who lied to her. *Who hurt you, Evie?* "I'll always be honest with you."

She bestows a sweet smile upon me. A sixteen-year-old blonde. So easily duped.

When I wave her on, she grows somber. "A little more than a month ago, everything got worse. Much worse."

"How so?"

"I discovered a new talent of sorts, Jackson Deveaux rode back into my life, and my mom . . . she got hurt."

Her voice breaks when she speaks of her mother, but the mention of that boy puts my back up. Something about the way Evie has described him—as if the Cajun is larger than life to her—makes me feel murderous.

So not only had he lived, he'd returned for her? I see the odds of her being my helpmeet dwindling.

Why did bad boys like Jackson Deveaux always attract girls like Evie? It'd been that way at my high school. The only attention *I* had received from pretty girls was their laughter when I'd shown up for class with a busted lip or an awkward new cast.

They'd spurned me for things I could not control.

I remind myself that I *took* control of my parents—and that I no longer have to worry about attracting a girl's attention; I have a captive audience of beautiful females.

Yes, these days Arthur gets *all* the girls. *I keep them in my basement.* I nearly chuckle.

Instead, I say, "Tell me about your mom." My tone is kindly and concerned, even as I'm thinking, *If you like bad boys, little girl, then you've found the baddest of them all.*

"I'll tell you the rest." Another abashed look. "But, Arthur," she says in that soft drawl, the one that makes my heartbeat race, "the same warning as before applies."

15

It was time.

A pitcher of water shook in one of my hands. In my other fist, I squeezed a clean length of bandage.

Still I hesitated, dreading what I was about to see. And I hated myself for being a coward.

The voices that hounded me—with their repeated chorus of twisted threats—quieted to a low, manageable buzz. As if to let me suffer the next twenty minutes with my mom all the more.

No distractions, no interruptions . . . "Bastards," I muttered. "Rot in hell, every single one of you."

Deep breath in. Out. Showtime.

With a breezy demeanor, I sailed into Mom's darkened room, placing the pitcher next to the washbowl on her dresser. "Good morning. How're you feeling?"

A ray of sun peeked through a broken louver on the hurricane shutter, highlighting her face. She looked so tiny in her big canopy bed, a shadow of the woman she'd been before the Flash. Her gaunt cheeks were much paler than yesterday.

If she truly had an internal injury like she thought, then that meant more of her blood had been collecting in the mottled, pulpy bruises beneath her elastic bandage.

"You ready for me to change your dressing?"

If I cried at the sight, I was going to hate myself forever. If I faltered in any way . . .

When I sat beside her on the bed, she raised her hand to cup my face. "How are *you* doing, honey?"

My bottom lip *almost* trembled. How badly I wanted to talk to Mom, to tell her all the things on my mind.

I hear more than a dozen voices. If I sleep, nightmares torment me. We're on the last of our food stores. Even now, I'm shaking from the effort not to ditch your room and run outside to scream into the wind with frustration. Our horse is dying of starvation. You're getting worse.

Are you *dying?*

Instead I said, "How am I doing? The *best*. Today is pea-soup day." My performance fooled no one, but I was determined to sell it. "So let's see what we've got here." I spread her arm across my shoulders, gently helping her to sit up while I stuffed pillows behind her.

Perspiration beaded her face—from her effort not to cry out in pain? We were *both* actors in our roles. And worse, we both knew it.

I started unwrapping her bandage, found the material damp with sweat. Every morning, I changed her dressing. Ever since she'd been attacked.

A week ago, she'd ridden out to check our dead neighbor's well levels. One of our water pumps was spitting sand, sounding like a straw at the bottom of a milkshake. So she'd decided to investigate, going out alone early one morning when I'd been asleep. In the note she'd left, she'd pointed out that Allegra could barely carry her, much less both of us, and she assured me that no Bagmen would be out in the daylight.

As long as she had her salt and made it back before sunset, she'd be safe.

Neither of us had even seen a Bagman, except in my drawings. At first I'd been petrified that they'd overrun us, but months had passed with no sighting. So I hadn't gone *hysterical* when I found her note.

To keep myself busy, I'd done a thorough cleaning of the house. I couldn't stand the ash that accumulated over everything, grew sickened if I let myself think I could be breathing someone's cremated remains.

As I'd been working, Mom had been miles away—stumbling upon three Bagmen in a pump house.

Two of the things had been licking at a wellhead. Another had stood between her and the door. It'd knocked her salt from her hand, so she'd charged, tackling it into the sun, both of them tumbling down cement steps. . . .

Now as I unraveled the first layer of bandage, I remembered how I'd listened to her tale, dumbstruck by her bravery. The badass Karen of old had made it home—without a single freaking Bagman bite, just a couple of bruised ribs.

Or so we'd thought.

Second layer of bandage. Like an idiot, I'd wondered if the attack might not be a *good* thing, a catalyst to jar her back to her ballsy ways.

Third layer. This task was testing me in ways I wasn't ready for.

Where had that thought come from? *Shame on you, Evie.*

Shame. On. You.

Final layer. *Don't you dare gasp at the sight. Don't inhale a breath. Calm. Act like it's better.*

Reveal. I clamped my lips together to hold back the surge of vomit in my mouth. *Swallow it back down, you stupid coward with your stupid shaking hands.*

The wound was hideous.

At first the injury had been just a cluster of bruises. Then it'd turned squishy. Now it looked tight, a sack of blood about to burst. Like a tumor growing out of her side.

The bandage was doing nothing but making *me* feel better—allowing me to think I was making a difference.

"It's . . . better today," I choked out. "I really think so." With wobbly knees, I crossed to the antique pitcher and bowl—the ones we'd previously used as quaint decorative pieces. Now back in service.

As I wet a cloth to clean her skin, I took a moment to collect myself, gazing in the mirror at her room's reflection.

This space was also a shadow of its former self. The burgundy and cream décor, the rich silk wall hangings, and the lace of her canopy bed were now all drab, the colors muted.

Despite my best efforts, ash continued to steal inside, steeping everything we owned. Layer by layer, that ash was erasing what we'd once known, erasing who we were.

I broke my stare, meeting eyes with Mom. Oh God, she'd been watching me when I was unguarded! *Shame on you, Evie.*

Had she caught a glimpse of the helpless frustration churning inside me? Of course—her eyes were glistening with unshed tears. But she said nothing, playing her role.

"Let's get you cleaned up," I said brightly, determined *not* to be helpless. Because wasn't that just another way to say *useless?*

Exactly as that Cajun boy had once described me. *Bonne à rien.* Good for nothing.

As I washed Mom's torso, I realized he'd been right. I couldn't cook, sew, repair, or hunt the vermin and snakes that had survived. I was a clumsy and inefficient caretaker.

Never in the history of mankind had there been a better time *not* to be useless.

But I wasn't going to be for long. . . .

Once I'd finished cleaning her up and rewrapping her torso as best as I could, I said, "Mom, I'm going out to find you a doctor today." I might as well have said I was going to find her an Internet connection. Or a rainbow. "If I ride fast, I can make it to the next parish before sunset."

The mere idea of heading away from this place, out into the world, sent a thrill through me. Then I felt guilty. How could I be excited about leaving my mom?

Was I so desperate to flee the misery at Haven House?

Every time I got that overwhelming urge to leave, I feared that I might truly be a coward at heart.

Or could it be more? *Had* something begun at the End, at the end of the world?

What I wouldn't give for an answer! Since I'd stopped taking my meds, I'd started remembering more about that last drive with Gran. But those tiny flashes of recollection were never enough to make sense.

I recalled that she'd asked me to take her Tarot deck out of her purse, to look at the Major Arcana. I remembered the smell of her purse—Juicy Fruit gum and gardenia hand lotion. As I'd shuffled through the cards, they'd felt so big. . . .

"What are the odds that there will be a physician, Evie?" Mom asked. "And even if there is, the doctor will never have whatever is necessary to heal me. Be realistic." Was her voice fainter than it'd been yesterday? "And your plan to ride *fast*? A week ago, Allegra was about to keel over just from walking to the neighbor's. She won't make the property line now."

Did Mom think I was just going to sit idly by and do crosswords with her? The last time I'd sat idly by hadn't worked out so well for us.

What if I could've somehow used my visions to save our friends and loved ones . . . ?

Hell, the only positive thing about the voices was that they kept me from dwelling on the past, on what could've been. More than a dozen kids spoke in my head at various times, as cryptically as Matthew always did. This morning as I'd debated bringing Mom breakfast (knowing she'd turn it away), they'd ranted:

—*Crush you with the Weight of Sins.*—

—*Red of tooth and claw!*—

—*We will love you. In our own way.*—

"Evie," Mom said, "I want you to dress up real nice and take a basket of cans over to Mr. Abernathy."

The former animal control officer of the parish? "A *basket*. What do you think we are—rich?" The cellar full of cans that was supposed to last us years? We were down to weeks, were already rationing to the point of constant hunger.

"Do this for me, honey. Relieve my worries."

In a mock-horrified tone, I said, "My mom's pimping me out to a fifty-year-old dogcatcher."

"He's only thirty or so. And he's a widower now."

"You're *serious*?" My mother, once so independent, now wanted me to go throw myself on the mercy of a man.

The woman who'd fought the old boys' network of farming—and *dominated*—planned to offer up her daughter.

Don't scream; keep the banter light. "Then why stop with a basket of cans, Mom? Don't you think showing up with a fourteen-year-old sister-wife in tow would be more appropriate?"

"He's one of the last people in Sterling, honey."

Outside, the daily winds were starting up, pelting the shuttered windows, rocking Haven House until it creaked and groaned.

When the wind stirred up the ash, obscuring the sun, the temperature dropped. I busied myself smoothing another blanket over her. "Then maybe *you* should go out with Abernathy."

"I'm forty-one and currently in no condition to go make nice with the boys. Evie, what if something happened to me? What would you do?" Ever since the attack, she'd been asking me this. "There's no one here to look out for you, no one to protect you. It preys on my mind, thinking of you alone here."

"I've asked you to stop talking like that. A few days ago, you told me you'd be fine. Now you're acting like I'm about to have to institute Darwinism or cast you adrift on an iceberg or something."

She sighed, and immediately started coughing. Once the fit subsided, I handed her a glass of water, making a mental note to go to the pump whenever there was a lull in the winds.

"Oh, Evie. What would you do?" she asked again.

I met her gaze, willing her to believe my words: "It won't happen, Mom." As soon as I left this room, I was going to march down to the barn. If Allegra could take a saddle, I was riding out for a doctor. "Why don't you concentrate on getting better and leave the worrying to me?"

I kissed her on the forehead. "I'm off to finish my booby trap."

This was a believable lie. Though no one had ever trespassed—or even visited—Haven since the Flash, I'd been preoccupied with securing our home, with keeping Mom safe.

Her expression grew wary. "Evie, that's so dangerous, and you're . . . you're . . ."

"All thumbs? Even I can follow a guidebook with pictures."

"But the storm?"

The ash was disgusting but manageable. I dragged my ever-present bandanna from my neck up over my face, then made finger guns like a bandit. Mom smiled, but didn't laugh.

"Get some rest," I told her. "I'll be back to bring you lunch."

"Don't forget your salt," she called weakly.

My smile disappeared the instant I was alone. We were out of food, out of luck, out of time.

Back in my room, I donned my oversize Coach sunglasses and a hoodie, then strapped my shotgun over my back. Between that and the salt in my pockets, I was prepared for potential bad guys—and Bagmen.

Salt was supposed to repel the zombies—if we believed the few haunted-eyed stragglers who had passed through Sterling. They'd also said that plague had hit the North, nonstop fires raged out west, slavers ruled the bigger cities in the South, and cannibals had taken over the Eastern Seaboard.

Hearing tales like those made me thankful to be here, tucked away at Haven—even as I suffered the overpowering sense that I should be somewhere else, doing something else.

But what could possibly be more important than watching out for Mom . . . ?

Once I'd opened the hurricane shutter covering my window, I loosed the fire escape ladder, watching it unfurl down the side of the house.

This window was our only entrance. Early on, I'd braced all the doors with lumber, painstakingly nailing down the shutters on the first floor.

I closed my window behind me, then climbed down the swaying ladder into the swirling ash, like I was in the gym class of the damned. The sooty ground crunched when I hopped down.

At once, I had to lean into the wind or get tossed.

The only things constant about the new weather patterns? There was never any rain. For most of each day, we had windstorms. And after the storms faded, cloudless blue skies and that scorching sun returned.

At night, there was perfect stillness, with no insect chatter, no rustling leaves or swaying branches. Wretched silence.

Unless a quake rumbled somewhere in the distance.

When I passed the remains of the once mighty Haven oaks—now twisted black skeletons with leafless fingers—I slowed to run a hand over a crumbling trunk.

As ever, I felt a pang; they'd given their lives, protecting us.

That last night of rain before the Flash had saturated the thirsty, aged boards of Haven House and the barn. Between that and the cover of the oaks, the structures had been saved from the sky fires—though most wooden buildings in the parish had burned to the ground.

It was almost a blessing that I couldn't see more than a few feet in front of me. At least around the house we had the *semblance* of trees. But the fields . . .

My six million strong, destroyed utterly. I heard a sound, surprised to find it was a soft cry—from my own lips.

At the barn, I opened the double doors just enough to squeeze through without the wind catching them.

Inside, I drew down my bandanna, marching to Allegra's stall. So help me, I'd *make* her take a saddle, and then we'd be off.

I didn't see my horse in her stall—not until I was standing just before it, because she lay on her side, ribs jutting even worse than I'd realized. Her breaths were labored.

She could barely lift her lids, but she tried to, wanting to acknowledge me.

Did she ever wonder why I never brought her apples anymore? Was she scared? How could I let her suffer any longer?

Her expressive eyes rolled back, and she passed out. No Allegra; no doctor for Mom.

The grief and frustration welling up inside me had to have an outlet. I threw back my head and screamed at the top of my lungs.

I screamed. And screamed.

When my throat burned like fire, I finally stopped, choking out to the voices, "Come on, then! It's your turn!" I jerked around in a circle. "There's still some of me left to torment. Don't be shy."

Three different voices obliged, all speaking at once:

—*Eyes to the skies, lads, I strike from above!*—

—*I watch you like a hawk.*—

—*I'll make a feast of your bones!*—

I recognized Ogen's grating hiss. I'd figured out that at least some of the voices belonged to characters I'd had visions of.

I recalled the winged boy I'd glimpsed the night of my party. Maybe he was the one saying, *I watch you like a hawk.*

And the sparking, electric-looking guy? Had those been his lightning javelins? Perhaps that was his Irish-accented voice saying, *Eyes to the skies, lads.*

I'd seen those boys and the blurry-faced archer lying in wait. Now they were in my head among many more. Could any of those kids possibly be real?

Boys with wings and lightning javelins. Horned creatures like Ogen. Death . . .

Before the Flash, I'd never been crazy. After? I was on a slippery slope and they kept pushing, pushing at me, until I was sure to fall.

I unstrapped my gun, put my back against the wall, and slid down, knocking my head against the wood. Over and over.

I'd always wondered why kids had done that at CLC—seemed like it'd freaking *hurt*—but now I knew why. That pain distracted me from my misery.

Yet it did nothing for those voices. They swarmed like wasps in my head.

—*We will love you. . . . Feast of your bones. . . . I strike from above!*—

"Matthew!" I called. "I'll take the migraine. Just come here. Please?"

Naturally, my attitude had changed toward him, toward all the visions. I craved his visits now. During his latest, he'd explained to me, *"He hurts when he helps."*

Did I have any idea what that meant? Nope, but I just liked that Matthew was nearby.

Another time he'd popped up just to inform me somberly, *"You are the only friend I've ever had."*

When he didn't come this time, I stemmed my disappointment, commanding myself to concentrate and block those voices out. *Think about what to do!*

Mom had once asked if we would eat Allegra if things got desperate enough. I'd thought the better question would be, *How can Evie look her horse in the eye, shoot it, then* butcher *it?*

I was about to find out.

If Allegra couldn't be used for transportation, then she'd be . . . food. Mom would have to do better with more nourishment; she sure as hell couldn't do worse.

This was the only thing I could do to help her.

Butcher my gentle Allegra.

With a cry, I dropped my face into my hands, my eyes brimming with tears. Soon I was sobbing worse than I had day one after the Flash, when I'd first suspected that most everyone on earth was dead.

Pain sliced into my scalp. Tears drenched my cheeks—and my *forehead?*

I glanced down, saw blood streaming into my palms. "Shit!" I'd cut my forehead with my razor-sharp claws, and now blood was pouring down my face. It dripped from my chin, saturating my bandanna.

Leaving a trail of crimson behind me, I squinted around for

something not dust-coated to dry the wounds with, but I couldn't see through the blood.

I frantically wiped my eyes, blinded by the cascade. Scalp wounds bled so much, and now I had *ten* of them!

Finding no makeshift bandage, I pulled my soaked bandanna up over my entire face, pressing the bunched seam at the top against the line of cuts.

I froze when I heard a whisper of sound to my right. Then another to my left. I sensed movement all around me, but was too terrified to flee, to yank down my blood-soaked blindfold.

Shuddering, I eased my hand toward my gun, patting the wet ground—and felt some creature straining against my palm.

A rat! *Several* rats? I shrieked, lurching away, tumbling onto my back as I snatched at the bandanna. Rats would eat me alive in this barn!

I swiped an arm over my eyes, could finally see—

My jaw dropped, my breath leaving me in a rush. At length, I was able to murmur, "Oh my God."

I was looking up at . . . *plants.*

Shoots of green were growing in the dust all around me. Wherever my blood had hit old oats or hayseeds, they'd sprouted.

I rose cautiously. It had been so long since I'd been near a living plant; I'd almost convinced myself that I *had* been hallucinating about my connection to them.

The voices tried to ring the Evie bell then, but I was so fascinated with my new discovery that for a few brief moments, I could turn down the volume.

As I gauged my sanity, the plants stretched toward a murky shaft of light. Could this be *real*? I tentatively touched a stalk with another drop of blood.

It shot higher, from seedling to mature in seconds. *"Life in your very blood,"* Death had said. My mind could hardly wrap around the possibilities. I needed—

"More *seed.*"

I took off toward the house, sprinting into the wind. By the time I'd reached the kitchen, my claws had retracted and my head had stopped bleeding, already healing.

Inside the pantry, I ransacked a box filled with seed packs. Mom and I had collected them, thinking we'd grow food for ourselves.

Nothing ever took for us. Nor for *anyone* that we'd heard of.

But now . . .

My thoughts raced as fast as my heartbeat. There was an area at the back of the barn where the roof had caved in, creating a space open to the sky. We'd meant to fix it, fearing rain would pour inside.

No rain ever came. Only sun, dust, and ash. But I could grow crops there.

I stuffed packs into my jeans pockets. If Mom had enough food— *good* food—then she would get better. Yes, of course! She wasn't healing as she should because she was weak with hunger.

My narrowed gaze turned toward the barn. I could fix that. I could even mend our horse, then set off to find a doctor.

Out of food, out of luck, and out of time? I could take advantage of this luck, grow new food, and *buy* time.

With nothing more than a razor blade.

After all, how much blood could one girl need?

16

I thought I'd heard a motorcycle.

This morning the winds were still. With no leaves, cars, or animal calls, sound carried differently now.

Can it possibly be? I wondered as I stumbled away from the house, weak from blood loss. Since my discovery last week, I'd been aggressively . . . farming.

That motorcycle sound stirred up memories from a former life, a time of comfort and plenty that seemed a thousand years past.

I could almost close my eyes, listen to that rumble, and pretend I still lived that existence.

Almost. The bitter scent of ash and the jarring voices in my mind made it hard to pretend.

You're just delirious, Evie. There was no motorcycle—any more than there would be planes in the sky.

Yes, delirium. Alas, that was an occupational hazard of being a blood farmer. Especially one with such bountiful crops as mine.

I'd believed the side effects from yesterday's bloodletting had abated. Apparently they hadn't, if I was imagining figments from the past.

But really, what was one more imaginary sound? *Join the chorus, roar along with the voices!*

I trudged onward to the barn, determined to get to work. The sky was clear for now. That unbroken blue above should've been beautiful to me, but it seemed like it was trying too hard to compensate for the lack of green.

To me, that blue sky seemed like a forced smile. . . .

I remembered Brandon once saying that his thoughts were on shuffle between me and football. Now my *life* was on shuffle, among three miserable tracks.

Track One. In the morning, I would bandage Mom's ribs. I might be deluding myself, but I didn't think they looked *worse*. Yet her thoughts seemed foggier, and she was sleeping all the time.

After making Mom comfortable, I would head to the barn for Track Two before lunch. My new rows of crops seemed to mute the voices, shoring up my sanity for precious hours—yet that came with a price.

Track Three. When I was alone in my bed at night, those voices *exploded*. As if my beloved crops had just forced them into a bottle of soda that would later be shaken until the top burst.

Until I wanted to tear out my hair. If I could somehow sleep through the noise, I was rewarded with lifelike scenes of the red witch. . . .

Just minutes ago, I'd completed Track One. I'd left Mom dozing fitfully after a crying jag. Hers, not mine.

The more her health declined, the more emotional she grew.

"Why didn't I . . . listen?" she'd wheezed. "Gran told me you were special, and I *laughed* at her. Why couldn't I believe in her—or you . . . the two people I loved most in the world?"

Though I'd often wondered that myself, I'd tried to soothe her, telling her that everything was going to be fine now.

After her outburst, I knew I couldn't reveal my new talent. For days, I'd debated it, but how would she feel when confronted with yet more proof that I was "special"? More crying, more coughing fits?

My pilgrim's bounty would be like a slap in the face to the woman who'd dispatched me to Child's Last Chance. So I'd decided to keep quiet.

If she was out of it, I could sneak her little bites of succulent honey-dew and strawberries. Yesterday morning, she'd murmured, "This must be a dream."

For other times, I'd simply pickled the vegetables and told her I'd found jars in storage or at a neighbor's.

Did I know how to pickle food? Hell no. But I knew how to eat pickles out of a jar, then drop the new veggies into the pickle juice.

At the barn doors, I opened the padlock. No, we hadn't had visitors or trespassers here; regardless, I'd been paranoid enough about the priceless contents of our barn to lock it.

Inside, Allegra whinnied with a touch more energy. At least she was on her feet. After an initial lack of appetite, she'd become the delighted recipient of constant melon rinds.

"Hey, girl." I ran my palm down her neck, touching noses with her. I'd allotted two more days before I'd risk a trip with her.

Too soon, and I could kill her, eliminating any hope of finding a doctor. Too late, and . . .

Don't go there, Evie.

In the back, I ducked under the fallen roof rafters to enter my garden, shucking out of my jacket. After rolling up a sleeve of my sweater, I pulled out my pack of razor blades from my jeans pocket, sliding one off the top.

I took a deep breath, then dragged the blade along the plump vein leading to my elbow. *If only the doctors in Atlanta could see me now!*

Ah, but those smug quacks were probably all ash.

As though kindling a fire, I used my blood to coax carrot seeds and potato eyes to life. I dappled drops over kernels, watching as sleek stalks sprouted ears of corn for me.

Yet too soon, dizziness and a bone-deep chill washed over me. I now understood why dying movie characters always whispered, "Cold, so . . . cold," as they bled out. Body warmth oozed out right along with the blood.

I sighed when my skin began healing. Though my hand shook, I reopened that tender vein with another razor slice, wincing with pain.

As the blood ran, I fought to keep my eyes open. The barn started to spin and that chill intensified.

Delirium *must* be taking hold, because I heard that imaginary motorcycle—roaring down Haven's shell drive.

Not imaginary? My first thought: Had the Cajun . . . lived?

From time to time, I'd thought of him, mostly to curse him for taking Mel's phone—even though I'd begun to wonder if I could possibly have gotten her back to Haven and into the cellar in time.

Did I blame him for her death? Whenever I imagined Mel incinerated in her car, I did.

It hurt less than blaming myself for my mistakes—for not *making* my mother see the truth, for not believing in my own sanity, for not warning people.

For not saying, "Hell yeah, Mel, you're staying *here* tonight."

The motorcycle was getting closer. No matter who it was, I needed to tidy up and get my shotgun ready. I wiped my arm clean, then shoved down my sleeve.

Gun in hand, I stumbled outside, locking the barn behind me.

The biker caught sight of me and slowed to a stop, canting his helmet. He had on a black leather jacket, worn jeans, and boots. A wicked-looking crossbow was slung over his back.

I recognized his build, the wide expanse of his shoulders. My lips parted in shock. *Jackson Deveaux.*

He was alive.

I tottered, as if the ground was shaking beneath my feet. Then I frowned. The ground *had* briefly quaked.

He parked, turned off his engine. When he removed his helmet, I saw that his jet-black hair was longer, his face not quite as tanned. His eyes were still that vivid gray, but had dark circles under them.

He looked weary. And there was a hardness to his features that hadn't been there before.

I didn't know how I felt about seeing him again. In my mind, he was a villain. But he was also a former classmate—for however short a duration. Hadn't I yearned to see someone my own age? This one was actually, physically *here*.

Did I need to talk with someone so badly that I'd suffer even Jackson's presence?

We stared at each other for long moments. He took his time surveying me, just as he had the first time he'd ever seen me.

How different I appeared now. My looks had gone from well-kempt cheerleader to apocalyptic disasterpiece. My clothes were unmended and stained with soot, my hair wild. I must've been pale as death.

In the deep voice I remembered so clearly, he muttered, *"De'pouille."*

I stiffened. *De'pouille* pretty much meant "hot mess" in Cajun. He was going to show up here and insult me? After our last encounter?

Like I didn't have enough to deal with! "I should have known you'd survive."

He climbed off his bike, then leaned back against it. "Why's that, Evangeline?"

"Reptiles and vermin fared well." I sounded *stoned*. I inwardly shook myself, forcing my eyelids to open wider.

"I see nothing's changed with you. Still south of useless."

"And nothing's changed with you. Still impolite and classless."

"You look a little *cagou*. Pale in the face. You caught the plague, you?"

No, just been doing some gardening. It takes blood, sweat, and tears. I almost chuckled, but pressed the back of my hand against my lips. At length, I said, "What do you want?"

"I'm on my way to Texas. Stopped here to barter." He unzipped his jacket, then took his flask from a pocket. "A couple of folks in Sterling say you've got stores of food. Figures that you and your mother would be sitting pretty here."

Sitting pretty? What did *that* mean? I couldn't think. Even in the sun, I was so cold my teeth were nearly chattering. "What are you talking about?"

"You knew what was about to happen, didn't you? I'm sure you prepared for it. That's why you got food still."

"Prepared?" My dizziness grew. "*If* we still have stores, it's because we were out scavenging while everyone else was praying." The winds were kicking up again, worsening my chill.

"You drew the Flash enough, in detail. What'd you have? Visions of it? Dreams? That's what you were doing in class each day."

Leave it to Jackson to be resentful of something that hadn't helped me whatsoever.

He narrowed his eyes. "No wonder you wanted that journal back—it was a goddamned playbook for the apocalypse. I saw Bagmen in your drawings before I ever saw 'em in real life. Saw the sun shining at night on one of those pages before it happened. Thanks for the heads-up, you."

"Oh, like you would've believed me! *I* didn't even believe my drawings were real!" I yelled, the frustration of the last week, the last several months, bubbling over. "I thought I was crazy! And so did anyone who knew about them!" When he looked unmoved, I bit out, "Let me tell you how prepared I was. I was so prepared that my boyfriend and his family became piles of ash. All our friends were destroyed. And Mel"—my voice broke, but I kept on—"she was a sister to me and she died alone, not three miles from my house!"

His hard gaze softened a touch—until I said, "I blame you for her death!"

"What the hell did I do?"

"When I first saw the light, I began to realize what was happening, that the things I'd seen might be real. I wanted to call Mel and tell her to get back here. But she didn't *have a phone!*"

"I didn't steal her phone, no."

"You just kept me busy while Lionel took it."

"If he did, then he's paid for it. He's as dead as she is."

"You were just as much to blame." I grasped my forehead, refusing to argue anymore. Jackson wasn't worth my time. Unless . . .

"Have you passed a doctor—any kind of medic—on your way here?"

"Why you want to know? You sick? Or your *mère*? They said something in town."

"Just answer me! Can you get a doctor here? We have things of value, things that would make the trip worth it."

"*Non.* That's not . . . it's not possible."

Swaying on my feet, I told him, "That's the only thing I'll barter for, Jackson. If a doc's not happening, then leave."

"You doan even know what I got to offer."

"There is nothing I want—or need—except for a doctor."

"And what about what I need? Maybe I'll just go *take* what I'm hunting for."

Fear skittered through me. He couldn't get anywhere near my mom. We were so vulnerable! I flipped the safety off the shotgun.

He casually took a swig from his flask. "You even know how to fire that thing, you?"

God, he infuriated me! "I told you to leave!" I raised the shotgun.

He pocketed the flask, rising from his bike. "Doan you aim that at me," he grated, starting for me.

As he stormed closer, he had that look in his eyes, the menacing one he'd given that drunken man.

The one promising pain.

Alarm flared. Which made me even madder. I had a loaded gun pointed at his head! He didn't know I couldn't hit the broad side of a barn. "Gee, Jackson, I guess the little doll's got teeth—"

He moved so fast he was a blur, knocking the barrel aside. The slightest touch of the trigger and the gun went off, kicking me back like a mule. I saw him lunge for me—too late—then felt my head snap back against the ground.

My vision was wavering as he crouched beside me, feeling the back of my head. "You'll live, you *coo-yôn*. Now, ain't you glad we got that out of the way?"

My eyes rolled back. Darkness.

17

The red witch stood atop a raised dais overlooking a crowd of shadowy figures.

Villagers. They cowered before her.

Aggression sizzled through her veins as she surveyed them. She would destroy them all, every last one, her wrath unfathomable.

Lifting her claw-tipped fingers to a clear morning sky, she called on nearby plants to release their thorns. With a shriek, she unleashed a tornado of them.

Like a swarm of bees, the tempest descended upon her prey. People shoved one another down, scrabbling over the fallen to flee, but none could.

The razor-sharp thorns bit into their faces, scouring their features off, their noses and lips. Inch by vicious inch, those barbs sliced at their flesh, flaying the meat from their bodies. Blood spurt, gristle covering the ground.

One woman's scalp was severed clean; her beautiful black mane of hair drifted on swirling winds. . . .

The witch's tempest scoured them deeper, deeper. Even without most of their skin, the people managed to survive a surprisingly long time—which she particularly enjoyed.

As she cackled with delight, they crawled in place, mired in the thickening puddles of remains. . . .

I woke in my bed, squinting at the amount of light in my room, shivers still racing over me from my latest nightmare.

My gaze focused on a trio of burning candles. Three candles? I'd never be so wasteful.

I shrank back when I saw a blurry outline of a person. Slowly, my eyes adjusted.

Jackson was *in my room!* I'd never had a boy in my room—much less *that* boy.

He still had his crossbow strapped over his shoulder. In his hand? Yet another candle.

As I tried to shake off the remnants of that dream and get my bearings—how had I gotten in bed? why was he inside?—I feigned sleep, watching him as he snooped around like he owned the place.

He gazed at the storm clouds I'd painted on the walls, strolled into my closet and rummaged around, then emerged to check out my dance trophies and recital pictures. He flipped through a supply of sketchbooks—all blank.

Drawing held little interest for me these days. The voices made it impossible for me to sit still. And besides, my brain was already stained beyond repair.

As if he couldn't help himself, he returned to the wall paintings, holding up the candle to trace his fingers over the clouds. The flickering light ghosted over a grisly-looking scar on his forearm.

I recognized that injury, had been in his home when a drunken man had slashed Jackson's skin to the bone.

I'd witnessed how brutal this boy could be—he'd nearly beaten the man to death in front of me. Yet he was now touching my paintings gently, almost *reverently*.

I felt like a spy, like this was a moment I was never supposed to share. It seemed . . . intimate. When he touched the cane, I swore I could feel him aching for those fields, for that rain about to fall.

He abruptly dropped his hands. Without turning, he said, "So this is where Evangeline Greene grew up."

"What are you doing in my room? How did I get into bed?"

He finally faced me, but ignored my questions. "That closet of yours—not quite big enough, no?"

I flushed to remember that he hadn't even had a bedroom of his own.

He opened the top drawer of my dresser. "How many ribbons and *bebins* can one girl have?" With raised brows, he lifted a pink Victoria's Secret bra from the next drawer. "I fondly recall this one."

Between gritted teeth, I said, "Drop it like it's hot."

"Oh, it's hot, all right." He smirked, but he did toss it back. "How do you even keep up with all the stuff you own? Doan know that I'd want to have so much, me. Must be a full-time job just to remember where everything is."

I recalled his home, his meager possessions, his few books—that worn copy of *Robinson Crusoe* by the couch that he'd slept on. . . .

"You were even richer than I thought."

Rich? Why would he bring that up? Then I remembered that he was a thief—and he'd shamelessly told me he would steal supplies from us! "Where is my mother?"

"Drinking the tea I made her and reading one of the last newspaper editions from back east."

"If you hurt her or upset her in any way, I will make you pay."

"Hurt her? When I found her, she was trying to get down the stairs, scared to death from hearing that fool shot you took."

"Oh, God!"

"Doan worry. I managed to get you up your tree-house ladder and save the day." He frowned. "You weigh a lot less than I thought. Anyway, I explained to her that you accidentally shot at me—which didn't surprise her—then I showed her how you were passed out, limp as a noodle."

"Mom!" I called. Just as I ripped off my bedspread to race into her room, she called back, "In here, honey." She sounded perfectly fine, even *better* than before.

My relief was short-lived when I saw Jackson eyeing my uncovered legs. With a gasp, I yanked the bedspread back over me. Why was I no longer wearing my boots and jeans? Had I taken them off?

Or had *Jackson*? He wouldn't. . . .

Oh, but he would. Under my breath, I hissed, "You undressed me?"

He gave me a bored glance. "Partially."

Gaze darting around the room, I demanded, "Where is my gun?"

"I put it away before you killed a white hat with it. You might've been clever with the ladder and the door braces, but a markswoman you ain't."

While I was working up the most vile and cutting insult I could imagine, he eased my bedroom door shut.

My eyes went wide. "What are you doing?"

Instead of answering me, he nonchalantly unstrapped his bow, then sat beside me in bed, his back against the headboard.

And there wasn't anything I could do about it. I stiffened, scooting to the edge of the mattress. He seemed even bigger than I'd remembered, taking up far too much of the bed.

"You know, I'd never hurt your *mère*, no. She's never done anything to me. Unlike her coldhearted daughter."

What had I ever done to him? *He* was the one who'd stolen from me and my friends, who'd bellowed at me in the rain.

"*Non*, Karen and I had a nice long chat."

"*Karen?*" He was on a first-name basis with Mom? How long had I been out? "She wouldn't let you just roam around our home!" Then I noticed that his hair was wet, his black T-shirt and worn jeans clean. So I added, "And if she did, she shouldn't have. She doesn't know you."

"I explained that you and me were history podnas in school." With a mean smile, he added, "I told her that you'd even been to my house— and met my mother."

I swallowed at the memory of that night, at the way his voice grew tight with anger just to mention it. He seemed to be daring me to say something about it.

When I didn't, he added, "After that, Karen was fine with my being here."

I clutched my bedspread. "I don't apologize for going to your house that night. You had no right to take my journal from me."

"I doan like unsolved puzzles, me. You wouldn't show me your drawings, so I asked Lionel to borrow them."

"Considering the journal's contents, you can understand why I wanted it back."

"How long have you had visions?"

His matter-of-fact question flustered me. "I don't . . . I'm not . . . how can you talk about this so—so calmly?"

"I had a cousin who could read the future in coffee grinds. My grandmother could predict hurricanes a month in advance."

It seemed like everyone in Louisiana had known somebody with "the sight."

"I'm not discussing this with you."

"No matter. Your mother explained some things to me."

Had she told him that my grandmother was a Tarot card fanatic who thought I would be the world's salvation? *Bang-up job I'm doing, Gran!* "What exactly did Mom explain?"

"That you're s'posed to be sweet and charming and funny." He pinned me with a look. "I doan see it."

"You need to leave Haven. Now." What if he saw the contents of the barn? "You're not welcome here."

He smirked. "Karen disagrees."

"I doubt she'll welcome you if I tell her you undressed me."

"Maybe she'll only *partially* welcome me."

Smart-ass.

"So now it's time for you and me to talk, Evangeline. I didn't only come here to barter. Came here to warn you."

"About what?"

"There's a wave of men coming down this way in a day or two. An army. Three thousand strong."

"So? That's great news." Then my heart leapt. "They must have medics!"

"I see the wheels turning, but it woan work out like you're thinking. Not with the Army of the Southeast."

"How do you know?"

"I was in the Louisiana militia."

"So let me see if I've got this straight. You joined the militia. There's still got to be action out there. Yet you're here. Doesn't that make you a deserter?"

He nodded without shame. "When my unit got taken over by that big ole army, we found ourselves with a new general and a new objective."

"Which was?"

In a toneless voice, he said, "The involuntary enlistment of women."

"I don't understand. To train as soldiers . . ." I trailed off at his expression. His eyes had a wary look to them, belying his tough-guy act. What could affect such a hardened boy like this?

The unthinkable dawned on me just as he murmured, "Not soldiers."

"I see." What all had Jackson witnessed out there on the road?

"There's no one to free them, to fight back. That army keeps absorbing any military unit it comes across, taking control of them. Texas must be next in their path. Nobody knows why they're marching there, but I figure if anyone can stop these men, it'll be Texans. I'm on my way to warn the militia there." Then he frowned. "You ain't seen any of this in your visions?"

"Stop talking about them like . . . like . . ."

"Like they're real?" Finally, he let that drop. "I got out ahead of the troops, but they're on my ass. They camped just north of Sterling. If there're no storms, they could be here as early as tomorrow. They're goan to take you and your mother if you doan leave."

"Why should I believe you? They might be riding in to save us. We've been waiting for this since the Flash."

"They're coming, Evie. I swear it." He lifted a chain around his neck, pulling a jet-black rosary out from under his T-shirt. The beads glinted in the candlelight. The unusual cross was small but ornate. "And I swear to God that you will wish they'd never laid eyes on you."

I almost . . . believed him. I vaguely noted that I'd seen that rosary before, then asked, "Did you tell my mom about this?" He nodded. "What did she say?"

He regarded his knuckles, running a finger over a scar. "That the decision to stay or leave was yours."

What if I decided to leave once and for all? *Away! Out into the world at last!*

As ever, I tamped down that impulse, guilt suffusing me.

And why should it be my call anyway? I never thought I'd crave authority so dearly! "Even if your story is true, I can't travel with her. She's injured, and we've got one—malnourished—horse. How am I supposed to get her away from an army?"

"You could ask me for help. Or are you too proud?"

"I would do anything to keep her safe." I met his gaze. "That big army will have medics, a *surgeon* even. One could be on his way directly to us this very minute. I'm not going to risk her life fleeing from the one person who could help her."

"You're not listening to me, Evie—"

"You're not listening to *me*," I bit out in a low, furious tone. "I said *anything*."

Suddenly I understood what had driven my mom to do whatever it took to get me well last year. All I'd thought about was how horrific CLC had been for me. I hadn't considered how agonizing it must have been for her to drop off her daughter there, leaving her behind.

"You can say *anything*—because you doan know what that means with these people." He looked like he was about to argue more, but whatever he saw in my expression made him think better of it. He muttered, *"Tête dure."* Hard head. "We'll talk after dinner, yeah."

"Dinner?"

"I brought gator meat. It's goan to melt in your mouth."

I fell silent. That would be the first meat we'd had since Allegra had hoofed a rare rattlesnake to death two months ago. Maybe if Mom got protein, it'd help her heal!

As if he could read my mind, he said, "Your *mère* could use a good meal."

Game. Set. Match.

Then I remembered that the cellar looked like a Thanksgiving circular. Would he find all of my stores? I'd meant to pickle the rest, so they wouldn't be so obvious.

"That's right, Evie. I figure with all those *fresh vegetables*, we ought to have a stew."

Shit! I jutted my chin, saying nothing. Would he tell Mom? *Had* he?

"And out in the barn, I found rows of crops. Real, live, honest-to-God crops. You want to explain that? I've been racking my brain, trying to figure out that puzzle all afternoon."

"You broke into our barn?"

"After you locked the doors right in front of me?" He gave me that Cajun shrug. "You ought to know by now that if Evie Greene's got something she doan want me to discover, I'm goan to come up with a way to."

"Did you tell my mom about them?"

"I figured out that she didn't know and kept my mouth shut."

"It would only upset her."

"Woan upset *me*. So tell me about these crops of yours. You paint them on your walls—do you coax them from fallow ground? Maybe you got other talents besides seeing the future?"

"Stop talking about that!"

"You tell anyone else about what's in your barn?"

"Of course not!"

He met my gaze, his eyes dark and intense. "Doan you *ever* tell another, no. You can't imagine what people would do for those crops. You hear me?"

Shivers slipped up my spine. "No one but you, that is?"

"I need to know how you got them plants to grow, Evangeline."

I narrowed my eyes. "Silver bells and cockleshells." *Blood streams and freaky dreams and dizzy maids all in a row.*

The corners of his lips curled. "You and your secrets. Ah, *peekôn*, just when I think I've solved one mystery about you, up comes another one. I will figure you out one day. *En garde, cher.* Consider yourself warned."

18

"I can't believe you just welcomed him into our home. Without even talking to me?" I demanded as I plaited Mom's hair.

She wanted to "look presentable" for our first cooked dinner in ages, and for our first company since the Flash.

She'd entreated me to dress up as well, to be respectful of the effort Jackson alone was making—since he'd refused all her offers of *my* help.

I'd scoffed, until she finally said, "Dress up, Evie. Or go downstairs and insist on making yourself useful."

An actual order from Mom? I'd chosen the lesser of two evils, dragging on one of the few nice outfits that still fit me, a Nanette Lepore wrap dress with complementing blocky heels. I even wore my diamond earrings and a coat of precious lip gloss.

With a pang, I'd donned the necklace Brand had given me the night before he died.

"How could I have talked to you about Jack?" Mom asked now. "You were knocked out."

"And you didn't suspect that he might have been the one to hurt me?"

"Honestly, Evie, his explanation made perfect sense—I'm surprised you haven't shot yourself in the foot by now. Besides, I have a good feeling about him."

"What did you tell him about me?" I finished her braid, smoothing a lock here and there.

"That you're special. That you have a purpose in this world. And that you'll need support in order to fulfill it."

Not *too* bad of a reveal. What mother wouldn't say that about her daughter? "Please don't tell him any more about us, about our business. He's not the nice boy you think he is. Not like Brandon was."

I thought back to the last time I'd seen my first and only boyfriend, recalling his smile as he'd gone off to do battle for me, saving me from getting gaffled. I should've told him that I loved him—instead of *"You're the best."*

And it was because of the Cajun that I'd never gotten to speak to Brandon ever again.

"Don't be so hard on Jack, honey. Everything's different now. He even said he's going to fix my car tonight. Imagine that." She sighed. "Having a car."

Early on, Mom and I had talked about going to North Carolina to find Gran. I'd asked her, "Do you really think she's still alive?"

Mom had cried, *"I have to."*

Three things had kept us here: the lack of a vehicle, our wait for order to be restored, and the ready sources of water.

The wells were getting low, and apparently, order wasn't forthcoming. But a car might be. "Do you believe what Jackson said about the militia?"

She nodded. "If there are so few women survivors, and if those men truly think there will never be another government . . . Evie, people with no hope for the future can be very dangerous." She paused, seeming to think of the exact right way to phrase her next words. "I know this is hard for you to understand, but things *can* get worse for us, for anyone who's left."

"But they'll probably have a doctor who could fix you right up."

She shook her head. "And they'll marry you off to some old man. If you're lucky."

"You were trying to set me up with animal control!"

"Until Jack came along. He's so considerate. Not to mention gorgeous! Did you get a load of his shoulders? And that rakish grin?"

I'd always thought of it as a *smirk*.

"He's strong, resourceful, and intelligent. He can take care of you."

And what about you? "If I have to marry some geezer to get you well"—*to save your life*—"then that's my decision."

"Forget it, Evie."

"Why do you get to sacrifice for me, but I can't do the same?"

"Because I'm your mother."

"You think I wouldn't do whatever it takes to get you medical attention?"

"That's precisely what I'm afraid of." She started coughing, which only steeled my resolve.

"Why don't we see how you feel in the morning?" I said, wondering if her side could get any tighter, any darker over the night. "We can decide then." I'd already decided.

I thought she'd argue more, but she let it go. "Regardless, we *need* Jack." At my bug-eyed look, she added, "You could get him to stay with us, if you were nice to him."

"I admit he's handy. But everything in me says not to trust him." He'd lied to me, stolen from me, played me for a fool.

"That's a shame. Because I asked him to look out for you—if anything ever happened to me."

I stilled. "You wouldn't. You just met him!"

"Like I said, I have a good feeling about him. And he told me he'd consider it! He likes you, Evie. He wouldn't have come back here to warn us if he didn't. Now, promise me you'll try to get along with him." I opened my mouth to argue, but she began coughing worse than before.

I hurried to rub her back, saying, "Okay, okay, I promise I'll try." Once her fit subsided, I handed her a glass of water. "I'll go see if he needs help."

Her expression brightened, easing the strain on her pale face. "Thank you, honey."

Still mentally grumbling, I headed down the shadowy staircase. At once, the voices grew louder. Oh, and now there was a new one among the chorus, a girl's.

—Behold the Bringer of Doubt.—

"Ugh!" I snapped under my breath. "What does that *mean*? Leave me alone!"

"You talking to yourself?" Jackson said. He'd paused on his way upstairs with a folding card table—so Mom wouldn't have to go down.

Which was . . . considerate of him.

He climbed to the step just below me and murmured in that deep voice, "Um, um, UM, Evangeline. You dress up all pretty for me?"

Strike *considerate*. "Hardly." When he just stared at me, I narrowed my eyes. "How long were you standing down there?"

"Long enough to know you're fixing to break that promise you just made. Now, be polite, honey."

You wouldn't know polite if it bit you in the ass. With a fake smile and cheery tone, I said, "Why Jackson, I can't wait for dinner! I'll go get the dishes!"

But he blocked me, resting the edge of the table on a stair. His eyes seemed to glow in the dim light, his expression intent.

He pressed one palm against the wall beside my head, leaning in close—just as he had all those months ago when he'd almost kissed me. When he'd stalled for Lionel.

I remembered how stupid I'd been that night. I remembered the excitement—and the attraction—I'd felt.

He'd been handsome then. Now he was gorgeous; was he even more devious?

"Damn, *cher*, you still smell like a blossom. Been so long since I've seen a flower that I'd nearly forgotten what they smelled like." He took a lock of my hair, rubbing it between his thumb and forefinger. "You're dressing up *and* using expensive perfume? Ole Jack senses a trap. Consider me snared."

"What's your racket? Why are you really here?"

"Maybe I'm not the bad guy you make me out to be."

"Which is exactly what a bad guy would say." I pushed past him, but he grabbed my arm.

"You listen to me, Evie. And let me tell you how this night's goan to proceed."

I gaped at his condescending tone. "How dare you—"

He talked over me. "We're goan to have us a grand dinner, as nice as you can think to make it, with you being sweet as an *ange*. After we eat, you, me, and your *mère* are goan to make the *veiller*"—spend the evening visiting—"till she goes to sleep. Then you're goan to give me an answer about tomorrow, and I'll get to work. Because I *am* leaving here ahead of that militia. *Comprends?*"

"I . . . I . . ." My face started to throb. Oh, no, no. *Not now!* Not in front of his shrewd gaze.

Grueling pain shot through my head. The staircase and Jackson began to disappear. The more I fought the vision, the worse my head pounded.

I tried to stumble away, to get to privacy, but he caught my arm. "Evie? What's the matter, you?"

Instead of the house, I saw blackened forest all around me. "Jackson," I whispered, now clutching him desperately. "Please, don't let it . . ." My legs gave way, and I was grasping at him, grasping—

But he was gone. Everything was gone.

I was outside on a freezing night, standing in a haze of smoke, with my eyes burning and my nose running. I could hear men screaming in terror all around me, but I couldn't see why.

When explosions rocked the earth beneath my feet, panic set in, *dread*. I had loved ones out in the chaos, but couldn't reach them, could do nothing to protect them.

Until *she* appeared. The girl with the bow.

Though I couldn't make out her features, I watched her move through the smoke like a wraith. She was glorious, a goddess. She drew back her bowstring, taking aim—

At me.

"No!" I cried. "Wait!"

Without hesitation, she loosed her arrow. I had time to close my eyes. And to hesitantly crack them open.

She'd shot a faceless man through his throat, a man who'd wanted to hurt me, to harm my loved ones.

When she turned to me, her skin was glaringly bright, but tinged with red, like a hunter's moon.

"I'm sorry," I murmured. "I didn't know."

She gave a bitter laugh. "You never do. The Archer *always* keeps an arrow in her quiver for you; interrupt my shot again, and I will give it to you directly."

I recognized her voice. She was the Bringer of Doubt. . . .

"Evie, bébé," Jackson said softly, bringing me back. *"I've got you."*

I blinked, and again. As the vision cleared, I found him gazing down at me. I was in his strong arms, on the floor at the base of the steps. He had a napkin pressed against my nose. It was bleeding?

I couldn't endure this for much longer. Many more nights of this, and I would *run* into that archer's sights.

"You had a vision, no?"

I muttered in realization, "It's never going to stop." I was as doomed as my mother if I didn't get help too. And my grandmother was the only one who would know what I needed.

I edged away from Jackson, but he wouldn't release me. "Tell me what you saw. Was it about tomorrow? The army?"

"No. It makes no sense." Who was that girl? An ally or enemy? Did she even exist? I pushed against his chest, snatching the napkin to hold against my nose. "Please, just let me go. *Now*, Jackson!"

"Go where?" he snapped.

Matching his tone, I said, "To—dinner." When he finally released me, I staggered away toward the kitchen.

Part of me wanted to dismiss the Archer as imaginary. Yet all my other visions had come true. Before the Flash, I'd listened to everyone but myself. I'd ignored what I could remember about Gran's teachings, even after I'd started to believe them.

Now I would trust *my* instincts—and they said this Archer was out in the world today.

Which meant that all the voices belonged to actual kids.

Girls with glowing red skin, boys who could fly. Why not? I could make crops sprout with my blood and control their movement with my mind.

Matthew was real, out there as well. My friend. One day, I'd find him.

But the rest of those kids . . . ? My instincts also said I might do well to avoid them.

When Mom finished her helping of stew, hope grew inside me.

For the last week, she'd picked at her food, but clearly her appetite was returning. Maybe she *was* on the mend.

"Jack, that was absolutely delightful."

To his credit, it had been. He'd stinted on nothing, cooking an incredible meal, schlepping table and chairs up for us to sit with Mom, making me break out the finest china and crystal.

When I'd collected three everyday settings, he'd frowned. "Come on, rich girl, I *know* that's not the best you got."

I'd been uneasy about the number of candles he'd lit—it was extravagant—but those flickering flames shimmered off the crystal and warred with the ash, painting the room with a kind brush.

Even Mom's cheeks looked like they had color.

"Thank you so much," she told him. "Or I guess I should say *merci*."

With a "rakish" grin, he said, *"De rien, cher."* It was nothing, dear.

She tittered. Was she tipsy? Likely.

To my astonishment, she'd offered him free use of the liquor cabinet—as long as he made her dinner tea "Irish." With a heavy hand, he'd dosed her dainty teacup from a bottle of expensive whiskey, then filled a Baccarat highball glass for himself.

All evening he'd been doting on her, while I'd been on pins and needles, wondering what his game was, wondering what he thought of my earlier blackout.

But if this was what it took to ease the strain on Mom's face, then I'd play along. For now.

"Jack, did you know that Evie speaks fluent French?"

He leaned back in his chair, looking smug. "I did indeedy."

She asked me, "Wasn't dinner great, honey?"

I forced yet another smile. Mom wasn't the only one who'd finished her helping. Instead of complimenting Jackson and boosting his ego, I asked him, "Who taught you how to cook?"

He grated, *"Nécessité."*

Mom picked up on the sudden tension, and said, "Maybe you can teach Evie?"

Grin smoothly back in place, he told her, "Something tells me she can't boil an egg."

Mom smiled but was quick to say, "Our Evie's a fast learner."

Our *Evie? Trying to get him to take mental ownership of me, Mom?*

When he just shrugged noncommittally, she said, "Did you ever come across kids your age when you were in the militia?"

"Only other boys."

"So our Evie is kind of a rarity."

He smirked against the rim of his glass. "Oh, she is that."

I glared.

"Doesn't she look pretty tonight, Jack?"

"Mom!" I felt like I was on match.com. "I'm going to do the dishes."

"That can wait. Honey, we should look at your baby pictures! Oh, and your first dance recital!"

Would this night never end? "They're all on the flash drive. We went paperless, remember?" Which meant they were completely inaccessible, along with all my e-books and e-mails. Even if we'd had a generator, few electronics worked after the apocalypse. Damn technology.

"I saved the hard copies. They're in the sewing room."

I was about to beg her not to torture me—or Jackson—like this, but she started coughing into her napkin.

As her face turned bright red, I helplessly rubbed her back. When her coughing finally eased, she looked . . . scared. She tried to hide it, but I saw blood, stark against her crisp white napkin.

I glanced at Jackson. Though his face was expressionless, I could've sworn a muscle ticked in his cheek.

"You want a sip?" Jackson offered me his flask as I watched him tinker under the Mercedes's hood.

I peered around, nervously running my fingers over the salt in the pocket of my hoodie. This was one of my first times out at night since the Flash. The quiet was so eerily complete that every sound we made was amplified, as if we were in an auditorium.

"Take the flask, Evie. You look like you could use it."

My heart was aching for my mom. I gazed up at her window, at the flickering candlelight visible through the shutter. I could read the writing on the wall. She believed she was dying—soon.

Earlier, as I'd helped her get ready for bed, she'd been sentimental, kept telling me that she loved me, kept reaching for my hand to hold.

She told me that my father would've been so proud of me. She made me promise that if anything should happen to her I would find my grandmother.

In other words, Mom hadn't believed *me* when I'd told her I'd get her well.

I accepted Jackson's flask. "Why the hell not?" When I wiped the rim with my sleeve, he scowled.

"Jesus Christ, Evie. You were goan to let me kiss you that night at the sugar mill, but now you woan drink after me?"

"I was *not* going to let you! And why would you even bring that up? Don't you think that should go into the forgotten column?"

He returned to his task. "It ain't every day a Basin boy makes out with a Sterling cheerleader. I would've been even more of a legend than I already was."

"Wow. You mean you had more of a motive than just duping me?" Cajun shrug.

With a roll of my eyes, I took a drink, clamping my lips against the burn. "You're not worried about Bagmen?"

He gazed up from under the hood. "Nothing can get the drop on me." Even now that crossbow was propped up nearby. I'd noticed that he never let it out of reach.

When I held the flask out to him, he said, "Hang on to it while I finish up."

"You really think you can fix this?"

"I worked on the militia's trucks. It's not hard if you know what you're doing."

"And you do?"

"*Ouais.*" Yeah. "So, did your *mère* send you down here to be nice to the Cajun boy?"

That was exactly what had happened. Just before I'd joined him outside, she'd given me a rare order: "Convince Jack to like you." She'd asked me, "Can you imagine how relieved I'd be to know you were with a strong, capable boy like that? We *need* him, Evie. Please, for both our sakes? Make up the guest room for him. Go help him with the car."

I hadn't wanted to leave her. "You don't want me to stay?" When she'd shaken her head, I'd kissed her good night. "I'm going to get you better. You'll see."

"Leave the candle lit, honey."

"Love you." But as I headed out to join up with Jackson, I still hadn't been convinced that I could let bygones be bygones.

I'd finally decided to call a truce for one reason. He'd patiently looked at every one of my baby pics. As Mom had cooed over every toothless image—*"Look at that smile!"*—Jackson had dutifully paid attention, though it must have been miserable for him.

He'd risen a notch in my estimation.

And I reasoned that if he was out to rob us blind, he wouldn't have gone through this much trouble.

With that thought in mind, I took another swig—this one didn't burn nearly as much—then said, "Mom likes you a lot. She wanted me to extend an invitation to stay with us. For as long as you like."

His tinkering slowed. "I'm surprised you're actually extending it."

"I've already made up the bed in one of the guest rooms." When he merely raised his brows, I said, "What?"

"Hell, Evangeline, I thought you were goan to make me sleep in the barn tonight."

"Why would you say that?"

"Because you still think of me as *the help*." Attention back on the car, he muttered, "You probably always will."

He was wrong. I didn't think of him that way; I thought of him as a criminal hardened by life. Plus, I'd never want him in the barn near my crops again. "Whatever, Jackson, you can do as you like."

"I'm not goan to be here when the army rolls in." He pointed a wrench at me. "Count on that. I doan suggest you two being around either."

"Why are you so certain they'll come here?"

"Haven House is the biggest building still standing in the area—and one of the oldest."

"Why's that important?"

"Wells and windmill pumps. You doan need electricity to get at the water. The general's been following some field guide to all the big farms in the South, and he always hits the ones with the older wells. How many you got? Two or three?"

"Five," I admitted.

"Oh, yeah." He grasped his forehead, smudging oil there. "They'll be here."

"I have a hard time believing there's this swarm of three thousand soldiers, and all of them are evil."

"They're not necessarily. That general is, though, his two kids as well. And if you doan follow their orders, you get executed."

"Or you become a deserter."

"You need to get past that word, Evie. You're starting to hurt my feelings. No matter, you stick around here long enough, and you'll soon find out why I *deserted*."

"*If* I could move Mom, and *if* you got this car fixed, I'd leave. I'd head out at dawn to find a doctor, then we'd go to North Carolina to reunite with my grandmother."

"What makes you think your good ole granny's alive? She's probably not."

"I just know she is." Like Mom said, I *had* to believe that. The alternative—never understanding all the mysteries surrounding me— was unbearable. To have no recourse from the voices . . . ?

I just stopped myself from shuddering.

Not to mention never seeing my grandmother again. The more I remembered of her, the more I loved. I could recall Gran's eyes—they were a twinkling brown, the color matching the darker striation of a pecan shell. The skin around them crinkled when she laughed. She'd laughed a lot. Used to hum all the time too, especially when she played with her well-worn Tarot deck.

"You *know* she's alive?" he asked. "Like from a vision?"

"I don't walk around seeing the future, Jackson. And most of the time, the things I see make no sense."

"Tell me about them."

"There's no pattern to when they occur. They're . . . painful," I said in the understatement of the year. "They feel like they're being shoved inside my head."

"You ready to tell me what you saw earlier?"

No, Jackson. No, I'm not. So I glossed over that question. "I have repeated visions featuring a boy who talks about nothing that makes much sense to me. I get lectured by this kid, who might as well be speaking another language." And still I felt such a strong bond with him. "In any case, a lot of the stuff I see has never come true." But give it time. . . .

"Maybe it just hasn't *yet*."

Perceptive Jackson. Changing the subject, I said, "What's it like out there on the road? Really like?"

He exhaled, allowing me to steer him away from talk of my visions. "Outside the cities, you can go days without seeing another living soul. Actually better not to. Two types of people left: them that want nothing to do with you and them that want to do you harm—the black hats."

"And inside the cities?"

"Lots of corpses. More survivors are dying out now, and the old ones ain't moldering like they normally would, just piling up."

I shivered at the mental image. "Is every place burned out like Sterling?"

"Not a damned thing's green, if that's what you're asking. Everything's covered in ash, but not every place is burned. Some towns look striped from the lines of flames that hit the ground. *C'est surprenant.*" It's uncanny. "Real finger-of-God stuff."

At my confused look, he said, "One house stands while the one beside it burned down. No rhyme or reason, like how a tornado strikes." He closed the hood. After wiping his hands on his jeans, he collected his crossbow and climbed into the driver's seat, setting the bow on his lap. "Hop in."

When I'd joined him inside, he said, "You'd never make it to North Carolina, Evie. That's heading right into the belly of the beast."

"Why do you say that? Because of the Bagmen?"

He met my gaze. "Maybe you'll never have to find out. Ask me nice, and I might take you to Texas."

God, his eyes really were breathtaking. As I stared into them, I allowed myself to imagine what it'd be like with him guiding Mom and me west. She liked him so much already.

Another thing I'd noticed? The voices were much quieter when he was near. I guessed they faded when more people were around to distract me.

I begrudgingly admitted that it might be *not awful* having him around. "Why would you help us like that?"

"Your *mère* has been kind to me."

"There has to be more to it than that."

Earlier, I'd told Mom, "Jackson wouldn't stick around here unless he had an angle."

She'd given me a soft smile. "His 'angle'? It's probably that you're a pretty girl and he's an eighteen-year-old boy."

Did he actually like me in that way?

"I got my reasons, me. That's all you need to know for now."

"Not good enough. By this time tomorrow, she could be under the care of a real doctor."

He hesitated, gripping the steering wheel, clearly wrestling with a decision. Snapping his fingers for the flask, he said, "Clotile lived through the Flash."

That was surprising. "How?" I handed him the whiskey. "And for that matter, how did you?"

He absently touched his forearm. "Wouldn't stop bleeding, this. Couldn't throttle my bike. So Clotile took me to an unlicensed doc in the next parish over, had a cellar office."

In a twist of fate, that drunk man had ended up saving both Jackson's and Clotile's lives.

"After the Flash, Clotile and me followed another survivor from the Basin, a reservist, to join his company. He talked us into serving our fellow man, and all that bullshit. But what else did we have to do? Besides, he'd figured out how to get his car to work, and we were hankering to put the entire wasted parish behind us. Though Clotile was a damned fine shot, the reservists stuck her in the kitchen and me in the fields, hunting Bagmen."

"You've *killed* them?"

"During the day, we exterminated them in their hiding places. At night, we patrolled on live bug hunts. I've killed hundreds." I narrowed my eyes, but he said, "It's true. If I never see another Bagman . . ."

He gave a harsh shake of his head, then continued, "Clotile and me had shelter and food, so we spent a few months like that. It felt good to be busy, to keep my mind off"—he glanced past me—"off dwelling on things. Anyway, two weeks ago, this big-ass army marched in, led by General Milovníci. Given the choice to join or die, my unit's leader surrendered the chain of command to Milovníci. I thought the general was weird, but his two kids were off the charts."

"How?"

"Vincent and Violet are twins about your age, with these vacant eyes, like a dead fish's. They dress alike, talk alike, and even got a matching tattoo—some Goth-looking design—on their hand."

—*We will love you. In our own way.*—

I struggled to block out the stray voice. Damn it, they'd been so quiet.

"But what do I know about politics, me?" Jackson said. "One general's as bad as the next, I supposed. I didn't have a dog in that fight, so I followed my orders and went out on patrol. When I returned, I passed the rest of the army's convoy—the *prisoner* detail. All women and girls, every one of them. I ran for Clotile, but they'd already taken her."

"To the general?"

"*Non.* That's where this gets . . . *étrange*. The twins had her." Jackson gripped the steering wheel again. "I found their tent and held up the guards outside, but there were too many—they surrounded me, slammed a rifle butt into my face. When I woke the next morning, I was being dragged from the brig to a firing squad." He turned to me. "See, the reason there're no male prisoners is because they execute any men who rebel. They do it in front of everyone, keep the rank and file in line."

"Then what happened?" I asked breathlessly.

"I got a sign from a couple of podnas. They were goan to help me out. So there I was, fighting the two guards holding me when I saw Clotile running from the twins' tent with a pistol in her hand. She'd fought them to get free." Voice gone low, he said, "But, Evie, they'd beaten her to hell over the night. Blood coming out of her nose, her ears, her busted lips. Her left arm hung limp. Her eyes were . . . they were frantic."

He seemed to shake himself out of that memory. "Now, Clotile, she'd been around the block. She'd seen some things in her day, but whatever happened in that tent had left her shell-shocked."

—*in our own way, in our own way*—

"She opened fire on the two guards holding me. Those cowards ran. So I was free, just had to get to her and get us the hell out of there. . . ."

"And then?" I reached over to touch his forearm, grazing that fateful scar.

"She shook her head at me, waving at me to run with my friends. I gave her the look that deserved and kept heading for her. Then the twins limped out of their tent. She looked over her shoulder and saw them, then met my eyes. My heart dropped in my stomach—I knew what she was goan to do. I was yelling at her, just to wait, just to give me time to *get* to her. She . . . that damn girl, she mouthed, *I'm sorry*." He swallowed. "Then she blew her brains out over the ground."

I forgot to breathe. To watch a loved one commit suicide?

"I sometimes wonder, me, what drove her to do it. Just to save my worthless hide? Or because she couldn't live with whatever those two had done to her?" He shook his head in confusion. "A *Catholic* girl. Taking her own life?"

When he finally faced me, he seemed surprised that I was on the verge of tears. "Doan you cry," he snapped, growing distinctly uncomfortable. "I didn't want to tell you that. I just didn't know what else to do to convince you." In a brusque tone, he said, "I doan like tears, me."

"I can't help it." We sat in silence until I'd gotten control of my emotions. "Why is it so important for you to convince me? Who am I to you?"

Another deep drink. "I've met people from all over, some down from Canada or up from South America. East all the way from the burning fields of California. And there're a couple of things that everybody agrees on—*nothing* grows anywhere. And there's no rain. I doan think there are oceans anymore."

"*What?*"

"Flash-evaporation. It happened to more than just the rivers and lakes. The Gulf Coast is a desert as far as the eye can see." As I digested this horrifying news, he said, "After Clotile died, I stopped pretending like there was something for me to keep goan on for."

"Jackson—"

"*Non*, let me finish. I decided to go west to see if there were some militias that might take on the general. I wanted a shot at him, at his son and daughter too," Jackson said, the quiet rage in his voice unsettling me. He was talking about murdering three people like he might talk about slapping three mosquitoes. "I knew I'd die trying, but didn't care. So I figured I'd stop by the farm of this *belle fille* I used to go to school with and solve one last mystery."

"Mystery?"

"Uh-huh. Over the last half a year, I've seen everything in your journal coming true. I had to know why."

"You and your puzzles," I said absently. "Why did you think I'd still be alive, when most girls died?"

"I knew." At my raised brows, he gruffly said, "I got ways, me." Before I could delve deeper, he continued, "But I never imagined what I'd find when I got here. In a backwater parish in Louisiana, there's this soft little girl hiding *crops* in a barn." Jackson held my gaze. "I'll be damned before the general gets his hands on them."

"When will they come?"

"If it's clear tomorrow, the first convoy of trucks will be here by noon at the latest. Why woan you believe me?"

"It doesn't matter if I do or don't. I can't move Mom! She's in terrible pain just rising from the bed—how am I going to get her down the stairs? What if I hurt her worse? I could kill her!" Struggling for an even tone, I asked, "What would you do if it were your mother?"

I'd just assumed she'd died when Jackson and Clotile had been at the doctor's. . . .

He stilled beside me. "Doan want to talk about her, no." He could talk about the horror that had befallen Clotile, but not about whatever had happened to his mother?

Could her fate have been *worse*? "Okay, then. I won't mention it again."

"What if I promise to find your *mère* a doctor in Texas?"

If someone had told me yesterday that I'd soon be considering this—trusting my mother's life to Jackson Deveaux—I would have laughed. "Can I just *think* about this until morning?"

"What for, you?"

He'd shared his agonizing tale with me. I could at least be honest about my hesitation. "I'm not used to making decisions like this," I admitted. "Mom pretty much took care of any tough calls for the first ninety-five percent of my life. I'm still stumbling here, and God knows I can't afford a misstep with this. Nothing matters to me more than her. Nothing."

"Evie—"

"She might take a turn for the better now that she's eaten so well."

He exhaled a pent-up breath, but that muscle ticked in his cheek again. "We'll talk in the morning. Early. Until then, I'm goan to be filling this car with supplies, readying to bug out fast."

"What supplies?"

"I'm goan to top off every container I can find with fuel or water. Goan to rummage for weapons and a few tools. And you better be packed, ready to go. Just in case," he added, but I knew he had no doubt in his mind that we'd be leaving.

"You're pretty confident you'll get this car to work, then?"

He nodded. "Now, what're we goan to do about the crops?"

I gazed away. "Do?" *We?*

"When the army finds them, that general's goan to want to know all about them. If you're here, he'll give you to the twins to torture until you reveal everything. If you're not here, he'll send trackers after you. One way or another, he will get answers. Is that something you want him to find out?"

Dear God, no. If that man was as evil as Jackson said, he'd probably drain me daily. I shivered.

"Evangeline, damn it, tell me about them, and I'll help you. How'd you do it? Voodoo? Magic? Government experiment?" When I remained silent, he grated, "Come on, after all I told you?" He made a sound of frustration. "Then at least answer me this: If I pack that box of seeds from your pantry, can those crops come about again?"

I could at least answer that, right? I worried my bottom lip. Mom thought we could trust him. *Take a leap, Evie.* We did need him.

So why did I still distrust him so strongly? Was it because of our history, or because he was so different from me, from the folks I'd grown up with? "You yourself told me you were a thousand times worse than everyone said. You acted like you wanted to kiss me just so you and your friends could steal from me and mine. How can I trust you?"

He cast me a disbelieving look. "You think that's the only reason I wanted to kiss you? You doan know much about boys, no. I would've taken you to bed that night so fast it'd make your head swim." Another swig.

My breaths shallowed. "L-like I said before, I'll address this in the morning. It might be a moot point." At his raised brows, I said, "All this is assuming you can get our car fixed."

"It's *been* fixed, *peekôn.*"

I held my breath as he reached for the start button. When the engine came roaring to life in the quiet of the night, I glanced at Mom's room again.

I imagined her tucked in her bed, about to doze off, dreamily smiling at the sound.

I rose at dawn, wide-awake.

I was too wired to be hungover, even though Jackson and I had sat in the car, passing his flask back and forth as I'd charged my iPod. He believed electronics that escaped a direct Flash hit didn't get fried: "Kind of like people." He'd been right about my iPod.

But when he'd asked about the crops again, I'd quietly thanked him for dinner and gone to bed. . . .

Now I slipped to the window, gazing out at the morning dust storm—a howler. Which meant those men would be delayed and I could hold Jackson off a little while longer. Maybe Mom was better, well enough to evacuate.

I poured water from my pitcher into my stoppered sink, hurriedly brushing my teeth and hair. After pulling on some jeans, a hoodie, and my customary bandanna around my neck, I left my room.

In the hallway, I slowed. Jackson was sitting at the top of the stairs, opening his flask. He didn't look like he'd slept, still had his crossbow slung over his back, his own bandanna smeared with soot.

I frowned when he closed the flask without taking a drink. He just stared at it in his hands.

Uneasiness settled over me, as if I were an animal sensing a storm. *Pressure. Danger coming.*

"Evangeline, your *mère*'s gone."

I narrowed my eyes. "Leave it to a cretin like you to joke about something like that."

"She passed away in the night."

Even as it felt like a vise was grinding closed over my chest, I snapped, "That's not funny! God, you haven't changed a bit!"

"She's passed on," he murmured again.

"No." Dread grew as I studied his tired face. "You're *lying*." I pointed my finger at him. "No!"

He just stared at me. As the world began to spin, I bolted down the hall, clamping onto her room's doorjamb as I careened inside.

One look and I knew she was gone. Her face was truly peaceful. For the first time since the Flash.

Some wretched sound slipped past my lips. *She's gone. My mother is . . .*

Gone.

In a daze, I stepped closer to the bed, realizing that she clutched a picture in one ghostly white hand.

I remembered the photo. It was of her, me, and Gran in front of Haven one Easter. I was standing between them, proudly displaying a basket full of eggs. The azaleas had been in bloom, dazzlingly bold in color. The air had smelled of new cane, gardenias, and a distant high tide.

Now, as I'd done a thousand times before, I sat beside Mom on her bed to talk. "You wouldn't do this." I barely recognized my voice. "You wouldn't leave me alone like this."

When she didn't answer, a sob broke free, then another. I collapsed over her, resting my face against her chest.

It was quiet. Still.

Tears dropped, soaking the collar of her nightgown. *"Come back, Mama,"* I whispered, praying that I'd hear a heartbeat stutter to life or feel her take a breath.

Still.

"We need to go," Jackson said from behind me.

Leave my mother?

"Evie, there's no reason for you to stay now."

I rose unsteadily, narrowing my blurry gaze at him. "She was getting better. And then you show up, and you want us to leave. . . ." Wiping my eyes, I demanded, "What did you do to her?"

He said nothing, his expression shuttered.

"What did you do?" I flew at him, pummeling his chest.

"I didn't do anything!" He just stood there, letting me hit him. "I came in this morning, and she was like this." Finally he caught my wrists. "She'd injured something inside her."

We'd suspected that, but . . . "How could *you* know that?"

"You think I ain't been kicked in the ribs enough to know an internal injury? Crawling to a hospital on Sunday mornings, me?"

"B-but she was recovering! And now . . . now she's . . . *d-dead.*" I sobbed that word.

"She's been dying for days. And she knew it! She was asking promises of me last night for a reason."

Some distant, rational part of me knew that he was right. Her injury couldn't possibly have gotten worse. I recalled the what-if questions. She'd tried so hard to get Jackson to like me—to want to take care of me. And she'd asked promises of me as well.

Because she'd known she was running out of time.

With no one to blame, my rage abandoned me. My legs gave way, and I slumped to the floor.

Jackson just . . . stared at me, as if he'd never seen grief. Instead of comforting me, he said, "You're leaving here with me in the next ten minutes." Then he strode to Mom's jewelry armoire and started shoving jewels into his pockets.

My mother lay dead, and he was ransacking her belongings. "What is *wrong* with you?" I cried. "Show some respect!"

He turned on me, yanking me to my feet. "I intend to. By saving her daughter's ass. We're goan to need things to trade. You just let me be the bad guy that rifles through the dead woman's jewels, yeah? I'll get my hands dirty, so you woan have to." He dragged me into my room, scanning the area. "Damn it, Evie! You didn't pack?"

I hadn't been about to pack for me but not for Mom, and I hadn't wanted to wake her.

Had she already been dead?

He stormed into my closet, hauling a suitcase out. "Clothes in here. *Now!*"

"I c-can't leave Mom like that! We have to b-bury her."

He scowled as if I'd said something absurd. Then he went to work on my own jewels, filching heirloom brooches and pearls. "You got anything else of value in this house?"

Confusion. "I-I don't . . ."

"Gold bars, windup timepieces, any guns I didn't see last night?"

I could only stare at him.

Cursing me in French, he yanked a clothes drawer out, dumping its contents into my bag before seizing another drawer.

Wordlessly, I watched him fill my suitcase, then force it shut.

Bag in one hand, my upper arm in his other, he started hauling me down the steps.

But he didn't understand. I'd never leave my mother as she was. "Help me with her, Jackson."

"We doan have *time* to do right by her. I got other things I have to take care of."

"Please, Jack."

"Those men are coming. As soon as the winds die, you'll hear the scouts fire guns into the air, and then the whole damned army'll start grinding forward. They'll take you, and there woan be a damn thing I can do about it."

At the foot of the stairs, I thrashed against him. "I'm not leaving her here like this! Especially not if they're as evil as you say."

His eyes darted. "You'll go with me if I bury her?"

When I nodded, he jerked his bandanna up over his mouth and

nose, yanked the bracing off the front door, then plunged into the windstorm.

As he raced toward the barn, I followed dumbly, covering my own face.

He emerged with a shovel, and I thought he would dig right there, but he found a spot beneath the windmill, where Gran's rose garden had once been.

After removing his crossbow, he stabbed that shovel into the earth. Ash erupted, swirling in the winds.

As he dug deeper, he railed at me in French, telling me that I was more trouble than I was worth, that we didn't have the luxury of burying loved ones, that if I didn't get stronger I wouldn't survive out there.

Feeling as disconnected from reality as I had during those last days of school, I sank down, nodding vacantly while he cursed me and shoveled.

Soon his forehead was beading with sweat, dripping down to wet the cloth over his face. Just as I wondered if his hands were getting blistered from the gritty shovel handle, he adjusted his grip.

Bloody palm prints now stained the wood. Had his new blisters given way?

"This is the stupidest *coo-yôn* move I've ever made." He seemed driven, *crazed* to get this done. He increased his pace until blood ran freely down the handle.

Yet then . . . the winds died down.

Ash settled over us like snow. We both squinted up. Gradually, the sky became unbroken blue. A forced smile.

We were out of time. Those men would be here soon.

A gunshot popped in the distance, then another and another.

"Putain!" Jackson ripped down his bandanna. "They're coming."

"How far away are they?"

"We doan have long. Evie, I can't do right by your mother. If it's too shallow . . ." He trailed off, then snapped, "Damn it, I can't do right by her." The way he was acting, you'd think he'd never failed at anything in his life. "She wouldn't want you to stay."

"I-I know." We had no choice but to leave her behind.

More guns went off, followed by rowdy yells. What sounded like a parade of trucks was rumbling our way. I shuddered when I heard a woman's *scream*—then male laughter.

I knew in that instant that everything Jackson had told me was true. "They really are as bad as you say?"

A quick nod.

I thought about poor Clotile. I thought about all the girls out there in danger because of this army. And I knew what I had to do. "I'll be back!"

"No! You can't . . ." Whatever he saw in my expression made him hold up two bloody fingers. "Two minutes, Evie."

I stole inside the house, up the stairs. In my room, I collected my backpack, my flash drive of memories, and the necklace Brandon had given me. For some reason, Jackson had skipped over that one.

On my way out, I gazed at my room, at my trophies and paintings, committing them to memory.

In Mom's room, I sat beside her one last time. I collected the picture she held, then took her hand, smoothing it against my cheek, over my tears. "I swear to you, I-I will get to Gran's. I will figure out why everything went wrong. And I'll do anything I can to fix it." With a whispered, *"I-I love you, Mama,"* I kissed her good-bye, pressing my lips to her forehead.

Leaving her behind was the hardest thing I'd ever had to do.

In moments, I knew I'd do something worse.

Jackson met me at the front door with a dangerous gleam in his eyes and a lighter offered up in his ragged palm.

I smelled gasoline, heard Allegra trotting a retreat away from the barn, neighing with nervousness.

The moment began to feel dreamlike, like I was outside my body. A haze fell over me.

"They can't see those crops, Evie. They'll come after you, tracking you. They woan stop. The crops have to burn, even if they're the last ones on earth."

"Gas is . . . everywhere?" I stared at his face, at the startling gray of his fierce eyes.

He nodded.

"This is *my* home, Jackson. The only one I've ever known." It had centuries of history, dreams both lost and found. "I'm not leaving it like this. Hand over that lighter."

He cupped my nape, bringing our foreheads together. "I know this is your home, *ange,* but just listen to me—"

"No, you listen!" Fury made my voice low, my words like a hiss. I pulled back from him. "They can't *have it.*" I didn't want those centuries tainted by these murderers, didn't want them seeing my mother so vulnerable. They didn't get to touch our possessions or rape women in my bed.

I couldn't allow Haven to shelter that army, to help make that force even more powerful than it already was.

I'd already planned to burn my home down with my mother inside. Jackson had just been one step ahead of me.

"Now. Give me that lighter."

His gaze widened, then narrowed on me. He cast me a look, as if we'd *finally* gotten on the same page. When he handed it over, he murmured, *"Ma bonne fille."*

I flicked the lighter and a flame danced; he took my free hand in his, readying to run.

With my heartbeat thundering in my ears and my blood racing through my veins, I whispered, "Jackson, I can make them grow again. . . ."

I dropped the lighter.

Once we were clear of the fire and any potential militia scouts, Jackson drove up on the parish levee, parking on the rise.

I stepped out of the car, shielding my gaze against the sun. From this vantage, I could see smoke billowing up from Haven.

My mother's funeral pyre.

Jackson muttered from behind me, "She's in a better place." And that was all he said on the matter.

In this, I believed him completely.

As I gazed over the wasted horizon—at the ash-clogged mire that used to be a flowing bayou, at the sooty plains that were once verdant fields, at the angry flames rising from Haven—I reasoned that she *had* to be.

—The Empress is in play.—

I woke to the voices whispering this phrase again and again. Yet now these characters sounded different, more alert, maybe even a touch less *smug*?

I blinked open my puffy eyes, disoriented. It was dusk, the winds were still, and Jackson had just parked . . . in a shipyard? "Where are we?" Had I really slept the entire day away?

"Not nearly as far as I'd like to be. Still in Louisiana."

"Why are we in a shipyard?" One that was on the banks of a dried-out bayou.

"People forget to loot the ships in dry dock. We're spending the night here." As he got out of the car, he readied his crossbow. He clearly knew what he was doing with that weapon, was as comfortable with it as I'd once been with back handsprings.

I wondered who'd taught him to shoot. *Nécessité?*

Before I could unbuckle my seat belt and climb out, he was at my door. "Stick to me like a shadow, you," he ordered.

Though I bristled at his tone, I followed him as he stalked deeper into the yard.

"I like the look of that one, right there." He pointed out a huge metal shrimp boat raised on a repair cradle, its paint blistered off.

"What's so special about it?"

"It'll take a ladder to reach the inside, and there's only one way in or out. Safe as a drum. Good money says there'll be canned food in the galley."

In minutes, we'd found a ladder and were climbing to the ship. He grabbed my arm, hauling me aboard, then dragged the ladder up behind us.

As we stole across the deck, old shrimp, crab, and oyster shells crackled beneath our boots, but the sound seemed to please Jackson.

Inside, there was a spacious captain's cabin, and three smaller cabins with bunk beds already made up. At least we wouldn't have to sleep in the same room.

After searching every inch of the vessel, we returned to the galley. Jackson rooted around, pleased with the haul: cans of soup, unopened boxes of crackers, discount-club packs of bottled water, sacks of beef jerky, and a bottle of Captain Morgan's rum.

"Knew this one was a beauty when I first saw it. I got a sense for these things. Now, doan get me wrong—no place is one hundred percent safe. You always got to be on your guard."

I made some sound of acknowledgment.

"I'm sure this ain't exactly what you're used to—as far as ships go—but it's a find all the same."

The last boat I'd been on was the Radcliffes', a seven-figure yacht called *Billable Hours.*

When the kitchen faucet actually produced water, Jackson explained, "From the tanks. You can't drink it, but you can grab a shower."

"Shower?" I perked up somewhat.

"*Ouais.* You open a couple of cans for us, and I'll go get your bag."

In a daze, I perused the food offerings, wondering what he would like. There were at least a dozen cans of soup. Seemed like such a windfall, but I knew from experience that I needed about fifteen hundred calories a day to maintain my weight. I selected a can of minestrone soup, wincing at the calorie count. Two hundred.

I could only imagine how much a boy like Jackson would need. We'd burn through this—and all the supplies he'd scavenged from Haven—before the week was out.

Just as he returned from dumping my suitcase on the big cabin's foam mattress, I cut myself on the rim of a can.

"Eck, girl." He seized my hand. "You're bleeding."

"I'll be fine!"

"Let me see." He held up my finger, sticking it into his mouth like I was a little kid. I snatched my hand back, turning toward the cabin.

He grumbled, "Damn, Evie, suit yourself." Then, louder: "Remember, doan drink any of the water. And save some for me."

Jack had set up a flashlight in the small bathroom, so I was able to search the medicine cabinet for a Band-Aid to conceal my healing. I found one among an aspirin bottle, packs of No-Doz, and an ancient-looking box of condoms.

I stripped off my filthy clothes, entering the cramped fiberglass stall. The drain was covered with little bottles of shampoo and slivers of Irish Spring soap.

Under the paltry stream of tepid water, I scrubbed as fast as I could. But I was coated with ash, reeking of soot.

Because Haven burned to the ground today.

Had that been just hours before? It felt like a week ago.

My mother died today.

I pressed the side of my face against the stall, struggling not to cry. I feared if I started, I wouldn't stop. . . .

The shower began to disappear, black dots tracing before my eyes. "No, no, no! Not another one," I whispered desperately, shoving the heels of my palms against my temples as my headache grew.

Blood trickled from my nose, dripping onto the shampoo bottles. I gazed down, riveted by the stark scarlet drops.

Drip, drip, drip—

"They know, Empress," Matthew said.

I flattened myself against the fiberglass stall. He was here! In the bathroom with me.

I jerked around, giving him my back, glaring over my shoulder. But he appeared to have no interest in my nudity.

"The Empress is in play," he said. "The Arcana sense it, like a disturbance in the Force."

"*Star Wars*, Matthew? Really?"

"You're a target. *Take her before she grows too powerful,* the bad cards whisper. But you talked so loud they thought you wanted to lure them to your farm." He tapped his temple. "Beware the lures."

His words spurred a memory from my last day with Gran: *"I hate taking you from home, sweetheart," she told me as she pulled her Blazer out onto the interstate. "Only the bravest—or most foolish—Arcana would ever go to Haven, home of the great Empress. . . ."*

"I talked loud? What does that mean?" I was not only receiving voices but *broadcasting* my own?

Matthew frowned. "*No one* is as loud as you. They talk back louder, goading."

"The voices are from the characters I've seen, aren't they? The archer, the flying boy. Death."

He nodded. "Major Arcana."

The trump cards of Tarot. "How can their voices be in my head? Am I some kind of clairvoyant?"

"Clair*audient*. All Arcana have a call. Like birds. I'm crazy like a fox."

Whatever, kid. "What do they hear me say? How do I talk *softer*?"

In a patronizing tone he replied, "*Inside* voice, Evie."

I pinched my forehead, irritated at the double meaning—which told me nothing. "Why would they want to *goad* me? What have I done to them?"

"You're Arcana."

"I-I don't understand. And I . . . I can't do much more of this 'Arcana' stuff!"

"I'll keep sending you visions." He touched his nose, murmuring, "Drip, drip, drip. You have to learn."

"*Sending* me? Are you saying I'm not . . . *foreseeing* you on my own?"

"I send you visions."

"Or maybe I'm deluded, and I'm imagining you saying this even now. Maybe you're not even real!"

He rolled his eyes. "Nooo. I send you visions. Not *your* Arcana power. Mine, mine, mine."

So now I wasn't even psychic? "Do all Arcana have powers?"

"Vast. Superhuman."

My eyes narrowed as a suspicion arose. "Are you sending me those nightmares, too? Because I am *over* them!"

"Never nightmares! Empress, we're behind. Find me."

I'd been planning to seek him out eventually. "But I have to get to my gran. Where are you anyway?"

"Find me before Death finds you."

"Or what?"

He drew his head back, as if this was obvious. "Or he'll . . . *touch* you. His power. You are the card that Death covets."

I shuddered, remembering the Reaper looming over me, reaching for me with his bare hands. "Why covet me? I don't understand." But Matthew had disappeared.

And all the water had run out.

"Damn it!" Jackson had asked me for so little—make soup and save water. I'd failed at both simple tasks.

Queasy with guilt, I returned to the cabin. His backpack now lay on the bed beside my suitcase. Surely he wouldn't expect us to stay in the same room?

I'd just finished changing when he opened the cabin door without a knock, stepping over the raised threshold with mugs of soup in hand.

His gaze roamed over me, over the cami top and gym skirt I'd been forced to wear. His packing had left much to be desired.

My wardrobe now consisted of a total of one pair of jeans and a hoodie—both of which I'd had on—about ten hair ribbons, more underwear than I could possibly wear in a lifetime, bras that barely fit, workout clothes, and one mismatched pair of socks.

He opened his mouth to say something, then thought better of it. *Too soon, Jackson, much too soon.*

After handing me a surprisingly warm mug, he sat at the cabin's built-in desk to sip from his own. I felt a pang to see that he'd had to wrap his injured hands in strips of cloth. He was covered in grit and ash from digging.

He'd tried so hard to help with my mom. . . .

"This is as good a time as any to talk about the coming days," he said.

I eased down onto the edge of the bed across from him. "Okay."

"I did end up making some . . . *assurances* to your mother. Kept 'em pretty vague, so I feel sure I can wiggle out of them without goan straight to hell. My worry is that *you* made promises to her."

"I did."

He muttered a curse. "Maybe to get to your grandmother?"

"That's the one."

"Let me explain the landscape for you, *peekôn*. Between us and North Carolina, you've got Bagmen, offshoot militias, and doomsday cults—who are feeling mighty righteous these days. The slavers control the cities—"

"Slavers are real?" We'd heard rumors. . . .

"*Ouais*. They round up people to dig wells, like slaves in a gold mine." At my bemused look, he said, "If they caught someone like me, they'd chain me in an ash-filled quarry with a pickax, or shove me into a mineshaft, and wouldn't let me out till I struck the water table. Course, if they captured *you* . . . it'd be different. Same with the cannibals."

"C-cannibals?" Again, there'd been whisperings.

When he nodded, I tried to imagine what modern-day American cannibals would look like, kept picturing them wearing body parts threaded on a necklace. Maybe they carried bloody clubs. . . .

Though these threats chilled me to the bone, I still said, "I start for the Outer Banks tomorrow."

"You might not have a whole lot of skills, but it seems like you got stubborn mastered. There ain't any way for me to talk you out of this, is there?"

"Not a chance." I didn't have a choice. Aside from my promise to my mom, I had to solve this Arcana mystery. *Because it's never going to stop.* "If you're set on Texas, I'll drive you until you find another car to repair."

"You got me *mal pris*." Stuck in a bad situation. "If I let you go by yourself, you're as good as dead." I opened my mouth to argue, but he talked over me, saying, "Come on, girl, you got no way to protect yourself."

I did once. I used to have soldiers on every corner, watching over me. I gazed down at my mug, remembering my shell-shocked cane and those valiant oaks. Gone forever.

Just like my mother.

"Look at me, Evie. You certain you want to go that way?"

"I am." And I was certain that I'd be better off with him. "Will you . . . will you help me?"

"*Mais* yeah," he said grandly. "I'll take you there. *But* I got conditions, me."

"Of course you do."

"You tell me your secrets. I got to know how you grew the crops. Got to know how you'll do it again."

Maybe I should motivate him? "I will tell you anything you want to know—as soon as I get to my gran's."

He hesitated before saying, *"D'accord."* Agreed.

My relief was tinged with suspicion. "You don't like me. We were never friends."

He didn't deny either.

"We might as well be strangers, Jackson. Yet you're willing to travel with me, risking your life?"

"Strangers? That's relative, ain't it? You know me better than anyone alive. And I know you better than anyone does except your grandmother."

Because Mom's gone.

"Hell, Evie, there's no one left but you. No one to speak Cajun to, no one who remembers the bayou, what it smelled like or how the sun—"

"Used to stream through the moss and cypress needles?"

"Exactement."

"Then we're agreed."

With an unreadable expression, he said, *"Bien.* Now, there are two ways we can go. The Army of the Southeast swept down from South Carolina to Louisiana—we can backtrack over their trail, heading up through Atlanta. The major roads will be clear of wreckage, and there'll be fewer Bagmen. On the downside, the troops will have picked clean the local gas stations and grocery stores. We got a good supply of water from Haven—if we ration—but fuel and food will be sparse. And sourcing burns up your daylight."

This sounded less than ideal. "What's the second way?"

"We could head north into Tennessee, then cut east. We'll miss their trail, but risk Bagmen and blocked roads."

I was surprised—and impressed—by how knowledgeable he was. "What do you suggest?"

"Backtracking. The trip will take longer, and it'll be lean going, but I think it'll be safer."

Take longer? Now that I was on my way to find Gran, impatience burned in me. "How long are we talking?"

"I drove the entire day—and we made all of sixty miles through the windstorms. The visibility was about five feet. It's goan to take weeks to get there."

My lips parted. "Are we going to stop before dusk every day? The winds go still at night—I could've driven a shift."

"Bagmen roam at night, so we doan."

"Surely if we're in a car, they can't catch us."

"If it was just me . . . but with you . . ." He scrubbed a bandaged hand over his mouth, looking as if he'd only just grasped what a huge responsibility he'd taken on. The responsibility for another person. "Have you even seen a Bagman? Other than in your visions?"

I hesitated, then shook my head.

"When we hunted them, we went out in groups of ten, trained and armed to the teeth. You and me? We can't risk meeting up with them. Especially not in numbers. If anything happens to me out on the road, you're done. No two ways about it."

"I managed to survive since the Flash without you."

"You were hidden away, with food, water, and a strong shelter. It's bedlam out there. Folks have lost their fool minds."

"I have a difficult time believing that everything good has just fallen by the wayside so quickly." Decency, morality. "It's only been seven months. People wouldn't have resorted to cannibalism already."

"There's—no—food, Evie." He stood, retrieving the flask from his pocket. "Even with so few people left, grocery stores were picked clean in days. There're no crops, hardly any animals. The better part of a year is plenty of time for a new food chain to come into play."

I rubbed my forehead. "Food chain?"

"The strong—like the militias and that army—got all the supplies and food. They're at the top. The slightly less strong are the cannibals. Near the bottom, the weak are starving. And the unlucky weak? They're somebody's dinner." He drank deep, holding my gaze. "So you think real hard about where you want me to take you tomorrow, *peekôn.*"

I tried to sleep in the silent ship.

Haven House was always—*had always been*—so noisy. I would never hear it creak and groan again. Would never hear the cane whisper me to sleep. Would never hear my mom's heels clicking across the marble floor.

Even the voices were quiet, as if they wanted me to experience my grief to its full, excruciating potential.

Or perhaps they were quiet because Jackson was mere feet from me, sleeping slumped over that desk. He'd told me we'd always stay in the same room on the road because, again, "no place is one hundred percent safe." His crossbow was at the ready.

I felt alternately uneasy and protected to have him so close.

As I lay on a too-soft foam bed in a too-quiet cabin, I relived the day. A trio of memories had been etched into my mind, and I knew they'd never be forgotten.

The proud look Jackson had given me when I dropped the lighter to burn down my home and cremate my mother.

The feel of his blistered palm when we ran hand-in-hand from the flames.

How peaceful Mom had looked in death.

Tears gathered and spilled—there was no stopping them. I imagined her last thoughts, imagined her clutching that picture. Had she known it would be her last night to live?

Why hadn't I stayed with her?

If she hadn't died in her sleep, then I could have been there to hold her hand, to see her . . . to see her through it.

Curling on my side, I wept, trying so hard not to make a sound.

Jackson suddenly shot upright. "You need to stop crying."

I kept crying.

With a harsh oath, he grated, "Out here, there's no room for this. You're too soft, Evangeline."

Yes, Jackson had only just begun to recognize what a weighty responsibility he'd taken on today—and now the reality was setting in. I sat up, swiping my forearm over my face. "I c-can't help it." Sooner or later, he'd get sick of me.

"Your *mère* died in grace. What more could you want for her? I only hope to go out so clean."

I cried harder.

"Damn it, Evie!" His brows drew together, his lips thinned. "To hell with it. Cry all you like, but I doan have to watch it!" Snatching up his bow, he stormed out of the cabin, slamming the door.

I stared after him, miserable, listening as he strode through the ship. But just as suddenly, he started back toward the cabin. I heard him slide down outside, sitting against the door. He exhaled a gust of breath.

I continued to cry; he rose to pace.

What felt like hours later, he flung open the door. "You know what PEWS is?"

I shook my head dumbly.

"Perimeter early-warning system. It's a way to hear enemies creeping up on you. Like the crackling shells out on the deck."

"O-okay?" Tears were streaming down my face.

But he wouldn't look at me, just started pacing again. "You can crush up lightbulbs outside your door, any kind of glass. A groaning staircase works just as well. That's part of the reason I always try to roll two-story houses. When I'm driving, you're goan to be looking for places for us to overnight, so keep that in mind."

I tentatively nodded.

"Now, Baggers can smell water from miles away, so they still flock to old bodies of—"

"Then wh-why are we in a shipyard?"

"A ship on blocks is too good to pass up. Bagmen are like rabid wolves—they can hunt, but they can't figure out how to use a ladder. Besides, every overnight has its own drawbacks. Any house with an open door? You have to wonder if a Bagger got in there first, like a moccasin coiled in your boot. Public building? You can't spit without hitting a fire exit. Fire exits equal Bagman entrances."

"Y-you know a lot."

"I do, Evie," he said matter-of-factly. "I know that Bagman scratches aren't contagious, but their saliva or blood in your own will turn you in less than two days. I know that the only way to kill them is beheading or a shot to the brainpan. I've seen 'em all dried-out and chalky, till you think they got to be dead—but if you toss a bucket of water on 'em, they'll come slithering across the ground to bite you. I know that they're not allergic to sun like everybody thinks. They just doan like it 'cause it dries out their slimy skin. Enough of an incentive and they'll brave the sun. I've seen 'em out past dawn licking dew from cars, or even from the ground."

As I shivered to imagine such a sight, he canted his head at me. "You paying attention? I learned this stuff, but I've paid for it. Giving it to you for free."

I would grasp at anything to occupy my mind. "I want to learn more."

"All righty." He hauled his backpack to the bed, taking a seat across from me. "Now, this here's my bug-out bag. Only critical stuff and survival gear." He dumped its contents onto the cover, his bearing seemingly *proud*?

My gaze flicked over energy gel-packs and protein bars, a canister of Morton salt, a Swiss Army multipurpose tool, a travel toothbrush, lighters, medical tape, a windup flashlight, glow sticks, three mini bottles of liquor, and a canteen.

Some items were more surprising: a small hammer and bag of nails, an envelope of photos that he didn't seem keen for me to see, and a pistol, snapped in a holster. "We'll turn your backpack into a bug-out bag too. And every night, we'll sort our resources." At my questioning look, he said, "So we know what to be looking out for on the road."

My tears were drying. "Like what?"

"If your bootlaces get busted, we woan pass by a corpse with decent lace-up boots."

I swallowed. This was my life now. "If you have a pistol, why do you carry only a bow and arrow?"

"Only?" he scoffed. "This is bolt-action." He reached for his weapon, showing me a magazine clip with six short arrows inside. "It's quiet, and the arrows are reusable. Not so great against militiamen, but perfect for Baggers. Besides, that pistol's only got one bullet—hanging on to it in case I get bit."

"Oh. When do I get my shotgun back?"

"Try never." I glared. "I'm goan to saw off the barrel. Carry it along with my bow for black hats. But here, I'll help you get started with supplies." He handed me the three mini bottles.

I raised my brows. "Jack Daniels?"

He met my gaze. "Is *always* good to have in hand."

I set them away, too tired and emotionally raw to deal with his innuendo.

But he scooped the bottles up, dropping them insistently into my lap. "Doan scoff at the liquor, Evie. What else on earth can disinfect, catch an enemy on fire, *and* get you drunk? Tell me, what could you use the empty bottles for?"

"Um . . . glass for a PEWS?"

The corners of his lips curved just the slightest bit.

DAY 230 A.F.

DEEP IN MISSISSIPPI

I sat in the parked car, surrounded by old corpses, watching Jackson fight through a windstorm. He had his bow at the ready, the shotgun slung over his shoulder, and a plastic gas tank tethered to his belt.

Empty, of course.

We hadn't made it out of Louisiana before we'd started running on fumes. That'd been nine days ago. Since then, he'd been scrounging a gallon here or there and sourcing for car parts. Already we'd burned through three pairs of windshield-wiper blades and two air filters.

With the constant stops—and the unrelenting windstorms—we averaged less than twenty miles a day.

Today, he was sourcing fuel at a lawn mower repair shop. He thought the militia might've overlooked it.

Surely they'd gotten everything else. Just as Jackson predicted, food *was* scarce. We were running out of cans. Luckily, we were holding steady on water, sometimes finding leftovers inside water heaters.

Kneeling up on my seat with my forehead to the glass, I squinted, keeping Jackson in sight. Visibility was poor. The car rocked, ash swirling over the corpses splayed all around, like sand over windswept dunes.

When he encountered a body in his way, he didn't veer his direction, just stepped right over it. He drove over corpses too.

At first I'd asked him to avoid them. After a couple of days, I'd realized how silly my request was. Without much moisture or insects, and few birds, the bodies had a lot of staying power, collecting over time.

He'd told me they were worse in the cities. I'd never imagined how many there could be.

Still, I was relieved to be out here on the road with Jackson, felt like some of the pressure of the last several months had been lifted.

Though my grief for my mom remained raw, it wasn't as debilitating as it'd been in the beginning. At least now I could stem my tears. They seemed to really bother Jackson, like he took them as a personal insult.

But then, he spent most hours of the day irritated with me anyway. I had little clue why, barely able to keep up with his moods. . . .

The winds increased. A plastic Christmas tree tumbled by; a blackened clothes dryer inched down the road. Debris battered the car.

Jackson was out in that wasteland, exposed to danger. The militia had indeed cleared the roads, bulldozing wrecks. They'd piled them up along the sides, until the streets were like corrals. Like deadly wind chutes.

When he bent down beside a riding lawnmower parked on the small lot, I fretted my bottom lip. But Jackson seemed to possess no sense of fear, working steadily at his task.

I watched as he jammed a clear siphoning hose into the mower's tank, swishing the tube around. He gave me a thumbs-up sign.

Clever, Jackson.

He'd turned out to be markedly different from how I'd remembered him at school. He was more hardened, and so possessed of himself that I sometimes forgot he was only a couple of years older than me.

Yet on very rare occasions, I caught a glimpse of an eighteen-year-old boy.

Some aspects of Jackson had remained the same. He was still dangerous, compelling, impossible to ignore—and *confusing*.

Though I wanted to be out there helping him, he always refused. Then he'd criticize me for not pulling my weight.

Sometimes I felt like I could never win with him, like he was purposely driving a wedge between us. But I didn't know why.

After positioning the gas container beside the mower tank, he pulled down his bandanna, taking the hose between his teeth. I didn't miss his hesitation to start the flow. Even if he was skilled enough not to get a mouthful of gas, he was still breathing the fumes—

Out of the corner of my eye, I spied a piece of sheet metal zooming through the air toward him, shearing everything in its path like a giant razor blade. I screamed, *"Look out!"* He couldn't possibly hear me.

He ducked all on his own.

I pressed my sweating palms against the window, exhaling a breath as he faced me. His sunglasses covered his eyes, but I knew we were sharing a *Holy shit!* look. Then he set right back to work.

Another gust shoved the car. More winds, more rocking, more ash. I was losing sight of him.

My heart dropped when he disappeared, swallowed by the haze.

Worry preyed on me. I hated this helplessness! Without him in sight, the voices threatened.

I tried to busy myself by studying the bodies around the car. Jackson had told me to pay attention to the newer corpses because "they give you the lay of the land."

At my blank look, he'd explained, "A bullet between the eyes means militia victim. You can tell how recently armed men have passed by. A body that's been beaten or strangled to death? Survival-of-the-fittest killing. Desperate folks are scrapping for resources, so you keep moving. Ain't goan to be no food around. A stab wound to the back? In-house. Family or friends offing each other. Again, keep stepping."

I could recognize the Bagman victims all on my own. Their faces were frozen in horror, their necks savaged. Apparently, a bite was contagious only if one *lived* through the attack.

I would forever keep salt in my hoodie pocket. . . .

—*Red of tooth and claw!*—

—I'll make a feast of your bones!—

I balled my hands into fists, struggling to tamp down the Arcana calls. It took exhausting effort. I'd grown to crave Jackson's presence, just for the peace he brought.

Other kids whispered, new ones:

—I descend upon you like nightfall.—

—Woe to the bloody vanquished!—

I even thought I heard Matthew's voice. *—Crazy like a fox.—*

So *that* was what he'd meant; the phrase was his own call. I'd thought he'd been spouting more gibberish.

And then Death spoke. *—Come to me, Empress. I've waited so long.—* I easily recognized him. He often talked directly to me, leaving my nerves frayed.

I rubbed my arms, hugging them around me miserably. Where was Jackson? What if he never returned? What if there was another piece of sheet metal . . . ?

I heard him just outside the car. Transferring fuel? Then he slammed the container into the back. After fighting to open the driver's-side door, he wedged himself inside the opening and into the seat just before another gust flattened the door behind him.

"Jackson, I was so worried!"

He yanked down his soot-stained bandanna, catching his breath.

The voices faded to a whisper, then . . . gone. As I hurried to open a canteen for him, I wondered if he could tell I was trembling. "I couldn't see you."

He took his time situating the sawed-off shotgun between his seat and the console, then laid his bow close at hand in the backseat. He glowered at the canteen before taking it from me.

After a deep drink, he wiped his sleeve over his mouth. "I kept *you* in sight," he said, his tone curt. He was mad, yet again?

"I'm just saying I was worried."

"Your bodyguard returned in one piece. You might want to look for a better one though. I only got a few gallons. And no food."

He turned on the engine. At once, the windshield wipers scraped the gritty glass, like fingernails on a chalkboard.

"A few gallons is incredible!" I reached over and squeezed one of his gas-stained hands. "We can finally make it to Alabama on that. And we'll find food tonight. I've got a good feeling."

He softened somewhat, digging into his pocket. "Got you this. Might help with the hunger." He offered me an opened pack of Juicy Fruit gum with three pieces left. The same brand my gran always loved.

Realization struck me. Every piece I enjoyed meant that there was one less in the world, never to be replenished. I met his gaze. "Thank you, Jackson."

He shrugged uncomfortably, color flushing across his cheekbones. At that moment, he looked very much like an eighteen-year-old boy.

I couldn't help but smile.

"It ain't like we're engaged or anything," he muttered. "Now let's get the hell out of here. Thought I saw a curtain flutter in a nearby house. We're being watched."

"There're people?" I cried. Sometimes when we sourced for supplies, casing houses, I'd spy a door slamming shut or a figure running in the distance. Unlike Jackson, I didn't believe that everyone was evil. But no one would show their faces. "*Live* people?"

He scowled at me. "Which are the worst kind."

Still, I craned my head around.

"What's your damned fixation with seeing others? I ain't company enough for you?"

And again, he's surly. "Of course you are, it's just—"

"Before you go wishing for someone else to talk to, keep in mind that we're about to drive near a big city—in other words, slaver territory. . . ."

Though we both hated backtracking, we were forced to retrace our route to get to the interstate. Jackson thought backtracking was a tactical error, and I had an OCD thing about it.

We traversed the same speed-bump corpses—*buh-dunk buh-dunk*—

and passed the same spray-painted road sign. Someone had written *Repent!* in red. Beneath it, another person had painted in black *Or WHAT?*

Then, back on the interstate, quiet stretched between us. Blissful quiet. I pulled out a yellowing copy of *Cosmopolitan* from the glove compartment, but found my attention on Jackson instead.

He was lost in thought, holding the wheel with one hand, absently tracing the scars on his knuckles with the other.

Was he still angry that I'd hoped to see other people? Frustrated that we hadn't scored food today?

How could he appear lost in thought *and* restless at the same time?

Over the last several days, I'd learned many new things about my Cajun bodyguard, but everything I'd discovered led to more questions.

I'd learned that he could go for long stretches in total silence. Whereas Brandon had been such an open book—thought to speech with no filter—Jackson kept his musings close to the vest.

What did a boy his age, an apocalypse survivor, think about over the course of the day? Why did he often trace the scars on his hands? Was he remembering old fights?

At other times, I suspected I was better off not knowing what went on in his mind.

I should just savor the quiet. The voices had been vanquished, which meant I was at peace. At least for a little while.

I rested my forehead against the window, staring out at the singed billboards advertising things we could never again buy—a trip to Hawaii, a new computer, permanent hair removal at a spa. Thank God Mel had made me go with her last year when she'd gotten herself lasered.

Pack of gum in hand, I closed my eyes. With each reprieve from the voices, I'd been able to center my thoughts, remembering more of my life before the clinic. During today's lull, I smelled the familiar sweet scent of the gum, my mind drifting to that fateful drive with Gran. . . .

"I'll return you to Haven well before your sixteenth birthday," she said. "Once you've been prepared for your destiny."

My destiny? Mint chocolate chip or butter pecan.

"There's a Tarot pack in my pocketbook," Gran said. "I want you to look at the cards. Really look at them."

"Okay." I rooted through her huge purse, past her gardenia lotion, but I got distracted by bubblegum—

"Evie, the deck."

I nodded, pulling the cards out, slipping some off the top.

"The most elegant cards are the trump cards, the Major Arcana."

"Major whatta?"

"Major Ar-kay-nah. It's Latin for greater secrets. You and I will have our share." She looked sad all of the sudden. "It's the way of our line." Shaking it off, she said, "The details of the images are important. They're to be read like a map."

I saw one card with a winged angel, one with an old man in a robe, one with a lion. A couple of cards had dogs on them.

I was struck by one picture of a fair-haired woman dressed in a poppy-red gown. She had a crown atop her head with twelve stars. Behind her, green and red hills rolled on and on.

Her arms were opened wide as if she wanted a hug, but her gaze looked mean.

Gran changed lanes, peering down at the card. "That's you, Evie. You're the Empress. One day, you'll control all things that root or bloom. You'll smell like them, and they'll recognize your scent."

I half frowned/half grinned up at her. Sometimes Gran said the strangest things. Then I shuffled through another couple of cards . . . until I saw him—a knight in black armor atop a creamy-white mount. The poor horse had bloodshot eyes. I loved horses—

"The details, Evie," Gran said in a sterner voice, checking her rear-view mirror again.

People were kneeling before the knight, crying and pleading. He raised some kind of stick over their heads, and they were scared.

"That one of Death frightens you, doesn't it, sweetheart?" Gran asked. *"Or maybe you get really angry when you look at it . . . ?"*

"Evie, you awake?" Jackson asked me.

I blinked open my eyes, the memory fading. "Yeah, what's up?" God, I could hardly wait to see Gran once more! At last all my maddening questions would be answered.

Jackson opened his mouth to speak. Closed it. Opened it. "Forget it," he finally said.

I shrugged, gazing out the window once more. It hadn't escaped me that Jackson was in the same situation that I was. Once we reached the Outer Banks, he'd have his puzzles solved too.

My secrets were driving him crazy. He'd continued to interrogate me about the crops and the visions. Yesterday he'd said, "If we do make it to North Carolina and we can camp somewhere for a time, what would I need to get for you? So you could make our seeds grow?"

"I'll tell you everything as soon as we get to my grandmother's. Until then, we need to be sourcing for silver bells and cockleshells."

Now he asked me, "Why are you always so quiet around me? You were a chatterbox with other people."

Chatterbox? "How can you say that? You hardly knew me." Oh, wait. Except for the fact that he'd once possessed the source of all-things-Evie.

Brandon's phone. How much had Jackson seen, read, heard? "In any case, I wanted to let you concentrate on driving."

"Uh-huh. You cried out again last night, mumbled some things in your sleep. What'd you dream of? And if you answer 'this and that' one more time, I'm slamming on the brakes."

"I don't remember," I said, even as I recollected my latest nightmare of the witch. All of them seemed to be from the same day, from nearly the same location. In this one, she'd been traveling the countryside with a besotted young admirer. He'd angered her over something. So— *of course*—she'd decided on murder.

"Come. Touch," she'd murmured to him. When he'd tripped

over his feet to reach her, she'd opened up her palm and a flower had grown—from her skin. With a sensual wink, she'd blown him a kiss across the bloom, releasing deadly spores.

He'd started choking, dropping to her feet. His skin had swelled until it split open in places. Putrid boils welled and spurted. She'd gazed on, cheerfully telling him, *"How artfully we plants beckon; how perfectly we punish. . . ."*

Each day, I hated her more. Then I frowned. "Jackson, what did you hear me mumble in my sleep?"

"You said, 'Come touch.' I thought this was a fine idea, until you added, 'But you'll pay a price.' What was that about?"

The admirable deviousness of briars. "I can't imagine."

"Liar." He glanced into the rearview mirror. "What's it goan to take to get you to trust me, huh?"

"Don't know," I said honestly. I wished I did. How badly I yearned to be able to confide in another! Maybe just to have a friend again? At least, one who was physically present.

But I didn't need to give Jackson more reason to ditch me. Though he'd accepted the visions easily enough, my hearing voices was a different matter altogether. My repeated nightmares of cold-blooded murder . . .

"You're always scouting for other folks, but you doan talk to the one you're with," he said. "Guess I ain't worth the bother."

"Maybe I'd talk to you more, if you weren't mean to me all the time."

"Mean? When? Is this because of the sunglasses?"

My old Coach ones were so scratched I could barely see through them. I'd sourced aviator glasses—still on a body. Again and again, I'd circled the stabbed corpse—definitely in-house—wanting those glasses so badly. Jackson had ordered, "You get your ass over there, Evangeline, and you pluck those off! Right now!"

"Yes, *mean*," I insisted. "How about when I forgot my bug-out bag that *one* time. You went off!"

"If I doan treat you with kid gloves, it's for good reason."

Kid gloves? Please. In the early days of our trip, he'd been decent but distant. But as the worst of my grief ebbed, his surliness increased.

If he ever came upon me sniffling with sadness or not eating when we did have food or not sleeping, he took it as a personal affront. "Bed not soft enough for you, princess?" he'd sneer, though I'd never complained. "Food not up to your standards?"

He especially didn't like it when I was quiet or lost in thought. Even though he was often the same.

Recalling all the times he'd appeared restless, I figured that he simply hated being cooped up in a car with me, being *saddled* with me. We were stuck together, watching the windshield wipers scrape, listening to the same iPod songs over and over.

Most of the tracks were from Mel's playlists. Oddly, Jackson didn't enjoy endless rap remixes of Alanis Morissette.

God, I miss that girl like an ache, like I miss Mom. . . .

Still stewing over my accusation of meanness, Jackson said, "You ain't perfect yourself, *peekôn*. You get your feelings hurt like this"—he snapped his fingers—"and you woan tell me anything about you. Most close-lipped girl I ever knew."

"Why am *I* always the one getting interrogated? You've rarely talked about yourself since we've been on the road." Yes, I had secrets, but he had such a huge advantage over me—Brandon's phone!

"Ask me something," Jackson said, though his grip on the steering wheel tightened, as if he were bracing for a punch.

"Okay. Was the cage-the-rage rumor true? Did you really go to prison?" If so, he might understand some of what my experience at CLC had been like.

Anger flared in his expression. "You got to go for the slam at every opportunity."

"What are you talking about? I asked for a reason."

"Which is to remind me of my place!"

"Jackson, I'm astonished you can walk upright with that chip on your shoulder."

"How about asking what my favorite book is? Or what class I liked best?"

"I figured you liked English a lot, and I thought *Robinson Crusoe* was your favorite book."

In a menacingly low voice, he said, "Sometimes I forget, me, that you were in my house."

"Fine, I'll try again. So, Jackson, what had you planned to do after high school?"

He slid me a narrowed glance. "Open a chop shop. Steal cars for parts. Isn't that what you expect me to say?"

"Forget I asked."

"What were you goan to do, then?"

"Marry Brandon, have a couple of rich brats, play tennis all day. Isn't that what you expected me to say?"

He seemed to be strangling the steering wheel. At least his hands had healed. When I'd insisted on cleaning and bandaging them last week, he'd been gruff, but I thought he secretly liked someone fussing over him.

Because it was such a rarity?

When I'd finished dressing them, he'd grumbled, "Surprised you didn't kiss 'em better." So I did, pressing a quick kiss to each bandage, just to shock him. Instead, his voice had grown husky as he'd called me *"ma belle infirmière."* My pretty nurse . . .

His moods were so changeable. That night he'd been flirtatious. Now he was brooding, filled with tension.

It seemed like the harder I tried to be nice to him, to make him happy, the more it backfired on me.

Silence stretched between us again. Until my stomach growled.

Jackson cast me another scowl. I'd also learned that the sound of my hunger really bothered him, as if I were pestering him for food.

"We're not eating for hours yet, princess." He knew I hated it when he called me that. "We agreed to keep heading for Atlanta, Evie. And we knew it'd be lean."

"I'm *not* complaining. I have never complained."

"No, but that stomach of yours is. I almost wish you'd start bitching at me." His knuckles were now white on the wheel.

"What good would that do?"

"It's better than you sitting here seething all day."

"Seething? Hardly!" He didn't understand. I could roll with a lot of punches now that the voices were quieted. "I was in a *great* mood earlier."

"Bullshit! Over what? You're exhausted, starving, and you doan know where your next meal's coming from."

"You didn't get decapitated by sheet metal and we scored some fuel. Win!"

"But no *food*." The wipers scraped louder across the windshield. *Grate, grate, grate . . .*

I threw my hands up. "All right, you talked me into it. I'm officially in a pissy mood."

"Damn it, you doan need to miss meals." Early on, he'd been giving me the lion's share, calling me a "growing girl."

As he'd explained: "Hell, Evie, I like where you're goan with this"—he'd motioned to indicate my chest—"I want to see where you end up."

Now he muttered, "Thought I'd be shooting some game." On occasion, we'd see a bird or a rabbit. "And you ain't exactly contributing to the pot."

No, but I *could*. If things got really bad, I'd grow food from the seeds in the back. Refusing to rise to the bait, I said, "It's getting late." The winds were dying down as the sun set. The ash started to settle, revealing a waxing moon. "Shouldn't we be looking for a place to overnight?"

"We need to get past this area. The gas took longer than I thought." He glanced over his shoulder, then back to the road, picking up speed. "Sick of these storms."

"What about the Bagmen? You said we can never drive past sundown." This afternoon, we'd crossed bridge after bridge. If they flocked to old bodies of water, at night . . .

"I'm changing the rule, adding: unless we're in slaver territory. We got to make up some time anyway."

My stomach growled more insistently.

"Suck it up, Evie! We can't risk looking for food right now. If anything happens to me, you're screwed."

"One more time, I'm not arguing with you about food, I'm not complaining, and I might surprise you by actually surviving without you."

"You can't hunt or ferret out supplies. You're a resource-suck. You're hopeless in the kitchen—"

"Here we go again." I could deny nothing. I was awful at cooking, couldn't seem to heat a can of ravioli without screwing it up.

"You should end each and every day with a 'Thank you, Jack. It's great to be alive.'" Another glance over his shoulder, another increase in speed.

"Clearly, I'm just a nuisance to you, a ball and chain around your ankle. I'm surprised you haven't gotten sick of me and dumped me already. I keep waiting for you to say, 'Screw this,' and ditch on North Carolina."

"I doan let puzzles go unsolved."

Which is why I won't tell you about the crops until you've gotten me where I need to go.

"Besides"—he flashed me a wolfish grin—"I ain't even slept with you yet."

My lips parted. "You're talking about having . . . sex. With *me*?"

I should have known this conversation would arise soon enough. It seemed like each night together, Jackson and I had grown *less* comfortable with each other.

If he felt relatively secure with our overnight, he'd sleep without a shirt. Those tantalizing glimpses of his chest—I always looked away—flustered me, making it difficult to sleep.

At other times, I'd cast wary glances at the bed, while he cast hungry looks at me.

"*Sex* is what you sit in this car thinking about?" Just as I'd suspected, I was better off not knowing.

His expression was bored, as if to say *Grow up*. "Why wouldn't I? I'm a red-blooded male, and you're the only game in town. Tell me you doan think about it."

I had. I'd fantasized about what might have happened at the sugar mill if we'd kissed, if we'd explored that sizzling chemistry between us. Then I would feel guilty and out of sorts. "I-I'm not having sex with you!" I finally answered. "I can't believe you would just put it out there like that."

Though I knew the world was different now, I still held on to the naïve idea that losing my virginity should be special—something I did with my boyfriend.

Not something I did solely because the guy with me was red-blooded.

He flashed me a knowing look, with a wicked glint in his eyes. "So you doan deny thinking about it?"

I sputtered. "That's the main reason you volunteered to help me—because you wanted to make me one of your *gaiennes*, one of your doe tags!"

"*De bon cœur.*" Wholeheartedly.

"All that bullshit about remembering the bayou and *Why-whoever-will-I-talk-Cajun-to?* was just lip service. You couldn't care less if we speak the same language or share a history!"

"I told you the truth. It's not my fault all that comes in a pretty blond package that I want to take to bed—"

BOOM! BOOM! Explosions sounded just outside.

The car careened out of control. He stomped the brakes, but we rushed toward an embankment.

My hands shot forward to grip the dashboard. "*Jackson!*"

23

"Hold on, Evie!" he yelled, arms straining as he fought the steering wheel.

The car swept up that embankment sideways—a ramp launching us off the ground.

Then . . . weightlessness. Jackson surrendered the wheel, shoving his arm over my chest. The engine revved as we rolled in the air.

My feet were above my head. When the ground suddenly punched the top of the car, I screamed; airbags deployed.

Still we plummeted . . . rolling . . .

Sudden *stop*. The car landed upside down. Windows shattered on impact, metal shrieking from strain.

Jackson and I hung from our seat belts. And it'd sounded like we'd landed on another car?

Even over the wheezing gaskets, our breaths were loud. "Wh-what just happened?" I peered out the window opening, disoriented. We were off the ground, by at least half a dozen feet.

At once, Jackson's buck knife flashed out, stabbing the airbags. "I hope you got your bug-out bag packed right. Now stay still."

"You're *not* going to cut my seat—"

He cut my seat belt.

"Ow!" I scrambled upright, hunching down on the roof of the car.

Then he cut his own belt, twisting to his back. "Evie, grab your bag and shut your mouth! You hear me?"

I reached back, rummaging until I laid hands on my pack. "What is going on?"

"We're in a heap of trouble." He grabbed his own pack, his bow, and the shotgun, then shimmied out through the window hole. Jumping down, he hurried to help me out.

As we crawled free from the wreck, comprehension dawned. We'd landed on an old car. All around us were more wrecked vehicles.

A graveyard of cars.

At once, flashlight beams started bouncing toward us. What sounded like a . . . *dog* bayed. While I marveled that one still lived, Jackson raised the shotgun, cocking it.

His lips were thin with fury, his gaze murderous.

"Those people aren't coming to help?" I whispered. "Maybe th-they know that road is dangerous."

"They ain't coming to help. They're slavers coming to hunt. They were just laying in wait."

Oh my God.

He gazed from the group nearing on our right—to the forbidding ruins of a forest to our left. Then his expression grew determined.

He gripped my upper arm and hauled me toward the murky tree line. I struggled to keep up, but mud—actual mud—was sucking at my boots. Which meant moisture.

Which meant Bagmen.

"Jackson, we can't go into that forest," I murmured between breaths, glancing over my shoulder. The men were gaining. In the erratic light, I could make out a few of them, regular dressed middle-aged guys. No manacles at the ready. They looked so . . . *normal.*

"Not a forest. Used to be a wooded swamp."

"What if those people *do* want to help us?"

"It was a trap." With one hand, Jackson swapped out the gun for his bow, bolting an arrow in place. "A spike strip took out all four tires. These cars were all wrecked on purpose."

"They wouldn't!"

"Oh, yeah. They might be too scared to follow us. An old swamp's probably full of Baggers."

"Forget that! You can't convince me that we'd be better off in there!"

He squeezed my arm. "The ones who set the trap are slavers—at best. At least the Bagmen usually go right for the throat."

I gaped, letting him lead me away from the approaching lights, the yelling men.

As soon as we plunged past the tree line, sounds echoed all around us. A snapping twig. The rustle of sooty leaves.

Dead branches crackled just to our left. Jackson released me with a shove, whirling around with his bow at the ready. "Run, Evie!"

With a cry, I stumbled forward. But scorched vines littered the ground, slowing my retreat.

Though I had no idea where I was going, I struggled on. The rising moon streamed shafts of light through the leafless trees. Shadows wavered all around me.

Where was Jackson? I'd never been more terrified. Had never felt more vulnerable . . .

—*I watch you like a hawk.*—

—*Blood will tell, blood will run.*—

—*Don't look at this hand, look at that one.*—

"No, no! Shut up, shut up!" *Slice.* Pain flared in my palms.

I gazed down, didn't know whether to laugh or cry. My thorns had grown back. Staring at my claws, I burst into a clearing, glanced up. Three Bagmen were mere feet from me.

I drew up short with a gasp. One stood while two smaller ones crawled on hands and knees, *licking* the mud.

Their heads swung in my direction.

They were even more horrific than in my visions. Pus seeped from their eyes, glistening in the moonlight. Their irises were as pale as cream. And their skin . . . battered and creased all over, like wadded-up paper sacks—but so slimy.

Blood and filth stained their slack mouths, their tattered clothes.

The standing one's runny gaze landed on my throat. With a shuffling gait, it lurched toward me. I backed away. Did I dare scream for Jackson? Were there more behind me?

The creature was picking up speed. In a panic, I dug into my hoodie pocket for salt, slicing the lining with a claw. My supply of salt began drizzling away, sand from an hourglass.

I managed to salvage a handful. Aimed it at the Bagman. Threw it as hard as I could.

Would the crystals sear its skin, blind it . . . ?

The salt dropped uselessly to the ground well in front of it.

Shit, shit! My gaze darted once more—

I heard a *twang.* An arrow suddenly jutted from the big one's right eye.

As the creature's body collapsed, a hand covered my mouth from behind. I jerked with fright, but Jackson whispered at my ear, *"Quiet."*

When I nodded, he released me to loose two more arrows, dispatching the remaining pair.

Three monsters, dropped like carnival targets. I'd seen his skill at fighting, but I'd never seen him shoot.

Yet as I was staring up at him with undisguised awe, he was frowning down at me. "Evie, what's on your face?"

"I don't know, ash? Did those men follow?"

He blinked his eyes. "No. But there'll be more Baggers in the hours till dawn. I need those arrows." He started for the ones he'd killed, but murmured over his shoulder, "You stick to me like a shadow, you."

Before, I'd bristled when he gave me that order. Now I whispered, "Not a problem, Jackson."

24

"Didn't you tell me you had a *good* feeling about tonight?" Jackson muttered as he shot yet another Bagman straggler.

After he'd taken out the first trio, we'd holed up in a dense stand of dead and fallen trees, protected on three sides. Jackson was guarding the fourth.

"Damn, Evie, what kind of psychic are you?" he asked when he rose to collect his arrow.

Might not be one whatsoever, jury's still out, I thought as I hurried to stay right behind him.

But I hesitated to approach the creature. Up close, it was even more revolting than in my drawings, with old blood running down its mouth and neck like a painted-on beard. Its mucousy-looking skin shed globs of reeking slime all around it.

If they were constantly excreting this stuff, no wonder they were always thirsty.

I could scarcely believe that this thing used to be a person. But it wore ragged jeans, a concert T-shirt, and one Timberland boot. A teenage boy.

Now Jackson's arrow jutted from its eye. Did the Cajun never miss?

"Remember how it smells, girl," he told me.

"It's rotten." When I was little, I'd had a dog who was addicted to rolling in the remains of dead animals. No amount of shampoo could erase the rancid scent. That was what I was smelling now.

"You grab the arrow, I'll move the body," he said, but still I hesitated. In the harsh tone he'd taken to using with me, Jackson snapped, "Over here, Evie. *Now.* I'll be damned if I'm goan to let you be scared of a *dead* Bagman."

Let me? Had he been so mean for days just to . . . toughen me up? Like a drill sergeant getting me ready for war?

Or possibly because I was getting on his *last* nerve. "Fine." I plodded forward.

Holding my breath, I reached for the short arrow, tugging at the end, but it wouldn't come out.

"*Yank* it, princess."

With a glare, I yanked harder, until it came free with a bubbling rush of red goo.

As I shoved the back of my hand against my mouth, working not to vomit, Jackson said, "This one fed recently. Otherwise it'd be chalkier."

I still couldn't believe I'd been face to face with these things. I could've been bitten. Hell, I could've died in the wreck or been captured!

Of course, the night was still young. . . .

When he started dragging the corpse away from our hideout, I asked, "Why are you doing that?"

"Bagmen drink their fallen. Not goan to invite them to a happy hour."

Learn something new from Jackson every day. "Are you certain their skin's not contagious?"

"I know it ain't with *me.* Just to be safe, you doan touch it, no." Taking the arrow from me, Jackson wiped it on the sole of his boot, then returned it to his bow's magazine clip.

Back in the dead-tree hideout, I said, "If I get bitten—"

"You will have my arrow in your brainpan directly, doan you worry," he said without a nanosecond of hesitation.

"Well. Good to know." I wondered if I could regenerate from a bite. *May I never have to find out.* "When the Bagmen go find shelter, will those men come for us?"

"Let's hope a windstorm dusts up," he said, never taking his alert gaze off the woods. "Their dog woan be able to track us."

"They looked like regular people." I could almost imagine they'd been part of a community watch on the trail of criminals, like I should've stopped and said, "They went thattaway!"

"Jackson, why'd they wreck all those cars?" And why'd they have to wreck ours? Right when we had some gas in the tank.

All our water, our seeds . . . gone.

"It's an easy way to provision," he said. "They're probably wanting women, too. I think that's half the problem."

"What's that supposed to mean?"

"Nothing."

"Tell me," I insisted.

"Everywhere I go, I meet crazy-ass *coo-yôns*. I've only run into one or two solid characters since the Flash. You remember when you asked me how everything went bad so quick? I think the lack of women is fuel to the fire."

I rolled my eyes. "Ohhh, men are now bad because they have, like, masculine 'needs' or some other crock?"

"I ain't making excuses for 'em. Just think you women civilize us men. Without you around, we . . . devolve or something."

Huh. His explanation made as much sense as anything I could come up with. "Jackson, I think you're a lot smarter than I gave you credit for."

He faced me with a scowl. When he realized I was serious, he said, "You'd keep me as a history podna now?"

Again, I thought that this was something he should've already forgotten. At least enough that it wasn't worth a mention. Still I said, *"Sans doute."* Without a doubt.

I could tell that pleased him. "You should try to rest up, *ange*."

There was no chance of sleep. "I can help you keep watch."

He gave a soft laugh. "I told you—nothing can get the drop on me. *Nothing.*"

"Wow. If only you felt confident on that score."

"I spent my whole life watching my six." At my frown, he said, "Watching my back."

I recalled that drunk man barreling into Jackson's house, a threat coming out of the blue. Had others come quietly? *"I sleep with one eye open,"* Jackson had once said.

And his comment about crawling to the hospital on Sunday mornings after being kicked in the ribs? I'd just assumed he was referring to injuries from his wild Saturday night bar brawls.

Or had he been talking about an earlier time in his life, when he'd been a scared little boy, beaten by his mother's drunken . . . *dates?*

Maybe that was why he traced his scars. They might be records of near misses or hard-earned victories. No wonder he could be so brutal.

I felt a spike of shame that I'd judged him for thrashing that man in his home. No more.

"Evie, bed down." Scanning the dark, he murmured, "You doan have to be scared. I've got you."

You do, don't you? Here we were in the Bagmen's lair, and I wasn't terrified for my life. Jackson would kill any that strayed too close. In fact, they should fear him.

I was with the boy that monsters should fear.

The idea was liberating. We were carless, with nearly zero supplies, fresh from a wreck and trapped in a swamp filled with bloodthirsty zombies—and yet I was beginning to feel optimistic.

As long as he had that bow, maybe *we* were the bogeymen.

I shrugged off my bug-out bag, marveling at how relieved I was to have it now. Because of Jackson riding my ass, I still had my flash drive, a full canteen, my jewelry, another change of clothes, some energy gel-packs and more. "I'm actually *not* scared. Can you believe it? If there was ever a time for me to be . . ."

"Maybe you're in shock."

"Maybe I'm safe with you." Grinning softly, I told him, "Thank you, Jackson, it's great to be alive."

"Smart-ass," he grated, but the corners of his lips quirked.

Curling up in the ashy leaves, using my bag as a pillow, I watched him. I'd always found him physically attractive, but not to the degree that girls like Catherine had.

Tonight I was starting to see why she'd sighed over him.

The moonlight illuminated his chiseled cheekbones and his black, black hair. His gorgeous eyes gleamed. He hadn't shaved in a few days, but the stubble only added to his looks.

When he turned his head, listening for something, I admired his profile, his strong chin and straight nose.

He was focused and ruthless, and seeing him like this made *me* want to sigh.

Never in a million years could I have imagined that Jackson Deveaux would end up being my protector, a refuge from the voices, and a . . . friend.

If I wasn't careful, I'd do something incredibly stupid, like fall for him.

He must have noticed me regarding him so closely. "Get some sleep."

"I'm too keyed up from the wreck. Never been in one before. Have you?"

"Motorcycle wrecks all the time. Hell, you almost made me crash."

"Me?"

Again his lips curled. "That first morning I saw you, I could barely take my eyes off your ass in that little dress." He scrubbed a hand over his mouth, as if he was remembering the sight even now.

Which made my breath hitch. I couldn't tell if I was flattered, embarrassed, or excited.

"Then I got a gander of that face of yours. Nearly hit a pothole and took a header over the handlebars, me." He shot me a glance, looking like he regretted saying so much.

Definitely flattered and excited—

He suddenly tensed. In an instant, he'd taken aim and shot his bow.

When I heard a thud in the distance, I swallowed. "You move the body, I'll get the arrow."

He helped me to my feet. "Now, Evangeline, I *know* you ain't about to leave that bag behind."

Once we'd returned from our tasks and settled back in again, I told him, "Jackson, I meant what I said earlier. Thank you for saving me tonight."

Another sideways glance to see if I was serious. "If you truly want to thank me, you'll tell me a secret."

Part of me did feel like I owed it to him, but on the other hand . . . "You already know so much more about me than I do about you. You investigated my room, all my belongings—down to my panty drawer."

He made a low *ooom* sound of agreement. "That I did."

"And you had Brandon's cell phone. Did you go through it?"

"Why would I?" he muttered, not denying either.

"I'm embarrassed by what you were able to see and read." And hear.

He just stared out into the night, sharing nothing of what was going on in that mysterious mind of his. But I could feel the tension rolling off him.

Finally he said, "Did you . . . did you really want to get hitched to Radcliffe? Have kids and play tennis?"

"I'd planned to leave Sterling as soon as possible," I said honestly. "Go to college at Vandy or UT Austin."

"Leave that boy behind?" At once, Jackson's mood seemed to improve.

"I was getting out, one way or another."

"Then maybe it wasn't true love on your part, no?"

I kind of wished it *had* been. I felt guilty that I hadn't been in love with Brandon, as if I hadn't appreciated how good our lives were, at least before I'd been sent away. "I don't want to talk about him anymore."

"Then tell me where you really were last summer, when you dropped off the face of the earth. You weren't at a special school, were you?"

Two realizations struck me—Jackson was one of the most perceptive people I'd ever met. And he'd studied every byte of data on that phone.

Surely he would notice that my text messages to Brandon had gone from countless to zero overnight—until the rare texts began to arrive over the summer. On the exact same days of the month, at the same time.

Though I'd told no one where I was, a clever boy could figure out that I'd been locked up *somewhere*. "No way I'm talking about that, Jackson. Not until you divvy."

He looked to be growing uneasy again, like he'd prefer facing an army of Bagmen over talking about himself.

"We don't have to do this," I assured him. "We don't have to get to know each other—even though we're on the road together and we might die tomorrow. As soon as we get to North Carolina, I'll tell you all my deepest, darkest secrets, and you can leave, still a stranger to me. If that's what you want."

He exhaled a gust of breath. "Ask, then." He dragged his flask out of his own bag, as if in readiness.

Surprised he was cooperating, I sat up. "What did you really want to do after school?"

"A podna of mine worked on an oil rig off the coast of Mexico. Eight-week stints. Great money." He flashed me a rueful grin. "*No* girls. I was goan to send money to Clotile, and she'd look after my *mère*." In a more somber tone, he added, "We had it all figured out."

A boy with hopes, dreams, and a *Spanish for Beginners* book. Just as I'd wondered all those months ago, he *had* planned on getting out of that hellhole. "You said Clotile . . . that she might be your sister. Do you know who your father was?"

"I knew *of* him, more like. Only met him once."

"Why?"

"He was too busy spoiling his legitimate son to spend time with me—or to send a single dime to *ma mère*. Told her he wouldn't admit culpability or some bullshit."

"Sounds like a lawyer."

With a contemplative swig of his flask, Jackson muttered, "Heh." Cajun for *Huh. You think so?* "By the time I learned I could nail his ass with a paternity suit, I was more concerned with telling him where to shove his money." His hand tightened around the bow stock. "I knew who my *père* was, but Clotile could only narrow hers down to three or so. My father made the short list. Blood or no, she was a sister to me."

"I'm sorry you lost her."

"And what about your dad?" he asked, changing the subject.

Another thing I'd learned about the Cajun? He didn't like messy emotions. His go-to response for just about every situation tended to be pure anger, with a side of action.

"I never knew my father," I said. "He disappeared when I was young. Went into the bayou on a fishing trip and never came back."

Jackson looked like he had an opinion on that, but wisely kept it to himself. "Am I done now?"

"Please tell me why you were on parole."

Another shrug. "One of my ex-stepfathers wouldn't take *non* for an answer. He terrified *ma mère*. And he paid for it." The fierce protectiveness in his gaze was staggering.

So Clotile hadn't been the only woman he cared about who'd been abused?

"I did to him what you saw me do to that other man—and then some."

"Bagasse?"

He nodded. "Knew I'd get sentenced; didn't care. He somehow pulled through, but he'd never be able to hurt another woman."

As I wondered what that meant, Jackson said, "Now can we get back to your summer away?"

He'd shared so much with me that I supposed I could at least tell him this. And hadn't I yearned to talk to someone about these things? But I didn't want him to look at me like those docs had. Because at some point in the last nine days, Jackson's opinion of me had become important—

"You went to a nuthouse, didn't you?"

"Wh-why would you guess that?"

"If anybody else saw that journal of yours, you'd have been sent up for true."

I glared. "Or maybe you guessed that because you saw my texts to Brandon, and put things together."

"You told me there was a reason you'd asked about me going to prison. I think it was 'cause you got locked up too, only you were with all the *fous*." Lunatics.

"Ugh! You are such a dick!"

"*Shh.*" His gaze darted, body tensing before he gradually settled down once more.

I never should have sidled around this subject with him! Now he thought I was mental.

"You go in for the visions—or the voices?"

I just stifled a gasp. "What . . . how did you know about the voices?" Why was I bothering to hide *anything* from this boy?

"I'm not stupid, Evie. I've caught you talking to yourself. A lot. Muttering for someone to leave you alone or begging them to shut up."

"I don't . . . it's not like that."

"Then what *is* it like?"

"Why should I tell you anything? You'll just make fun of me again," I pointed out, even as I was nearly shaking with the need to unload. "You'll call me a lunatic."

"I never called you a lunatic. I'm not making fun."

Did I dare confide this to him? I bit my bottom lip. "I'm not talking to myself—I'm talking to others. I do hear voices, tons of them. They all sound like they're kids our age."

"Do you think they're real?" he asked in a neutral tone.

I sighed, nodding. "And I feel like I'm connected to them somehow. Like we share a hive mind or something."

"Pardon?"

"Hive mind. Like how bees communicate."

"You're starting to confuse and unsettle me, Evangeline," he said, but strangely, he didn't look either at all. Did nothing faze him? "What they say to you?"

"Sometimes nothing but gibberish. Sometimes I hear these phrases repeated over and over. A girl says, 'Behold the Bringer of Doubt.' This Irish kid always says, 'Eyes to the skies, lads, I strike from above.' It gives me chills."

Jackson studied my expression, probably reading me like a book, while I gleaned nothing from him. Would he be even more likely to cut his losses now, to ditch the mental girl? "Why do you think it's happening?"

"I don't know. That's the reason I have to get to Gran. She will have all the answers."

"Is *she* psychic?"

Good question. "I honestly don't know. She could be." Or maybe she'd learned all this Arcana stuff from her own mother, information handed down through the generations.

Hadn't Gran told me she herself was a *chronicler*? Matthew had mentioned something about it as well.

"If your grandmother knows so much, then why the hell didn't she teach you before she packed up for the beach?" Jackson said. "Let me guess: There was some secret passing-down-the-baton ceremony on your sixteenth birthday that never came about—"

"She was sent away when I was eight. Everybody said she was insane. I was forbidden to talk about what she'd taught me."

"You *have* to remember something."

"Not enough. I was forbidden even to think about her."

"Nobody can control what you think about," Jackson said.

I gave a bitter laugh. "Oh, but they *can*." I recalled sitting at a cold metal table with my primary shrink. I'd glanced down, confused to see a puddle of saliva pooling. Even when dosed so heavily—with a billion milligrams of don't-give-a-shit drugs pumping through me—I'd been *humiliated* to realize the drool was coming from me. He'd asked, *"Evie, do you understand why you must reject your grandmother's teachings . . . ?"*

Jackson slid his gaze to me. "They get into that head of yours?"

How to tell him I'd been drugged to within an inch of my life in an echoing ward, then hypnotized until I could barely remember my name?

No, not *hypnotized*—that might've been beneficial. Hypnosis that made things worse? That was called *brainwashing*.

"Yes," I said simply. *Let's see how he likes that for an answer.*

He let it drop. "So, do you hear voices right now?" When I eventually nodded, he did a double take. "Like *right* now?"

"Don't look at me like I'm a freak, Jackson. I hate that look!" I squeezed my eyes shut, mortified. His nuthouse and *fous* cracks hadn't helped things.

Why had I revealed so much to him?

Oh yeah, because he'd shared with me. One difference: I didn't judge him.

"Did you just get your feelings hurt again? Damn, *cher*, I doan know my way around this with you."

I opened my eyes but wouldn't look at him. "Around what?"

"Being with a girl like you." Now I had to raise my brows at him. "Yeah, with your *bebins* and your girly ways. You got soft hands, and you're . . . soft. *But* I doan think you're a freak."

"How could you not?" I imagined what Brandon's reaction might have been if he were the one here with me tonight. Would he be able to handle my confession? Then I remembered that I probably wouldn't have survived this long without Jackson.

"Look, Evie, I saw some things before the Flash, things that couldn't be explained. Hell, my grand*mère* was rumored to be a *traiteuse*."

A kind of Cajun medicine woman. "Really?"

He nodded. "After the Flash, I'm ready to believe just about anything.

Do these voices make me uneasy? *Mais* yeah. Am I itching to know what causes them? *Ouais.* But that doan mean I think less of you for hearing them." He curled his forefinger under my chin, until our eyes met—and I could see he was telling the truth. "Just glad you told me a secret." He canted his head. "Though you got a thousand more, *non?*"

So many more.

One of those voices belongs to Death on a pale horse, and he wants to kill me. I communicate "clairaudiently" with a crazy boy who gives me nosebleeds when he thinks I'm not listening hard enough. Just about every morning, I wake up to the scent of blood and the sound of agonized screams.

My gaze dropped, and he lowered his hand.

"What're the voices saying now?"

"They're quiet enough to ignore," I said. "When I'm around others, they pipe down." I peered up at him from under a lock of hair and admitted, "But never as much as they've done around you."

"Evangeline," he sighed. "It ain't ever goan to be easy with you, is it?"

Though I feared more and more that he would get sick of me and leave one day, I answered honestly, "Nope."

25

DAY 235 A.F.

DEEPER IN MISSISSIPPI

"Do you need to slow down?" Jackson yelled over the winds.

I shook my head, wanting to continue on. We'd left Haven almost two weeks ago; I was beginning to fear we'd never get out of this state.

Bandannas over our faces and sunglasses in place, we meandered through another deserted town, with a windstorm whipping around us—and tremors beneath our feet.

Lucky for us, the storms had become more sporadic and shorter, lasting just an hour or two a day. A blessing, since we remained carless.

Even if Jackson could fix a vehicle, the tank would be empty.

On foot, we'd started seeing gaunt-cheeked survivors every now and then, peeking out from behind barricaded windows. Much to Jackson's annoyance, I always gave them a tentative wave. But none of them had wanted anything to do with us. . . .

"You stay right behind me," he said now, pressing on. He would always walk first, blocking the wind for me, insisting I draft behind him.

During the worst part of the storms, I would curl my forefinger around one of his belt loops, which always seemed to amuse him.

I did so now, dumbly following his broad back down yet another "main" street. During daylight hours, Jackson usually had the shotgun in hand, with his bow and bag slung over his shoulders.

Today, he also carried something far more exciting—

Without warning, my head started to pound. My nose itched.
Matthew.

My bandanna was continually bloody on the inside, courtesy of his
appearances. Jackson might keep the voices in check, but Matthew
showed whenever.

And with each visit I'd become more convinced that he was, in fact,
sending me visions. I didn't believe I'd ever been clairvoyant. He was
the only one with that talent.

Now blood began trickling to my upper lip. These moving visions
were the worst. I'd learned to just keep walking, even when Jackson
disappeared and all I could see around me was Matthew's basement.

—*Find me, friend.*—

I clamped my lips shut, willing myself not to speak out loud. *I told
you, I have to find my gran first. Where are you, anyway?*

—*On your way.*—

Truly? What city are you in?

—*Arcana means secrets; keep ours.*—

I don't understand. If I had a can of ravioli for every time I told
Matthew that . . .

—*Have you seen the red witch?*—

Unfortunately, I dream about her all the time. Is she alive today?

—*She arises. She's coming for you. The Empress fights the red witch.
Learn her strengths and weaknesses.*—

Do you expect me to face her?

—*Evie, you must be ready.*—

Apparently. *God, why do I put up with you?*

—*The same reason I put up with you.*—

Which is?

—*We are friends.*—

Once he was gone, I furtively washed the blood away with water
from my canteen. I'd just finished as the storm faded. When the ash
settled over the town, the temperature began to rise on the shade-free
street. The odor of refuse boiled up from the ground.

I unzipped my hoodie and pulled down my bandanna, surveying the area. I could see so much more around me. Not necessarily a good thing.

Of course there were bodies. But it was worse than that. . . .

Over his shoulder, Jackson muttered to me, "Bedlam."

I was beginning to understand his compulsion to solve puzzles. Every few feet, a new mystery taunted me.

An eighteen wheeler lay *atop* a house. On my right, someone had painstakingly nailed a wedding dress and veil to a front door. A dingy sleeve waved in the wind.

To my left, a dead man and young boy were positioned in a front yard, as if they'd been making snow angels in the ash right up to the end.

On the side of a dumpster, someone had spray-painted: *Eye of a hurricane, listen to yourself churn* . . . Whatever.

I struggled to assign meaning to things, to read clues. But post-Flash, little made sense. I had to wonder if Jackson might not be right, that maybe everyone was bad now. Or at least crazy.

Up ahead, there was a moaning Bagman, chained by the neck to a refrigerator, crawling in place, its pants rotting off. Who in their right mind would think chaining up a Bagman was a good idea?

Its skin was chalkier than the ones I'd seen in the swamp, and it moaned louder.

Jackson paused before it, offering me his crossbow. "Shoot it."

I shook my head.

"Come on, it'll do you some good to take one out."

"No, Jackson." Did I think the Bagman needed to live? Not at all. But I didn't want to be the one dispatching it. What if I . . . *liked* killing it?

The witch enjoyed killing more than anything. *I'm all about life.*

With a scowl at me, Jackson shot it in the temple, then retrieved his arrow. Great. He was mad again.

But he surprised me a short while later, when we had to cut through the cracked open fuselage of a jumbo jet. He took my hand, helping me over the debris. I grimaced at the bodies still fastened into seat belts, still hunched in a crash position.

"Hell on earth, huh?" he asked when we were clear.

I nodded shakily. "About the only way to describe it."

"You know, at first, I wanted you to see stuff like this all the time, so you'd get harder."

My drill sergeant. "And now?"

"Now I wish you never needed to get harder. But it's just goan to keep getting worse," he said, continuing on.

I believed that. I'd be even more despairing over our circumstances if it wasn't for the knowledge that every step took us closer to North Carolina—that and my growing fascination with Jackson.

It was mind-boggling to me that I'd known him at school and had never guessed how remarkable he might be.

Unfortunately, my fascination was slipping toward infatuation. I told myself it would never work between us—best not to complicate things.

So why had I been absolutely thrilled when Jackson had begun *carrying my bag*?

Last night, we'd been forced to stay in a library—one of those fire-exit capitals—but at least this one had been locked up. As we'd meandered through the stacks with his windup flashlight, I'd teased him, "You carried my bag today. Does that mean you like me, Jackson? Hmm? Isn't that what a *beau* does?"

His shoulders had stiffened at my tone. "Or maybe I help you along because you would slow me down otherwise."

"Oh," I'd said, on the verge of getting my feelings hurt "like that." But then I'd wondered if maybe Jackson had snapped at me because I'd found a chink in his tarnished armor.

Which would mean that he *did* like me, and did think of himself as my beau.

That would also explain why he got so mad whenever my stomach growled. A boy like Jackson would be protective of any girl he thought "belonged" to him, and frustrated that he couldn't provide for her.

Of course, this was all speculation. More likely, as Jackson repeatedly told me, I just didn't understand boys whatsoever.

After all, why *would* he like me? I was still the same old Evie, the one he'd ridiculed and cursed. I wasn't exactly this team's critical asset. On the road, my skill set consisted of fussing over any injuries he sustained, biting back every complaint, and occasionally speaking French with him; it seemed to relax him.

He'd considered me useless before the Flash. When he'd first seen me afterward, he'd summed me up with one word: *de'pouille*. I had no illusions that I'd changed his opinion of me.

Still, when I found a copy of *Robinson Crusoe* on the library shelves, I'd secretly slipped it into my pack to give him later.

"Behind me, Evie!" Jackson snapped. He had his gun against his shoulder, aiming toward a house. I didn't ask, just hurried behind him.

A middle-aged man stood on a front porch with his own rifle aimed back at us. Three preteen boys cowered behind him. Everything in the guy's bearing said, *Keep walking, strangers.*

So we did, Jackson easing past, me walking behind. Yet then the man's gaze darted from Jackson's gun . . . to me, and lingered.

At once, fury seemed to roil within Jackson. "Lower that piece, old man, or I'll drop you where you stand."

The man didn't comply. Faceoff.

Then Jackson bit out, "Your boys'll be next—and I woan waste bullets on them, no."

At the cruel threat, the man swallowed and gazed longingly at me. Eventually, he lowered his gun.

Keeping him in sight, Jackson squired me down one nerve-racking block. Another. *Clear.*

Only then did he spare a glance at me, scowling at my loose hair. "Start looking for a hat—or a pair of scissors."

Cutting my hair? Despite the heat, I shrugged back into my jacket, pulling the hood over my head.

"He actually thought about trying to steal you," Jackson grated. "To steal you *from me*."

I shivered. Something told me the man hadn't been sourcing for just a nanny.

We walked on, both of us silent. Jackson was still seething, and I remained on edge. We'd just seen what were probably the last four survivors in this town.

All male.

Sometimes I thought I was being stubbornly foolish to believe my grandmother was still alive. But then I'd remind myself that I'd survived the Flash and so had Mom. Maybe there was something in our genes that had saved us?

And Gran would have known to take shelter, to make any preparations she could.

In my heart, I believed she lived. Which meant I had to reach her. At times in the last few days, I'd stared at the picture my mom had held, fighting to recall more of Gran's teachings.

Slowly, so slowly, I was piecing together that last day with her. I'd recollected more details about all the cards she'd made me study, but especially Death's.

Against a crimson background, the Reaper had been clad in that black armor, scythe at the ready, riding his pale horse. He carried a black flag, emblazoned with a white rose. His victims—man, woman, and child—had all been on their knees before him, with their hands clasped in pleading.

Though the image had been eerie, I remembered being enthralled with that card more than all the others—even my own. Which had made Gran . . . *nervous*?

When she'd asked if that card frightened me, or made me really angry, I'd shaken my head firmly. "It makes me sad."

Gran hadn't liked that answer at all. "Why would you feel that way, Evie? He's a villain!"

"His horse looks sick, and he has no friends. . . ."

Now I cast my mind back, delving for more. Yet it seemed like the harder I fought to remember, the further those memories danced out of my grasp.

One thing I'd recalled? Gran's voice from long ago: *"Sometimes you have to let things unfold, Evie."*

I suspected I was putting too much pressure on myself, blocking all my own efforts. But I didn't know how to stop. . . .

Jackson drew up short. "Look there, Evie." He jerked his chin at a motorcycle ahead, lying on its side, clean of ash.

"Jackson, careful."

"The rider got bagged." He pointed out a dried swath of blood and telltale slime leading from the motorcycle to a darkened bay in a fire station. "They dragged him over there, into the shadows to feed." With a shrug, Jackson lifted the bike upright, engaging the kickstand. "Key's in it."

My eyes darted behind my shades. "Let's go!"

"Nuh-uh, not without this bike." He ran one palm along the frame, as reverently as he'd explored my paintings. "Do you have any idea what this is?"

"Should I care?"

As if he were speaking to a child, he said, "It's a *Ducati*."

"So?"

His expression said I'd just blasphemed or something. "This is the bike to end all bikes!" His words thrummed with excitement; he was *so* the teenage boy at this moment, flipping out over a motorcycle. "And to find it today? It's a sign, Evie. Things're turning around for us." He hopped on, cranking it.

When the engine fired, his lips curled. "She's got a nearly full tank, too."

"Can't we put that gas into a *car*?"

"None of them around here will be fixed already." He rifled through the bike's storage compartments, ruthlessly tossing the dead man's mementos and pictures to stow his own bag and bow within easy reach.

It even had an empty leather holster for Jackson to stick the shotgun. "Perfect fit." He turned to me. "You ready?"

"I've never ridden on a motorcycle before."

"*Pardon?* I didn't hear that right."

"It's true. My mom never let me." I frowned at the small space on the seat that was left for me. "Um, my hood will come off, and I don't want to cut my hair."

"We'll make an exception for this ride. Come on, you." When I tromped over to him, he reached for my hood, pushing it back over my head. "You're not scared, are you?"

In answer, I raised my chin and awkwardly climbed behind him. Our bodies now had, like, forty points of contact. I surveyed his back, wondering where I was going to put my hands.

Just when I realized how tightly my jeans had stretched over my thighs, I saw his head dip, his gaze locking on my right thigh, only moving to swing a glance over at my left.

He bit out a choked sound, then put his big, tanned hand flat on my knee. Even through the denim, his palm was scalding.

"Jackson!"

He balled it into a white-knuckled fist. The idea that I'd affected him in such a physical way made my breaths go shallow.

Without warning, he reached his arm back and wrenched me even closer to him, until I was flush against his body from one of my knees to the other and up to my chest.

Then his hand dipped back between us! Before I could sputter a protest, he'd snagged his flask from his back pocket. Shoving it into his boot, he murmured, "It was getting in the way."

Of *what?*

"This is where you put your arms around me, *cher.*"

"Maybe this isn't a good idea."

"Evie. Arms. *Now.*"

I rolled my eyes. After a hesitation, I finally reached around him—

Just as he rose up to disengage the kickstand.

My clasped hands brushed over him . . . *there.*

He sucked in a breath, his muscles gone rigid with tension; my face flamed as I yanked my hands back.

"If you touch me like that again, Evangeline," he began in a husky tone, dropping to his seat once more, "in the space of a heartbeat, I will have you off this bike and onto the closest horizontal surface. And I woan be picky, no."

Over my gasp, he explained, "I been strung tight for days, *bébé.*"

He must have suspected I was about to scramble off the bike like it was on fire—his hands, so rough and callused, captured mine, setting them well above his waist.

"Just so we understand each other." Then he took off.

Strung tight? What exactly was I supposed to do with that knowledge? I sat stiffly behind him as we gained speed down the lonely road, through the town and beyond—passing a forlorn playground, a wide-open clapboard church, a field with bleached cattle remains.

But with each mile, I started to relax. I'd noticed that whenever Jackson and I touched, the voices went silent. Not just muted. *Why?*

I sighed, deciding to ponder that another time. For now, I just enjoyed the quiet. And the air blowing was like being in air-conditioning again. It almost smelled *clean.* I closed my eyes and raised my face.

"You like this?"

I opened my eyes to find him watching me over his shoulder. I bit my lip and nodded.

He gave me that sexy jerk of his chin, then shifted gears to go faster.

Adrenaline rush! I loved the speed, the feel of the bike, the way he could make it move so effortlessly. "Faster!"

He raised his brows over his shades. "Hold on tighter, you."

As soon as I locked my arms around him, he floored the engine until the front wheel briefly left the ground. I yelped, then threw back my head and laughed.

How long had it been since I'd laughed like this?

Around corners, we'd lean in together. When he opened it up on a straightaway, I ducked down with him.

But soon I grew less interested in the ride—and more interested in the driver.

As his too-long hair whipped in the wind, I caught glimpses of the tanned skin on the back of his neck. I wondered what it would be like to kiss him there, to brush my lips against that smooth skin.

Jackson was often so rude, so *crude*, but all that could be forgotten when I thought about how warm and strong he felt against me. Or when I recalled how brave and intelligent he was.

Mom had said I could do a lot worse than Jackson Deveaux.

At that moment, I concluded she'd been right.

What would it be like to have him as my boyfriend? As I tried to imagine it, I sighed, pressing the side of my face against his back, fully relaxed against him. Soon exhaustion caught up with me. The constant rumble of the engine lulled me. My lids grew heavy.

"Sleep if you want." Again, he covered my hands with one of his own. "I've got you."

I loved it when he said that to me. "Are you sure?"

"I'm goan to find us a *bonne* place tonight. We'll have us a grand ole time."

Though I was curious what Jackson would consider a "grand ole time," sleep overtook me. . . .

26

When I woke, a full moon was high in the sky and Jackson was only now slowing.

"We haven't stopped for the night!" I darted my glance around. We looked to be in a rich subdivision. "What about Bagmen?"

"There weren't any," he said. "The night's so bright, maybe they think the sun is out. Who knows?" He sounded *drunk* as he eased the bike to a stop. But he didn't smell like whiskey—at least not more than normal. "In any case, the road was clear."

"The road to where?"

He booted the kickstand down in front of an intimidating driveway gate, with *lit* gas lamps on each side. "I guess to *here*," he said, scratching his head with a bemused grin. "Hey, check out the security on this place, Evie, the fences. They'll be secure against brainless Bagmen." Then he murmured, "Just not against us."

When he climbed off the bike, he left me feeling cold and out of sorts. "Why would these lights be on, Jackson? This feels like a baited trap. How about we pass this one by?"

"Bet there's loads of food inside." He was already wedging his crossbow between the two gates, using it as a lever to pry them apart. "Watch and learn, *peekôn*." With a click, the flourishing crest in the center parted, the gates swinging free.

He turned back to clasp me around the waist and set me on my feet. "We'll walk the bike from here." Once he'd pushed it past the fence, he shoved the gates back together behind us. Another click sounded as they sealed shut.

When the house—a gargantuan brick mansion—came into view, he whistled low. "Damn, Evie, you ought to feel right at home here."

I narrowed my eyes at the landscaping lights. "Those are *electric*."

"They've probably got a gas generator."

"One that would've had to be filled up recently, right? This place must be occupied."

He hadn't even slowed. "Or maybe we'll get lucky. What if the owner left to go source supplies and ran into trouble? He might've gotten attacked by roaming Bagmen. Like the rider of this bike."

I rubbed my arms. "I've got a bad feeling about this."

"The last time you had a *good* one, we lost everything we owned, nearly got enslaved, and spent the night in Bagman Swamp. I'm goan to take my chances here," he said. "It's too late to find another place to stay, anyway. If there's someone here and he's decent, we'll barter jewelry. If he's not decent, we'll take it. Kick him out."

"You're going to steal a house from its owner?"

"This house?" He smirked. "*J'pourrais.*" I might.

After we'd parked the bike near the side entrance, he cased the house with his crossbow in hand, taking in every detail before he approached the double doors. "Hasn't been rolled yet. Still locked tight."

With the end of his bow, he hit one of the glass sidelights that flanked the door, busting out a pane. The noise seemed startlingly loud.

Instead of entering, he stood motionless, cocking his head. After long moments, he reached in and opened the door, inhaling deeply. The air smelled fresh. No Bagmen around?

Weapon raised, Jackson finally entered the house, with me close behind.

"This is a mistake," I whispered, trying to recall something Matthew had repeated in all his mutterings and ramblings. It was tickling at my brain. "Why is staying here so important to you?"

"'Cause you'll like it here. Soft girl like you belongs in a place like this."

"I'd prefer the shrimp boat."

"I'll make a note."

Lamps burned low, lighting the interior enough for us to search the lavishly decorated house. It looked like a movie producer's Hollywood pad. Even *I* was impressed by the wealth.

Every room was even more luxe than the one before. "This feels like a trap," I repeated.

"Trust me, Evie, this place is goan to be a beauty. Remember? I got a sense for these things. And just think, if there's power *and* a well, there'll be a hot shower."

I nearly moaned at the idea of piping-hot water. But when a breeze wafted from overhead fans, I still said, "Why is the occupant so wasteful? Eventually, the gas *will* run out."

"Heh."

"Why *heh*?"

"The gas was already running out before the Flash. But I bet every room in your big ole mansion was cold as an icebox all summer long."

"This situation is more *acute*."

"If you think you could die tomorrow, why not go all-out? Part of me admires the owner for this."

Sometimes when he said things like that, I was reminded of how different we were. Like fundamentally different. "We'll have to agree to disagree. . . ."

We searched both wings upstairs and down, finding even more delights. The bedrooms had closets full of designer clothing and shoes. The garage housed camping supplies, hi-tech survival gear—and a colossal storage tank of gas.

No car, though.

In the enormous kitchen, Jackson opened one of the two refrigerators, which was surprisingly well-stocked with jellies, condiments, and drinks.

He briefly closed his eyes at the feel of cold air, then said, "Come here, you." He shoved me in front of him so I could feel it too, then stood behind me with his hand on my shoulder. "Admit it, this was worth it just to feel the icebox."

Though I was still wary about being here, I reminded myself that Jackson was the bogeyman, as long as he had that bow. So I closed my eyes too, and we just stood there for long moments.

Then I felt him reaching past me. "Jesus, *chilled* long-necks. Okay, that's it, I'm on the lookout for three bears." He snagged a couple of bottles, twisting off the tops. Pressing a beer into my hand, he led me into the biggest pantry I'd ever seen. "Find us something to eat, woman."

I arched a brow, but did inspect the goods, enough to last two people for months—canned and boxed foods, airtight cartons and bags, fruit juices. After hastily stuffing my backpack with PowerBars—just in case we had to flee—I perused the shelves for dinner.

A jar of maraschino cherries had my mouth watering. I snagged them, as well as a couple of cans of black olives, a carton of Pirouette cookies, and a bag of giant pretzel sticks, making a picnic on the counter.

For our main course, we enjoyed beer and pretzels. For dessert, Jackson hit the cookies, while I dug into the cherry jar. When I dropped one in my mouth, my eyes rolled with pleasure.

"You like *cerises*, huh?" He eased closer to me. "I've got an *envie* for a cherry." A craving.

Cajun innuendo, Jackson? "Here." I smiled sweetly, holding one up by the stem for him. "Enjoy the only cherry you'll get from me."

"Sounds like a challenge." With a wicked gleam in his eyes, he nipped it from my fingers with his even white teeth.

Flustered, I took a swig of my beer. But he pressed his finger to the bottom of the bottle, tipping it until I'd finished it with a gasp.

"Are you trying to get me drunk?" It was working. I'd always been a lightweight, and now one beer had me pleasantly buzzed.

"Sans doute." Without a doubt.

Okay, he was definitely flirting with me. Because I was the only game in town and he was . . . strung tight? Had to be. *Still the same old Evie here.*

He finished his own beer, chasing it with a shot from his flask. "Let's see what's outside." He collected his bow in one hand and my free hand in his other, then led me to a line of towering french doors.

We exited one onto a huge screened lanai that was like a wonderland, with gazebos and an outdoor kitchen. The moon was full overhead, lighting the area gently, until it looked untouched by the apocalypse.

Escorting me farther outside, he declared, "We are *home*, Evie Greene—"

He fell silent at the sight of a pool, sparkling in the moonlight. A *filled* pool.

Water. A death trap.

"Christ," he muttered, darting his head around. "Moon or no, why ain't we swarming with Bagmen?"

I pulled on his hand. "Jackson, we've got to go!"

"Stay here." He strode to the side of the pool, crouching down to dip a finger. After tasting the water, he rose with a thrilled expression. "It's saltwater, *bébé.*"

Salt? "Then they'd be repelled, right?"

He nodded. "And the water's *warm.*"

"Where'd it all come from?"

Propping his bow against a lounge chair, he said, "Private well. Just like you had at Haven."

But we hadn't wasted it *to swim.* "Jackson, please. The owner could return at any minute!"

"Why would someone be out this late if he's coming back?" Jackson kicked off his boots. "Finders keepers."

"You're not going in!"

In answer, he pulled his shirt over his head, revealing rigid planes of muscles. Yes, I'd caught glimpses of him shirtless before—but this was the first time I'd utterly lost my breath looking at him.

His face and his broad chest were still tanned, his eyes seeming to glow in the moonlight. That onyx rosary around his neck glinted with his movements.

He was stripping before my eyes, yet I couldn't look away. I bit my bottom lip. Any minute I would turn my back. Any minute . . .

As he began to unbuckle his belt, his stomach muscles rippled.

I grew weak in the knees. *Any minute.*

When he reached his zipper, he cocked his head and met my gaze.

I was frozen, could do nothing but stare. He raised his eyebrows at me in challenge, his fingers inching his zipper down.

A second after I'd finally found the presence of mind to turn my back, I heard his belt buckle ping on the tile floor, the rustle of his dropped pants. Eyes wide, I snapped, "This is foolish, Jackson—"

In the space of a heartbeat, he'd snagged my pack off my back, looped an arm around my waist—and hauled us both into the pool.

27

I broke the surface, sputtering, shoving water out of my face. "Have you lost your mind? Ugh! I am *not* skinny-dipping with you."

In a scandalized tone, Jackson said, "*Skinny-dipping?* Evangeline and her dirty mind." He glanced down. I could see he'd left on a pair of dark boxer briefs.

"Oh." Had I sounded disappointed? "Still, I'm not all right with this. We should be—what do you call it?—watching our six."

"So you do listen to me on occasion? Who'd-a thought . . . Look, I'm not goan to let anything happen to you. I'll hear anyone coming in plenty of time."

When I remained unconvinced, he said, "I told you, no one can get the drop on me. Doan you trust me?"

I didn't have much of a choice. "You couldn't have let me remove my boots?" I dragged them and my socks off, flinging them near his bow.

"You're right. I should've let you strip." Then he splashed me in the face.

I sputtered again, but he was grinning. Not a smirk—a *real* smile. As I gazed at his lips, I found my own curling in response.

I pointed behind him. "Oh, look!" Then I splashed the back of his head.

He faced me with his eyes wide. "Now you've done it! You mess with the bull . . ." He chased me around the shallow end until I was squealing with laughter.

It felt incredible to act like normal kids again. To flirt and play.

The voices were blessedly quiet.

Just before he caught me, I dunked under, swam around him and yanked back on his ankles. He couldn't have known that in another lifetime, I'd been a terror in the pool.

He acted like I'd tripped him, sinking like a stone. Once he broke the surface, he looked surprised—and delighted—that I was messing around with him.

I'd never seen this playful, grinning side of Jackson before, had never seen him without his customary restlessness. I recognized then that I'd never witnessed him *happy* until now.

And, damn, it was a good look on him. "You're smiling."

"I should be." His wet hair whipped over his cheeks. "Best day I've had in a long, long time." He began edging me toward the side of the pool, and I let him. Streams of water slid down his broad chest and rock-hard torso.

I want to follow those streams with my lips. . . . Okay, so maybe Jackson wasn't the only one strung tight. "Um, best day?" When my back met stone, he kept easing closer until I could feel the heat coming off his body. I had to crane my head up to meet his gaze.

His grin turned smug as he said, "Got me a new bike, a *jolie* girl who's sweet on me, and a mansion for us to live in."

Then I realized that I had a very real problem—add it to my tab. Jackson Deveaux was nearly irresistible like this. "Sweet on you? Please."

"I can tell."

"How?"

"You smell like honeysuckles when you're liking ole Jack."

Oh my God. Just as I'd been told, I *did* smell like flowers. No wonder everyone had kept complimenting me.

"When you're mad," he added, "you smell like roses. Excited? Sweet olive. I'm still figuring out the rest."

Even as he continued to stun me with his insight, I muttered, "Th-that's ridiculous." How was I going to hide my secrets all the way to North Carolina?

"Is it?" He inched even closer.

"In any case, it's not like *you* are sweet on me."

"C'est vrai." That's true. "But I do know that it's slim pickings out there."

I glared, unable to tell if he was teasing. "Melt my heart, Cajun."

He reached forward, clasping the edge of the pool on both sides of me, boxing me in.

"What are you doing?"

"Getting ready to kiss you for the first time."

Heart stop. *Form words, Evie.* "Y-you told me something like that at my party, but I didn't fare so well that night."

"Me neither. God, I'd wanted me a taste of you." His smoldering gray gaze was locked on my lips.

I wetted them, just as I had then.

"Do you know how many nights I've thought about almost kissing you? I remember every detail about you. I couldn't tell if your eyes were blue or green. Your lips were so red—it was sexy, but I couldn't decide if I liked it. 'Cause it wasn't you, not really."

That almost-kiss hadn't been just a trick! He'd felt the same excitement and attraction that I had.

"Evangeline, you're like . . . like a *peekôn dans ma patte*."

A thorn in my paw. How appropriate. *I guess that's my nature, Jackson.*

"And I can't quite shake it, no." His eyes were completely mesmerizing.

For the first time in months I wanted to draw—just to capture that look forever.

"Let's take this off, *cher*." When he reached for the hem of my soaked hoodie, I found myself raising my arms so he could pull it free, leaving me in my white cami.

Which was now see-through. I might as well have been wearing nothing.

When his gaze dipped, his lids went heavy and his Adam's apple bobbed. In a hoarse voice, he said, *"Mercy me."*

I'd never been looked at like this, had never been utterly certain that a boy was gazing at my body—while imagining how he wanted to touch it. My face and chest flushed with embarrassment.

Just when I was about to duck under, he said, *"Non*, you let me look." His accent was getting thicker. "Waited a *long* time to see you like this."

"But we've only been together a couple weeks."

He grazed the backs of his fingers along my cheekbones, as if my face was made of delicate porcelain. "Uh-huh," he murmured as he leaned down to gently press his lips to mine. His were so firm and warm. I could just taste the bite of whiskey.

He felt perfect . . . the kiss, *right.*

He parted his lips, coaxing me to do the same. Once I did, he leisurely stroked his tongue against mine . . . and again. Relaxed, wicked flicks.

Energy filled me, pleasure radiating. This was addictive—nothing *meh* about it.

Our tongues tangled, over and over, until I couldn't stop a moan. I wanted more of him. I wanted this never to end. I *needed* more.

I was losing control; why wasn't he? His kiss was sensual, but deliberate, as if he had all the time in the world.

As if he has something to prove?

Just when that thought arose in my foggy brain, he drew back with a cocky smirk. "There. Now that's what I'm talking about." He rubbed his thumb over my bottom lip. "You're not laughing now, are you—"

"More." I reached up, tunneling my fingers through his dark hair, clutching, dragging him back to me.

He rasped, "Evie?" just before our lips met again, our tongues . . .

I ran my hands down his back, over his flexing muscles. I couldn't stop touching him, couldn't keep my body from moving against his. With each sweep of my palms, he deepened the kiss. So I did it again. And again.

Soon I was gasping and he was groaning. His hands cupped my waist, descending to my wriggling hips. He squeezed them, then reached for my ass, gripping me with splayed fingers, wrenching my body even closer to him. Was he shuddering against me?

No more control for either of us.

I loved his abandoned groans, loved that I could *feel* them because we were pressed so tight together. Just as he'd promised, we were breathing for each other—and still I couldn't get enough.

For me, this was the game changer, a line in the sand. Life before our kiss; life after.

He wrapped his strong arms around me, hauling me up, crushing me against his solid chest. I dimly realized my feet weren't touching the bottom of the pool any longer.

He broke away to kiss my neck, saying against my skin, *"Tu me fais tourner la tête! Ton parfum sucré, tes secrets."* You drive me mad! Your sweet scent, your secrets. Heated licks followed. "Ah, Evie, you taste as good as you smell."

I breathed, "Jackson . . ."

He pulled back, letting me slip back down to stand on my own. His voice was raw as he said, "If you want me to kiss you again, you call me Jack."

I couldn't think. I made some sound of agreement.

"Say it."

My head tilted back, and I whispered, "Jack."

He cupped my face with his callused palms, so that I stared directly into his eyes. There was something *possessive* in his expression, something masculine and . . . older that I had absolutely no idea how to decipher—all I knew was that the intent look on his face made my heart race. "You said you wanted more?"

Of his kiss? "God, yes."

He exhaled a pent-up breath. *"Bien."* Then he lifted me again, cradling me in his arms. As he climbed the pool steps, he grazed his lips along my neck, keeping me in a haze of bliss. At my ear, he rasped, *"T'chauffes mon sang comme personne d'autre."* You heat my blood like no other.

I quivered with delight, only vaguely wondering where he was taking me. And maybe why he'd swooped down to collect his jeans along with his ever-present bow.

My back met cushions. Gazebo? Reclining lounge chair for two?

Ah, more kisses! He licked my earlobe, making me cry out, my back arching. Was that *my* zipper?

I felt weightless for a moment, then cool air breezed over my damp legs, up to my panties.

He hissed in a breath. *"Ma belle fille."* My beautiful girl. He followed me down, lying half on me, half on the chair.

When he fiddled with something in his jeans pocket, I murmured, "Jack?"

He raised himself over me with one straightened arm, flashing me that wolfish grin, so sexy he robbed me of thought. "I'm goan to take care of you, *bébé*." He produced a condom in a wrapper, holding it between his white teeth as he rubbed one hot palm up my torso, rolling my cami higher.

He looked roguish and wicked and oh-dear-God-did-he-have-a-condom?

For *me*?

"Wait!" Everything was moving too fast, spinning out of control. "Wh-what are you doing?" I hadn't agreed to sex! I shoved against him.

He'd teed me up to be his next *gaienne*—without a word about me being his *girlfriend*. And what if that condom broke? I could have sworn it'd come from the shrimp boat medicine cabinet. Who knew how old that package was!

His brows drew together. "What's the matter, you?"

"I'm not just going to have *sex* with you!" What if I got pregnant?

I was fuming all the more because I'd *loved* kissing him, and then he'd gone and skipped over all the bases—the ones that I had *never* gotten to experience—and gone straight for a home run.

"Why you acting like sex with me is a fool idea?" he demanded, his expression exasperated.

I shoved his chest again until he drew back. "Where do I even begin?" *Your ancient condom pack, our lack of a defined relationship, the fact that you were going about things at light speed—even though this is my first time.*

Damn it, why'd we have to stop kissing? I just needed to think, with a clearer head.

But his own anger was already seething. "You *told* me you wanted more."

"Of your kiss!" I brought my knees to my chest, wrapping my arms around my legs. Without him against me, I was shivering with cold.

A couple of weeks ago, I'd told myself that I would save my virginity for my boyfriend, no matter how naïve that sounded. Today, on the bike, I'd imagined what it'd be like if Jackson was mine.

There was *something* between us, something exciting and . . . combustible. Then I frowned. Tonight, he'd told me lots of things to let me know he was attracted to me. But not that he *liked* me.

Hadn't he talked about it being *slim pickings out there*?

Even if there were no other girls for him to be with, I still wanted Jackson and me to get on the same page about what was going on between us. If we didn't have some kind of understanding worked out, then sleeping together would only complicate things.

And I couldn't let anything get in the way of reaching North Carolina.

So how to broach the subject of a relationship? "Jackson, you know that I've never . . . I've never done that before. And I was kind of looking for something *more* to go along with it." Hint, hint.

Realization lit his expression. "You *still* think you're too good for me. You'd let Radcliffe get first pick, but not me?"

I gasped. "Don't you dare bring him into this!" Again, I thought of how happy-go-lucky Brandon had been, how many good times we'd shared at the beach, out on the water. Always laughing . . .

Those times with Brandon had been the *last* of the good times for me. Before the apocalypse, before the Arcana . . . My eyes watered.

Jackson saw my reaction. "You're still in love with him!" He shot to his feet, then stabbed his legs into his jeans. "You were ready to lie down with that boy 'cause you thought him twice the man of me. But what the hell did he ever do besides drive a nice car or throw around a ball? I saved your life!"

I rose as well, darting for my soaked jeans, snatching them up my legs with difficulty. "Did you save me just so I'd sleep with you?"

"The idea might've crossed my mind! Hell, Evie, you're probably the last girl on earth for me. Would it *kill* you to put out?"

"I can't believe you just said that!" I felt like such an idiot! Believing we had a connection? The Cajunland player had merely intended to score another doe tag—and I was the only game in town. I stormed off for my hoodie, then worked it over my head.

"Believe it!" He closed in on me. "Remember, I'm the *cruel* and *classless* boy from the wrong side of the bayou. That's all I'll *ever* be to you!"

We were in each other's faces, but I refused to back down. "When you act like this, it's hard to see otherwise! Thank God I had the good sense *not* to become more involved with you."

"Good sense? That's one thing you'll never be accused of having! Getting more involved with me is the smartest thing you could ever do. I'm the one who keeps you safe. *Me*"—he thumped his bare chest—"remember? 'Thank you, Jack, it's great to be alive.'"

"Admit it, this is the real reason you volunteered to help me—because you wanted to sleep with me!"

"Yeah, I'd pegged you for a snob, but I didn't figure you for a miserable tease!"

"A *tease*? Did you believe I was a sure thing because we're in a hell-on-earth situation? Or because every other slore you've been with has given it up? Tell me!"

He gave me that shrug. "A little of both."

I wanted to *strangle* him!

"Why's everything always got to be so hard with you?" He turned to punch a wooden gazebo column, rocking the entire structure. When he faced me again, his chest heaved, his scarred hand bleeding. "You're goan to make me crazy!"

"Well, then suck it up! Just like you said, I'm the best there is. It seems like you'd be a little nicer to the last girl on earth. Maybe you should—oh, I don't know—try to be pleasant or boyfriendlike or, or . . ."

"Court you?"

"Well, yeah."

"Maybe I have been—every time I've rescued your ass! And every night I've kept watch over you! But you just take all that for granted. Because you're *gâtée*!"

"I am not spoiled!"

"Never knew a girl as spoiled as you—coddled your whole life. But that shit stops *now*."

I rubbed my arms, dripping and dejected in my wet clothes. How had we gone from kissing to a fight like this? "What do you *want* from me?"

He pinched his forehead, saying in an odd tone, "I might've wanted something from you—but it's clear you're never goan to give it to me."

Were we still talking about sex?

"You know why my *mère* drank?" he demanded, his voice a harsh rasp. "Because she wanted and waited for things that would never be. I swore I'd never do the same. In the past, whenever I felt my mind wandering in the wrong direction, I shut those thoughts down." He raked his fingers through his hair. "I got to do that now, me."

"I don't *understand* you."

Suddenly what sounded like a sonic boom went off in my head.

—BEHOLD THE BRINGER OF DOUBT.—

As I tottered on my feet, Jackson lunged for his bow, swinging it around, aiming it behind us.

"Wh-what is it, Jackson? Is someone here?" He couldn't have heard the voice, and I'd detected nothing around us.

He jerked his chin in the direction of a shadowy walkway. "Out there."

"How do you know?"

He grated, "Experience."

A girl moved out of the shadows, with her own bow raised. "Seems that I have company."

A bow? In moonlight? When I saw her completely, my jaw slackened. Standing on the other side of the pool was the girl from my visions. Though her face had been blurry before, I'd recognize that beach-volleyball-player figure anywhere.

For a split second, a still-shot image seemed to be superimposed over her. I saw her as that red-tinged archer, poised like a goddess in the moonlight.

I swallowed. The image looked just like a . . . Tarot card.

I blinked. In the next instant, she was just a normal teenage girl. A gorgeous one. Her long mane of silvery-blond hair shimmered, her dark eyes watchful.

She wore a black halter, cropped khaki shorts—which showed off mile-long legs—and biker boots.

A leather quiver circled her freaking thigh, Lara Croft–style.

"What are you two doing in my home?" Her voice was exactly like it'd been in my head. Had she experienced visions of me as well? Heard my own Arcana call? Whatever it was . . .

I'd believed the Arcana were all real kids. She was undeniable proof that they existed.

Her eyes flashed to me—and they might have widened just a touch before her expression grew shuttered, her attention back on Jackson.

"Apologies," he said, giving her a once-over. "Didn't think anyone was here." He looked like he dug what he saw.

And she *certainly* did. In a purring tone, she said, "I'll drop my bow if you do, handsome."

After a hesitation, he began lowering it.

I wanted to cry, "No, I don't trust her!" But she popped her arrow from her bow and dropped it into her quiver.

Now that the immediate threat had eased, she raked her gaze over him, lingering on his bared chest. "That's a sweet Ducati you've got."

Had Jackson's shoulders straightened? "Just picked her up today."

Brushing her hair back, she said, "I'm Selena Lua."

I now knew the name of one of the voices. Because she was standing right before me. One of the *Major Arcana*. What else could I find out from her? I had to talk to her in private. . . .

"Didn't I tell you," Jackson muttered to me, "that this place was goan to be a *beauty*?" While I bristled, he said to the girl, "I'm Jackson Deveaux, *you* can call me Jack." He tossed an offhanded wave at me. "That's Evie."

With only another brief glance my way—and no glimmer of awareness—Selena returned her gaze to Jackson as though magnetized. "I don't get many visitors. If you want to, I'm cool with you staying the night here."

I'll bet you are.

Jackson turned to me with a devilish smile. In French, he said, "All of a sudden, Evie, you're not the last girl on earth for me."

Selena's Arcana call was "Behold the Bringer of Doubt."

Right now, I was awash in it.

"Here you go, Evie. Fresh towels." She placed a stack of them on the bathroom counter of my luxurious guest suite. "Toiletries are in the cabinets. And there's plenty of hot water, so enjoy!"

All my life, I'd gone out of my way to make friends. And here was another *girl*. At last! I hadn't seen one in months, much less a girl that I was linked to in some way.

So why did I intensely dislike her?

Earlier, when I'd shaken hands with Selena, her voice in my head had gone from jarringly loud to *silent*. As if snuffed. Maybe I was supposed to find each of the speakers, to silence each voice—and preserve my sanity?

Her expression had betrayed nothing out of the ordinary. In fact, she'd acted a little unnerved that I'd kept staring at her. But I'd gotten the weirdest feeling that her behavior was fake. Her eyes seemed almost *too* blank of recognition.

Yet then she'd graciously welcomed us into her home. She'd gone out of her way to make friends with me, as kind and generous as she could be.

My visions of her had told me nothing *definite*. In them, she'd frightened me, but she'd also saved my loved ones.

I began to suspect that my dislike was based in . . . petty jealousy—because Jackson's attentions had turned on a dime to focus on the leggy Selena.

Now he leaned his shoulder against the bathroom wall, ignoring me completely, drinking another beer as Selena chatted about how great it was to have company. She'd been alone here since the Flash and was nearly "stir-crazy."

"An occasion like this calls for a cookout," she said, clearly thrilling Jackson. "I was out hunting earlier, bagged two quail today. Get ready for a feast."

"Thank you, Selena," I said. "And thanks for the clothes." She'd let me raid her closet for "as many outfits as I liked."

"It's nothing, sweetie. Now, come on, handsome. Let's go see your room."

On the road, Jackson and I had never been separated. "His room?"

Giving him yet another admiring glance, she purred the words, "He'll enjoy the best view from a suite—in my wing."

"I'll be alone here?"

Jackson still hadn't looked at me.

"Don't worry." Selena gave a laugh, bumping her hip against mine. "I've scrubbed the surrounding woods of Bagmen. Lots of target practice." She winked at Jackson; he grinned. "I've also got salt lines around the grounds. Motion sensors as well."

Wow. A regular superheroine. At Haven, I'd managed to brace my front door.

"Let me know if you need anything else," she said. "We'll have dinner on the lanai in an hour."

I parted my lips to say something to Jackson—anything to get him to stay—but he just gave me that curt chin jerk, then followed Selena to *their wing* of the mansion.

So much for his insistence that we always sleep in the same place.

Once they'd gone, the voices buzzed anew. I fought to dampen them, telling myself that *nothing* could ruin my first real shower since the Flash.

Wrong.

Under the hot water, my cheeks stung where Jackson's stubble had abraded my skin, reminding me of how much my night was shittily declining.

Surely he couldn't transfer his interest from one girl to another just like that. We'd had *something* between us, right? *So says the girl with such little boy experience.*

After I'd showered and dried my hair, I slipped on a dark jean miniskirt—that nearly hit my knees but was tight over my ass—and a body-conscious red tank. I decided to go barefoot. None of Selena's shoes had fit, and I refused to pull on my wet boots. Besides, it *was* a cookout by the pool.

I assessed myself in the mirror, my mood lifting. *Not bad, Greene.* My eyes looked bright, my hair clean and shiny. The tank molded over my chest, which Jackson would surely appreciate.

This wasn't over. One last glance, then I set off downstairs.

Out on the lanai, Selena and Jackson were drinking beer and grilling the quail—while discussing *bowstring tensions.*

Instead of announcing myself, I decided to observe them from the shadows, doing recon on Selena.

My mood soured once more when I saw her man-eater outfit: a slinky, off-the-shoulder couture blouse, a micromini, and four-inch heels. Her eyes danced as she gazed at Jackson.

With his face clean-shaven and his new clothes—a black hunter's T-shirt, broken-in jeans, and boots—he looked even more gorgeous than usual.

She laughed at something he said, grazing her fingers over the scar on his forearm, having no idea what that mark meant to him—to *me.* . . .

Another joke, another laugh, another round of beers popped open.

Another brush of her fingers. She seemed to be taking every opportunity to touch him.

He was *letting* her. Just an hour ago, he'd been trying to sleep with me. Now here he was getting drunk with this strange girl in the moonlight.

The Bringer of Doubt? Oh, she'd brought it.

Evidently he didn't figure *her* for a miserable tease. And she was lapping up the attention. Why wouldn't she? Jackson was handsome, strong, an incredible protector.

Not that Lara Croft needed any help in the protection department. Her longbow was propped up right next to Jackson's crossbow, both within easy reach.

How quaint.

She didn't even know how wicked a kisser he was.

Jackson seemed to be hanging on her every word as their conversation moved on to motorcycle engine horsepower and tire treads.

Tire. Treads.

How could Selena know all that stuff? It was like they spoke a foreign language that I could never learn.

My heart sank when she drank out of his beer, then gave the bottle back, as if they were a couple.

Back at Haven, I'd wiped his flask with my sleeve.

His attraction to me truly had been just about slim pickings. He'd liked me out of *nécessité*. As he'd readily admitted. *But give him a choice . . .*

He would never want to leave this realm of beer and electricity and leggy archers.

And I needed him to get to Gran's. *Only* to get there. For no other reason. *At all.*

Maybe I shouldn't roll over and let her have him so easily. I recalled how possessive I'd been about Brandon. I thought of what Mel would say: "Stop being a puss and take your toy back. What are you—minced meat?"

Selena asked him, "Will you say *back there* again?"

He complied. With his accent, it sounded like a rumbly *bag dare.*

"Cajun is sooo hawt, J.D."

J.D.? Okay, that was the final straw!

I strolled out onto the lanai, fake smile in place. "Dinner smells delicious."

Jackson's gaze moved over me. I thought I detected approval in his expression, but then he looked away as if he could barely stand the sight of me.

"Just in time, Evie," Selena said. "I've got everything ready."

I surveyed the outdoor table, immaculately set with nice silver and crisp napkins. Covered dishes steamed with mouthwatering aromas.

"We're having quail, asparagus, and mushroom risotto. Hot apple cobbler for dessert."

I smiled thinly. *Martha Stewart called, wants her shtick back.* "Can I help?"

Jackson snorted. And Selena play-slapped his chest, like he was her mischievous boyfriend.

At that, the initial *mrowr pfft pfft* I'd felt transformed into *I will cut a bitch.*

No, no, no. I had to think about this rationally! She might help me discover more about the Arcana.

But then, Jackson's assistance was critical to my getting to Gran's, to finding out *all*, and I was losing him.

Ever polite, Selena opened a sweating beer bottle for me. "Here you go."

The last thing I needed was to lose control, but I politely took a sip. "Cheers."

"You guys take a seat. J.D., you're over here." She pointed out the chair right beside hers, which put me on the other side of the large table alone.

When they dug in, Jackson *groaned* at his first bite. *And she can cook, too.*

My mouth should have been watering, but I was too nervous. I kept imagining how dangerous—and lonely—the road was going to be without him.

That was the only reason I felt like crying. *Not* because he'd told me he was going to take care of me, making it sound like a promise.

"Aren't you hungry?" Selena asked me.

"Doan worry about her." Jackson spooned more risotto onto his plate. *"Plus pour nous."* More for us.

Seemed he was no longer concerned about this growing girl's ultimate bra size. Because he'd *shut those thoughts down. . . .*

Over dinner, I learned of all the things that J.D. and Lara Croft had in common. I thought about proposing a new drinking game: Take a swig every time Selena said to Jackson, "No way! Me too!"

They loved to hunt and fish. Both had been shooting a bow since they were little. Selena modestly admitted that she'd been training for Olympic archery before the Flash struck.

Jackson looked far more impressed with that than he had with my dance trophies.

She and Jackson were both soon to be nineteen. Once she'd realized I was more than two years younger, Selena had started talking to me in a patronizing tone, like I was their plucky, annoying tagalong. "Oh, no, J.D., I gave her a beer!" she'd cried, jabbing him with an elbow. "Should we take it away?"

I hadn't wanted my beer. Now I dared her to reach for it.

Wonder of wonders, Selena was also an ace motocross rider, had even raced against the boys.

In fact, she gleefully told Jackson, "I rode so much each weekend that my family got me my own industrial-size tank of gasoline. It's still half-full. Hey, we could go off-roading tomorrow, if the weather holds. You won't believe the trails I could take you on, J.D."

It was as if Selena had been factory-made for him. Any hope I'd had of keeping his attention was doused.

I didn't care—I *didn't*. Even if he'd liked me, I had nothing to offer him and wouldn't want some Cajun biker thief anyway. A drunken one. Though I hadn't finished my beer, he and Selena were pounding them.

As if she felt my eyes on her, Selena faced me. "If you don't like the quail, I can cook you something else. I've got a bunker full of cans, freeze-dried foods, and jarred vegetables. Just let me know, honey."

Honey? No one called me that but my mother. Thinking of Mom, I forced myself to be polite. "You're so considerate, but I'm full." I turned to Jackson. "Can I talk to you after you're done eating?"

He glanced up, looking maybe a shade less pissed than before. "About what?"

"The trip tomorrow."

His eyes narrowed. "*Non.* Nothing to talk about."

My face heated at his dismissive tone.

Selena blinked in confusion. "The trip tomorrow? Where are you headed?"

Had Jackson not told her? I felt like I couldn't dodge answering now. "North Carolina."

"J.D. told me you might stay for a spell."

"Did J.D.?"

He merely raised his brows at me, his expression saying, *What are you goan to do about it?*

I began to comprehend that I was truly about to be on my own.

"So what's in North Carolina, Evie?" Selena wanted to know.

"I have family there. A grandmother."

"Well, you don't have to leave so quickly. I would love the company, even for a couple of days. And it's really safe here—no Baggers, no militia-types." She touched Jackson's forearm for the thousandth time. "There's still game around here. The three of us could clean up."

"Evie? *Hunt?*" He gave a mocking laugh, and, God, how it stung. "She can't shoot, no, can't do much of anything." He drunkenly snapped his fingers. "Oh, wait, she's an expert at looking down her nose at folks."

While I sat there burning with humiliation, Selena glanced from Jackson to me and back.

I'd made an effort to be pleasant. And look how well that had turned out. I couldn't compete with the heaven-sent girl who loved every single thing he did, who could talk expertly about all the things he was passionate about.

So what did I have to lose? "I'm also good at *keeping secrets*," I murmured to him with a serene smile. "Apparently, that drives some boys crazy." *She shoots; she scores.*

His sneer deepened. "Secrets doan keep a bed warm at night."

Enough. "If you're going to be a dick, *J.D.*, I'm going to bed." To Selena, I said, "Thank you for the dinner. Sorry I couldn't be better company. But enjoy this one, such a *classy* guy. A real gentleman."

His knuckles whitened on his bottle.

As I took my plate to the kitchen sink, I heard Selena snickering at something Jackson said. Was he telling her a story about my clumsiness? My cluelessness?

Dejected, I headed back toward my room, listlessly viewing the family pictures in a hallway gallery. Selena was in *none* of them. I didn't see a single picture of her shooting her bow in a tournament or proudly gearing up on a motocross track. Odd.

Back in my room, I found some computer paper and a pencil in a desk drawer. I was itching to sketch Jackson as he'd looked when he gazed down at me in the pool, his face lit by the moon.

It hurt too much to draw him; it hurt too much not to. I'd just taken up the pencil in my shaking hand when a knock sounded on the door.

How badly I wanted it to be him! To have him come sleep in the same room with me, as we'd done for weeks.

But he'd never knock. "Come in."

Selena meandered inside, visibly tipsy. As good as a Bayou Bessie.

"Hey, Evie, can we have a girl chat?" Instead of sitting at the foot of the bed, standard protocol for girl chats, she crossed to the dresser, checking her nearly waist-length mane of hair in the mirror.

"Sure. I've got something I wanted to talk to you about as well."

"Oh? What's that?"

"Earlier when we met, you looked like you recognized me. Did you?"

She gazed at me through the mirror with an indulgent expression. "Um, *no*. When would we have met?"

"It just seemed—"

"I was surprised because I was seeing a *girl*, Evie. You're the first female I've seen after the Flash. There're never any girls anymore."

That made absolute sense. So why did I get the feeling she was lying? "What did you want to talk to me about?"

"I wanted to make sure that you and J.D. aren't an item."

"Excuse me?"

"Sometimes guys say stuff to other girls about being single or whatnot . . . well, you know how it is, girlfriend. I wanted to confirm with you."

I tried to make my tone casual. "What'd he say about us?"

"I asked if you two were exclusive, and he emphatically said no."

I was so naïve! When he'd told me he was going to *take care of me*, he'd meant it in that *other* way—the one usually accompanied by vulgar hand gestures or waggled eyebrows.

Sure, I'd known Jackson had been a player, but I'd stupidly imagined there'd been something special between us. He'd just wanted to get laid.

Even postapocalypse, some things *did* remain the same.

As Selena gazed at her reflection, pinching her cheeks for color and tugging down her blouse to show more cleavage, I realized his chances were promising.

He'd probably use that condom of his this very night. My face grew hot with unshed tears. Wanting nothing more than to get rid of her—for now—I said, "He's right, Selena. No ER with us."

"Oh, thank God," she said with a relieved breath. "I *really* like him, Evie. I never expected to meet a guy. Here. With you. Much less that he'd be a perfect match for me." In a softer tone, she added, "I always assumed I'd be alone forever. I just never expected . . . *him*."

For the first time, I got the sense that she was being sincere. And that made me wonder: Had she been expecting *me*?

Seeming to snap out of her thoughts, she made her manner brisk. "I'll let him know you were just as emphatic, and clear the air of any misunderstandings. See you in the morning!"

Yes, in the morning I would investigate this girl more. For now I planned to choke on tears and voices.

29

DAY 236 A.F.

—Need to talk to you.—

The next morning, I heard Matthew in my head, just seconds after I awakened.

I was groggy and puffy-eyed, yawning after my fitful sleep. "Matthew, you won't believe this, but one of the Arcana is here, the Bringer of Doubt."

—La Luna. She's the Moon Card. The Archer.—

So if every Arcana had supernatural powers, hers was archery? *The Olympics frowns on performance enhancers, Selena.* Or it'd used to. "Meeting her was wild," I told Matthew. "I heard her call so clearly, then poof, her voice in my head went silent. And when we first met, I saw something flash over her, like a picture."

—Tableau. A card. How we recognize each other. But Evie . . .—

"I *knew* it. I've been hearing her voice for months, and now I'm in her house? This is too weird." I stretched my arms over my head, surprised my migraine wasn't worse. The pain was manageable—even though he sounded much louder than normal. Had I cut some of the distance between us?

"So is the Moon good? Or evil, like Ogen?" I wished Matthew would say she was just like El Diablo, or worse than! I'd be forced to get Jackson away from her.

—Good or evil?— Matthew sounded confused by my question. *—She's the Moon. But Empress, we need to talk . . .—*

"What's up?" Rubbing my eyes, I swung my legs over the side of the bed and eased to my feet.

The bed disappeared behind me.

"Matthew?"

I was no longer in Selena's guest room. I found myself standing with Matthew in his basement playroom, but water was rising around our calves. His khaki pants and long-sleeved button-down were soaking wet. He was shivering.

A flashlight burned from a peg on a nearby wall, allowing me to see him clearly. His face and hair were dripping, his brows drawn together.

I'd known he had even features and deep brown eyes. But now I could see lighter flecks in his eyes, could gauge the strength of his lean physique. He was almost as tall as Jackson.

"Why are we down here and where's all this water coming from?" Obviously, there were still big reserves of water out in the world—we just had to find one.

Then *secure* it.

"Tremors," he said. "Pipe burst. Water tower."

"Then the whole place could flood?" When he nodded, I said, "Matthew, you have to leave this room immediately!"

He remained motionless, like a dog that had been commanded to sit in the middle of a busy freeway. "Can't." He looked so pitiful, so lost, his big brown eyes darting.

"Yes, you can! Get out *now*," I ordered him, wishing I could shake his shoulders. The protectiveness I felt for him staggered me.

Beanbags floated past our legs as the water steadily rose. "Can't," he repeated. "Mother locked me in."

"Why would she do that to you? Does she *know* your basement is flooding?"

He nodded. How could she condemn him to drown?

"Mother knows what's b-best for Matthew." He rubbed his palms over his upper arms. "Mother knows I won't stay in the car. Shouldn't have fixed engine. Bad, Matthew, BAD!"

"I don't understand what you're saying! Kid, just *listen* to me. Is there a window? There has to be a way out! You're strong—go break down the door!"

"Clock stops. Don't have to see the future to know that."

"What does that mean? Like, you'll die?" The idea rocked me. I had this friend out in the world waiting for me. Now I was going to lose him?

"Mother's dead. I follow."

No, he can't die! "I'm coming for you! Where are you?" *Please be close enough for me to reach in time. . . .*

He gave me a sad smile. "I've always been on your way." The vision wavered, then changed to a time before the Flash.

He was in a backyard, at a barbecue with other kids, but they wouldn't talk to him. So he wandered off, standing all alone as a *rocket* blasted off in the distance.

"Rocket? Oh, dear God, you're in Houston! Or . . . or *Florida!*" Just as I started to despair, I saw a hilly dirt road scored with washboard ruts. Hilly?

Then I clearly saw the T-shirt he'd worn. HUNTSVILLE SPACE CAMP. "Huntsville! In Alabama?" Only one state over.

But all the way north.

"Matthew, how long ago did it start flooding?"

"Couple of hours." So roughly one foot every two hours. Maybe?

I could make it to Huntsville in time—*if* I could talk Jackson into driving me and the winds cooperated. "I'm coming for you, kid. Just hang on!"

Once the vision faded, I hurried to dress in another borrowed outfit—jeans too tight over my ass and too long and a T-shirt. I yanked on my damp boots over a pair of spotlessly white socks.

Minutes later, I was jogging down the stairs with my packed bug-out bag.

I found Jackson in the kitchen, shirtless, wearing only his new jeans. He sat with his head in his hand at the breakfast counter, while Selena—clad in a short silk robe—happily scrambled powdered eggs for them.

She poured him a tall glass of some orange drink, then doused it with a healthy splash from a vodka bottle. He took the drink without a word, blearily downing half of it in one gulp.

When she rubbed a knuckle in his hair, I realized that I was probably witnessing their morning after. And I wanted to vomit.

This domestic scene dashed any lingering hope that Jackson wouldn't sleep with her. He'd found a girl who would "put out." And I knew he would never leave this Shangri-la of hunting and gourmet food and sex.

Not for the irritating former cheerleader who couldn't heat soup. The one who always made things so difficult for him. The miserable tease.

But for Matthew's sake, I would still try to get Jackson's help. *Even if he didn't pick* me.

Hoping to ward off my tears, I assumed a cheery air. "Good morning, guys."

He swiped his forearm over his mouth. In a murderous tone, he said, "Where you goan, Evangeline?"

"Same place I've always been going, Jackson." *Just need to make a quick stop on the way to save a boy's life.*

Selena sat at the counter and crossed her long legs, unconcerned when her robe split all the way to her upper thighs. But hey, Jackson had already seen the goods, right? "Evie, I talked it over with J.D. last night—and you're more than welcome to stay here as long as you want. Like, even permanently."

They had talked it over, and *they* were extending the invitation. My claws tingled—as if they were waking up. "Thank you for the offer, but I have to get going."

"You'd really leave all this food and water behind?" she asked. "The electricity and security?"

Yes, her estate was perfect. *Too* perfect. A place like this could tempt a girl from her mission if she wasn't careful.

"North Carolina is cannibal and plague territory," she continued. "What's the rush?" She seemed very serious about getting to the bottom of this.

Jackson hadn't told her the details? Not during their beer binge last night, or their—what was it called—their *pillow talk*?

I had to admit I was surprised. "Like I said last night, I'm going to join my grandmother there. I belong with her."

Selena took a sip of Jackson's drink. "Why would you believe she's still alive? I hate to say this, but she's probably not, you know?"

Jackson threw his hands up. "Just what I told her!"

"There's got to be more to this than a long-lost granny," Selena said. "She'd never want you to sacrifice the safety you could find here just to try to locate her. All that's out there is death and more death."

—*The water's rising!*— Matthew called, making my head throb.

Fighting for focus, I muttered, "She *is* alive."

Jackson's scowl deepened. "You're not even goan to consider staying here? Not even for a few days?"

Days? My temper flared. I didn't have *hours*! "You know I have obligations. I keep *my* promises." I bit my tongue as soon as I said that.

"Ohhh," Selena said, "this is because you two had a spat last night? No offense, honey, but it seems totally rash for you to go running off like this."

She made it sound like I was flouncing away in a huff. As I commanded myself to rein in my temper, the strangest thought arose: *She's needling me so I'll justify my leaving, so I'll spill why it's so important.*

But why would she care? And if she was deceitful, did that automatically mean she was dangerous?

Even if I'd been tempted to level with Jackson about what was at stake, I feared he'd tell her.

"Thanks for your concern, Selena, but I'm going." I faced Jackson. "Are you going with me?"

He narrowed his eyes. "She said you're welcome to stay."

Calm. Breathe, Evie. "Then this is where we . . . split up?"

"I'm good here."

Don't cry, don't cry. Swallowing my pride, I said, "Okay, but would you please just drive me as far as half a tank will take us, and then you can come right back?"

He crossed his arms over his chest. *"Non,"* he answered, studying my expression.

Somehow I forced myself to turn to Selena and utter the words: "Can I please borrow your motorcycle, if I swear to bring it back?" *As if I can drive one.*

"Sweetie, take anything else you like, anything. But that's my only transportation."

With a sinking feeling, it dawned on me that these two weren't going to assist me whatsoever. They were happy to let me walk out that door, to face the road alone.

Which meant they were just wasting my time. Matthew's precious time.

"Okay, then, I have to go." Yesterday Jackson had found a motorcycle out on the road. Maybe I could find a car? A freaking ten-speed? "Oh, I almost forgot." Yanking open my bag, I snatched out that copy of *Robinson Crusoe* and tossed it across the counter. *"Bonne chance,* Jackson."

Just before I turned toward the door, his brows drew together and that muscle ticked in his jaw.

Selena called, "Evie, at least let us set you up with some supplies or camping gear."

My shoulders stiffened, but I kept going. Outside, I muttered, "Let *us* set you up?" *I already cleaned you out of PowerBars, bitch.*

I jogged to the end of the drive, telling myself that I didn't have time to cry over Jackson. Matthew's fear was palpable, his voice growing louder and louder until all the others were dim. Maybe that was because he was so close to me?

Or was it because I was learning to focus on just one at a time?

As I triggered the entrance gates to open, I imagined Jackson running after me, begging forgiveness. But I made it off the property and onto the street, alone.

He hadn't even said good-bye.

I needed to get to a gas station, grab an Alabama map, then hope for a miracle in the form of a working car.

Shit. I probably should've asked for my shotgun back. But I'd gotten used to Jackson handling the weapons, and I'd never learned to shoot anyway.

Would my claws be enough to protect me? If I could ever get them to flare on command?

By the time I'd reached the first crossroads, I felt a slight breeze. Dreading the coming winds, I stood in the middle of the intersection, trying to guess which direction I should take.

I rubbed my pounding temples. I needed to go north. Which was *where* exactly?

Four possible choices. I was totally turned around, not surprising considering my sense of direction—as well as the fact that I'd been asleep when we'd arrived here last night.

I gazed up at the sun, as if I could determine my way from its position. I bet Selena could.

Hey, Matthew, I'm going to need some help here.

Again I got that flash of the rocket, accompanied by a new wave of pain.

No, no—I need help getting out of this subdivision!

I was starting to panic, ordering myself to choose a damn direction, any direction. I'd just taken a turn to the right when Jackson came striding around the corner with that menacing gait.

He'd pulled on a white T-shirt, inside out; his boots were unlaced. The shotgun was strapped haphazardly over his shoulder. He wasted no time insulting me. "You're a fool, Evangeline Greene!"

So much for begging for my forgiveness. Between gritted teeth, I asked, "Jackson, I don't suppose you came out here because you've changed your mind? About driving me for half a tank?" It was a long shot, but . . .

"Came out here to see if you were *coo-yôn* enough to go off alone. You doan even know where North Carolina is!"

I didn't have time for this! "I figure I'll head *north*." I kept walking.

"Then why are you heading *west*?"

I jogged back to the intersection and adjusted my bearings, but he just laughed. "Now you're marching south, *peekôn*."

I did an about-face.

"There you go," he called, following me as I picked up speed. "North! Guess that saying's true: Even a blind pig can find a truffle every now and again."

Ooh! I glared over my shoulder, but continued on. Great. The winds were increasing.

"Why are you so set on leaving?"

"It's not like I just sprang a trip on you," I tossed back at him. "I've told you from the beginning that I had to do this. And now you've made it clear that you want to stay here indefinitely."

—*Water! Rising!*— Matthew's urgency was like a banged gong reverberating through my mind.

I barely resisted the urge to clasp my forehead. "What do you want, Jackson? What more is there to say? I asked you for help, and you wouldn't give it to me!"

"So you just took off." In a low voice, he said, "I'm *that* easy to leave behind?"

"Seriously?" I snapped. "After last night?" At once, I regretted it. What he and Selena did was none of my business.

"Damn it, Evie!" He caught up to me with a scowl. "What is so all-fired wrong with me trying to sleep with you? You act like I'm stupid for even considering it!"

—*Empress!*— I couldn't think, quickening my pace even more.

But Jackson kept at me. "I'm good enough to travel with, to fool around with, but not to have sex with? You can take the girl out of Sterling . . ."

"That's not . . . it's not something I'm just going to throw away on a boy like you."

He stopped cold. I couldn't help but glance over my shoulder again.

He'd clenched his fists until tendons strained in his neck. "Like *me*?" He threw back his head and bellowed to the sky before facing me. *"What is so goddamned wrong with me?"*

He lunged forward, seizing my arm. "'Cause I didn't have money? That it? 'Cause of where I'm from? From the first day we met, you've looked down your nose at me. You've laughed at me, you've messed with my head."

"Money?" How had we started talking about *that*? The whole concept of it was fading from my mind, having as much significance to me as movie tickets or search engines.

My temples were aching, the wind bombarding me, confusion bombarding me. When had I messed with his head? "What are you *talking* about?" I flung off his grip, trudging forward again.

He followed. "In school, you treated me like I was something you needed to scrape off the bottom of your boot!"

I didn't bother hiding my bewilderment. "I was always nice to everyone. *Everyone.* We just got off to a bad start. And things went downhill."

I slowed when I came upon another intersection. All the estates around here had gates, all of them looking similar. Was I heading *deeper* into this neighborhood? I took another right.

So did Jackson. "Tell me you never think about the difference between how I grew up—and how you did. Or what you saw in my house that last night!"

"Oh, I think about it. And I regretted judging you for beating that man. Or at least, I did before you were such an asshole! Why are you dragging the past into this anyway?"

"Because you said *a boy like me*!"

"Yeah, a selfish boy like you."

"Selfish? *You* are calling me selfish?"

"In the pool, I thought you were asking me if I wanted more kissing—then the next thing I see is a *condom*? You couldn't have cared less if I was freaked out because you skipped over *all* the bases I'd thought to expect, or nervous about your ancient-looking protection, or—or not ready to go that fast! In general. I didn't expect you to declare, like, love for me forever or anything. But for my first time, I'd hoped for more than 'It's slim pickings out there.'"

He drew his head back, looking confounded. "Why didn't you tell me any of that?"

"I started to! But you got all pissed—shocker—and I was angry that you'd interrupted things . . . things that I'd . . . really *liked*." God, this was embarrassing! "None of this matters anyway. Looking back, I'm grateful it turned out the way it did."

"And why's that, you?"

"I don't want to be with a boy who can replace me at the drop of a hat with a strange girl he knows nothing about!" Though I was yelling at him, he seemed to be growing less and less angry.

"Those are the only reasons?" he said over the wind.

I cried, "That's not enough?" *Another* intersection?

—EMPRESS!—

I flinched with pain this time, taking another right. "And how dare you call me a miserable tease, Jackson! *You* are the tease. I thought things were great until you snatched the rug out from under me! So we both were hoping for something we didn't get."

Jackson and I were lockstep, out of breath, staring at each other. Then he just nodded.

"Nodding?" I nearly shrieked the word. "You're nod— Ugh! I don't *understand* you!"

"Just taking your point, *cher*." He looked like all his anger had just evaporated.

While mine had ramped up. "You've accomplished what you came out here to do. You've confirmed that I'm a *coo-yôn*. No reason for you to stay with me any longer!"

He didn't say anything, just hurried in front of me, striding backward, blocking the wind with his back. All considerate-like.

He was making *me* crazy! "I can't keep up with your moods! Shouldn't you be back playing house with Selena?" With a sinking feeling in my stomach, I realized that I'd taken so many rights I was almost back to her place.

"Well." He rubbed his chin. "I never thought I'd see this."

"See—*what*?"

"The day when Evangeline Greene was jealous over ole Jack."

"I am not!"

He laughed. "Your eyes are green with *jalousie*. It's an awful feeling, ain't it? How it rips at you inside."

"Sounds like you're talking from personal experience?" He said nothing, just kept staring at me. "Doesn't matter. I couldn't care less who you get with."

—*EMPRESS, EMPRESS, EMPRESS!*—

I stumbled, palm flat on the ground before I righted myself. Okay, that one *hurt*. My eyes watered and my nose started to run.

Jackson lunged forward to catch my arm. "Evie!" All of a sudden he was yanking off his shirt, balling it up to shove it at my face. "Your nose is bleeding, *bébé*."

"Oh." I held the shirt against my nose, hating how much his scent comforted me.

"Another vision?" His brows were drawn with concern. "This is why you're in such a rush, then?"

I dropped my gaze to his chest, staring at his rosary, realizing where I'd seen it before. His mother had been wearing it, the night of the Flash. He wore it to remember her? "Why should I tell you anything?" My voice was thick.

"Because if you tell me the *truth*, I might just get you wherever you need to go."

The truth? I scanned my surroundings for any alternative—

And saw a familiar flourishing crest. I was at Selena's once more. Shit! Back where I started from.

"You can trust me." He pulled me closer.

"But I don't trust *her*, Jackson." Should I reveal that she was one of the voices? That I'd had disturbing visions of her? I recalled Matthew's mysterious comment: *Arcana means secrets; keep ours.* Had he been warning me to keep my mouth shut to non-Arcana? Jackson was the only non-Arcana person I knew in the entire world. In any case . . . "If I tell you something, you might tell her."

"I think she's solid."

I wanted to scream, "Of course you would! Because you slept with her!" But I bit my tongue. Without him, I would never make it out of the neighborhood—much less to Matthew's in time.

"Evie, I woan tell her anything you doan want me to. I haven't told her anything more than I've had to."

So he *hadn't* revealed anything about my visions or my grandmother. Seeing no other choice but to trust him with at least *some* of this, I said, "Do you remember the boy that I sometimes see, the one who lectures me? He's not far from here. And he's calling for me. Loudly. Jackson, I saw him trapped in a flooded basement. He'll drown soon. And I get the feeling that . . . that I won't be alive much longer without his help." When Jackson didn't reply, I added, "I just know it's imperative that I reach him today."

"You believe you're goan to die if you doan find some strange kid you've never met? And you think *you* can find him?"

I adjusted the T-shirt against my nose and raised my chin.

Jackson gave a decisive nod. "All right."

"Excuse me?"

"See how easy that was? In the future, just *tell* me what you need, and let's see where things shake out, yeah?"

I gazed away. *I might need you. For more than a bodyguard.* "Why go with me? I know you want to stay here with her." *Deny it, please deny it.*

He didn't. "You and me started this thing. Guess we should finish it. And I got puzzles to solve, me. Besides, I plan to ask Selena if she'll come with."

"What?" She would. I had no doubt that she'd follow Jackson anywhere.

He started leading me back to the mansion. "You're not the only one who can keep secrets. And why wouldn't I invite her—since you couldn't care less who I might be with . . . ?"

30

Hundreds of Bagmen. All in one place.

"*Nom de Dieu,*" Jackson murmured, booting the Ducati's kickstand into place. We'd just driven up on a rise to get the lay of the land around Matthew's home, an isolated ranch-style house situated in a valley below.

And found a horde of zombies teeming around it.

Selena pulled up behind us. Naturally, she'd been up for the trip. She drew off her electric-blue helmet, shaking her long hair free. "What are you guys staring at?" When she caught a look at the swarm, she whistled low.

The nearly full moon was high in the sky. Almost midnight. It'd taken me forever to home in on Matthew.

Once we neared the space center, I'd listened for his voice, directing Jackson closer. Sometimes we'd make a turn, drive for a mile before I realized Matthew was growing fainter. Then we'd be forced to back-track. The winds—though still not nearly as bad as usual—hadn't helped.

Jackson had told Selena that we had to make a stop on our way to North Carolina, and the girl had said nothing about our fitful progress. She seemed to trust Jackson implicitly—while I probably would've been mouthing off in the same situation.

"Is this our 'stop'?" Selena asked with a hint of amusement.

Could she not sense Matthew's closeness or hear his call? Or was she again fishing for information?

"There's a boy inside," Jackson said. "Somebody Evie was supposed to check on."

Her eyes lit up. "A boy for Evie?"

"It's not like that," I hastily said. "I haven't even met him."

She adjusted the bow strapped over her shoulder, popping the top on her quiver. "What do you think the Baggers down there want?"

They were mindless with thirst, banging their hands against the door, the boarded-up windows, even the melted vinyl siding.

"There's got to be water inside," Jackson said, shooting me a look. "Maybe a flood."

—*Running out of time, Empress.*— Matthew's voice rang clear with our proximity, but I could tell he was weakening. "He's trapped in there. We've got to save him."

"We'll wait until dawn, till the Baggers scatter for cover," Jackson said.

Considering their frenzy, Matthew was going to be done for soon—water or not. "They'll break in way before then." Already they were denting the garage door. "We have to go now!"

He gave a harsh laugh. "Not in a million years, Evangeline."

When Selena hopped off her bike, heading to the very edge of the cliff, he muttered to me, "You didn't mention anything about Bagmen."

"I didn't *know* about them! But I do know he'll drown soon."

Selena called, "I don't see any lights or movement." Rejoining us, she asked, "Are you sure somebody's even home?" But again I got the feeling that she already knew the answer.

Jackson smoothly said, "Right before you drove up behind us, we saw a flashlight signal." He would lie to her for me? I eased closer to him.

"Then let's go save him," Selena said.

We both turned surprised glances to her. She was . . . agreeing with me? Immediately, I tried to work out her angle. She must know that one of the Arcana was inside, must believe Matthew would prove valuable to her in some way.

Selena plucked her bowstring over her shoulder. "You planning on living forever, J.D.?"

"I thought we were of one mind about some things," he told her. "Like survival being foremost. Us goan down there is the opposite of survival—it's suicide."

"If you guys can come up with a plan, I'm in." At his disbelieving look, she shrugged. "Maybe I can't stand the thought of some kid, in the dark, thinking he's counting down the last minutes of his life. He's got to be pissing himself."

Jackson turned to me again. "Evie, come on!"

I crossed my arms over my chest. "With or without you, Jackson."

He ground his teeth, shoving his fingers through his hair. "Jack Deveaux ain't *ever* goan to argue with two women. Always come out the loser on that score." He paced. "If you got any ideas, Evangeline, now's the time to share them."

I gazed down at the structure. One-story with vinyl siding. Older-looking. "I have one, but you'll just ridicule me."

"*Sans doute.* But let's hear it anyway."

"Stupidest, *coo-yôn* idea!" Jackson snapped as he sped down the highway in our freshly appropriated van, an older Econoline. "Risking my hide for a stranger!"

He was livid about this, but at least he was cooperating.

We'd found the van in the closest subdivision. As Jackson had swiftly done repairs, he'd said, "*If* I actually do this before coming to my senses, there's no reason for you to go with me, Evie. Or you, Selena."

"You'll need an extra bow." Selena had patted hers proudly.

"I'll need you to stay here and take care of Evie."

As I rolled my eyes, Selena had defiantly flipped her hair over her shoulder. "Save it, J.D. I'm going. Which means Evie is too."

When he opened his mouth to protest, I'd said, "Sounds like ole Jack's about to argue with two women . . . ?"

We'd siphoned some gas from the bikes, hidden them to pick up later, then headed toward Matthew's again.

Now Jackson yanked the wheel, careening onto the hilly dirt road that led to the house. The sharp ruts bounced the van so hard my teeth clattered.

"Easy, J.D.," Selena protested from the back. "No seat belts back here, *remember*."

Jackson had been adamant about sticking me in shotgun for this jaunt, had met my eyes as he'd yanked on my seat belt to test it. At once, Selena had started bitching that the only seat belts were in the front.

Now he said, "I want this remembered, *peekôn*. You holding the hell on?"

I nodded. "Bagmen ahead." Already we were driving past stragglers, the crowd of them growing thicker and thicker.

He didn't try to dodge them. The first we struck gave a guttural wail as it ramped up over the hood and into the air. The second one must not have fed recently; its body exploded into dusty chunks, coating the windshield.

When the house was in sight . . . we still didn't slow. "Kids, doan try this at home," Jackson muttered, his expression intent. Did he possess no fear? Instead, he looked as if the house had personally insulted him and he was about to make it pay.

I swallowed. As our targeted exterior wall loomed, I suddenly doubted this plan, wanting nothing more than to call it off.

Too late.

Impact. We crashed into that wall. *Through* it. Siding and boards battered the hood as Jackson slammed on the brakes.

Halfway inside the house, the van jolted to a stop. My body pitched forward, the seat belt wrenching the air out of my lungs.

As I fought for breath, I cracked open my eyes. One headlight remained intact, casting a muted glow over a living room. Drywall plaster clouded the air, but I could still see the outdated carpet and furniture. And cardboard boxes—they were everywhere, piled high against every wall, stacked throughout.

Retro Cracker Barrel meets Hoarders.

"Evie! You all right?"

As my breath returned, I gave him a thumbs-up signal.

"Selena?"

She gave a determined nod as she readied her bow.

Though the back half of the van plugged the hole we'd just made, sealing the Bagmen out, they'd already started banging on the back windows, moaning with thirst.

We wouldn't have long.

Jackson collected his own bow, shouldering his pack. "Then let's move." Leaving the engine running, we filed out into the house. "Where's this *coo-yôn* goan to be, Evie?"

"He has to be in the basement."

"Where's that?"

With all the boxes, I couldn't spy out a door. And with all the noise—the moaning Bagmen pummeled the van, the engine still revved in the confines of the room—I could barely hear his voice in my head.

When I bit my lip, struggling to concentrate, Selena shoved me out of the way. "J.D., I'll go right. You're left. I'll find you two directly." She clicked on the spy flashlight hanging from her belt, then slipped away.

Jackson too raised a flashlight, bow at the ready. "Let's go, Evie," he said, adding, "And, *peekôn*—"

"Like a shadow," I finished for him.

He led me forward, following a path through masses of boxes. Some of them were stacked so high they looked like they'd topple over on us.

We passed a boy's room, decorated with a space theme. Jackson's light shone over wallpaper depicting the galaxy and intricate mobiles of the planets dangling from the ceiling. Space shuttle posters adorned the walls. High-tech-looking computers and video game consoles were neatly organized.

Jackson gave a harsh laugh. "I've never been in a nerdery before."

Matthew's voice was growing fainter still, filling me with dread.

Selena returned, slipping up beside us. "There's a dead woman in a car in the garage. Car's out of gas. Ignition *on*. She's only been croaked a day, tops."

Suicide? What had happened here?

Jackson was unfazed by the suicide, instead wondering, "Who the hell fixed her car?"

Selena shrugged. "I found the way into the basement. There's water rushing down there."

Jackson met my gaze. We both knew my vision was coming true. "Selena, show us!"

With a nod, she took off through the obstacle course of boxes.

Jackson and I followed her to a nondescript door at the top of the basement stairwell. Pitch blackness greeted us. Snagging two glow sticks from his bag, he snapped them, tossing them below. They landed in water.

From their eerie green glow, we could see that the stairs led to a short hallway with two doors. Water was cascading from the *top* gap of one door, spouting from its old-fashioned keyhole as if from a pitcher. . . .

Selena said, "It's deep in there."

Jackson turned to me. "Unless that boy has gills, he's not goan to be alive."

"Oh, God!" I didn't hear Matthew in my head at all. Silence. "Please, you have to get him out of there!"

"You lost your mind?"

"Please, Jack!"

"Damn it, girl." A harsher oath followed as he shoved his bag into my chest, then tossed Selena his bow. "Want this remembered," he muttered, pushing past us to descend the steps four at a time.

We followed. "Can you break it down?" I cried.

He sloshed through knee-high water to reach the bowing door, sizing it up. Then he brandished the buck knife he always carried.

"It's solid oak," Selena said. "No way you can pierce it."

"Not goan to." He swiped water from his face. "You both head back up. *Now*."

As Selena and I ascended the steps, he worked the blade into the seam between the doorknob and the frame. His muscles rippled as he wedged it in, until only the hilt was visible.

Then he backed to the wall, bracing himself, and kicked the knife sideways. Once. And again—

The door exploded outward. A flume of water rushed over Jackson; a limp body rode the current, as if the basement had spat it out.

"Jackson!" I screamed.

He broke the surface and seized the pale boy, hauling him back to the steps.

"Is he alive?" I asked, squinting as Matthew's "tableau" appeared over him—a smiling young man carrying a knapsack and a single white rose. He had his vacant gaze raised to a blinding sun, about to walk off a cliff, a small dog nipping at his heels.

I shook myself and the image faded. I didn't want to see Matthew's tableau; I wanted to see him *safe*!

Jackson felt the boy's neck, then hovered a hand over his mouth. "Breathing. Just knocked out."

My legs nearly gave way.

Selena said, "The water's still rising, J.D."

Jackson gave a quick nod, heaving the kid over his shoulder in a fireman's carry. When he bounded up the stairs, I marveled at his strength.

"Come on, you!" he snapped at me. "We ain't out of this yet."

By the time we returned to the van, the Bagmen were rocking it so hard you could see its shock absorbers. Getting inside was like boarding a boat in rough seas, but we managed to slide open the side door.

I scrambled across the floor in the back, motioning for Jackson to let the boy down gently—

He dropped him like a dead alligator, attention already on other things as he determined the situation. "They're too thick behind us, and we're wedged in," he said. "Stay here. I'm letting them in."

"What?" Selena and I cried in unison, but he'd already slammed the side door and loped off, wending around the boxes.

Shortly after, I heard what sounded like him kicking a door down. A sharp whistle followed. Gradually, the van stopped rocking.

Then came Jackson hauling ass around the corner, a line of Bagmen in pursuit. He hurtled some boxes, purposely knocking others over to slow the creatures down.

Selena leaned out to cover him, but the Baggers all stopped at the entrance to the basement, drawn by the undeniable call of that water. . . .

Once Jackson had hopped in the van, he shoved it into reverse and gunned the engine. Tires squealed. The smell of burned rubber filled the air as we inched out.

And then . . . we shot backward in a rush, leveling any Bagmen stragglers.

Part of the house caved in behind us. But there was enough of an opening for newcomers to crawl in.

None chased the van. As I gazed out the back windows, I saw them begin to teem into that hole, like ants in reverse.

Once we were back on the dirt road, heading out, Selena cried, "We did it!"

Jackson's eyes were dancing with excitement. "Hell, yeah!" He slapped her raised hand.

With disaster averted, I cradled the boy's head in my lap.

"Let's pick up the bikes, J.D., then break open that fifth to celebrate!" She turned up her iPod, to some kind of irritating industrial music.

Grinning, Jackson glanced back at me in the rearview mirror.

I mouthed, *Thank you so much.*

He shrugged, his demeanor brusque, then looked away.

I peered down at Matthew's face, startled by the overwhelming tenderness I already felt for him—as if I'd found a long-lost brother.

Something drew my attention to his arm. The sleeve of his plaid button-down had rolled up, revealing a silver MedicAlert bracelet circling his wrist. It was stamped with the word AUTISTIC and an emergency contact phone number.

For some reason, I didn't want Selena or even Jackson to see this, didn't want them to judge him. I whispered to Matthew, "You won't need this anymore."

I reached down to unfasten it; as soon as my skin made contact with his, a vision softly appeared inside my head, fluttering down into my consciousness like a tossed scarf.

The van disappeared. I found myself in the boy's home watching a scene unfold.

Just before dusk, the house began quaking. Then came a deafening metallic pop, sounding like a manhole cover had exploded. Water rushed downstairs. It wasn't long before Bagmen streamed into the yard, beating at the house.

The boy stood in that creepy time-warp living room alone. Waiting. Though he was so tall, and at least my age, he looked young and lost among all those hoarded boxes. Hours passed, and still he waited. The yard was now thick with zombies.

When a middle-aged brunette finally emerged from her bedroom, he met her gaze, not bothering to hide his emotions. *Vulnerable. Pleading.*

"Matthew," she said in a high voice, adjusting the prim skirt-suit she wore, "why don't you go check on the pipe? See if you can't fix the leak? I'll go secure the garage."

His soulful eyes misted. "Yes, Mother," he rasped, dragging his feet down the stairs and into that flooding basement.

Once he'd trudged through foot-deep water to find the burst pipe— a massive one that he could never *fix*—he heard the woman murmur from the basement hallway, "Mother knows best, son."

As the water continued to rise, he faced her. His expression was heartbroken.

But not surprised.

Not even when she forced the door closed behind her and locked him inside to drown. . . .

"Slap that boy awake," Jackson told me.

We'd just broken into a four-bedroom brick McMansion for the night. After searching the place, Jackson had returned to the van to ferry a still-unconscious Matthew to one of the twin beds in a guest room.

"I want to know how he got himself into that fool bind." He leaned his shoulder against the wall, hitting the fifth that he and Selena had broken out to celebrate our successful rescue mission.

I sat beside Matthew, shaking his shoulder. Then harder.

Nothing.

"He'll wake up soon enough." Selena snapped her fingers for the bottle. "Come on, J.D., there's a dartboard downstairs."

Jackson nodded. "Evie, let's leave him for now."

"I don't want him to wake up and not know where he is." Not after the day he'd had. *Mother knows best.* I shivered. "You guys can go and play—"

"My friend came for me."

My gaze darted down. Matthew's whisper had been . . . *out loud?* After so long hearing his voice in my head, it sounded so rich, so authentic.

He was awake, his eyes open. Utterly familiar to me.

Shooting upright, he yanked me into his arms to hold me close, his breath shuddering, as if he'd been aching to see me.

Over Matthew's shoulder, I saw Jackson's frown turn into a scowl.

In a pissy tone, Selena said, "I thought you told us that you'd never met this boy."

"I-I haven't."

"Empress," Matthew sighed against my hair.

I stiffened, wishing he hadn't said that out loud.

"Why did you call her that?" Jackson demanded, while Selena canted her head with curiosity.

Matthew drew away from me to face him. "Why *don't* you?"

I couldn't tell if his tone was challenging or merely puzzled. Apparently neither could Jackson. "Tell us your name."

"Matthew Mat Zero Matto." With a sly look, he said, "Empress knows my name."

Jackson asked, "Where'd the water come from in your house?"

"A pipe." Then he explained to Jackson, "Water travels in pipes."

Jackson pushed up from his spot against the wall, clearly reaching his limit of patience. "You hit your head or something, boy?"

"Jackson, please."

Another scowl from the Cajun. Then he muttered to Selena, "He's slower than Christmas."

"Christmas," Matthew began grandly, "is . . . slow."

In a loud voice, Selena enunciated to him, "I am Sah-lee-nah Loo-ah. This is Jackson Dah-voh."

In a bored tone, Matthew said, "Dee-vee-oh and Luna." He turned from them without interest to gaze at me. "You came for me."

"*We* did, Matthew," I said. "Jackson's the one who freed you from the basement. Selena played a huge role as well."

Shrug.

"The only *coo-yôn* in the world who could drown himself after the Flash," Jackson grated. "And you owe me a buck knife, boy."

"Come on, J.D.," Selena said, "we'll let these two *crazy* kids catch up. I'll bet you the other fifth I packed that I can beat you at darts."

Smart girl, packing whiskey—for the boy nicknamed after it. *Well played, sage foe.*

Jackson gazed from Matthew to me, looking unconvinced.

Impulses warred inside me: my curiosity's need to ask Matthew questions in private, and my jealousy's need to separate Jackson from Selena, to find out what had happened between them last night.

Curiosity won. "You guys go have fun," I said. "We'll be fine. I think I'll be able to talk to him better alone."

Selena started dragging Jackson away.

"You yell if you need anything. I'll be listening," he added darkly for Matthew's benefit. Then in French he murmured to me, "We need to talk. Tonight."

"Gawd, you are sexy," Selena cried, "when you speak French!" And then they were gone.

Slore! Jackson was right—*jalousie* did rip at you inside.

I made my face expressionless before I faced Matthew again. "Hey, kid, you need to be a little nicer to those two. Unfortunately, we're kind of dependent on them."

He chuckled at that.

"Can you hunt? Or shoot?"

"Had a slingshot once!"

"Okay, then, neither can I. But they both hunt. They'll source food and protect us. So, seriously, we *are* going to have to rely on them."

He grinned. "Empress has a sense of humor this time." It was one thing to be called Empress in my head, quite another in real life.

Matthew truly was here. With me. "Thank you for the visions, kid." That was a sentence I'd never thought I would say. "You saved my life from the Flash."

He nodded gravely. "I *am* a lifesaver."

"But I *couldn't* have been one. I mean, I couldn't have prevented the Flash, right?"

He gave a bark of laughter. "That's just crazy talk."

Guilt easing . . . "Matthew, exactly how psychic are you?"

"So psychic that other psychics should be called Mattics."

I smiled, excitement coursing through me. "What all can you see?"

He gazed up at the ceiling, his eyes going vacant. "The last two monarch butterflies are thousands of miles apart and flying *away* from each other. A boy is skateboarding across old Lake Michigan. The next card is close. Don't look at *this* hand . . ."

"Look at *that* one," I finished. "I know it. When you hear the voices, do they go quiet whenever you make contact?"

"Don't want them quiet. Dee-vee-oh makes them quiet for you. Whenever he helps, he hurts."

"Do you want to elaborate on that?" He gave me a wide grin. Apparently not. "So you can send your visions to anyone? And you can spread them through touch?"

His hair was drying, now flopped charmingly over his forehead. "Messages."

"Did you send them to other Arcana?"

He looked insulted. As if I'd accused him of cheating on me. "*You* are my friend and ally."

"So why'd you send me visions of *Selena*? What did that one in the woods mean?"

"Mean?" he asked in a baffled tone. "Is it bedtime?"

"Um, not quite. Tell me this, is Selena good like us or bad . . . like Death?"

"She's the Moon," he said matter-of-factly.

Obviously this subject was a dead end. I raised a new one. "Can you see my grandmother?"

"*Tarasova,*" Matthew murmured.

Just as she'd described herself to me. "Is she okay?" Nothing. "We're on our way to find her. She has all the answers."

"You have matching questions."

Surely he'd tell me if she hadn't survived—since we were going there? "If you're psychic, and I can control plants, what are some of the other Arcana powers?"

"Vast."

"Are we genetically altered or something? How did we get our powers?"

"We are born."

Okay. "Does Selena have other abilities besides her archery?" Other than always looking perfect, bike racing, and cooking like *Top Chef?* "Does *she* know what we are? Is she *literally* the Bringer of Doubt? And how many Arcana are there? Why was that vision of Death more lifelike than all the others?"

Instead of replying to any of my questions, Matthew yawned widely, his eyes less clairvoyant-y—more a sleepy, childlike brown.

Though I burned for answers, I sensed that pushing him on any subject would help as much as pushing my own memories had. In other words, not at all.

Sometimes you have to let things unfold. But I had to know one thing. "When you were knocked out earlier, I saw a vision of you today. You didn't look surprised when your mom locked you in. You saw your future?"

"Not my own. Never my own. Hers."

He could only see *others'* futures? "You didn't want to, um, inter- vene with her?" Maybe to keep her from attempting to murder her son and committing suicide?

Had she snapped under the stress? Or had she wanted to spare him a ghastly Bagman death—with a drowning instead? Why wouldn't she just take him with her in the car?

Then I remembered; Matthew had already told me. She'd known he wouldn't *stay* in the car.

"Wouldn't have mattered with her. Not for long." With glinting eyes, he whispered, "I see *far,* Evie."

So she would have died soon after? Or maybe her fate would have been worse?

Even as I debated whether there *was* a fate worse than death, I wondered how Matthew handled making these excruciating decisions for others.

You poor boy. I reached forward to smooth his hair from his forehead, as my own mother used to do to me. How could I feel this much affection for him so quickly?

But then, we had known each other for months.

He blinked up at me with endless trust. "I believed you'd make it in time." Another yawn.

Watching him yawn was equivalent to watching a puppy dozing off—about the cutest thing I'd ever seen. *Will I ever see a puppy again?* "Why don't you try to go to sleep? We'll have hours tomorrow to talk."

"Don't leave me."

"I won't, I promise."

His lids grew heavier. "It begins with me . . . and ends with him."

"Ends with who, Matthew?"

He'd already drifted to sleep.

I headed toward the other twin bed, lying down, reflecting on the hectic day. Of course Selena had wanted to come with us: "Hell, J.D., I could use some adventure." She'd had her survival gear, high-performance clothes, and high-energy food packed in minutes. Bitch.

At least she had let us rummage for sleeping bags and portable food of our own.

And she was certainly equal to the journey, handling her own bike like a professional stuntwoman. In fact, she'd wanted me to ride with her—no doubt to prevent me from clinging to Jackson like a dryer sheet.

But in a tone that had brooked no argument, Jackson had said, "Evie's with me."

Had I reclaimed his attention from Selena? I couldn't decide! At times, as we'd sped north, my thoughts had turned to the night before, but then I'd remember that Matthew's life was at stake, and I'd feel ashamed.

Now I could mull it all I wanted to. Facts: Last night, Jackson had been drunk and pissed off at me. She'd been all over him. This morning, when Jackson had shepherded me back to the mansion, Selena had acted indignant, like a spurned girlfriend.

Three possibilities. One, they'd been at it like minks and would be again tonight. Two, they'd gotten together, but now Jackson regretted it. Or, three, he'd kept his hands to himself, and Selena was psycho-jealous over nothing.

I had to know. Yet while nothing they'd done or said convinced me they were a couple, they'd also done nothing that would allow me to rule that out.

"Empress?" Matthew said, waking.

"Did you have a bad dream, kid? Are you hungry? We have food."

Gazing at me intently, he rose—then climbed onto the bed with me.

"Whoa! What are you doing?"

He took my hand, covered it with both of his own. At once, I relaxed. Being with him like this felt normal, natural. *Familiar.*

"They play, Evie."

"Who?" I grew warm, unable to keep my eyes open.

The last thing I heard: *"The Arcana."*

32

Matthew and I were standing at the edge of a great charred field. Above us, continuous lightning bolts fractured an ink-black sky.

He was still holding my hand in his, allowing me to experience his foresight. This scene was even more vibrant than the ones he'd sent my way. In fact, it was *seamless* from reality. How could he even tell reality from a vision?

He whispered in my mind, *"Hit or miss."*

From his thoughts, I knew that we were here to secretly observe a battle of the Arcana—one happening *right now*, somewhere out in the world.

There were five Arcana, divided into two small alliances. Already, it neared its conclusion.

Had Matthew foreseen who would win?

He shook his head. *"Future flows like waves—or eddies. Can't always see. But bet on* him *to win."* Matthew pointed to the field, to the tall, armored male striding across the sooty earth, a sword in each hand. *"Death."*

Exactly as I remembered him from Haven, the Reaper wore a full set of black armor and a helmet with light glowing behind the grille.

He was awing, and so clearly at ease with those swords. A perfect killer.

Had I actually once looked at his card and pitied him?

All around him, lightning javelins exploded, spitting electricity. Far in the distance, the sparking outline of a boy's form blazed in the night. "Eyes to the skies, lads!" he yelled as the spears came down faster and faster.

Just as I wondered what his name was, Matthew whispered, *"Joules. Master of Electricity. The Tower Card."*

Bolts were striking all around Death, but he didn't alter his course, didn't even hunch down in the fray. Occasionally he'd deflect a javelin with one of his swords.

I caught sight of his target—a black-haired girl who looked even younger than me. She was limping across that barren landscape, dragging a leg, struggling to escape him.

I feared it was a lost cause. Though she had weapons—a trident-looking blade in each hand—he wore armor. I didn't think she could pierce it unless she could reach his helmet grille.

And her body had already been damaged in some way. I squinted at the veins of black forking over her olive skin. They grew thicker and thicker until they intersected in large patches.

"Touch of Death," Matthew explained.

Out of breath and whimpering, she twisted to keep the Reaper in sight.

"The Temperance Card," Matthew whispered. *"Calanthe. She wields the Weight of Sins."*

She stumbled, losing her balance, collapsing to her back. A cloud of ash wafted up, haloing her body—

A trident blade came flying out of the soot, twirling end over end, directly for Death's helmet.

With a flick of his wrist, he batted the blade away with his sword. Like a gnat.

Once the ash settled, I could see that her expression was one of utter terror—this girl knew she was about to die.

When those javelins rained down with even more force and number around Death, I realized that Joules was trying to save her. He was hurtling spears on the run—because a horned beast stalked him.

I recognized the skulking creature on my own. Ogen, *El Diablo*—the Devil Card. Death's repulsive ally.

Yet Ogen's body was now morphing, expanding—first into a colossal ogre, then into a giant. His brutish strength was unbelievable.

Joules kept up his maddened volley, retreating from Ogen. If that creature seized the boy . . .

Death spun his swords all around him, deflecting the bolts with uncanny speed. He was striding through a shower of lightning—and his demeanor seemed bored.

Just before Death reached Calanthe, a blur from above started to dive down like a comet. A flying boy! I'd seen him before, with his old-timey clothes and majestic black wings. I'd *heard* him before as well: *I watch you like a hawk.*

Through Matthew's thoughts, I discovered that he was Gabriel, the Judgment Card. Also known as the archangel, his MO was to hover above the battle, choosing the perfect moment to attack. Then he would dive, increasing his missilelike speed, leveling off just above the ground.

Now he was plummeting so fast, he displaced the air with a whistle. With his first flyby, he knocked Death's helmet away. At once, Calanthe hurled her remaining blade at the Reaper's face—as if according to plan.

But he dodged it with ease. How fast was he?

I wanted to see Death's face, but ash swirled all around, obscuring it. His long white-blond hair concealed his features as well.

Losing little velocity, Gabriel bowed his back, muscles and tendons straining as he looped his body into the air once more. His speed was still a shrill whistle as he made his second strike.

But the Reaper was too fast even for the archangel. His swords flashed out, slashing one silken black wing, sending the boy careening across the night sky.

I heard Joules yelling—clashing with Ogen? No more javelins to blitz Death; nothing to save the girl now.

Could we help her?

Matthew whispered, *"We're not* here, *Empress."*

So we could only watch as Death took her life. With his armored back to me, he loomed over Calanthe. When she began to beg for mercy, he gave one curt shake of his head, and she trailed off.

With a weak cry, she raised one hand, as if to wield some kind of power against him.

"Crush him," Matthew murmured. *"Weight of Sins."*

A haze erupted around her, ripples of energy seeming to flow out from her, bombarding Death.

He *laughed.* "I'd have to consider my deeds sinful for you to have power over me, Calanthe." He lopped off her arm with one of his swords, while his other arced around for her neck. *Slice.*

I gazed away, my eyes watering.

Matthew squeezed my hand. *"She fears him no more."*

Across the field, Joules howled with grief, retreating as Ogen gave chase.

Leaving Death alone with his kill.

When he turned toward his red-eyed steed, awaiting not far from our secret spot, I glimpsed Death's face for the first time.

Surprise rocked me. Death was the most beautiful boy I had ever imagined.

Looking to be no more than twenty years old, he was tall and broad-shouldered with a breathtaking face. I imagined some might describe his features as *noble.* His eyes glittered like . . . stars.

How could someone so evil look so divine?

He jammed his battered helmet onto the saddle pommel, and exhaled a gust of breath. Every line in his bearing screamed *weariness.*

Yet then he stilled, craning his neck to look directly at Matthew. "I've been around long enough to sense your unblinking gaze, Fool." His voice was a harsh rasp. "You allowed her to see me at play? Perhaps I won't kill you *last* after all."

Then his attention turned on me. "Don't worry, Empress, Matto remembers his debts. He'll show you to me as well." His accent sounded Eastern European, or maybe Russian? "I'll watch all your battles and discover your cunning tricks. After tonight, I'll whisper in your mind more freely than any of the Arcana."

I was speechless, still awestruck by his face.

Which seemed to take him aback. "Are you *weak*? Our game is no fun if you're weak. Are you faint of heart and short of courage?"

Matthew squeezed my hand, prompting me to croak, "No." It sounded like a question.

Death narrowed those glittering eyes. "I've waited endless years to battle you again. Will you not face me?"

Face him? What was I supposed to "battle" him with?

Behind him, that field might as well have been a lunar landscape for all the plants that grew. Should I attack an armored knight with my thorn claws?

Just as he'd once said, I *did* have life in my blood. But even if I had time to grow seeds, garden plants couldn't withstand those swords.

How much blood would it take to grow an acorn into a formidable ally?

"Remember, Empress," he said. "Death always defeats life. It might take time, but I will *always* win." As he mounted that mighty steed, he pinned me with his hypnotic gaze. "When your blood bathes my sword, I'll drink it just to mock you. . . ."

I woke with a gasp, back at the McMansion.

Matthew looked groggy, slow to come out of his vision.

"What the hell, kid?!" We'd not only witnessed a murder, we'd talked with the killer! "Wake up." I shook his shoulder. He seemed a hundred times more exhausted than before he'd slept. "Why does Death expect *me* to face him?"

He ran his hand over his forehead. "The ancient battles must be fought, the markings earned, the bad cards defeated."

My senses were on high alert after that disturbing vision, my patience at an all-time low. Striving for an even tone, I said, "*Why* must they be fought? Maybe we have—oh, I don't know—enough on our plates after the Flash!"

"The battles begin at the End," he said yet again.

"The Flash marked the beginning?" Right when the voices kicked up. Had the apocalypse awakened the Arcana? I swallowed. *Or vice versa?* "What caused the Flash, Matthew?"

"Sun."

I exhaled in relief. Okay, a solar flare made sense. Then I remembered . . . "Isn't there a Sun Card?"

Shrug.

Patience, Evie. "Is the Sun good or bad?"

"The sun is a star."

And wasn't there a Star Card too? *Moving on . . .* "How did Death see us?"

"Old. Knows my glimpse."

"How old is he?"

"Really."

"Matthew!" I rose, pacing.

"Twenty-one centuries or so."

"Twenty-one! Is he immortal?"

Another shrug. "Just hasn't been killed in a while."

Back and forth I paced. "But he knows you. Are you . . . his age?"

With a roll of his eyes, Matthew informed me, "I'm *sixteen*."

Patience! "Then tell me when you two met."

"Twenty-one centuries ago."

I pinched the bridge of my nose. "You're killing me, kid."

He shot to his feet, clamping my shoulders. "Never kill you!"

"It's just a figure of speech, Matthew." I eased out of his grip.

"Oh." He sank back on the bed. "I've seen the games, the past. I've seen Death. In some ways, I'm wise," he said, looking anything but.

"Crazy like a fox," I murmured. "Okay, so say I have to fight in some kind of supernatural 'ancient battle.' What's the purpose? What do we get if we win?"

My mind raced as I imagined what kind of prize might be equal to the risk. Maybe there was a protected haven on earth, one that still had rain and greenery?

Death was some kind of otherworldly knight; did he possess an untouched fortress somewhere? Then I remembered his plane of unbroken black, cluttered with ruins. Not precisely where I'd choose to live.

Maybe there was some way to go back in time and stop the apocalypse! Hadn't Gran believed I was going to save the world? I needed to know the stakes.

My heart dropped when Matthew said, "If you win, you get to . . . *live.*"

"So there's no way to improve our lot? Just more danger and worry heaped on my shoulders?"

"Danger! And worry!"

"No. I *refuse* this. I didn't sign up for this shit! I never opted in. But I sure as hell can opt out."

"No refusal. You are Arcana. Learn your powers. *Use* them."

"Nuh-uh, I'm a girl with no dog in this fight," I assured him. "I'll raise a white flag, seek a truce. *You* can help me with Death, since you know him."

"I'm in his pocket, so he's in my eyes."

"And that means *what*?"

Matthew nodded. "No truce. No peace. He is *Death*. He knows one thing—killing."

"Then I'll run." Was that what my life would be like from now on? Fleeing from an armored serial killer, always looking over my shoulder, dreading his approach? How long could I keep that up?

With a shiver, I thought of Matthew's eulogy for Calanthe.

She fears him no more. . . .

"I doan like the feel of this," Jackson muttered, clenching the van's steering wheel, squinting to see the road. Only now he wasn't peering through an ash storm . . .

Fog blanketed us. The mountains flanking the interstate were bathed in it.

I hadn't seen fog since before the Flash. Unfortunately, that wasn't the only weather change we were contending with. Over the last six days since we'd rescued Matthew, the temperatures had dropped to nearly freezing.

The windstorms had grown less frequent, but when they hit, they were fierce.

Biting winds in the Deep South—in May? Seeing our breaths smoke put all of us on edge. For all we knew, the entire earth was about to freeze over in a new ice age.

I had only my hoodie, Jackson a thin leather jacket, and Matthew? A sleeping bag. Selena, of course, had her all-weather-performance clothes.

From her position in shotgun, she studied our map. "We're going the right way, J.D. Maybe the fog's throwing you."

Each day, Jackson and Selena took the front seats, sticking Matthew and me in the back with their motorcycles. Like luggage.

Matthew was currently lying on a sleeping bag on the floor, whistling the *Star Wars* theme song, completely oblivious to our disquiet.

"The tank's teetering on E," Jackson said. "That map doan show any towns for miles. It was rural here."

"The map's old," Selena said. "There could be strip malls just ahead. And I guarantee you that we'll find more gas than we did in the places we've already passed."

After Matthew's rescue, we'd decided to go north into Tennessee before heading east to North Carolina. Backtracking south along the same desolate—and supply-free—highway in Alabama wasn't an option.

We had only a few energy bars left between us. Water was getting scarce.

Though we had officially deviated from that big army's swath of destruction, we still hadn't found any food in this area.

What *had* we found? More Bagmen. We'd see them crawling along the side of the road, reaching for our van.

"We can always use the gas from the bikes," Selena suggested.

Jackson shook his head. "Wouldn't get us ten miles in this thing. Besides, we got to conserve those tanks."

I noted the tense set of his shoulders, the clench of his jaw. He was weighed down with so much responsibility. I wished I could help in some way. I might not be able to—but Matthew could.

As Jackson and Selena debated routes, I rearranged our box of weapons and empty gallon jugs in the back so I could lay out my sleeping bag next to Matthew's. I dropped down beside him, curling up for warmth. The back of the van was drafty.

We faced each other, whisper-distance away. "Matthew, talk to me," I murmured. "Are we going the right way? Will we find food soon? Give me something we can use."

Jackson and Selena had no idea what kind of resource they possessed, still treating him like an idiot.

Like a fool.

Matthew glared. "They don't deserve it," he snapped under his breath, sounding more like a sixteen-year-old boy than a visionary. Then he started back up with the *Star Wars* theme.

Whistling sucked.

And there went Selena, turning on that grating industrial rock. He whistled louder; Selena cranked the volume.

If there were any more tension in this van, it would explode. The four of us had about hit our limit of each other.

Jackson had taken an instant dislike to Matthew, scowling whenever the boy clasped my hand in his as we walked, calling him *bon à rien* at every opportunity.

On the surface, Selena appeared to ignore Matthew completely, but when she thought no one was watching, she studied the boy with an alarming intensity.

The vision Matthew had sent me of her still gave me chills. But he didn't seem to fear her in the least, which made me feel better.

I'd forced myself to put all my worry—and jealousy—over Jackson and Selena on the back burner, focusing my attention on Matthew. I believed he was without continuous care for the first time in his life—and he was struggling.

Most of the time, he didn't appear to be experiencing our reality. He talked to himself, giving a stray laugh here and there. He slept fitfully, no doubt overwhelmed with those visions of his.

He'd shown me one battle. I'd never asked for a repeat.

Whenever we could talk without Jackson and Selena overhearing, I'd been delving about the Arcana. I'd found out that the Fool could see not only the futures of others but also their pasts and presents. I'd learned that there were many more kids like us. But not what our purpose was.

If we were all in some kind of war with alliances and battles, then what had started the fight? I knew this was life-or-death—I'd seen Calanthe beheaded—but had other kids already died?

Had Joules and Gabriel survived that night?

Basically, Matthew had revealed just enough information to make me want to pull my hair out. A typical conversation:

"How many Arcana are there?"

"Cards?"

"Yes, cards."

A firm nod. *"Arcana."*

"Okay, then. So what came first—the kids or the cards?"

His answer: "Gods."

I could almost think he was doing it on purpose just to frustrate me, except that *he* got exasperated with *me*—as if he were trying to teach me a new language and I kept forgetting how to say "the."

I reached for his forehead now, smoothing away that mop of hair. "Matthew, let's hold off on the whistling for a bit."

He drew a deeper breath, his expression defiant.

"Pretty please?"

He glowered, but did go quiet.

A relief. Ideally, I wanted us to be so quiet that Jackson and Selena forgot we were here.

"Empress fears Dee-vee-oh and Luna will throw me away."

"What? No way." I *might* have had a brief worry a couple of days ago when I'd heard Jackson tell Selena, "That boy can't fight, hunt, keep watch—or shut up. He's a resource-suck." *Just what he called me.* "He's always hungry. We're burning through any food we find."

Selena had replied, "But Evie likes him so much, J.D. Surely you can see how strongly she feels about him."

My attachment to Matthew wasn't like that at all—and she knew it— but I couldn't contradict her without outing myself as an eavesdropper.

Then Selena had added, "Why don't you tell her that we'll keep him along, but only if she agrees to head back to my place. Otherwise, we'll be forced to cut the deadweight."

Selena, you snake in the ash.

Yet Jackson had told her, "I'll think about it." How much sway did she hold over him?

Deciding there was no chance the two up front could hear us over that music, I whispered, "Matthew, can Selena literally bring doubt?"

"She's the Moon." He began staring at one of his hands, turning it this way and that, seeming to examine every contour. Which usually meant he was done with a subject.

I'd asked him if Jackson had been with Selena—and I'd received the same response. I still couldn't tell if they had. The two of them got along great, but never betrayed that anything deeper was at work.

At least Jackson didn't. Selena was clearly head over heels for him.

She might not be the only one.

If I could find out for certain that he wanted more from me, and that he hadn't slept with our constant traveling companion, I'd tell him that I was falling for him. . . .

Now Matthew gave me a disappointed look. "Empress lies about them throwing me away."

I exhaled. "I'd never let anything happen to you. If they toss you out, I'll go with."

I'd told Jackson as much. Big mistake.

Yesterday, in one of the rare moments when both Matthew and the clinging Selena had been out of earshot, Jackson had gruffly muttered to me, "Do you think that boy can take care of you? Can protect you on the road?"

I'd blinked in confusion. "Uh, will he *need* to?" Then doubts had arisen. "Ohh, I see how it is. The tribe has spoken. You and Selena are going to lighten the load. Will you at least give me notice so we can be ready?"

Jackson had drawn his head back, his jaw muscles bulging. "You believe I'd abandon you?"

"I might have accidentally overheard you and Selena talking. You called Matthew a resource-suck, said he was burning through the food." Would Jackson look at Matthew through "greater good" glasses? Especially with Selena's influence and doubt-mongering?

"That's *fact*," Jackson had said. "Something *I* tend to consider in decision-making."

"Like deciding whether to maroon him?"

"And what would you do if I did?"

"Go with him," I'd said without hesitation.

"You'd choose to go with him over me?" For the scarcest instant, I'd thought I saw something fierce and chillingly possessive in his gaze, then—

Gone. His expression had grown shuttered once more. He'd said in a scathing tone, "Maybe that's what I should do! Let you two make your own way, one more useless than the other. If I wasn't so sure I'd be sending you to your grave, I'd probably cut bait now!" Then he'd stormed off, leaving me shaken.

We hadn't spoken more than a few words since, though I often caught his gaze on me in the rearview mirror.

Now I told Matthew, "I don't want you to worry about getting abandoned, okay? Promise me."

"We don't need them," he said. "You need your allies."

"Okay, I'll play. Who are they?"

"Arsenal!"

"*Shhh, kid.*" As much as I felt like a big sister and best friend to Matthew, he could nettle me like no other. I imagined this was what it'd be like with a sibling on a long road trip.

In a quieter tone, he said, "You need to practice your powers. Phytomanipulation."

This was something new! "Does that mean plant control?"

"I'm hungry."

Patience. "Matthew, if I'm supposed to practice, are you going to be my coach?"

"Yes!" he said brightly. "Flex your thorn claws."

Suddenly self-conscious that another person knew about them, I made fists. "I can't just force them out." The last time they'd appeared was in Selena's neighborhood. "Or *can* I?"

He gave a long-suffering sigh.

I focused my attention on my fingernails, imagining them transforming. Nothing happened. I concentrated again. Same result. So I gave up. "You said I had other"—*possibly easier*—"abilities? What are they? What's my Arcana call?"

"I don't see your claws." He peered at my hands, then began studying his own. *Topic finished.*

"Oh, I get it. We're on a new reward system." I lay back in a huff, staring at the van roof.

Maybe I should just let things unfold. We could be at Gran's in less than two weeks. I could wait till then to bombard her with all my questions.

What am I? Why am I this way? What is my purpose?

Can the world be . . . saved?

Suddenly Matthew shot upright, his face paling. "Death sends his regards."

At once, Selena turned down the music. I saw Jackson's eyes narrow in the rearview mirror.

Matthew asked, "Why aren't you preparing for Death, Evie? We've talked of what the future brings."

Oh, no, no. If our cryptic exchanges weren't enough to make me batty, Matthew also liked to talk about his visions of Death. A lot. Which kept me on edge—Jackson as well.

And Jackson didn't even know that Matthew referred to a real man, a psychotic knight who'd vowed to execute me and drink my blood.

This morning Jackson had told Matthew, "You mention death one more time, and I'll knock you into next week. *Comprends?*"

"Already been there," Matthew had answered. Now he told me, "You have to be ready for Death, Evie."

Jackson said, "I warned you, *coo-yôn!*"

Selena touched his forearm, casting him a fake, pleading, *Be-patient-for-Evie's-sake* look.

Her personality had been grating on my nerves, scaling new heights of annoyance. But as ever, I was filled with doubts about her. How fitting. I didn't feel I could trust her, but I sensed I might have to . . . depend on her?

Matthew asked me, "This time will be different, won't it?"

Though I had no idea what he was talking about, I promised, "Yes, Matthew. Let's just lie back."

"You won't kill me?"

Jackson shot me a look in the mirror.

Under my breath, I said, "I'd never hurt you!"

"Death won't wait forever." With a confident nod, he added, "Strike first or be first struck."

When Jackson gripped the steering wheel harder, I said, "Hey, let's talk about something else. Did you ever get to see the space shuttle in Florida?" Nothing. "How about those rascally Ewoks, huh?"

"I'm in Death's pocket, so he's in my eyes," Matthew said again. "He sees you even now. You'll meet the Reaper soon."

"*C'est ça coo-yôn!* Jackson snapped. "That's it! I've had enough of your crazy-ass talk—"

The engine rattled.

Sputter. Clunk. Done.

Everyone fell silent as Jackson steered the van off the road—as if another car might need to pass. Once our momentum crept to a standstill, we all sat wordlessly, even Matthew.

Without gas, we'd be walking. In the raw cold and fog. There was only one house in sight, a modest brick structure that had surely already been rolled.

Just as I'd been in the days before my mom had passed, we were shit out of luck—and I felt like heading to the barn for my daily primal scream.

Selena piped her lip to blow her hair out of her face. "What are we going to do now, J.D.?"

"We passed a militia camp in a valley, not far back. They'll have gas."

I hadn't seen anything. Of course, I'd been trying to keep Matthew quiet. "How do you know it's a militia?"

"Several big fires. I saw them even through the fog. They got no fear that others might spot them, which means it's an armed group." He climbed out of the van, immediately tucking his chin and pulling his jacket close around him.

I followed him, sucking in a shocked breath. The temperature had dropped even more since this morning.

"Hate this cold," he muttered.

Though none of us was accustomed to these temperatures, at least I'd been skiing with Mel and her family each winter break.

Jackson had never known a cold like this, had never been outside of Louisiana. When Selena had asked him what his favorite ski resort was, he'd shared an amused glance with me in the rearview mirror. "Wouldn't know snow if it hit me in the face," he'd said. "Bayou boy, me, born and raised. . . ."

Once Selena and Matthew had climbed out, Jackson said, "We'll stop at that house for the night, raid the camp in the morning."

"How are we going to steal gas from them?" I asked.

"We?" Jackson raised his brows. "*We* ain't goan to do nothing. *You* are goan to sit somewhere safe, you. Once the Bagmen get scarce at dawn, Selena and me will ride the bikes in closer."

She beamed.

I glared, feeling as useless as ever, embarrassed by my ineptitude, especially compared to her.

Whenever Jackson called Matthew *bon à rien*, good-for-nothing, it only reminded me of all the times that he'd called me the same.

A worthless little doll with no teeth.

34

I shot up with a gasp, fresh from a nightmare. When I blinked open my eyes, my claws were extended, glinting in the dim moonlight that streamed through a dirty window.

Beside me, Selena and Matthew slept on. Earlier, the three of us had laid out sleeping bags around a cold hearth—we hadn't dared to build a fire—then divided an energy bar. While we'd tried to sleep, Jackson had taken up watch in an adjoining room.

I stared down at my claws as I remembered my dream. The witch had been surrounded by shadowy figures, burning with that aggression, that overwhelming compulsion to kill them.

So she'd twirled in place until her leaf-strewn red hair spun around her head, emitting something into the air. *Spores?* Once she'd stopped in place, she'd assured her victims, *"There is no shame in surrender."*

I'd expected the villagers to choke, writhing like her young admirer had. Even when sleeping, I'd braced for more ghastly images to stain my brain.

Instead, her victims had dropped to the ground with happy sighs, curling up on a grassy field, warmed by the sun.

Where was the fractured bone? The bits of flesh? The shrieks? The people had simply gone to sleep.

Yet they would *never* wake up.

Experiencing this dream was almost worse than the most gruesome ones. Her subtle evil haunted me. There hadn't been a single shriek—because not one soul had been aware enough to fight for his life. . . .

As my claws began to recede, I wiggled my fingers, watching the light play over the thorns. I realized I was growing accustomed to them. The sight didn't shock me at all anymore. In fact, I felt . . . numb.

I was gradually becoming more like *her*. The abilities I'd once considered a gift now seemed more like a curse.

Once my nails returned to normal, I rose, seeking Jackson. Seeking comfort. I just needed to be near him, knew it would make me feel better.

In the next room, I drew up short to find him sleeping on his watch, sitting upright on a cushioned window bench.

One of his long legs was bent, his crossbow balanced precariously on his knee, his other leg stretched out in front of him. He rested his head against the window. Had I ever seen him sleep?

No. Because he'd been watching over me every night. Well, except for at Selena's. I wasn't yet sure where he'd slept then.

He had dark circles under his eyes and his brow was creased with worry. So much responsibility. I felt a pang. No wonder he drank so much.

I climbed up on the bench, kneeling before him, and smoothed the backs of my fingers along one cheek. Still he didn't wake. He must be exhausted.

I felt a welling of tenderness for this boy—my cursing, hard-drinking, ladies'-man protector.

I sighed. Was he *my* protector? Could he possibly prefer *bonne à rien* over flawless Selena? As much as I hated to admit it, she suited him better. In fact, I didn't see how *anyone* could suit him better than she did.

If I found out they'd had sex, would *I* still want *him*?

So many questions swirled between us, so many secrets. I was involved in some kind of battle that I wanted no part of, I was a marked target because of abilities I'd never asked for and didn't know how to control, and Jackson was the only thing in my life that made me feel sane, made me *want* to fight for a future.

Tilting my head, I grazed my thumb over his bottom lip, remembering our kiss. What I wouldn't give to go back to that night, to explain my fears to him, to ask him to go slower.

"Hey," he suddenly murmured. His eyes were hooded, a lazy smile beginning to curve his lips. "Now, this is what I like to wake up to, *peekôn*."

If I'd thought happy and smiling was a good look on him, a sleepy Jackson tugged at my heart.

He set away his bow, then looped an arm around me to drag me to his chest. When I relaxed against him, he brought his knees up on both sides of me.

Against my hair, he rasped, "*Honeysuckle*. You liking ole Jack right now?"

"Yes," I answered honestly, luxuriating in his heat, his strong arms around me. I wanted to burrow even closer to him.

"Ah, *bébé*, I feel like I ain't seen you in weeks."

"I know, me too."

He cupped my face, meeting my gaze. "If I'd known I would wake up to this, I'd have gone to sleep earlier." Then he tensed. "Wait. Why was I *asleep*?"

He scrambled to his feet, sending me tumbling before he caught my arm and steadied me on the bench. "What the hell! I fell asleep on watch?"

Selena stirred in the next room but didn't wake.

"Jackson, you haven't been getting any rest for days. Weeks, even. You passed out."

"And *you* got the drop on me?" He snatched up his bow, scanning out of the windows. The coast must've been clear, because he lowered the weapon. "We could've been surrounded by Baggers. I doan know what happened. This has *never* happened."

"Nobody can go this long with so little sleep."

"I have in the past." He sank back down on the bench, gazing out. "A fine job I'm doing taking care of you."

"You *have* been! I owe my life to you."

"How long can I keep you safe? It's only goan to get worse and worse. We're heading into places where folks lived off the land and hunted, where there weren't Wal-Marts on every corner with aisles of cans to live off of. They're goan to be starving, Evie. Desperate."

The new food chain . . .

"I'll be taking you straight into danger, and it might be for nothing. You got to be wondering if your grandmother's even alive."

"She *is*."

"Why you sound so confident about her? You've had more visions, haven't you? Damn it, why haven't you told me?" In a surly tone, he added, "Bet you told *coo-yôn*."

How to reply to that one?

"It's like you two communicate in some way I can't understand." He exhaled a breath. "I got to accept that, me." Then his brows drew together. "Why's that boy always talking about the future? You said he lectured you—why would he be lecturing a psychic like you?"

I began pulling at a new hole in my jeans.

"Is he . . . like you? Can he see the future?"

Though I might not tell Jackson my disturbing secrets, I couldn't lie to him anymore. "I don't have visions of the future, Jackson. I am not psychic." But I also couldn't tell him Matthew's secrets.

Jackson flashed me a disappointed look. "I *saw* your drawings. I've watched you get nosebleeds."

I bit my bottom lip, gazing out through a filmy windowpane.

When I glanced back, he had that analytical look on his face. *Uh-oh.* "The day we rescued that boy, you told me you didn't think you'd be alive for long without his help. He ain't simple, is he?" When I eventually shook my head, Jackson added in a mutter, "I'd kinda hoped he was."

"He's just . . . different."

"When are you goan to come clean with me? What is he to you?"

"I started seeing him just before the Flash. We *do* communicate differently. He's one of the voices I hear."

"Heh. You haven't had a single nosebleed since we picked up that boy."

I swallowed, uneasy with where this was going.

"This is like those puzzles we used to do in school. If some things are true and some are false, you can figure out a solution. If you haven't told me any lies tonight—"

"I haven't!"

"—then I can back my way into the truth. One. You said you can't see the future, but you didn't answer when I asked if that *coo-yôn* could. Two. For some reason, you think *his* help can protect your life. Three. You once told me your visions felt like they were being shoved into your head. Maybe 'cause they were?"

Cunning, perceptive Jackson.

Realization lit his expression. "You've been growing plants somehow, and *he*'s been seeing the future? It makes sense."

I just stared at him.

"Did he send you those visions to protect you?"

Why bother denying it? "He tried to get me ready for the Flash. I barely listened to him."

Jackson tensed. "Then why does he keep talking about you *dying*, Evangeline?"

Oh boy. "When he talks about me meeting Death, he's doesn't mean it like you think. More like I should be prepared to face a big-bad or something. I know it sounds weird, but he considers Death to be a . . . person. Someone who can be defeated."

A measure of tension eased from Jackson's shoulders. The idea of a fightable adversary was something he could handle. "So *both* of you got gifts." Then his face fell. "*That*'s why you like each other so much."

"It's not like that with Matthew and me. He doesn't see me in that light."

"He's a sixteen-year-old boy, Evie. He sees you in only *one* light! Trust me on this, *cher*."

"Well, *I* look at him like a sibling."

"Like I did with Clotile?" he asked, and I thought he was holding his breath.

"Exactly. He's a kid brother to me."

Jackson briefly closed his eyes. At the memory of Clotile? Or from relief at my words? Both?

Had he truly believed I was interested in Matthew? I could only imagine what all Selena had told him when I wasn't around. *Doubt-mongering bitch.*

Jackson met my gaze. "Got something for you." He reached for his nearby bag, rooted around inside, then produced a bottle of Sprite.

My lips parted as he handed it to me. "Did you know that was my favorite?" He might as well have presented me with a piece of price-less jewelry. Just like with the gum, every time we drank a soda or ate a candy bar, there was one less treat in the world, never to be replenished.

"Of course. I *did* see you at five lunch periods. I've been saving it for when you could enjoy it—alone."

I unscrewed the top, handing it back to him. "*We* will share it."

"Oh, you'll drink after me?"

My cheeks flushed. "Sometimes I can be immature, Jackson. I know it's not always easy to be patient with me."

As we passed the bottle between us, he grew serious again. "I'm not goan to be able to keep charging forward blindly. And there's so much more than you're telling me. Why woan you trust me? Is it because of the stuff I did back in school?"

Arcana means secrets. "It's not you, Jackson, it's me."

He scowled at that, about to question me more, but the sun had begun to rise.

"I got to head out to work, me," he said. "I'd leave Selena here as a guard, but her bow shoots better from a distance, and I need her for cover. I can't get in and out of a camp full of soldiers without her."

"I understand."

"You woan have to worry about Baggers today. And hell, *coo-yôn* can probably see any threats coming, huh?"

"Don't worry about me. Just please be careful." Though I knew he was brave and resourceful, I didn't want him to go, dreading the danger he was about to wade into. "I want you to make it back, okay?"

"I could almost think you really care about me."

"I do really care!"

"About having a bodyguard to protect you."

"You're more than that to me," I said quietly. "And you have to know that—so why are you acting like you don't?"

"Then prove it." He eased closer, until our faces were inches apart. "Tell me your secrets."

God, I loved it when he looked at me like this, with his eyes so steady and . . . *affectionate*?

"Trust me, *ma belle*. Can you do that?"

Ma belle meant "my pretty," but also "my girlfriend." So how did Jackson mean it?

Just then, glaring beams of sunlight hit us through the window, like . . . *winter* sunshine.

The spell was broken between us. Jackson shifted back to his usual restless self, his mind on his upcoming task. "Just think about it, Evie. We'll talk when I get back."

We woke Selena and Matthew, both groggy and in pissy moods. I was too nervous to care much.

Jackson deemed the house too plain a target, so we camouflaged the van down the road for Matthew and me to hide in.

Before Selena and Jackson departed, he gripped Matthew's upper arm, telling him in that steely tone, "You're goan to stay here and *watch out* for Evie. Earn your keep for once. You see a chance to kill or die for her today, then you *take it*."

When Matthew merely stared at him, Jackson reached into the weapon box and pulled out a sheathed machete, handing it to the boy.

Matthew laughed and dropped it.

Jackson's fists clenched, his temper at the ready.

But Selena quickly said, "They'll be hidden here, J.D. They'll be fine."

Jackson turned to me. *"On parle quand j'reviens."* We'll talk when I get back.

"Prends soin de toi," I replied. Take care of yourself.

Selena didn't like this exchange whatsoever. "Hey, handsome, we don't need to take both bikes. Wastes gas."

When Jackson agreed with a shrug and mounted up, Selena slung her bow over her shoulder and hopped on behind him. With exaggerated relish, she wrapped her arms around his torso, pressing her long legs against his.

My spot. That was where *I* belonged. My claws grew slowly, menacingly, and it felt *good.* I tucked them into my palms so no one could see, but Matthew chuckled behind me.

Over her shoulder, Selena cast me a triumphant expression. And when she laid her head against his back, I was certain he could feel her smiling against him.

35

"Are you ready to tell me if Jackson will be safe down there?" I asked Matthew as we waited in the van, bundled in our sleeping bags for warmth. The fog was setting in, chilling me to my bones.

"You'll see him again." When I exhaled with relief, he said, "You think about him too much."

Tell me something I don't know, Matto. And that'd been *before* Jackson had called me *ma belle.*

To be Jackson Deveaux's girlfriend . . . I was giddy from the possibility, too scared to hope.

Then I nibbled my lip as doubts crept in. *What about the Arcana war, Selena, Death, the red witch?*

"When Dee-vee-oh helps you, he hurts you."

"You've told me that before, but not what that *means.*" No answer. "He did save my life—and yours. He's protected us. He's taught me about Bagmen and sourcing." Nothing. "Matthew, I feel stronger around him."

"Practice with your claws," he said. "*That* will make you feel stronger."

"I don't know how to make them appear, because someone won't tell me." Right now they were emotion-based and uncontrollable.

"How does the red witch flex her claws?"

I glared. "And speaking of disgusting things that repel me, how long am I going to suffer those nightmares? Can you look into the future? *Why* do I see her?"

Though I had no interest in fighting Death, I was almost tempted to face the witch. Then the nightmares would end—one way or another. "Matthew?"

He began staring at one of his hands. Subject closed.

So I posed the same question I'd been asking for days, "Can you please just tell me if Jackson and Selena were together?"

"You'll find out soon enough," he answered in a testy tone.

Baffling answers from the king of cryptic!

"You're thinking of him, and you haven't even heard the card," Matthew said.

"What card?" I asked, beginning to prepare our lunch. In other words, I pulled out a squished energy bar from my pocket to halve with him. My stomach was already growling for it.

"Nearby. Don't look at *this* hand. But you can't hear him because of Dee-vee-oh."

"Why would I *want* to hear the voices? I don't know this new card, don't feel an attachment to any of them but you. I *hate* the voices."

"Then you'll die, with their gloating whispers in your ear."

"Matthew, that was ... harsh." And eerie. It was times like this when I realized how little I truly knew about this boy.

"Death is expecting you," he said for the umpteenth time.

"Then he'll have a damned long wait!" I snapped. The mere mention of that knight set me off. "Death schooled those other Arcana, and they were strong, united. Even committed to each other," I added, remembering Joules's howl of grief. "I will never face him. Get it out of your head, because it will never happen. *Never.*"

Silence groaned between us, cold seeping into the van.

Regretting my tone with him, I tamped down my irritation and changed the subject. "If we're going to have this cold and fog, maybe we could actually get some rain, too."

Matthew shot upright, eyes wild. "No, no, no! Never say that! Take it back!" He clasped my shoulder, squeezing *hard*.

"I take it back! You're hurting me!"

"You don't want rain!" His gaze darted, his expression horrified. "The rain is worse."

"How can that be?"

He yelled, *"WORSE!"* His voice boomed in the confines of the van, paining my ears. "For *you*. For us! Can't be stopped though." He released me, looking wounded, his face leached of color. "Why would you hope for hell, Evie?"

"I-I'm sorry." This was the first time he'd ever frightened me. I kept thinking of him as childlike, and he was in some ways. But he was also volatile, and as strong as a full-grown man. "What does the rain do, Matthew?" Was precipitation even possible anymore? Surely if there was fog . . .

"The game changes. Not in our favor," he whispered. "We grow so weak. They grow so strong."

"Who?"

"All our foes laugh *now*. But once the sun hides? You've never known terror, not like you will when the rains come."

I shivered from cold—and fear. "I need more of an explanation. Matthew, I need you to clarify these things to me."

"You're not ready. You listen poorly. We sit inside this van—because *you listen poorly*! We are behind, with rain on the horizon."

"Okay, okay, but I'm ready to listen better now. Tell me what we should be doing. What do *you* think we should do? I want to know."

"Too late. Our capture starts soon."

"C-capture?"

"We need the card in the cage."

Glancing up through the windshield, I asked, "What are you talking . . ." My words trailed off, my heart dropping.

In the wafting mist, a ragtag group of militiamen—all armed to the teeth—stalked closer.

Like a hunting party.

"Matthew, you follow me now," I whispered as I strapped on my bag and crawled to the back doors of the van. "Grab the machete. We've got to slip out, *quietly*." I cracked open one door, wincing as the hinges groaned—

Three shotguns were pointed at my face.

"Looky what we found," the leader of our captors announced as he shoved Matthew and me through the crowd in their camp.

On the long trek here, I'd determined that he was as dentally challenged as he was odor-enhanced. Apparently this entire encampment was.

These militiamen were what Jackson would call *cou rouge*.

Because they were seriously red of the neck.

During our capture, Matthew hadn't fought whatsoever. In fact, as they'd snared my wrists with those plastic zip ties, he'd put his hands behind him, making it easier for them to bind.

I hadn't *wanted* him to resist—we'd been surrounded by aimed rifles—but maybe he could have made a show of displeasure?

We'd been abducted, our van looted, *my* bag ransacked. The leader had stolen all my jewelry and whiskey bottles, tossing the rest.

Now as the head Cou Rouge maneuvered us through the camp, I kept my eyes open for Jackson and Selena—and tried to ignore the way men stood when I passed, ogling me with lecherous eyes.

They all seemed to have winter-weather gear, though many of their jackets sported what looked like bullet holes. I frowned. Bloody ones— often in the back.

My lips parted with realization. Bullet holes from where they'd gunned down their victims, then stripped their clothes.

"She smells good enough to eat," one man said as he grabbed his crotch.

I shuddered with revulsion, so tempted to try my claws. They could easily slice through those ties. Matthew had once told me they could even cut through metal.

But then what? These men had guns. I was a slow runner, and I'd never leave Matthew behind.

I'd probably end up cutting myself anyway. And what would I do if dead grass sprouted green under my drops of blood?

Cou Rouge marched us past numerous RVs with their generators humming, scores of tents, and vehicles of all kinds. Cookout fires abounded, with men barbecuing what looked like small mammals. Despite the circumstances, the smell of grilled meat made my mouth water.

I also spotted plastic cans of gas everywhere. I'd decided this militia was rich with fuel—even before I saw an actual *tanker*. They safeguarded it in the center of the encampment like a golden idol.

And that wasn't all. Near the tanker was a raised cistern, its iron sides dripping. *Filled with water.*

Cou Rouge stopped before an improvised jail cell, a cage made from wooden packing crates nailed together. Only one boy was within. At least Jackson and Selena remained free.

Shoving Matthew and me inside, Cou Rouge padlocked the door and posted three guards. "Don't be leavin' this spot," he ordered them. "Not for any reason."

The other prisoner was around our age, with freckles on his nose and chin-length dirty-blond hair. *This* boy was the card in the cage I was supposed to be listening for? The one we'd needed to find? He seemed so *unremarkable.*

"'S'up," he said mildly as we sat on the cold, ashy ground. "Name's Finneas. Call me Finn. . . ." He trailed off as he stared at me, then Matthew.

He was seeing our tableaus; I knew because I was beholding his. For a split second, Finn was clad in a red robe, holding a wand to the sky while pointing to the ground with his other hand. On a table before him lay a pentagram, a chalice, a sword, and a cane. A bed of roses and lilies grew at his feet, vines trailing above.

—*Don't look at* this *hand, look at* that *one.*— Then his call grew silent. Was he hearing ours?

And was the boy associated with plants in some way? Matthew's card also had a flower on it, a white rose!

Of course, so had Death's card—an emblem on the black flag he carried.

While I was blinking, regaining my focus, Finn said, "Whoa. I think I just had an acid flashback." He sounded as if he belonged on a beach in Cali.

"I-I'm Evie. This is Matthew." I indicated him with a jerk of my chin.

Matthew met his gaze and said, "Card. Arcana. Secrets. Card."

"Whatever, dude."

"Um, Finn, I couldn't help but notice that you seem really calm."

Matthew, too, looked unaffected by our predicament. He began inspecting the grain on one of the boards.

"I am calm, blondie."

"Even though these men are probably slavers or cannibals?"

"Nah, homeowners' association gone awry."

I frowned at his flippant tone. "What do they want with us?"

"They're going to use me and your weird companion here as cistern diversion."

"I don't understand."

"Bagman bait. The woods around here are thick with Baggers. At dusk, they advance on that cistern in this big wave of creep—unless live meat runs past and distracts them. Then the hicks pick them off. Oh, and while we're out running for our lives, you're going to be married off to, like, *all* of this militia. *Mazel tov.*"

Dread swept over me—for both Matthew and myself. "H-how many soldiers are there?"

"Hundreds."

"Hundreds?" Even if Jackson managed to figure out what happened to us, I didn't know if we *could* be rescued.

"They're just waiting for nightfall. Then you're s.o.l., sister. There's only one other chick in the entire camp. But she's the chief redneck's

daughter, so they consider her off-limits, kind of a Smurfette situation."
He exhaled, grinning up at the slats of the cage roof. "*Smoking* body
on that one—but shy a few teeth. Still, I'd do Hickette with a flag over
her face."

"Excuse me?"

Matthew chuckled. "Do her for his country."

"Matthew!" I cried, frowning at him. I'd thought of him as more . . .
innocent.

Finn laughed with him, the two of them apparently fast friends.

Ugh. Teenage boys! Jackson had told me I didn't understand them. I
realized then that I probably never would. "You two are joking around,
not concerned about this at all."

"I just had a hot blonde dropped into a *Caged Heat* scenario with
me." Finn waggled his brows. "A *chesty* blonde—with *all* her teeth. As
my Flash-fried redneck cousins used to say, 'I'm happy as a pig in shit.'"

Plant association or not, this self-important, smirky boy was getting
on my nerves.

When he relaxed back against the side of the cage, I said, "You
probably have someone coming to save you?"

"I can get out of this at any time."

"Really?"

"I only let them capture me so I could get close to that daughter. I'm
a magician, hotness. Getting out of binds is what I do."

"*The* Magician," Matthew said.

Finn's chest puffed out. "Damn straight, dude."

If he was an Arcana, then he had powers of some sort. Still, I
couldn't buy his total lack of worry. "Well, we have friends who are
coming for us," I told him under my breath, my words full of assur-
ance. "We'll be rescued soon."

But time kept passing. One hour. Another.

For afternoon amusement, some soldiers set up target practice
nearby—three moaning Bagmen impaled on spikes. One Bagger looked
freshly turned, one had no legs, and the other no arms.

The soldiers opened fire and the Bagmen writhed and gurgled. Chunks of slimy skin flew off the targets, plopping near the cage, fouling the air.

I held my arms over my head to block out the gunshots, the moans....

By late afternoon, I caught myself wondering why Jackson and Selena—two hard-core survivors—would risk their necks against tremendously shitty odds to rescue their pair of deadweights?

How strong was Selena's influence over Jackson?

As much as I wanted to believe in our rescue, my current predicament—freezing, huddled in a cage, starving—wasn't boosting my optimism.

Much less my *future* predicament.

And Matthew would say nothing to help. Did he not understand what was about to happen to us?

By sunset, I was awash in doubt. Why wouldn't Jackson and Selena just run off together and be happy, without all the hassle, without all the danger? How many times had Jackson told me I was more trouble than I was worth?

I wondered how I would recover if he'd truly abandoned me here.

I wondered how I'd feel if he got killed trying to save me from these ignorant militiamen.

My eyes watered. At that moment, I hit my limit of fear and confusion and . . . and *people*. I was sick of them! Sick of danger lurking around every corner.

"Is *everybody* evil now?" I murmured to no one.

I had the strangest urge to shove my fingers into the dirt and feel them . . . *take root*. What if I could tap the earth and become a soldier at attention? I wouldn't even have to be a girl anymore, just a part of something so much bigger.

If I surrendered, there'd be no more worries about Jackson, no more fears about facing the red witch—or Death.

Such a seductive pull . . . as alluring as a ripe berry. I gazed at the sooty ground with contemplation.

Then I grew ashamed. What would Mom think of me now? The

woman who'd tackled a Bagman would never surrender like this.

"Yeah, everybody's totally evil now," Finn said, jarring me from my thoughts. "What, didja miss the memo? Dickwads. Pretty much uniformly, in my experience. All evil, all the time. But not *me*." In a grand ringmaster's tone, he breathed, "I'm *mischievous*. . . ."

I turned to Matthew. "Once again, anytime you feel like contributing, please do. We need to figure out our own escape."

He nodded winningly. "Cards."

"Yes, Matthew, but you really need—" A wail sounded from the nearby woods. I shot up straighter. "What was that?"

"Bagmen at the gates, baby," Finn said, excitement flashing in his hazel eyes. "It's almost showtime. I've only seen this from a distance before."

Suddenly the earth quaked, an explosion rocking the camp. I cried out. The deafening blast was so strong my teeth clattered.

Bits of debris rained down through the slats of the cage. Smoke billowed. Men yelled from all directions, barking orders for fires to be put out.

Matthew yawned as a larger explosion followed.

When we heard a raging *whoosh* from that giant cistern toppling over, I shared a stunned glance with Finn.

Bagmen in number. A cistern of water.

"We'll be overrun," he said. "A pretty ballsy distraction. Did your people make with the mayhem?"

Chaos had broken out among the militia. "Yeah. Our people."

Smoke and fog blanketed the air until we could barely see five feet away.

But we could hear panicked soldiers all around us, fighting to secure their encampment. Then we heard a strangled yell: *"Bagger breach!"* They were past the militia's defenses.

Guns popped, men screamed—and Bagmen howled as they swarmed the camp. The trio of guards in front of us shifted nervously, guns rattling in their shaking hands.

"Evie!" Jackson?

"I'm here!" He'd come for me!

An arrowhead suddenly jutted from one guard's back. I just choked down a scream as he collapsed, twitching on the ground.

Jackson's arrow.

The two remaining guards grew spooked, rifles at the ready, but they couldn't see their enemy to fight.

Another arrow protruded from a second guard's neck; he twirled toward us, patting his throat in bewilderment before he drowned on his own blood. The third guard got wise—and fled.

Then I spied Jackson sprinting through the smoke, hell-bent for our cage. He shoved soldiers out of the way, battering them with the end of his crossbow.

He skidded to a stop right before me, scanning me for injuries. "*Bébé*, are you okay?"

I nodded wordlessly.

"I'm goan to get you out of here."

"The door's padlocked, Jackson."

"*Putain.*" But that didn't stop him. He drew back his mighty fist and punched the boards, again and again, ripping at them to get to me. Splinters and blood flying.

I glanced behind him, caught sight of that third guard returning. Right when I was about to scream, Jackson yelled, "*Selena, my six!*"

The tip of a long arrow emerged from that guard's chest. He'd just pitched onto his face when Selena came running up. My vision had come true. *Sure enough, she saved someone I . . . love.*

"Come on, J.D.!" she yelled. "It's going to blow!"

What was going to blow? Something bigger than the current earth-shaking explosions?

As Jackson freed Matthew and me, Finneas gawked at Selena—probably from witnessing her tableau, possibly because she was so freaking gorgeous anyway. "*Another* chick? Hellooo, hotness." Though we were surrounded by a melee, Finn took his time checking her out. "Dude. It is *raining* hot ass today. Screw the toothless daughter—I'm coming with you guys."

His bindings fell away. Sure enough, he'd escaped them.

Jackson grabbed my upper arm, and we started running, back in the direction of the van. I thought.

As we sprinted past the worst of the fray, I noticed several flaming arrows plugged that gas tanker. *Time bomb.*

"Come on, Evie!" Jackson was hauling me along; the rest of our group had run ahead. "You got to be faster than this!"

"Trying!"

He had just slowed, probably to toss me over his shoulder, when a soldier emerged from a bank of haze—with a rifle pointed at Jackson's face.

It was Cou Rouge, the one who'd taken me. He wasn't more than a few feet away—and he had Jackson dead to rights. "Just be steppin' away from her, all nice and easylike, and we'll let you go."

Jackson evinced no fear. "Not goan to happen."

"We only want the girl."

"Well, now, that's a problem," Jackson grated, "'cause I just *got* her."

Cou Rouge shrugged. "Suit yourself." His finger tightened on the trigger.

Oh dear God, he was about to *shoot*, and Jackson couldn't stop it, *I* couldn't do anything—

The man pulled the trigger. *Click.* Nothing. *Click.* Nothing.

Empty?

Cou Rouge gaped at his gun, then at Jackson, at the chilling expression on the boy's face.

The same look I'd seen that night in his house, the one promising pain; now it seemed multiplied by a thousand.

I was seeing how much Jackson was about to *savor* the pain he promised.

Cou Rouge gave a whimper just before Jackson lunged forward, one of his brutal fists connecting with the man's jaw.

The man went down from a single hit, limp. But Jackson hauled him back up, beating him more, seeming mindless with rage. "Only want the girl?" Another blow shattered the soldier's nose. "Worst thing you could ever have said!"

"Jackson!" I cried. "Please, let's go!"

The man's face grew unrecognizable, shapeless, and still Jackson beat him. I wasn't witnessing a fight, or a rescue. I was beholding *punishment*.

A sentence.

When Matthew casually trotted back for me, catching my arm, Jackson yelled, "Get her out of here! I'm right behind."

"Come with us, please!" I screamed as Matthew forced me away. "Nooo, Matthew! Go grab him!"

Matthew chuckled at that, then shoved me forward.

"Go back, go back!"

He just continued squiring me through a minefield of explosions, brawls, and Bagmen, maneuvering me in different directions.

One time he yanked me back against his chest—just as a bullet whizzed past, missing us by inches. A few seconds later, he palmed my head, shoving me to my knees, and I heard some kind of shrapnel whistle directly above me.

I realized he was seeing a maze of present and future, a web of occurrences visible only to him.

As if he were fate itself. . . .

Still I begged him to go back for Jackson—until I spied soldiers pursuing us.

By the time we'd spotted Selena at the edge of the charred woods, dozens of militiamen were on our trail, calling for their comrades to "Get the girl!"

Selena intercepted them, with two rifles tucked against her sides. She blasted away at them, allowing Matthew and me to dive into a nearby ditch for cover.

A handful of shots sang over our heads, then stopped abruptly. From their shouts, it seemed our pursuers had realized Selena was a *she*, and ordered a cease-fire.

Selena didn't follow that order. When they took up positions in a gully opposite us, she emptied her guns at them. Then she dropped into the ditch with us.

As the soldiers decided what to do—they couldn't risk *two* females by storming us—Selena snapped, "Where the hell is J.D.? Damn it, there was *one* person I wanted to see come out of the camp. Not you two."

I cried, "He wouldn't come with us!"

"And you took no for an answer? I would've *made* him come with me! You're not good enough . . ." She trailed off, her attention seized by something beyond our makeshift bunker.

I turned to find Finn strolling past the rednecks to hop down with us. "Yo."

I found my voice first. "You just . . . walked right by them?"

With a cocky air, he brushed off one shoulder, then the other. "Told you I was a magician." Then to Selena, he said, "Finn's my name. Getting you back to my pad's the plan. You just tell me when this stalemate gets old, because I can seriously change this channel."

Selena didn't seem nearly as shocked as I was. She merely patted her bow and said, "As can I."

"You think you can take out more than I can?" Finn scoffed. "You're on."

Should I point out the obvious? "Kid, you don't have a *weapon*."

He chucked me under the chin. "Not to worry, sugartits, I got this."

With a roll of her eyes, Selena charged up the rise, her bowstring singing.

Finn followed, and began to . . . *whisper* to the rednecks?

The sound of Selena's archery was uncanny. In the smoke and confusion, I peeked up over the ridge and saw her shooting arrows with an impossible speed.

A *supernatural* speed.

Her skin was glowing with that blood-tinged hue—like a hunter's moon.

Beside her, Finn raised his hands, softly chanting in a language I'd never heard. His breaths seemed to be searing, as if he were diffusing the air with heat. I perceived *power*, and he was directing it at our attackers.

The shooters he addressed stumbled on their feet, looking as dumbfounded as I felt, because the soldiers beside them now resembled Bagmen.

The rednecks began murdering *their own comrades*.

Somehow Finn was making these men look like their enemies.

And his ability seemed like the most natural thing in the world. I *needed* to witness this, needed to reach the memories that felt just on the verge of surfacing.

As Selena picked off stragglers, she winked at Finn; he grinned back. They accepted their powers, readily accepted such abilities in others.

"Arcana," Matthew murmured at my ear.

"Yes," I breathed. "This is real? Not another vision?"

"Real."

I possessed abilities. These three kids did as well. Matthew had his live-streaming foresight, Selena could run and shoot like a goddess of the hunt, Finneas could create illusions.

And me? I smelled my own rose scent steeping the air—so lovely, almost intoxicating. I glanced down to find my claws had flared.

Matthew cast me a relieved look. "Thorns."

"I can go help Jackson, fight with him!"

He shook his head firmly. "You don't attack. You await, you *beckon*." Beckon?

Come, touch, but you'll pay a price. I remembered the witch's besotted admirer. She'd beckoned him.

The admirable deviousness of briars I'd once admired? Was that guile mine as well?

I heard a twig snap behind us and whirled around.

Matthew was staring at the end of a rifle, the barrel just inches from his face.

I glanced up at the slavering soldier who brandished it. I didn't dare think he would run out of bullets too. He would capture me and kill Matthew. I had to stop him!

"Beckon, Empress," Matthew whispered.

And then . . . I *did*.

I raised a trembling, delicate hand to the man, palm up. A fragile lotus bloomed directly from my skin, right before his riveted gaze. I blew him a kiss across its petals—and the rifle dropped, abandoned.

Because the soldier was clamping his neck, face gone bright red from the spores closing his throat and robbing his lungs of air.

As he thrashed on the ground, helpless, the lotus disappeared; my claws grew, sharpening—but now they were dripping like hypodermic needles.

"Poison." Matthew grinned. "Lethal."

I gaped. Ten thorns working like ten needles?

"Pierce him."

For the briefest instant I wondered if it would feel *good* to plunge them into flesh.

No! "I-I can't! Matthew, I can never be like her."

"You fight her, you'll face her. You must."

Sink to her level? I feared I would literally become my worst nightmare, losing myself forever. "Matthew, what if I can't come back . . . ?"

Selena trotted over with a glare and drilled an arrow into one of the soldier's wide, disbelieving eyes—

The tanker blew, shaking the world like an atomic blast.

37

When we realized Jackson wasn't at the spot where he was supposed to meet Selena, Matthew had to hold me upright.

He can't be dead, can't be dead.

But if he'd gotten caught in that blast, how could he have survived?

I'd just stifled a sob when Finn asked, "So what do we do now?"

"We wait for Jackson," I quickly said. "Or we go back in for him."

"This is your fault!" Selena snapped at me. "God, will you turn off that scent?"

"Just shut up and let me think!"

With his lids at half-mast, Finn said, "I dunno. I really like the way she smells." When he lifted a lock of my hair and inhaled, Selena rolled her eyes.

"So what's up with you guys?" he asked, still sniffing me. "Are you like the Super Friends?"

Matthew said, "Cards. Cards! *Cards.* Cards—"

"Stop, please." I jerked back from both boys. "Just let me think! Finn, can you get back into the camp, or disguise me?"

Selena scoffed. "They'll *smell* you, little shop of horrors. I still can't believe you left him behind!"

Neither could I. "Why don't we save the blame for later—for now we need to *FIND JACK!*"

"Evie?"

I whirled around.

Emerging from the smoke, Jackson stumbled toward us, covered with grit and ash, his clothes blood-spattered. One of his calves was burned severely.

I gave a cry of relief and ran toward him, wanting to help him, but his furious gaze made my steps falter.

"Jackson?"

Still quaking from his fight, he just held up one finger, warning me away.

So volatile. Had he just killed a man with his bare hands?

Finn broke up the tension. "Okay, now that the gang's all here, let's start making tracks back to my totally secure pad."

An hour later, we learned that Jackson did not agree with Finn about the security of his pad.

It was a weekender, secluded in a blackened forest, overlooking what used to be a *lake.* A Bagman draw.

But Finn vowed that no one would bother us—just as they hadn't on our trek to get to his place.

Selena, Matthew, and I had known that Finn was disguising us. Jackson hadn't. He'd limped along, bow at the ready, taking point. No one, not even Selena, had dared to approach him. We'd held back, agreeing not to discuss our new discoveries around Jackson. . . .

At the front door, he said, "You doan board your windows here, boy?" He cautiously entered, motioning for me to follow right behind him. Matthew trailed me.

Inside, I was looking less at the windows and more at the Sam's Club warehouse of goods stored here. Yes, that militia had been rich; apparently, Finn had taken full advantage of his abilities.

Wares were piled high: batteries, boxes of chocolate bars, Coleman lanterns, crates of bottled water, cereal.

Selena snidely observed, "Kind of looks like your mom's old place, Matt."

Matthew squeezed my shoulder, just preventing me from a screeching girl-fight attack. Even Jackson frowned at her.

"No need to board up any windows," Finn told Jackson as he fetched three Duraflame logs—from a towering pile of them. He bundled them over to a fireplace with a stone hearth and antlers above the rough-hewn mantel.

Jackson eyed him cagily. "And no one can see the *smoke*, either?"

"Seriously, Cajun-type guy. We're camouflaged here. I've stayed at this cabin for weeks, stealing from that militia."

As the fire started warding off the chill inside, we raided Finn's food, dragging our fruit cups, Doritos, and Chef Boyardee cans in front of the hearth.

But not Jackson. With ash and blood still streaked all over, he rummaged till he'd found a fifth of whiskey.

Bow strapped over his back and bottle clenched in one mangled hand, he limped to a bench before the fire, sinking down. He sat with his elbows on his knees, staring at the flames, drinking heavily as we finished stuffing ourselves.

I put together a selection of food for him, but he declined with a sharp shake of his head, turning up the bottle instead. Then he leveled bloodshot eyes at Finn. "How have *you* been getting in and out with all this stuff?"

Finn shrugged. "Candy. Baby. I even made it out with one of their trucks. It's out back." When Jackson looked incredulous, Finn said, "What can I say? I'm *crafty*. I've had that Tahoe gassed up and ready to take me back to Cali. But it's been so easy leeching off those reds that I guess I got lazy. Plus, I like to play pranks on them—more of a *compulsion* really. Not to mention that I've had this excruciating boner for Hickette."

Casting a significant glance at Selena, he added, "I'll never set my sights so low again."

Seeming unfazed by Finn's *colorful* personality, Jackson swigged that bottle. "Somebody want to explain to me why those soldiers were shooting each other?"

Jackson had seen that? I glanced at Finneas, counting on him to have a ready answer.

He smoothly said, "Inbreeding?"

God, this night must be awful for Jackson. Probably nothing was making sense to him, puzzles left and right, and we were hiding all the pieces from him.

"You been north of here, boy?"

"I have. All over the Carolinas. And I will *not* be going back."

"That's where we been goan." Jackson must be getting buzzed for his accent to sound so thick. "To the Oudder Banks."

"Bad idea, Cajun. There're three ways to get there from here, each one worse than the last. You can either hold your breath through the plague colonies, slip through Slaverville, or take the mountain route." Something flashed in his expression, something somber, which seemed out of place on his animated face. "That's where the cannibals really like to hole up."

"You've *seen* them?" I asked.

"Oh, yeah. And it's, like, totally worse than you can imagine. Their steady diet of grilled Homo sapiens really screws with their heads. And the miner cannibals in North Carolina? They're the worst! Dude. They don't even *grill.*"

Selena said, "The Outer Banks are looking less and less like my future."

"We sure will miss you, Selena," I said, sugar and snide.

When Jackson unsteadily rose, favoring his good leg, I shot to my feet to help him. "We need to get your burn bandaged up." No response. "Jackson? Please eat something." He glowered. "What's wrong with you?"

"I wonder, me." Without another word, he took his bottle and bow, then limped out on the porch.

He so clearly wanted to be alone. Deciding to let him go for now, I returned to sit with the others.

When only the four Arcana remained, Finn asked, "So how long have you guys known you were different?"

In an airy tone, Selena said, "Awhile now."

Matthew answered, "Different?"

I replied, "Um. Just found out recently." All of us were hesitant to offer more, all of us on guard.

"So, what I really want to know is *how*. And *why*." Finn gazed from one of us to the next. "Shit. I was hoping you guys could tell me something."

Selena shook her head. "I've got nothing. Ask Matthew. The way he was dodging bullets, he must be a clairvoyant."

Matthew said, "Kill the bad cards."

Bad cards. He'd said that a lot. Maybe the Arcana war was simply a matter of good versus evil.

As I gazed over this group, I wondered if perhaps *we* were supposed to band together, like a hand of cards—playing to our strengths and shoring up our weaknesses. As I'd witnessed in that battle of Arcana.

Matthew had told me I was fated to fight Death. I'd vowed never to face the Reaper; would I reconsider if I had backup?

Hell. No. Death and Ogen had been unstoppable together.

Then I noticed all eyes were on me. "I don't know much more than you guys. But I do know we're connected to Tarot in some way." I asked Finn, "Have you ever seen a Tarot deck?"

"Yeah. It gave me the wiggins. Picked it up and put it right back down."

I nodded, knowing the feeling. Well, except for the fact that I'd apparently loved to gawk at Death's card when I'd been little. "The trump cards are called the Major Arcana, the big bosses of the deck. They represent us. I think. I'm the Empress, Selena's the Moon, Matthew's the Fool. And you're the Magician. There are other kids too."

Finn muttered, "Rad-ick-ull." Then he launched into a spate of questions.

How'd we get our powers, what are we supposed to do with them, how do we find the other kids?

"I wish I knew," I said with a pointed look at Matthew. "But I don't. I think my grandmother will, though."

"Tarasova," Matthew said in an awed tone. "Mistress of the Tarot, wisewoman, chronicler."

What had he once told me? *"Beware the old bloodlines, the other families that chronicle. They know all!"*

If my family chronicled, did that mean Gran knew all?

Selena glared at me. "*That* was the pressing urgency to reach Granny! You wanted to get the scoop on all of us. Why would she know anything anyway?" Again I got the feeling that she knew exactly why my grandmother would know.

"I didn't want to *scoop* you, Selena! I want to figure out my abilities, my life, the world." I needed to get to Gran more urgently than ever. I recalled that disturbing impulse in the militia's cage: *not to be a girl at all . . .*

That call to surrender, to go *dormant*, scared me as much as my ability to hurt that soldier with the lotus.

"So what? We have abilities," Selena said with a dismissive wave. "Why do you think there has to be a *reason* behind it, any more than there was a reason for the Flash?"

I drew my head back. "Are you . . . are you *joking*? You have to feel that some force is putting us in each other's paths. Don't you sense that this is just starting?"

Matthew picked up a fruit cup and handed it to me, like a reward. *Evie gets a cookie.*

"And what exactly are your abilities again?" Selena asked. "All I saw were some ugly, deformed claws—how helpful! Oh, and you smell good. Big asset! Those rednecks could've tracked us by your scent."

I *hated* her! When my claws flared, itching to make contact with her eyeballs, Matthew eased between Selena and me. "You're brimming tonight," he told me. "It wouldn't even be fair."

Selena smirked. "That's right—"

"Not fair to *you*," Matthew said, which shut her up. "Archer in close quarters? Against poison?"

"She's *poisonous*?" Selena cried in a horrified tone.

A *fake* horrified tone. All my instincts screamed that Selena already knew this about me—that she knew more about me and all the Arcana than I could even imagine.

What if Selena had some kind of guidebook or her own Tarasova wisewoman, one who hadn't been locked up? Selena might have total control over her powers, might have been practicing her entire life.

Her archery skill was unmatched. What other abilities did she possess?

I recalled Jackson's strange behavior when we'd arrived at Selena's house, how bright the moon had been, seeming to call to us.

Beware the lures. Maybe Selena could manipulate moonlight the way I did plants. Had she used it to lure me to her house that first night—unaware I'd be with Jackson? She'd said, *"I never expected to meet a guy. Here. With you . . . I just never expected him."*

"Poison?" Finn leaned away from me, but excitedly said, "For real?"

"My, um, *claws* are." When he raised his eyebrows, I displayed them, all ten deadly thorns.

"That is righteous, blondie! Hey, we need to come up with superhero names. How about capes—and *codpieces*? Just think about the idea for now, chew it over for a bit, let me know," he said. "Hey, do you guys ever hear . . . voices?"

I groaned. "All the time. I thought I was going crazy."

"Duude," he said in agreement. "And before the Flash, all kinds of freaky shit was happening to me. I started speaking this weird language. And stuff started transforming—but only in front of me. I saw my cat walking on the ceiling, saw lava coming out of a faucet. The worst? I

was doing this girl, and suddenly she looked like my gym teacher!" He shuddered.

And I'd thought I had it bad. Matthew and Finn had also suffered. "What'd your parents think?" I asked, wondering if Finn had gotten institutionalized too.

"Dad couldn't handle my 'erratic behavior' anymore, so he pawned me off on Mom. Same result. They were just about to break out the straitjacket—or, worse, military school—when she got the brilliant idea to ship me from Malibu to North Carolina to rough it with my redneck cousins."

So Matthew and I hadn't been the only ones deemed "damaged" by our folks. It made sense, though. I wondered what Selena's story was.

"Yeah, Mom figured they'd toughen me up mentally," Finn said. "I can't even make this shit up. Mental health—through the chugging of Natty Light, the chasing of hot hick ass, and the killing of ducks and bucks."

At least Finn was forthcoming. Though the boy was abrasive—and had he really called me *sugartits?*—he was starting to grow on me. Especially when compared to Selena.

I was just about to ask him what my Arcana call was when Selena said, "I don't hear voices, you two crazycakes."

After days with this girl—stifling my irritation, trying to rub along—I'd reached the end of my patience. "If you're going to lie, I'm not doing any more reveals with you."

"I have never heard *voices*," she scoffed, worse than my primary shrink ever had.

I stood, bristling. "You're a liar, Selena. But that's what you do best, isn't it? Deception's your MO, right?"

She shot to her feet as well, on guard. "What are you talking about?"

"When we first met, you behaved as if you recognized nothing about me, but I think you knew exactly who—and what—I was all along. If you're so bent on acting ignorant, then that means you know a whole hell of a lot more than you're letting on. Do you know our powers?

Maybe you had some kind of teacher or a book. Maybe you were taught everything we're hoping to discover."

She leaned in aggressively. "Prove it."

"Now, now, ladies, you two know the rules." Finn rose, holding up his hands like a referee. "No fights outside of a Jell-O ring."

I twirled my be-clawed fingers in front of her face, and eventually she backed off.

"So tell me what his story is." Finn jerked his chin in Jackson's direction. "He's not one of us?"

After a final threatening look at Selena, I said, "I don't think so. I haven't seen him do anything superhuman."

Selena flipped her hair over her shoulder. "Because you haven't experienced him in the right situation, honey." Her tone dripped with innuendo.

Was this the proof that I'd been waiting for? Or another lie? Maybe they *had* gotten together—at least on the night we'd stayed at her place. And possibly more often.

Though I did believe Jackson was interested in me again, I didn't know how I could get past *them*. Between gritted teeth, I said, "Then tell us what card he is, Selena."

She sighed. "My Jack of Hearts."

Claws aching, I snapped, "Wrong—deck—hooker."

Finn groaned. "This can't be happening! So you're both digging that Cajun dude? *Both* of you? Come on, pussycats, that's just not right! Spread the wealth."

"To you?" Selena raised her brows.

"Precisely. I'm your guy, Archer. You and me." He winked. *"Think about it."*

She looked at him as she might at a pesky insect.

Unperturbed, he asked, "In any case, do we continue to keep our shit secret from the Cajun?"

"Secret," Matthew hissed.

"Right, dude. Guess that answers that. . . ."

By the time we started getting ready for bed an hour later, I was beyond exhausted. Though there were three rooms in the back, I made pallets for Matthew and me by the fire. I wanted to stay near Jackson. He remained just outside on the porch, still drinking.

I'd gone out there once, but he'd held up that finger again. *"Want to be alone, me."*

Now I crawled under my blanket, shivering as the events of the day caught up with me. Still, I was determined to wait up for him. If he didn't let me tend to his injuries, they might get infected. Plus I yearned to talk to him, to find out what was going on in that mysterious mind of his.

To find out what tomorrow would bring.

I also wanted to stay up because I was on edge after my fight with Selena. She'd laid her blankets on the other side of the hearth. Despite the fact that Finn had a bed in the back, he'd unrolled his sleeping bag directly beside her. Much to her annoyance.

He'd repeatedly tried to coax her to his bedroom. The poor guy must have burned through his entire repertoire, but she'd shot him down completely.

Selena only had eyes for Jackson. . . .

Matthew burrowed down beside me, sleepy-eyed and adorable. We lay facing each other—the front door in my peripheral just in case Jackson walked in. I told Matthew, "Get some sleep, kid."

"Big night," he whispered.

Yes, it had been. He reached over to take my hand.

And my lids slid closed.

38

The villagers taunted the red witch from aboard their fleet of ships.

They'd anchored offshore, out of reach of any trees, vines, or thorns. The becalmed sea was unfavorable for her spores.

As she watched from the beach, they called her the "Countess of Chaff" and the "Queen of Famine." As if the crop failures had been her doing.

The dazzlingly blue water was flat as a mirror under the sun. When she drew back her hood, light bathed her face, invigorating her. A glorious day for retribution.

Yet everyone knew that unless she could walk on water, there was no vengeance to be had.

Death had arrived at the shore to observe her, always fascinated with her Empress gifts. Astride his stallion at the top of a sandy rise, he took off his helmet, looking like a god.

"And what shall you do now, creature?" he called. Sunlight lovingly highlighted his flawless features, his long blond hair. "The sea is her dominion—not yours."

The witch tapped her chin with a thorn claw, reminding herself that it was not yet time for her encounter with Death. She turned her attention to the sailors, the last remaining survivors of the village she had plagued with spores and a tempest of thorns.

Now the sailors grew bolder, more boisterous. They mocked her, lewdly exposing their genitals.

Death's glittering eyes were locked on her face, ever watchful of his foe. He would enjoy a show indeed.

"Though it's not my way . . . if they shan't come to me, I must go to them." She strode purposely down the beach. At the sea's edge she didn't slow, simply stepped upon the surface, blithely walking on water.

The crews fell silent. A stray gasp here, a whimper there.

She glanced over her shoulder at Death. His mien was impassive, those starry eyes giving away nothing.

Sea plants rising up from the deep held her afloat.

The sailors were finally jolted into action, but no wind caught their lax sails. They frantically rowed, yet her underwater allies trapped the ships in place.

Then came the men's impassioned pleas to gods old and new.

But it was too late.

Once she'd neared enough to see their faces, she waved one tattooed hand. At once, giant ropes of slimy sea plants burst through the surface, exploding up from the abyss.

As the men screamed, she grinned back at Death. "No, the sea is not my dominion." Her powers over the ocean paled in comparison to a certain other Arcana's. "But I can borrow it from time to time."

Those plants danced above the ships, raining water, positioned to strike. Grown men whimpered for mercy, begging "the lady" for her grace.

She threw back her head and laughed with pleasure. "I shall give you as much mercy as you afforded me." These villagers had tied her to a wooden stake and begun burning her; she'd felt the lick of flames before she could revive the stake into a tree, freeing herself.

She'd meted out retribution to most of them, all but these sailors. When she recalled the smell of her burning flesh, she waved her hand once more.

The ropes of green slapped across the decks, crushing the masts, bludgeoning men. Blood pooled on the decks, pouring along the ships' gutters. Thick cascades of crimson splashed the sea in a froth of pink bubbles.

As the plants coiled around the ships like giant tentacles, cracking the vessels in half, sailors plunged into the water.

More of her allies awaited them, slithering around their ankles, jerking them down. The witch tormented the men, dunking them under, then allowing them an exquisite taste of air, a chance to scream, a second to reach for the indifferent sun—before dragging them to the deep.

She didn't stop until all were slain.

By the time the sea stilled once more, it was stained red.

When the witch returned to shore, Death inclined his head regally, then spurred his pale mount, leaving her.

She turned back to gaze over her handiwork. In the perfect stillness of the blood-slicked sea, the witch spied her reflection. Staring back at her was . . .

Me. I shot awake, out of breath. It'd been my reflection. Mine!

Shuddering, I darted my gaze around the firelit cabin. *Just a dream, just a nightmare.* I hadn't been there. It hadn't been *me* annihilating an entire village.

Matthew dozed beside me. Selena and Finn slept across the room. One of Finn's hands rested on a lock of her hair.

Jackson wasn't here. Still outside?

I pushed away my blanket, then stumbled toward the lantern-lit bathroom. I couldn't handle more of these dreams! They were like ghastly horror movies on loop in my brain.

And in this one, the witch had made it sound like *she* was the Empress—when she'd had a conversation with Death.

Was I now to have nightmares about both of them? I recalled the way his glorious face looked in the sun and shivered.

Why didn't Selena have to deal with shit like this? Yet another reason to hate her.

Inside the bathroom, I reached for the dimmed lantern, turning up the light. Something was smeared over my hand? I rubbed at my skin, but the smudge didn't fade.

A trick of the light, a shadow? Did it go past my wrist? I shoved my sleeve up. An ivylike marking stretched the length of my arm.

With a gasp, I whirled around to the dust-covered mirror above the sink, frantically swiping the glass with the bottom of a fist.

I glanced at my reflection, tottered on my feet.

The red witch stared back at me. My eyes were . . . green. My hair? A glossy red, threaded through with leaves.

Those glowing glyphs ran all over my pale skin.

Nearly hyperventilating, I staggered closer to the mirror. No, I didn't look like the witch *exactly*. It was still me, just with similar traits.

My thoughts raced. The witch must have been . . . she must have been another Empress. One born in the past. The ships she'd destroyed had looked like galleons.

Matthew had told me there were ancient battles—and he'd never said I was the *first* Empress.

The red witch and the Empress were one and the same.

Deep down I'd known it. I had to have. But Matthew had told me that the witch was arising, that she was coming for me. That I'd fight her.

I guess I *had* been fighting her this entire time, resisting the realization. Indeed she had been coming for me. Even now I could feel her arising—*inside* of me.

Surely Matthew had sent me those nightmares? Or were they included in the Empress package?

As I peered at my emerald eyes, I recalled other details about the Empress card.

Rolling hills had stretched behind her, but now I realized her empire had been awash in green and red—from both crops *and* blood. Her hair had been strewn with blossoms, vines—and strands of red.

Her hands had been upraised, arms spread wide, beckoning. Yet her gaze had been deadly, her eyes saying, *"Come, touch . . . but you'll pay a price."*

Recognition hit me. *That's my Arcana call.*

The glyphs began to move, to swirl over my skin, shimmering from gold to green and back. *Mesmerizing.*

As I watched, I recognized that a part of me was still high from the power I'd experienced in that dream; just recalling the witch's feats made my aggression surge.

To be able to crush a fleet of ships . . . ?

In fact, as I reflected over all the nightmares I'd experienced, I could almost admire the witch's *zeal.* At least it was pure.

And her victims *had* tried to burn her. Of course she'd retaliated.

No, no! What was I *thinking?* She'd wiped out an entire village. They'd probably had reason to burn her!

I felt something tickling my arm and glanced down. A delicate ivy vine was budding from one of the glyphs.

When it snaked from the surface of my skin, briefly peeking out, I gave a cry and leapt back, tripping over a rug.

Pinwheeling my arms, I careened back toward the tub, plunging into the shower curtain. As I sat with my legs sprawled over the side of the tub, panting in disbelief, I heard heavy footsteps pounding down the hall.

Oh, God, Jackson!

Outside the door, he said, "Evie, you all right?"

"Uh, fine. Just tripped in the low light!" I struggled to my feet, then returned to the mirror. "I'll be out in a minute. O-okay?" As that unnatural aggression began to fade, my disgust mounted. *I am the . . . red witch.* I dropped my head in my hands, on the verge of sobbing. *The things I've seen her do . . .*

What would Jackson do once he discovered this about me?

No. I would refuse this! Just as I'd declined Death's challenge, I would deny this curse. I'd never asked for it. I considered it a disease, robbing me of my identity.

Was I doomed to be either a cowardly freak—the dormant girl in the cage today—or a monster who murdered?

Yes. I sensed that I had only so much time before I was trapped, as either one alter ego or the other. Unless I could get help.

"*Bébé*, let me in." Jackson was still outside?

I gaped at the door, at my reflection, at the door. "G-go away!" I cried, ripping leaves from my hair and stashing them in a clothes hamper. *Breathe through the panic, Evie, breathe.*

"What's wrong, you?"

"Nothing!" Gradually, my hair and eyes began to revert, the glyphs fading. *Hurry, hurry!*

"Let me in!" He banged against the door. "Or I'm coming in."

"I . . . I . . . just wait!"

"Back away, then."

"No, Jackson—"

The door came crashing down. Splinters shot into the air, the door-frame battered.

My lips moved soundlessly. Finally, I managed to say, "What is wrong with *you*?" I darted my wide-eyed gaze toward the mirror. . . .

My appearance was back to normal.

"I thought I heard you cry out earlier!" He swooped down to collect his bottle from the floor in the hallway, though most of it was gone. "Scared the devil out of me."

He was still filthy. His bow was strapped crookedly over his back.

I shimmied past him into the hallway. The other three were awake, regarding us with curiosity.

I peered hard at Matthew. He'd known what I was all along, had known I'd realize it tonight. *"Big night,"* he'd said. Grinning from ear to ear, he gave me a thumbs-up sign. I slitted my gaze at him.

"Want to talk to you," Jackson told me.

"Huh? Okay," I said tonelessly. My body felt bruised, my mind numb. Did viciousness always simmer within me, just waiting to be unleashed? If I killed like the witch, could I ever come back from it?

Maybe I *should* have taken root today.

"Talk to you *alone*," Jackson added sternly, as if I'd argue with him, or someone else might.

Selena clearly didn't like this, but she kept quiet. Finn eased beside her, offering her a rare Snickers in consolation. She rolled her eyes at him.

Jackson snagged the bathroom lantern, then ushered me to one of the bedrooms in the back, closing the door behind us.

He scowled at the unfortified window, handing me the lantern and his bottle. Then he yanked the mattress off the single bed, shoving the wooden frame over the window. Using the hanger rod from the closet, he braced it in place.

Satisfied, he collected his bottle from me and started pacing.

"Please, let me look at your leg, Jackson." Did I sound as deadened as I felt? "And your hands, too." I hung the lantern on a coat hook, ready to examine his injuries. I was still worried about infection.

Plus, doing something productive might keep my thoughts occupied. *I'm the red witch.* "You've probably got splinters embedded in your knuckles." Now that he'd been drinking so much, maybe it wouldn't hurt him too badly when I got them out. "You can talk while I work."

He shook his head hard. "*Non.* Got something I need to say, me."

I'd never seen him *this* brooding. "Go on, I'm listening."

"When you got captured, I didn't know . . ." He trailed off, had to chug whiskey before he could continue. "If it'd be like . . ."

"What?"

"Like it was with Clotile."

"Oh, Jackson, no. I was okay. I'm unharmed."

"Didn't know if I'd get there too late," he said with a shudder. Then he crossed over to me, until we stood toe-to-toe. "Evie, if you ever get taken from me again, you better know that I'll be coming for you." He cupped my face with a bloodstained hand. "So you stay the hell alive! You doan do like Clotile, you doan take that way out. You and me can get through anything, just give me a chance"—his voice broke lower—"just give me a chance to *get* to you." He buried his face in my hair, inhaling deeply. "There is *nothing* that can happen to you that we can't get past."

Nothing? I gazed at the ceiling in misery. *If only that were true.* But how could he possibly accept these changes in me—when *I* couldn't?

I transformed so drastically I might as well be a different species.

Or a plant. I choked back a hysterical laugh. A different classification altogether.

What boy would want a girlfriend with claws? *Hey, Jackson, you probably won't want to drink after* me.

Still I couldn't stop myself from asking, "When you say *we* . . . ?"

He pulled back, gazing down at me, his eyes blazing. "I'm goan to lay it all out there for you. Laugh in my face—I doan care. But I'm goan to get this off my chest."

"I won't laugh. I'm listening."

"Evie, I've wanted you from the first time I saw you. Even when I hated you, I wanted you." He raked his fingers through his hair. "I got it bad, me."

My heart felt like it'd stopped—so that I could hear him better.

"For as long as you've been looking down your nose at me, I've been craving you, an *envie* like I've never known."

"I don't look down at you! I'm too busy looking *up* to you."

He seemed amazed by my declaration. "For true?"

"Yes!"

The corners of his lips curled for an instant before he grew serious again. "You asked me if I had that phone with your pictures, if I'd looked at it. Damn right, I did! I saw you playing with a dog at the beach, and doing a crazy-ass flip off a high dive, and making faces for the camera. I learned about you"—his words grew hoarse—"and I wanted more of you. To see you every day." With a humorless laugh, he admitted, "After the Flash, I was constantly sourcing ways to charge a goddamned phone—that would *never* make a call."

I murmured, "I didn't know. . . . I couldn't be sure."

"It's you for me, *peekôn*."

My face fell. A thorn. He might have feelings for me, but that didn't mean he *wanted* to. And he didn't even know about my vile alter ego.

341

How could this be happening? Why did I have to discover I was one in a line of cackling, murderous psychopaths—on the night I'd learned of his feelings? I bit back a sob. "W-we both know your life would be so much simpler without me! I *am* just a thorn in your paw."

He nodded easily. "And it reminds me of you—every move I make, I think of you."

My lips parted. Again I realized that he was the only thing in my life that made me feel sane, made me *want* to fight for a future.

"Evangeline, I've got to feel you with my every step." His shaking hand closed over my nape, squeezing. "Or I go a little crazy, me."

Despite everything, I felt a tendril of hope. Jackson wanted me. I wanted him. Which was all that should matter, right? He never needed to learn what I was. Gran could teach me how to rid myself of this curse, or how to keep it buried forever—without slipping to that cowardly other side.

With her guidance, this didn't have to be an either-or situation. I could learn how to be a normal again!

And we were only weeks away from the Outer Banks. There was still time. Optimism filled me. . . .

Until I recalled yet another of the many barriers between us. "What about Selena? Didn't you two get together?"

He shook his head. "She's all right, and if I'd never met you, I might've looked twice. But I only flirted to make you jealous. To see if you felt the same way about me at all."

"The same way?" Half of me wanted to be kissing Jackson; half of me wanted to hear anything else this beautiful boy wanted to tell me. I threw my arms around his neck, squeezing him close, uncaring of the dried blood and mud.

He stiffened at first, as if in surprise, then closed his arms around me with a groan. "Ah, I know that smell. Honeysuckle."

I felt laughter bubbling up inside me. "Yes, yes." I went to my toes to smooth my lips along his neck, to press kisses across his proud, weary face.

His eyes slid closed, his expression one of bliss. He rasped, "I'm goan to protect you, *bébé*."

"I know. I know you will."

"Never taking you to North Carolina. *Jamais*."

I stilled, drew back. "What are you talking about? I have to find Gran."

"Come on, Evie, we both know she probably didn't make it. We haven't seen another woman on the road. I woan let you be in danger like today."

He wanted to call off our journey now? *Running out of time . . .* I pulled away from him, trying to keep calm.

"I got plans for us, see. We're goan back to Selena's. You can take your *coo-yôn* pet with you. But we're goan south. Back to warmth, away from plague and cannibals. You can teach me how to court you. 'Cause I doan know my way around that. You can be happy living with me. You *will* be."

Yes, I would. Just as soon as I was freed of this curse! "All of this is bigger than me, Jackson. I have to figure . . . have to figure *myself* out."

"Then *tell* me what's happening. Be honest for once. *Trust* me with your secrets. I've laid mine bare."

Tell him what I was? Or, dear God, *show* him?

Selena had been magnificent as the Archer, all grace and speed, with a goddess's poise. Matthew had his to-the-second foresight, a master of fate. Finn's talents were nearly inconceivable.

Mine? I sprouted eerie claws. I grew things through the spilling of my own blood. I could be *poisonous*. When I controlled plants, they were snakelike and shuddersome.

And what about tonight with the lotus? I'd called Selena deceptive. Wasn't that my MO as well?

Unlike me, the other kids just seemed *enhanced*, like demigods. If I revealed to Jackson what the Empress truly looked like, how could I bear to see his disgust? I grew nauseated even thinking about showing him.

What if he saw me—and made the sign of the cross?

He had feelings for me, but only because he didn't know what I truly was. He desired me—*not* the witch. "I want to tell you," I whispered. "But I can't. Not yet." *Just let me have this for a little while.*

His expression hardened. "Then you're coming with me. We'll talk about what you got to 'figure out' when you can trust me."

Real alarm spiked. Would he prevent me from leaving? Drag me back to Selena's? "I *am* going to North Carolina. And I thought you and the others would be there with me."

"It's so damned easy for you to make these decisions! When you're not doing any of the dirty work!"

"I'm stronger than you think. If push came to shove, I could help our group."

"Help *us*? Doing what? Are you goan to *pretty* the Bagmen to death?"

"Again, I might surprise you!"

"You can't hunt, can't fight. You're too soft!"

"You can't say that about me anymore. You don't know me—"

"Because you woan tell me!" He flung the bottle against the wall.

I felt like I'd shattered right along with it. "L-let's talk tomorrow, when you're sober. O-okay?" Trembling, I turned toward the door.

"Damn you, girl, you listen to me!" I faced him again, found him wild-eyed.

"Jackson, I will go insane if I don't discover what I'm supposed to do!" *And how to save myself!*

"I *know* what you're supposed to do. You stay with me, as mine. We'll grow food, we'll live our lives. We'll build something together."

How badly I wanted that too. My tears gathered and fell.

The anger sailed from him. "*Non*, doan cry, you." He covered my shoulders with his palms, rubbing me with his thumbs.

"Th-there's more to this," I insisted.

"Then *tell* me, *bébé*." The anguish in his voice was almost my undoing. The startling gray of his glinting eyes . . . "*Trust* me."

When I remained silent, quietly crying, his hands tightened on my shoulders. He threw back his head and roared like a madman. Then he met my gaze. "You keep your secrets from the one person you could actually depend on." His voice raw, he rasped, *"J'tombe en botte, Evangeline! J'tombe en botte."* I fall to ruin. "I can't keep doing this! You're coming with me, or we'll part ways in the morning."

"Let's just talk about this—"

"Vow you'll come with me, or I've got to shut these thoughts down. I can't keep running after you, goan against all my instincts, no. Can't keep wanting and waiting. I know what that will do, I've *seen* it."

"I-I don't have a choice."

He released me, jamming his shoulders back. "Then I doan either. I am *done* with you, girl."

"What does that mean?"

"I—am—*done!*"

The last word was still echoing between us when he limped out of the room and slammed the door behind him.

30

"You knew I was the red witch!" I snapped to Matthew under my breath.

He'd entered the bedroom directly after Jackson left, sitting without a word for what felt like hours until I'd stopped crying.

Finn had also dropped in, bringing a couple of blankets and starting a fire in the little hearth for us. "Obviously you're off the menu, blondie," he'd said, "with your boy troubles and all. So be a sport, and tell me the swiftest way to get in Selena's pants."

Once he'd realized I was in *no mood*, he'd raised his palms. "Hey, hey, 's'cool. Don't worry, I'll devise something. Wish me luck." Then he'd winked and disappeared. Literally. He'd turned himself *invisible*.

Now I paced while Matthew sat on the floor, studying a piece of broken glass by firelight. "You could have told me that I was her." I was still reeling from *all* of the night's revelations.

"You're not her."

"Not *yet*? Because she's strong and vicious. And I'm not, right?" I said, my tone hurt.

He inclined his head. "One day you'll be known as the Poison Princess, the May Queen. Lady Lotus. Queen of Thorns. Phyta."

"As in phytomanipulation?"

"You can *make* plants too. Phytogenesis. Without seed."

This was titillating—until I remembered that such a talent was likely designed with murder in mind. "You did send me all those nightmares then?"

He frowned. "Nightmares? No. Just . . . dreams."

"Who was she? Was that me in another life or something?" *Say no, say no.*

"Past Empress from long, long ago. She didn't keep secrets. She was known by all. But they burn what they fear," he said, his thoughts drifting.

"Matthew!"

"I updated the dreams for you. Because you can't speak middle English."

But you can? "Those *dreams* were about to drive me insane. Why would you make me experience such evil things?"

"Not *evil*. Arsenal." With a sigh, he repeated, "Arsenal, field of battle, obstacles, foes."

So he'd shown me all four things, either through visions or nightmares. "Arsenal? As in what I'm capable of?" I grudgingly admitted that the only reason I'd been able to create that lotus was because I'd seen the witch do it before.

The field of battle was a burned-out earth. The foes were other Arcana, like Death. Were the Bagmen the obstacles? "One problem, Matthew. I'm *not* a killer. I'm never going to *use* that arsenal to harm another. I swear to you, *it will not happen*."

"Hmmm," was all he said.

"This is a curse! One I'm going to rid myself of. Because of it, I had to push Jackson away. I can't stand this, Matthew. I want him so much. Tell me what I'm supposed to do."

"Take tricks. The markings must be earned."

"I mean about Jackson. He doesn't *want* to part ways with me any more than I do from him. He has feelings for me, deep feelings." He'd wanted me from the start.

He'd returned to Haven for me, saving my life. He'd kept watch over

347

me, protecting me. Even when he'd been so exasperated with me.

He'd done so much, given me so much, and I hadn't even given him my trust.

Hadn't he earned it?

"Jackson was right, about everything," I said. "I *should* trust him. I *should* tell him my secrets."

I'd been a coward, dreading his reaction—but could it be worse than this? He was *hurting*. And that was unbearable! My eyes watered just thinking about his voice. "I'm going to fix this. I have to tell him everything."

Matthew turned the shard, twisting it upside down. "Secrets. You listen poorly."

"After tonight I have two choices. I can keep these secrets. Or I can keep *him*. Which means I'll be telling him the truth, even if I have to . . . to reveal what I am." Queasiness roiled again.

I reminded myself that Jackson said we could get through *anything*. He said there was *nothing* that could happen to me that we couldn't get past. I didn't ask for any of this—surely he would understand that!

"Matthew, when I explain my confusion and fears, he'll *want* to take me to Gran's. So I can get cured."

Together with Jackson. A partnership. With no more secrets between us.

"I'm not going to give up on him." *On us.* "And I am through letting Selena worm her way between us."

"I'm sorry you want him," Matthew began in a careful tone, as if he was trying very hard to say the exact right thing to me. "I feel your heart—it actually *aches*. I wish it didn't, Evie. You cannot have him."

I glared down at him. "Why would you say that?"

"You don't want to be Arcana. But you *are*." He gazed up at me with those soulful eyes. "Jack's *not*."

"So what are you, like, a card purist or something?"

"He's a weakness. You use him as a crutch. When he helps, he hurts."

How could that be? He made me feel *hope*. "Jackson might be the only thing that's keeping me from turning into a monster."

Matthew shot to his feet, towering over me. "Into what you were meant to be!"

I gasped. "He *does* keep me from turning!"

Matthew's gaze slid away.

Jackson had quieted the voices, and then had acted as some kind of anchor for me—yet another reason why I should be with him.

I already wanted nothing more than to start a life with him; now it felt fated.

Matthew sank down on the bed, looking exhausted. "If you don't embrace your powers, you can't win."

"I don't accept that, don't accept my part in this war." When Matthew looked to argue, I cried, "No one can force me to fight!"

"You will *want* to, you will *need* to. There's a heat in battle. It's your nature."

"I will ask Jackson for his help—"

"Not a card."

"—and once we've gotten this disease under control, we'll run together. You can run with us, Matthew. Surely you don't want to go to war!"

"Jack versus Death? Who wins? You might survive, I might, Luna might, Finn might."

"That's why we'll run where Death can't find us."

"He sees you even now. He listens to every word you say, every thought that drifts through your mind. No escaping him."

"I don't believe that I'm locked into this, that I'm trapped through no actions of my own."

"You can't control your powers. Lady Lotus made us sleep last night. Any longer? Jack sleeps forever."

"What are you talking about?"

In a sly tone, Matthew murmured, "Lotus. Sleep forever and ever."

"No," I whispered, even as I remembered my nightmare. The villagers had lain down, falling unconscious. When I'd awakened,

Jackson had been out cold. Had I released some kind of spore in my sleep? "Ah, God, I did *that*?"

When I'd come upon Jackson in that window seat, I'd mused that he looked so handsome—and he'd been on the verge of dying because of me! "Then why won't you help me control my powers?"

"Oh, you'll learn. *Soon.*"

I shook my head hard. "I owe this to Jackson. I'm going to warn him about the danger. If he still wants to be with me, I'll do whatever it takes to protect him from other Arcana. From myself. But he has to know."

It's only fair, I reasoned, though I felt my hopes for our future plummeting.

"A storm on the horizon," Matthew said ominously. "And we're already behind. They laugh at us. They *should.*"

"Then let them laugh," I snapped. "I'll be back."

As I walked into the hall, I thought he muttered, *"Good-bye, Evie,"* but I kept going.

Passing another guest room, I heard a groan from inside. Gasping, scuffling? Had a Bagman gotten in? A militia soldier?

Claws going sharp, I opened the door. . . .

Couldn't believe my eyes.

Bile rose in my throat.

With his strong, protective arms wrapped tight around Selena, Jackson was kissing her for all he was worth.

DAY 246 A.F.

REQUIEM, TENNESSEE

"What better way to shut those thoughts down than with another girl?" Evie asks softly, her eyes glistening with unshed tears.

We sit in silence as I wait for her to compose herself. I could use a moment as well. So many things she's said have perplexed me, making my head ache. My focus grows hazy. Just as she has striven to resurrect memories, so too have I.

I crave one of my elixirs, though it's not nearly time for one.

"As I slipped away, I realized that Jackson *had* warned me."

"So *he* is the one who hurt you."

"I don't blame him. He asked for so little from me. And Selena will never harm him with uncontrollable powers. She'll protect him. I believe that she loves him."

Though I'm running out of patience, I want to hear about the last two days, want some questions answered. "What happened after you found the two of them kissing?"

She flinches at my words. She might not blame the Cajun, but deep down, she still feels betrayed.

She's about to know more betrayal.

"I . . . I . . ." She frowns, seeming surprised to have lost her train of thought. Right on schedule. With just ten more minutes of tape left. "So I . . . scribbled a note to Jackson, telling him that I had to continue, that I hoped he would be happy with Selena. I asked him to please look out for Matthew, to explain to the boy that it's safer for everyone this way. For some reason, I'm convinced Jackson will protect him."

"How did you get here?" I ask, my tone growing curt. My head is splitting. And her earlier blathering about voices has reminded me of a time before my tonics.

I never want to return to that time of shame—when *other things* divided my laserlike focus.

Before I ruthlessly eliminated the distractions.

Evie presses the heels of her hands against her eyes, rubbing. After blinking several times, she continues, "I stole Finn's truck, figuring that he could easily get another one with his abilities. I drove till it ran out of gas two days ago. Then I just followed the road, hoping I'd find someone who would help me. I-I've been a wreck, Arthur. So confused, crying nonstop." Her voice grows fainter. "I have never in all my life needed kindness like I did from you today. Thank you."

No. Thank *you*. "I'm surprised you didn't want to bring Matthew with you."

"I wanted to so much. But how could I take him away from all of Finn's food and safety? From the promise of security at Selena's? Jackson was right—sending everyone into trouble *was* easy for me to do. Bringing Matthew north would've been selfish."

I steeple my fingers. "But I thought you had powers now. You could protect him. What about the lotus?"

"It takes so much concentration. I think Matthew helped me with that, helped calm me. But I wouldn't want his life to depend on it."

Yet another power she can't demonstrate.

She draws her leg up on the chair again, but it slips down. She doesn't repeat the effort. "And I don't *want* to use those powers, not if I risk turning into that witch."

"Do you really think you can survive in this world on your own?"

"I have to try."

"An army led by a sadistic family almost 'enlisted' you, forcing you to burn down your home, with your mother's body inside. Then men who wanted to enslave you wrecked your car, risking your life. That militia caged you so you could be used by hundreds of soldiers."

She pales, murmuring, "And somehow through all that, I managed to hold on to my . . . my *humanity*. I've kept the balance so far."

"You believe that's because of Jackson. Now what happens? Your anchor's gone, fled into the arms of another."

Her eyes water once more, yet she juts her chin. "M-my gran will help me the rest of the way."

"You're not tempted in the least to embrace your"—pretend— "abilities? So much strength to be tapped?" She can imagine such awesome power all she wants, but it won't change the fact that she has already been defeated. She lost this match hours ago.

Evie told me that her mother's view of the world had gotten rebooted violently. Evie's is about to be as well. The optimistically cheerful girl— who never complains, who wants to be friends with everyone, who still waves at strangers—will disappear this night. One way or another.

"I can't embrace those abilities, Arthur. I don't think . . . don't think that the good can be separated from the bad . . . risk is too great. I don't *want* to become a killer."

"How do you know if you've never tried killing?"

"I . . . I'm sorry. What did you ask?" Her head bobs once, but she fights to stay awake. *Defeated.*

Thinking about loose ends, I say, "Did you ever remember the answer to that doctor's question? I want to know why you should have rejected your grandmother's teachings."

"Not yet. Feel like I'm sooo close."

Alas, you've run out of time. Now I must make a decision.

Should I keep her as a subject—or a companion? As I gaze at her heavy-lidded blue eyes and her waves of glossy blond hair, I again consider giving her a place in my bed, rather than in the dungeon.

Though she will never leave this house alive, at least she would survive longer than the scholar.

Jackson wanted Evie to teach him to court her; perhaps she could teach me how *not* to kill her.

Or would she be too much of a distraction from my work? I have *never* tolerated distractions.

It is time to decide her destiny, to play God with her future. I ask one last question: "Are you in love with *Jackson*?" Earlier, when she described that kiss with him, I barely quelled the urge to slice off her lips.

Subject or companion, Evie?

She seals her fate when she whispers, "Every time I close my eyes, I see his. Even after what happened . . . Jackson still has my heart."

Rage boils up inside me. "Not quite, dear. But *I* will have it. I will squeeze it in my hand."

She can barely keep her head raised. "Hmm?"

"It's time, Evie." I rise, slipping one of the scalpels from my case.

She squints at it, but the sight doesn't even register in her foggy brain. She slurs, "What's that?"

"A scalpel, which I will use to carve up your pretty face if you don't stand this instant."

She gasps, opening her eyes wider, shaking her head to clear it.

I have to admit that this is my favorite time with a new capture. I can only imagine the nauseating, sinking sensation as comprehension dawns. That gut-wrenching sense of betrayal.

Then the bone-chilling terror. "Stand. This instant, girl."

With a cry, she rises on quaking legs, collapses back in her chair, then attempts again. Adrenaline is beginning to pump through her system. She's a touch more alert, but her movements remain sluggish.

"Arthur, wh-what're you doing?"

I snatch her upper arm. "Walk. Now."

"Oh God, oh God, where are we going?" She shuffles clumsily beside me.

"Into the dungeon."

"D-dungeon?" She sways as if she'll faint, but I yank her upright. "Wh-why are you doing this? What'd I do?"

"You entered my lair, as good as offering yourself up to use for my studies, for my . . . experiments. Your body equals knowledge not yet harvested. That is your only value."

"Experiments?" She sounds like she'll vomit, but I have a powder in the lab to prevent that.

Ever mindful of my corduroys. "You were doomed as soon as my front door closed behind you. I need you, Evie. My work is everything. I must know everything."

"Please don't hurt me, Arthur! You heard my story—did I survive all that just for you to . . . hurt me now?"

"You told me lies. All lies! Again and again, I was on the verge of punishing you. You cannot lie on your patient history!"

As I unlock the cellar door, she cries, "What's down there?"

"Below. Now!" I force her down the stairs. She trips, almost pitching into a fall before I catch her.

Once we've made it down to the lab with all my simmering potions, I relish her horrified look. Then I drag her past the plastic sheeting into the dungeon. "Your new home."

With her pupils the size of dimes, she stares at the other girls, huddling against the walls. "You . . . kidnapped them?" Then she catches sight of the scholar's remains.

Evie tilts her head at the putrefied body, as if she can't reconcile what she's seeing.

Here's the part where comprehension dawns. . . .

Her eyes go blank, her trembling hand shooting up to her mouth. *Realizing that will be you one day?*

"Come, Evie, let's get you settled." I shove her toward the scholar's corner, pointing to the decomposing pile. "Fish out your new collar from that mess."

She recoils. *"Wh-what?"*

"Accept your fate, and you'll live for a time."

"You don't want to do this to me, Arthur."

"Retrieve the collar NOW!" I yell, spraying spittle. The other girls

ball up into fetal positions in their nests, all openly crying.

But not Evie. She chokes out one word: "No."

The other girls whimper, the youngest crying for her mother as usual.

"No?" With a flick of my wrist, my scalpel will bring my new subject to heel. "Just for saying that to me, I'll cut out your tongue and put it in a jar for you to see every day." I advance on her, rage clouding my vision.

To herself she whispers, *"Ah, God. I'm lost."*

"Utterly lost! This is the last time you will ever disobey me." I reach for her with one hand, my scalpel raised in the other—

"Come, Arthur," I dimly hear her murmur. *"Touch."*

What's this? She's recited those words before, in her timid girl's voice, but hearing them in this new sultry tone rocks me.

She finishes, "But you'll pay a price." A streak of movement between us.

Just as I perceive her irresistible rose scent, four parallel slashes appear across my torso.

I gape down, dropping my scalpel. Hot blood gushes from me. *My* flesh is a curtain, one opened to my probing gaze. "H-how?"

Evie straightens, unaffected by any drugs. Her eyes are alert and bright . . . green. A line of vine appears over her cheek and down her neck, blazing across her pale skin like a glowing green brand. Locks of her hair are turning red.

Tipping each finger is a razor-sharp thorn, now dripping with my blood.

She hadn't been hallucinating. Evangeline is filled with power, thrumming with it.

I clasp my palms over my wounds; blood spills between my fingers. "Y-you made me believe you were lying—or delusional!"

"I told you not *all* of my tale was true. For instance, I left out the parts concerning *you*."

"Me?"

356

"I didn't want to have to hurt you, Arthur. But you left me no choice!" She is visibly shaking, *seething*. "Not after you struck out at me. Just like Jackson said, I am DONE!" The entire house begins to quake, plaster raining from the ceiling. "I am *sick* of this world, sick of being attacked and kidnapped!"

Blood loss is making me cold—just as she said.

"All I ever wanted was to be normal. But tonight I've accepted that's not possible. Even without Death and the Arcana, I now know that I have no hope of it. As soon as I saw these girls chained down here, it suddenly hit me—I'm not like them. I'm *not* normal. I don't have to be trapped. I just have to become the vicious Empress I was born to be. And as you pointed out, the one thing holding me back— Jackson—is gone."

She stalks closer. I stumble back toward the lab. I have tonics to heal myself. This isn't over!

"During the last two days, I had a lot of time to consider my choices. I thought about my fierce mother. She would have embraced these powers. I thought of Clotile—what she wouldn't have given for them in her final moments! And then telling you my story solidified my feelings."

I'm almost to the plastic sheets. If I can reach my workbench . . .

"I'm ashamed that I thought about surrendering, burying myself in the earth to hide from men like you. But no longer. The Empress doesn't get collared, or caged, or tortured. How artfully she beckons, how perfectly she punishes. *I* punish." Evie's fury begins to ebb, the house settling. "I'm not going to get mad at you for poisoning me. I'm simply going to make you pay a price."

"How . . . how did you know?"

She makes a tsking sound. "Using a *plant*-based toxin in the chocolate? I could smell it, could sense what it'd do. Remember my titles? I don't *get* poisoned, I *do* the poisoning. I'm the *Princess* of it." Leaves are now tangled through her wild red hair, those spellbinding glyphs winding along her arms as well. She's a pale, terrible goddess. "I poured out my mug when you took the tray away. Probably wouldn't have affected me anyway. Oh, but you? You're *definitely* poisoned from my claws. Dying right now."

"No. Not possible," I bite out, though I already perceive her volatile toxin racing through my veins. Now *I* feel the betrayal and terror I'd only been able to imagine before. "Why visit this upon me? Why come here?"

"As I drove north, I began hearing a new voice. Yours." She taps her chin with a sinister claw, saying, "I might have forgotten to mention that one tiny detail. In any case, yours grew louder, above all the others, above even Death's—who was quite chatty once I was alone at last." She frowns, shrugs. "But your voice was drawing me near. *A wise man in the guise of a boy.* Does that sound familiar?"

I make a strangled sound. "You couldn't have heard me."

"You're one of the Arcana, Arthur. For the longest time, I couldn't figure out which one, couldn't remember my grandmother's cards well enough to match one to your tableau. Not until I saw your experiments down here in your creepy little lair. You're the Hermit. The old man holding a lantern."

"One among your number?" I draw my lips back from my teeth. "Never!"

"You're denying it, just like I did. No wonder Matthew grew so frustrated with me."

"If you believe I'm one of you, then you came here intending to do me ill!"

"No, I sought you out, hoping you knew your destiny as one of the Arcana and could teach me mine, hoping that you'd actually be good— unlike most everyone else I continue to encounter. But I was prepared to defend myself if you weren't."

One of my knees gives way; I reel and catch myself on the operating table. I spy my reflection in the stainless steel. I am . . . transformed. I see an aged man, holding a lamp in the dark. My own *tableau*? Then my appearance returns to normal.

"Arthur, you *are* the Hermit, also known as the Alchemist."

"Alchemist?" A dull roar begins in my head. *The* Alchemist. That's all I've ever wanted to be!

Yes. That is who I've always been. Never has it been clearer to me.

Of *course* Evie looked special to me when I first encountered her— because I'd seen her card. I hadn't envisioned her with open arms in my bed; I'd seen the Empress's tableau—the one with her beckoning.

"I kept dropping hints, waiting for you to recognize some aspect of my story, for you to make a move." She tilts her head, and that length of silken hair sweeps over her shoulder, drowning me in her luscious rose scent, threatening to subdue me even now. "My guess? You're so high from your wacky concoctions that you haven't been hearing the voices." She leans down, tells me in a confiding tone, "Drugged till your brain is soup? I've been there, buddy."

"*High?* I wanted focus!" Bloody saliva flies from my mouth. "The voices . . ." Suddenly I remember that hated cacophony, those useless repetitions. "They distracted me!"

"It's like Matthew said. If you don't listen to the voices, then you'll die with their gloating whispers in your ear."

Just as the other Arcana have supernatural abilities, so do I. Reminded of that, of the powers I wield, I lurch toward my lab.

Behind me, the girls beg Evie to free them, though they sound as petrified of her as they've ever been of me.

As Evie stupidly obliges them, I hunch over my workbench, grasping for every vial I can reach. I guzzle their colored contents, one after the other.

Black to counteract her poison. Blue to make me stronger, more aggressive, faster. Red to heal my wounds.

I have underestimated her; she's done the same with me. If I can get upstairs, I can reach the weapons strategically stockpiled throughout my home.

I will sear her to a puddle, just like Father.

Though she must hear me slamming through my potions, she has no fear, patiently telling my subjects—*mine*—that she's going to cut their chains with her claws now. "Don't be afraid," she assures them. "You're almost free."

Three slashes later, the girls clamber out of the dungeon, giving me a wide berth, fighting each other to get up the stairs.

I start for the stairs myself, crawling across the floor, fleeing to buy the elixirs time to work.

"Where were we?" Evie asks as she appears from behind the plastic sheeting. She's brushing her hands off, as if she'd just dusted.

At the base of the stairs, I twist to keep her in sight. "Why toy with me?" *Must keep her talking.* Already I can feel one potion neutralizing her toxin. Under my clutching arm, my torso begins to heal. "Why act as if the poison had taken hold?"

"Just as I told you, sometimes I play roles. I portrayed a breezy caretaker when my mom was dying; I pretended indifference about Jackson and Selena, though I was about to go mad with jealousy. I acted drugged so you'd show me what you planned to do to me. And what was down in your cellar."

"Why tell me your story?"

"Did you not listen to me *at all?*" she asks with a sigh. "My MO is to await, remember? To *beckon.* You had to make the first move." As I fight to climb the steps, she calmly trails behind me. "And it took me a while to wrap my head around the idea that you'd tried to drug me—that only one of us was leaving this house alive. Besides, I needed time to recuperate from my busy day . . . gardening."

"Gardening?" I frown, can't make sense of her words.

"Then you struck. You tipped the scales."

At last, strength begins to pump through me, my muscles swelling. "This isn't finished. I'll strike again. I'll slaughter you, girl."

"Will you?" Her expression is hard, her green eyes devoid of pity. "Don't you see, Arthur? Jackson was wrong. It might not be my way, but I *can* hunt. I'm hunting you."

Arthur is inching up the stairs, wheezing, still threatening me at intervals, baring his bloody teeth.

Had I ever imagined it could come to this?

I arrived here an emotional mess, fresh from sobbing for two days. Little wonder. I've never been alone like that before, friendless and without family. I'd never felt the stab of betrayal from a boy.

Yes, I came here seeking answers from Arthur, but I was also yearning for more—a sympathetic hug, a pat on the back, any scrap of kindness.

And worse, I still *expected* it.

I've been good to people in the past, and even after the Flash—after all the times I've been wronged—I still nurtured this naïve belief that people wanted to be good to me too.

When I first gazed at Arthur with his aw-shucks modesty, I thought: *New friend.*

As simple as that.

God, how badly I *needed* a friend. Instead, I found a psychopath.

Even now those three girls are upstairs shrieking for help, unable to get out of this lair. I hear the youngest one bawling, begging for her *mother*. I can only guess how long he's been torturing them.

Tonight Arthur has changed me forever. He's pushed me over the edge, forcing me to become what had once been my worst nightmare.

I am altered. Before Arthur. And after. There's no going back.

I hate him for that.

As we reach the top of the steps, he weakly lunges across the threshold, landing on his lacerated belly with a grunt. Then he begins to scrabble crablike across the floor, half looking at me, half looking at the front door he's keen to reach.

When he nears the entrance, the girls scream and bolt into a corner.

At the door, he drags himself to his knees, stretching for a doorknob that isn't there.

"Caught by your own trap? You creepy, filthy fiend."

Darting glances over his shoulder at me, he reaches into the back pocket of his pants, snagging a pair of pliers.

I continue stalking closer, which makes him more and more agitated. This power is heady. No wonder the red witch laughs so much. I'm beginning to see the appeal. "I followed you around town before I came here—but you knew that, didn't you? What you didn't know is that we were both getting ready for this meeting."

Matthew warned me of lures; the Alchemist used several to coax me into his lair, and I was wary.

The bright lantern on his house—a light in darkness. The stew I'd smelled—a feast when I was starving. But while he'd been stoking his fire in anticipation, he'd left me plenty of time to call for my special kind of backup.

Just as I'd seen the red witch do.

With my blood, I revived dead plants—and it felt *delicious* to bring them back to life. Then I'd practiced with them.

Arsenal.

Now roses, vines, and oaks await just outside, ready to storm the Alchemist's hold. A tornado of thorns swirls above. "You thought I was so pale and weak," I tell him. "Yet I was only recuperating from blood loss. Thank you for giving me the TO."

At that, he bobbles his pliers up . . . up; they land several feet away. In a panic, he grips the metal rod—all that remains of the inner half of the doorknob—twisting with all his might. Blood begins to drip from his palm.

"Ask yourself, Alchemist, do you really want to make it out that door?"

Over his shoulder, he sneers, "You are an aberration, a freak! That's why your precious Jackson chose another, because he could sense how wrong you are! He spurned you."

I don't deny that. *Fair's fair.* Hell, it could be true—what do I know? Apparently, *nothing* about boys.

Even after seeing Jackson kiss Selena, I still miss him. I wonder how long that ache will last—

Arthur begins to rise, lumbering to his feet. This is . . . surprising. I'd heard him drinking stuff downstairs, but I didn't figure he could counteract my poison.

When he stands, I realize his torso is healing with a speed matching my own regeneration.

"I'm not without talents, Evie." Before my eyes, his muscles are growing, straining against his clothing.

He casts me such a triumphant smirk that I wonder if he can outgun me and mine.

"You couldn't guess how strong I'd be." With a bellow, he plucks the door from its frame like a piece of lint.

He hurls it overhead at me; I scream when it connects with my shoulder, slamming me into a wall.

As my vision wavers, I imagine that I hear Jackson's echoing voice in the distance. *"Evangeline!"*

I breathe through the pain, grappling with the weight of the door, frantically squirming to get out from under it. I'm still so weak in body, a scrawny little girl!

"Evie! Answer me, damn it!" Jackson is here? How has he located this town? *"Where are you?"* I can't process the anguish in his booming

voice, his desperation to reach me. Why would he come? He was finished with me.

Then he yells to someone, "Tell me *exactly* where she is, boy! Or I'll gut you, I swear to Christ!"

Matthew's here too?

Arthur rushes from the doorway across the room. Instead of escaping, he's pressing his advantage. I watch in disbelief as he vaults clear over a table, skidding to a stop before a china cabinet. By the time I get free and make it to my feet, he has snagged *stoppered vials*?

He lobs them at me. They shatter, splashing their contents across my skin.

Acid.

The pain. Paralyzing. Mind-numbing.

I shriek. The skin on my upper arm, one thigh, one calf—dissolving. I drop to my knees. Consciousness dims.

"Evangeline!" Jackson's agonized roar is like a beacon, focusing me.

Arthur stalks closer, vowing, "I will *melt* you inch by inch, will make you beg, just as I did Father."

I struggle to rise, to ignore my hissing, burning flesh as it begins to heal.

When the Alchemist sees my skin regenerating, he mutters, "Not possible."

I gasp out, "You keep saying that . . . about things that are . . . already occurring." He hasn't witnessed even a *fraction* of my powers. The idea makes me proud, smug. I stagger to my feet.

Ready to end this, I call on my soldiers, loosing them into the fray. Battering-ram limbs beat down doors and windows so that vines can snake inside, overrunning every room.

Just as Matthew said, there *is* a heat in battle, and I feel it pumping inside me. *Glorious!* I yell from it and my soldiers respond violently.

Thorny stalks drape the front of the house. Behind me, a wall of green roils, a twining mass. As we creep forward, Arthur freezes, gaze blank with horror.

Just before we reach him, he whirls around, sprinting for the exit. He doesn't get two steps outside before a limb shoots in front of him, blocking his way. Ivy flies at him from the sides of the porch, coiling around his torso, the tips boring into his skin.

"Nooo! Stop this, you freak!"

A rose stalk creeps along the ceiling like beading water. Descending with vicious stealth, it slithers around his neck.

When it locks tight, I murmur, "Your new collar, Arthur."

More stalks bind his legs, ascending to his arms as if he were a trellis, wringing a high-pitched scream from his lungs. Tightening like barbed wire, they dig their thorny fangs deeper, *deeper*, until his lungs can't expand enough for a second scream.

He peers back at me over his shoulder, his eyes pleading.

How many girls have begged him not to hurt them? How many has he poured acid on?

How many has he maimed?

He'd been planning on doing it *to me*—

Suddenly he thrashes, freeing one arm with that insane strength. From his pocket, he snatches one last vial of acid.

Before he can strike, I wave my hand: the order for execution.

The vines holding his body slingshot in different directions, ripping him in half.

In a spray of arcing blood and splintering bone, the Alchemist is no more.

Two separate halves. Deposited on opposite ends of the porch. A puddle of crimson in the middle.

I've won the day, but the victory has taken its toll on me. When I totter on my feet, my soldiers press against my back, steadying me like a bookend. As I'd seen the red witch do, I stab my claws into one rose stalk, siphoning the life I'd given it back into my body, speeding my healing.

"Evangeline!" Jackson nears.

Why have you come here? Why, why? Fleeing from him is no longer an option. I won't hide what I am anymore.

"Bébé, answer me! *Please...*"

I spy him sprinting down the street, Matthew close behind. They're not alone. Selena and Finn follow.

When the four slow in front of the house, the web of briars parts to reveal me standing at the head of the steps. Half of my bloody T-shirt and the legs of my jeans have dissolved, baring my regenerating skin and glowing glyphs. My red hair whips from the tornado of thorns above.

A vine curls about my neck affectionately. I rub my cheek against it, petting it, my poisonous claws glinting.

Behind me, the thorny barbed wire, the vise of vines, and the battering-ram oaks all await my command. They choke every opening of the Alchemist's lair, until the shape of the house is unrecognizable.

I gaze down at the other Arcana. Matthew is proud. Selena is lethal, icy. And not surprised at all. Just as I'd suspected, she knows all about us. About *me.*

Finneas appears stunned—and guilty? He mutters, *"Never thought you'd walk in."*

Off to the side, lips parted and eyes wide, is Jackson.

Walk in...? Just then, the three girls begin fighting their way past the vines in the front doorway. With another wave of my hand, I allow them passage. They run out of Arthur's house past me, screaming for their lives.

Then something draws my attention down. A new marking appears on my hand, not one of my glyphs, but a small tattooed illustration. It's the Alchemist's symbol, a glowing lantern—his lure.

So odd to see it on my skin, yet familiar in a way. Just as Matthew told me, the battles must be fought, the *markings earned.*

Make a kill; earn a tattoo trophy. I swallow, going light-headed as a memory bombards me. At last, I recall the answer to that chilling question.

The doctor asked, "Do you understand why you must reject your grandmother's teachings?"

I nodded, slurring my words: "Because she wants me to do bad things to other kids."

The rest of that car ride with Gran blossoms in my consciousness, the scene as fresh as the day it was created:

Just as the cops blared their sirens behind us, she told me, "Every few centuries, a new life-or-death game begins. You must trump the twenty-one other Arcana, Evie. Only one can live."

"What does that mean, Gran?" I asked, panicked.

"At the end of the game, your hands will be covered with their symbols." After pulling over to the side of the road, she gently cupped my chin, meeting my gaze with grandmotherly affection in her twinkling brown eyes. "Because you're going to kill them all. . . ."

Kill them all.

This is what I am. Deep down, hadn't I known I might have to murder Arthur? It was the Alchemist who'd been doomed the moment he'd "trapped" me.

I now wear his symbol, will forever. I have entered the game, whether I wanted to or not.

No wonder Matthew asked me if I was going to kill him. And what of Selena? Has she kept us around, planning to murder us in our sleep?

Maybe she waits for us to attract more Arcana, like Finn. I wonder if the Archer finds it challenging *not* to kill us until the time is right.

I turn to Jackson, meeting his stunned gray gaze. *This is what I truly am. . . .*

I notice a blood-soaked bandage wrapped tightly around his hand. He's injured himself? I look closer. Not a bandage. Clutched in his grasp is . . . my poppy-red ribbon.

The ribbon he's saved since before the Flash.

He's not standing near Selena, and he's come here for *me.* Do I believe what is right before me—or my memory of them kissing? What if I'd misinterpreted things?

Oh, God. *Finn.*

Had I walked in on Selena and the Magician—disguising himself as Jackson?

Am I grasping at straws because I still want Jackson so much? It's possible that he never touched her, right?

For a dizzy moment, I wonder if Jackson and I still have a future. I ache for it. He can bring me back from this.

He can save me—

The house groans beneath the weight of my vines and limbs, the frame snapping. The foundation quakes. Though I'd practiced with my new powers, they are not yet completely under control. My weakness makes me clumsy with them.

I begin to withdraw my soldiers in a churning, snakelike retreat, but before they can fall back, dormant once more, they've ruptured the entire house wide, like a broken egg.

Jackson's jaw slackens. His gaze darts from one half of the house to the other; then he squints at something off to the side.

Oh. Part of the Alchemist. *The little doll's got teeth, Cajun.*

What will he say? Do?

I nervously rub my thumb over my claws until blood drips anew. He told me we could get through *anything.* Can I trust that?

Save me, Jack. . . .

He stumbles back, making the sign of the cross. Just as I once predicted.

With that one gesture, he has broken my heart utterly.

—And yet I could not be prouder, Empress— seductive Death whispers in my mind.

I hear him so clearly; he must be close. I now have nothing to lose, no reason to live in fear of him. *Watch your six, Reaper, I'm on the hunt.*

A rasping chuckle. *—Your Death awaits.—*

I start laughing, and I can't stop.

Jackson pales even more. I hope he deserts me now and takes the other three with him, out of my reach.

Because otherwise, the Empress might just kill them all—
Moisture tracks down my face. A tear?
Rain.
As Jackson and I stare at each other, drops fall between us. . . .